Beloved authors Kasey Michaels, Gayle Wilson and Lyn Stone join forces for this delightful collection filled with three breathtaking tales bound to sweep you into the Regency world of rakes, rogues and romance!

In His Lordship's Bed by Kasey Michaels

In a twist of fate, an innocent young lady and a handsome rogue were caught in bed together. But before their unavoidable marriage could begin, they found themselves facing an altogether unexpected challenge...love!

Prisoner of the Tower by Gayle Wilson

After twelve long years, a widow and a jaded earl were reunited against all odds. But as the past threatened to destroy their newfound happiness, would love be enough to save this battle-scarred man from a lifetime of loneliness?

Word of a Gentleman by Lyn Stone

In order to collect her inheritance, a daring debutante needed a husband. Could she convince her childhood sweetheart—now a penniless ex-soldier—to elope with her in exchange for a share of her fortune?

KASEY MICHAELS

Kasey Michaels is the *New York Times* and *USA TODAY* bestselling author of more than sixty books. She has won the Romance Writers of America RITA® Award and the *Romantic Times* Career Achievement Award for her historical romances set in the Regency era, and also writes contemporary romances for Silhouette and Harlequin Books.

GAYLE WILSON

Winner of the Romance Writers of America's RITA® Award for Best Romantic Suspense, the Kiss of Death Award, the Daphne du Maurier Award, the Texas Gold Award, the Laurel Wreath for Excellence and the Dorothy Parker Award, Gayle Wilson has written over thirty novels for Harlequin and Silhouette Books. Gayle writes historical romance set in the English Regency period and contemporary romantic suspense. She lives in Alabama with her husband and an ever-growing menagerie of beloved pets. Gayle loves to hear from readers. Write to her at P.O. Box 3277, Hueytown, AL 35023 or visit Gayle online at http://suspense.net/gayle-wilson.

LYN STONE

Lyn Stone loves creating pictures with both words and paints. Her love affair with writing and art began when she won a school prize for her poster for Book Week. She spent the prize money on books, one of which was *Little Women*. She rewrote the ending so that Jo marries her childhood sweetheart. That's because Lyn had a childhood sweetheart she wanted to marry when she grew up. She did. And now she's living her "happily ever after" in Alabama with the same guy. They traveled the world, had two children, four grandchildren and experienced some wild adventures along the way. Whether writing historical romance or contemporary fiction, Lyn insists on including elements of humor, mystery and danger.

KASEY MICHAELS

GAYLE WILSON   LYN STONE

the Wedding Chase

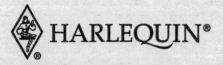

HARLEQUIN®

TORONTO • NEW YORK • LONDON
AMSTERDAM • PARIS • SYDNEY • HAMBURG
STOCKHOLM • ATHENS • TOKYO • MILAN • MADRID
PRAGUE • WARSAW • BUDAPEST • AUCKLAND

ISBN 0-373-83575-2

THE WEDDING CHASE

Copyright © 2003 by Harlequin Books S.A.

The publisher acknowledges the copyright holders of the individual works as follows:

IN HIS LORDSHIP'S BED
Copyright © 2003 by Kathryn Seidick

PRISONER OF THE TOWER
Copyright © 2003 by Mona Gay Thomas

WORD OF A GENTLEMAN
Copyright © 2003 by Lynda Stone

Visit us at www.eHarlequin.com

Printed in U.S.A.

CONTENTS

Dear Reader,

My name is Eleanor Olgesby, and please excuse me if I'm not at my best, for, to be frank about the thing, I am not in the best of moods.

There are a myriad of reasons for this descent into the doldrums, beginning with the fact that my sister, Francesca, has married the most cheeseparing man in creation. Not only have I had to leave London in the middle of my first Season (so much cheaper to order about a sister-in-law rather than hire a maid, you see) to escort her to her husband's country home now that she is nearing the day when she'll bring the man's first heir into the world, but I also have had to share a badly sprung rented carriage with that complaining woman, as well as a single bedchamber at a most inferior inn.

Hmm…from the sound of this, one might think I am a hideously spoiled young woman, wealthy beyond her dreams, but that is not the case. I just enjoy crisp, dry sheets and my own bed without Francesca's freezing toes in it, thank you very much.

Not that I could hope to have a moment's rest from Francesca's incessant whining that I be at her beck and call all day, and definitely all night. Now the widgeon has demanded the tin of sugarplums sitting inside the carriage, and here I am, outside in a muddy inn yard after midnight, my feet freezing inside these thin slippers, stumbling around in the dark with a tin of sugarplums and a guttering candle.

All I want is to get back into bed and please, please, have a few hours of rest. Goodness, it's dark inside this inn. The innkeeper must share Walter's cheeseparing ways—and there goes the candle! Pfftt! And I've stubbed my toe, and—oh, wait, here's the door to our room. It must be our room; I've counted down three doors. I'm sure I have.

Ah, she's asleep. Well, good, even if I am standing here with the sugarplums she no longer wants. And she's warm, too. I'll just snuggle against her, back to back, and drift into dreamland….

IN HIS LORDSHIP'S BED
Kasey Michaels

To Jean Herman, who keeps us all functioning.

CHAPTER ONE

ELEANOR OGLESBY could be a dreamer.

She could dream about palaces and princes, fairy godmothers and magic spells.

She could lose herself in a fantasy and forget that the real world existed.

Sometimes.

But not, alas, today.

Today, Eleanor Oglesby was most reluctantly being driven away from London at the height of the Season, trapped inside a badly sprung rented coach, forced to attend her older sister, who was traveling to her husband's ancestral home for her coming confinement because she "Couldn't bear, just couldn't *bear* it if the infant arrived early and Walter missed the birth."

At least Francesca would come out of that "confinement" with a brand new son or daughter— No, definitely a son. Walter Fiske had decreed it, and so it therefore must be.

Eleanor, on the other hand, would merely be released from her own "confinement" just in time for the King's birthday, the end of the Season, and yet another coach trip back to her ancestral home.

Not that Eleanor didn't love her sister, or babies, for that matter—but she definitely was not enamored of the top-lofty and rather bossy Walter. And not that the Season had been running along that smoothly, seeing that Eleanor was petite, brunette and brown-eyed, and the favor this Season ran to tall, blond and blue-eyed.

She was not in fashion, and the saddest part was knowing that gentlemen she might have otherwise considered handsome and appealing were all competing like fools for the honor of drooling on the shoe tops of all the tall, blond, blue-eyed debutantes, just because they were in fashion. Half of these females giggled and the rest could be dumb as redbricks. But fashion was fashion. That knowledge had not only depressed Eleanor, it had depressed her admiration for the supposed smarter sex.

Still, she liked London. Adored London, in fact. And this was to have been her first Season. Wasn't it just like Francesca to pick now to give silly Walter Fiske his heir? She might even have done it on purpose, counted out the months on her fingertips—Francesca had never been accomplished at sums—just to be sure she would be delivering that heir smack in the middle of Eleanor's first Season.

Francesca could be like that.

With their mother long dead, it had naturally fallen to Francesca to take over the rearing of Eleanor, four years her junior. The secret pinches, tickles and nasty remarks Francesca had employed to torment her sister for this added burden were still not quite a distant memory.

But they had both grown up, eventually. Francesca, now three and twenty, had been married for two years. And those two years, which Eleanor had spent alone with her father in Kent, had probably been the happiest of her life.

That was because her father was hunt mad, and mad for fishing, for billiards and for gallons of port shared with male friends—all of which kept him away from their home for months on end, leaving Eleanor to her own devices.

But she had to be chaperoned for the Season. Oh, yes, quite definitely, and a woman must monitor her wardrobe, her hair, her deportment. Some man of sense must vet all of her invitations so that the fool child wouldn't innocently accept an invitation to stroll the Dark Walk at Vauxhall, or to attend some risqué masquerade where disguised ladies of the evening mingled with the *ton*.

Who better, their father had said before haring off to Scotland, to take his dear Eleanor in hand than his so-sensible Francesca and her fine, upstanding husband? Which had brought Eleanor and Francesca back together again, neither of them exactly overjoyed by either the prospect or the reality.

So Eleanor had been tutored in the dance, her manners had been frowned over, much to her frequent embarrassment, and she and Francesca and the ever-frugal Walter had been installed in the Oglesby town house in Mayfair, Eleanor champing at the bit to be out and about, and Francesca repeatedly complained about her altered shape, her swollen ankles and the fact that her dearest Walter had been unexpectedly summoned to his father's estate because of something to do with poor field drainage.

Since Walter had deserted the theoretical ship, it had been left to Eleanor to do the entirety of the care and feeding of Francesca. Francesca, who quite obviously believed herself to be the first woman on earth to give birth, stated—again, repeatedly—that Eleanor "owed" her for the years she had helped raise such a wild, contrary and perpetually ungrateful brat.

"Does this mean I get to pinch you when nobody is looking, then say I have no idea why you're crying?" Eleanor had asked with her sweetest smile.

Francesca hadn't spoken to her for three days, which had suited Eleanor straight down to the ground.

But now Francesca was speaking to her again. *Repeatedly.* Incessantly. The hair-witted woman never shut up!

Even as they rattled and bounced their way through the countryside in Walter's idea of a "fine, closed carriage," Francesca was running her tongue nineteen to the dozen, when all Eleanor could do was close her eyes and hope her stringy mutton stew partaken of three hours earlier at a most inferior inn wouldn't come rushing back up for an encore.

"You will, of course, defer in all things to me, Eleanor, while we're at Fiske Hall, and during the worst hours of my confinement, to Mrs. Thistledown, who has been with the family for eons, and brooks no nonsense from flighty young girls, let me tell you."

"Yes, Francesca," Eleanor said, then bit her lips together, because the mutton was knocking on the back of her teeth.

"And you will *not* refer to Walter as 'Fiske-the tight-fist' behind his back, the way I heard you muttering under your breath last week when Walter forwarded our travel arrangements to us. This is a perfectly fine coach."

"It smells like moldy hay and sweat," Eleanor said. "I feel it only fair to warn you, Francesca, that if you don't soon let me drop a window I could be very, very ill. *Messily* ill."

"Oh, for pity's sake, stop your whining. Drop the window. But if I catch cold, it will be on your head. I carry the heir, remember?"

"How can I forget?" Eleanor sniped. "You remind me every five seconds." She removed boxes and bags from beside her on the worn velvet seat in order to scoot over and drop the window, only to find that it was stuck shut. "And why should I have expected anything else?"

Eleanor rearranged the mountain of luggage, scooted to her left this time and tried the window on the other side. It was likewise immovable. Francesca forestalled any further investigation by quickly stating that no, her windows would *not* be opened, not under any circumstances.

Eleanor took a lace-edged handkerchief from her reticule and dabbed at her top lip, which she knew to be moist. All of her was moist, and she so longed for a long soak in a bathing tub that just the thought nearly brought her to tears.

"My sugarplums, Eleanor," Francesca ordered. "They're under your feet, in that tin."

"I don't understand," Eleanor said, because although she was a nice person, really, currently she was in a foul, foul mood. "Are you merely pointing out a bit of information, as if I was not already painfully aware that my side of this woefully undersize coach is piled high with luggage and I am only sort of *stuck* on the seat as an afterthought? Or are you saying that you're hungry, yet again, and that you would be so very appreciative if I, your dear and only sibling, would please be so kind as to reach down and get the tin, open it and then offer its contents to you? Perhaps," she ended, her eyelids slitted, "you'd also like me to *chew* them for you?"

"No wonder you were such a wallflower," Francesca shot back nastily. "The hair and eyes had nothing to do with it. You're just a horrid, horrid child, and everybody knows it."

"Sugarplums?" Eleanor asked sweetly, pulling the lid from the tin and all but jamming the tin into her sister's nose.

And so it had gone for two days—one day, if theirs had been a better team of horses rather than the broken-down nags currently in the traces. And so it went until after dark on this day, until the coach finally limped into yet another benighted village and stumbled to a halt outside the meanest, smallest, most tumbledown and undoubtedly inexpensive inn there.

"Ah, how charming, even nicer than last night's inn," Eleanor said, squinting through the clouded—and quite immovable—window to the muddy courtyard and the slovenly ostler who was eyeing the coach as if to say, "And I suppose you want *me* to do something about this?"

"Don't be facetious, Eleanor," Francesca warned tightly. "Walter is economical. You don't become wealthy by tossing money around for temporary lodgings."

"Or dry beds, privacy, edible food and on and on," Eleanor groused as she opened the door and kicked down the steps. She'd already learned that their hired driver thought any of these chores beyond the scope of his duties. For what Walter was probably paying the man, Eleanor was just glad the fellow dealt with their luggage at each stop.

She stepped into the inn yard—literally into it—feeling her half-boots sinking a good two inches into the muck, and held out a hand to her sister. "Come on, Francesca. You've been longing to use the facilities for at least an hour and moaning about it for twice that long. Just step carefully. This could be quicksand.''

"Oh, *yuk*," Francesca said, grimacing, as her own half-boots sunk into the muck. "I didn't know it had rained.''

"Neither did I, which is why I don't want to think about what might have made this yard so muddy. Just please do hurry up, Francesca. Difficult as this is to believe, I think something in the air just might smell delicious. Wouldn't some roasted beef and pudding go down nicely?''

They were halfway to the inn door when three men walked up, one of them hastening to open the door for them.

"Thank you, sir, I— Oh, my, aren't you Nicholas Marley, Earl of Buckland? Why, of course you are. Forgive me for being so forward. I'm Francesca Oglesby Fiske, Walter Fiske's wife?''

Eleanor watched as Lord Buckland looked down at Francesca, who had foolishly attempted a curtsy.

Hair for brains, that was Francesca, Eleanor thought as she quickly grabbed her sister's elbow and helped pull her upright before she tumbled forward into the mud.

Lord Buckland bowed and then introduced his two companions to "Mrs. Fiske," but not to Eleanor. First, probably because Francesca hadn't introduced her. And second, because he must have thought the wrinkled, sweaty and put-upon-looking Eleanor was her sister's companion, not her sibling.

And, in truth, that was what she was, since Walter had pointed out that there was a plethora of maids at Fiske Hall and he could see no reason to transport one from his father-in-law's domicile then have to put down the blunt to get her *back* there once the trip was accomplished, what with Eleanor being so...handy?

Still, ignoring her would be just like Lord Buckland. Arrogant, insufferable man. Eleanor had observed him from her wallflower status against the walls of more than one ballroom, watching the tall, dark-haired and exceedingly handsome man as he sailed through society, leaving a flotilla of sighs and wishful dreams in his wake.

He was just the sort of man she loathed...when she wasn't slipping him very neatly into her dreams about handsome princes come to rescue her from her lonely tower.

As the two sisters entered the dim foyer of the inn, Buckland and his friends brought up the rear, then quickly disappeared into what Eleanor believed she could wager her quarterly allowance with no fear of losing it, had to be the single private dining room in this miserable, forsaken excuse for an inn.

She even smelled the heavenly aroma of roasted beef before the door had entirely closed behind Buckland, and would have wagered her *next* quarterly allowance that the man had brought his own chef with him, and the meal she and Francesca would be offered in the common room would have been lately hopping, arthritically, through the woods, then conveniently expiring of old age just at the back door of the inn, precisely in time for dinner.

Eleanor peeked into the common room, to see it stacked jowl to jowl with well-dressed London gentlemen. How odd. But then she overheard the one closest to the door talking about the "fine mill here tomorrow" and realized that this small village must be the site for a boxing match. Of course. There was nothing surer to bring the gentlemen of the *ton* out of London and into scruffy, undersize inns than the chance to see two of their fellow men pummel and bloody each other.

"We'll have to take our supper in our rooms, Francesca," she told her sister, who had been in a deep yet very quiet discussion with the landlord. Eleanor was sure he was their landlord, for he wore a huge, greasy, leather-brown apron, and he'd already been handed a small handful of coins, doled out by Eleanor, who had been doled out to herself by Walter's solicitor, coin by cheeseparing coin—complete with written instructions on how and when to spend every last bent penny.

"Yes, I've already deduced that, Eleanor," Francesca said, looking at the short, steep flight of stairs, then sighing. "I don't understand. Walter gave me strict instructions to give each innkeeper an extra ten pence, to assure us the best rooms, but it didn't help last night, and the horrid man back there just laughed and handed it back. As for dining in our rooms? Definitely. The inn is immensely over-crowded, and although they are all gentlemen, I'm sure it would not do for females to be too obviously in their midst. Walter mustn't have known.''

"Probably not," Eleanor said, following her sister up the stairs. "He probably reserves the worst rooms in the worst inns quite regularly."

Francesca paused at the head of the stairs and turned to glare at her sister, tears in her eyes. "Stop it, Eleanor. Just *stop it.* I'm wretchedly tired, my ankles are swollen, I'm dragging this…this *lump* with me wherever I go. I'm facing a confinement with no real idea as to exactly what that entails, except to be fairly certain I'm not going to enjoy it. I don't need you to remind me every five minutes that this has been a horrid trip. Simply *horrid.*"

"Ah, Frannie, I'm sorry," Eleanor said, gathering her sister into her arms, giving her a gentle hug. "Come on, let's find our room and I'll scare up a tub for you."

"I won't fit," Francesca said, sniffling. "I don't fit anywhere anymore. I'm just a great big fat *lump.* I can't even wear my rings. Everyone must think I'm some…some fallen woman, not even wed. I just want to go home, Elly. I just want to *go home.*"

"And we'll be there tomorrow, I promise," Eleanor said, taking the key from her sister and in-serting it in Number Three. "Now, let's get you bathed and into bed. And I promise not to be a beast, all right?"

"You weren't having a successful Season anyway," Francesca said as she sat on the single chair in the room and let Eleanor tug off her half-boots—which wasn't an easy chore.

"Thank you so much, Frannie, for reminding me of that fact yet again," Eleanor said, holding the muddy half-boots by their laces and looking around for a place to put them. Not that the small room could be much damaged if she went outside, gathered some mud in a pail and decorated the walls with it.

"Dark hair was in vogue when I came out," Francesca went on, not seeming to realize that she didn't have her sister's sympathy at the moment, and really shouldn't push. "I could have had my choice of five gentlemen."

"And yet you chose Walter. Life is strewn with mysteries, isn't it?" Eleanor said, then figuratively bit her tongue as her sister, never the steadiest trooper in any battle, burst into tears.

"WHO WAS THAT, NICK?" Sir James Donaldson said as he picked up the first of what were sure to be many mugs of home-brewed ale. "Fiske? Can't say as I know him."

"Neither can I, Jamie, not really," Nicholas said, tipping back his chair as he propped his own mug of ale on his flat belly, then lifted his Hessian-clad feet onto the tabletop. "But the lady seemed to know me, so I was polite. God knows, I'm always polite to females.''

''That's not all you are to females, Nicky,'' Beecher Thorndyke said, turning around his own rude chair and straddling it. He was drinking lemonade, still nursing a curst hangover from the previous evening. ''Gave me a bad turn for a moment, you know, wondering if you'd put the bun in her oven and she'd tracked you down.''

''Very amusing, Thorny. I always tell everyone what a wit you are,'' Nicholas said, his dark eyes flashing. ''She's Walter Fiske's wife, poor thing. I vaguely remember him from school, I think. He believes he's my friend.''

''We all believe we're your friends, Nick,'' Beecher Thorndyke said. ''It's safer that way.''

''Good one, Thorny,'' Sir James said as Sylvester, Buckland's valet cum traveling chef and general factotum, placed a large platter on the table, then turned to frown at his employer, who immediately removed his feet from the table. ''Ah, your master, Nicky. It never ceases to amaze me how Sylvester runs your life for you. Wouldn't be surprised if he cut your meat, stap me if I wouldn't.''

Nicholas smiled at Jamie's quick attempt to divert Thorny's attention, letting Thorny think what he wished to think, just as he let everyone think what they wanted to think. All except Jamie, who knew. Jamie, who'd never tell.

''You know what, Thorny?'' Nicholas said once

Sylvester had delivered all of their platters, already mounded with vegetables and ready for the beef they'd serve themselves, and left the room. "I think I'm going to get drunk tonight. Very drunk, well and truly drunk. It's the only way I can seriously hope I'll find a moment's sleep in that godawful thing upstairs the innkeeper has the audacity to call a *bed*."

"You brought your own sheets at least," Jamie pointed out. "I think I could have drowned in mine last night, they were so damp. And Thorny here snores. Even Sylvester has a room to himself, I'll wager, while I'm forced to share. It's so bloody unfair."

"At least my feet aren't cold," Thorny said, reaching for the serving fork. "Good thing the last mill's tomorrow and we can be out of here. If I'm going to share my bed, I'd rather my companion didn't have to shave every morning. Gad, how I miss females."

"Now I'm crushed, Thorny," Jamie said, winking at Nicholas. "Then I suppose those rumors about you are untrue? Good. Nick, old fellow, would you pass me that key to my chastity belt? Damned thing has begun to chafe, anyway."

All three men laughed, Thorny joining in just a little late because the joke was at his expense.

By ten that night Nicholas had made good on his promise and was a full three sheets to the wind, and most happily so. He said his good-nights to his friends, promising to meet them at six, to ride out to the site of the mill, and staggered off to bed, candle in hand as he mounted the stairs.

"Good evening, Sylvester," he said, putting down the candle once inside the small room, and saluting his valet. "I'm drunk. Isn't that wonderful?"

"My delight knows no bounds, my lord," Sylvester said, helping Nicholas out of his jacket, then motioning for him to please sit down so he could deal with his Hessians. "It does a man good to indulge at times in the company of friends, and since you're so strict with the bottle most times, I imagine the headache won't present too much of a problem."

"You didn't have to come along, you know. You don't even like mills," Nicholas said, unbuttoning his waistcoat and shirt, not too surprised that he was having a devil of a time trying to loosen each button. "I'm three and thirty, Sylvester, not three. I can manage to muddle through for a few days without your exemplary services."

"Yes, that's true. I suppose I could have spent the time at Buckland darning socks."

Nicholas winced. "You could accept my offer of an estate for yourself, damn it, and stop being my bloody conscience. Oh, damn it, I'm sorry, Sylvester. I didn't mean that."

"You didn't pull down your drawers and sire me, my lord. That was your father," Sylvester said, carefully folding Nicholas's jacket over his arm. "You owe me nothing. There are times I wish our father had not left behind that note, informing you of our relationship. Some things are best left unknown.''

"I'd drink to that, if I thought I could swallow so much as one more drop,'' Nicholas said, slipping out of his buckskins to stand there in his small clothes, which he then stripped off, leaving himself completely and unashamedly nude. "My valet of these past ten years is really my brother? I always knew the man was a bastard.''

"Not he, my lord. *I* am the bastard. I've taken the liberty of turning down your bed, my lord. I think you might be happier for a good night's sleep?''

"Probably not, but the mere hope comforts me,'' Nicholas said, aiming himself toward the bed under the eaves. "I'm sorry, Sylvester. It's just that Thorny said something earlier, innocently enough, and I—''

"Think too much?'' Sylvester offered, watching as Nicholas dropped back against the pillows, closed his eyes.

"You do know,'' Nicholas said, not opening his eyes, "that you are the only person in this world, save Jamie, who is not afraid of me?''

"Secretly, my lord, I shudder in my boots at the mere sight of you.''

Nicholas chuckled. "Good night, Sylvester.''

"Good night, my lord. Sleep well.''

"ELEANOR?"

Eleanor moaned, turned onto her side, trying to arrange her body around the lumps in the mattress rather than rest *on* them.

"Eleanor? Aren't you awake?"

"No. I'm sleeping."

"Silly, you wouldn't be talking to me if you were asleep. Except, of course, for when you were ten and walked and talked in your sleep."

"You still believe that?" Eleanor smiled in the darkness. "It was just my way of getting past you and down to the kitchens for the last of the apple tart. You mean, you never knew?"

"You're a horrid person, Eleanor, and were, even as a child. No, I didn't know. But, now that you're awake, I'd like to know where my tin of sugarplums is, if you please."

"It could be in Jericho for all I care," Eleanor grumbled, pulling the sheets up closer over her shoulder then shoving them back down again, as they didn't smell quite fresh. "I'm not getting out of this bed until sun is shining through that dirty window. At least then I can be fairly sure that the bugs in this hovel have scurried back to their holes."

"Bugs?"

"Bugs, vermin, very possibly bats. Does it really matter?"

"It most certainly does! What if I were *bitten?*"

What if *she* should be bitten? With not a thought to her sister? How like Francesca. Eleanor sort of pursed her lips and moved them back and forth across her teeth, trying to figure out if she should be incensed or amused. She settled for amused. "Don't worry, Francesca. They'll probably just go after the sugarplums."

"But that's the point," Francesca persisted, to Eleanor's chagrin. "I've already gotten up, looked for the tin. It's not here. It has to still be in the coach, don't you think? And I need those sugarplums, Eleanor. I don't think I could sleep a wink if I don't have at least three. Red ones."

"Red ones," Eleanor grumbled, sitting up in the bed. "Let me take a crazy guess here, Francesca. You want me to go out to the stables, locate our coach, and fetch you three red sugarplums?"

"No."

"Good," Eleanor said, settling against the pillow once more.

"I want the entire tin," Francesca said, ripping the covers off her sister. "Please, Elly?"

Their father, lacking the control of a wife, had sometimes slipped in the presence of his daughters, mouthing words best confined to evenings of cards with his fellows. Francesca had pretended to be temporarily deaf at these times, but Eleanor had all but raced for her copybook and taken notes.

A small litany of nasty words played inside Eleanor's head now as she slipped her legs over the side of the bed and aimed them toward what she hoped was the location of her slippers. "I don't believe I'm doing this," she muttered as she shoved her arms into the sleeves of her dressing gown. "You will never ask me for another favor as long as you live. *Never.*"

"Of course," Francesca said, undoubtedly smiling in the dark, for the woman at least maintained enough common sense never to gloat so openly in the daylight. "I would never ask such a thing from you, Elly, were it not that I so *crave* my sugarplums. I am forever in your debt."

"I know you wouldn't, until the next time," Eleanor muttered under her breath, lighting the single bedside candle, which did little to illuminate the darkness. "Ouch!" she said, smacking a shin against a piece of furniture as she made her way to the door. "Heaven forbid this miserable inn could extend its largesse to include a glass for the candle, so I'd have more light."

"There is almost a full moon," Francesca offered. This time Eleanor was pretty sure she heard a giggle at the end of that announcement.

"Don't push me, Francesca. And don't get out of bed to lock the door behind me. The vermin, remember?" That, and the thought that Francesca could lock the door then refuse to let her back in until she apologized for every supposed insult since their childhood, which was always a consideration.

Francesca did things like that. But, then, Francesca never thought far enough to realize that, for instance, if she kept Eleanor on the other side of the door, that meant Eleanor could pop a sugarplum into her mouth for every minute she was kept locked out. Eleanor always won, in the end. But, sometimes, it simply wasn't worth the bother.

She closed the door and turned to her left, sliding her hand along the wall, counting the doors until she felt the rude banister of the stairs that led to the entryway of the inn. Three doors and then the banister. She'd remember that. Not that she had to; their room number had been chalked on the door.

She hugged the wall as she made her way down the steep flight, then quickly sneaked outside before one of the gentlemen staggered out of the common room to see her in her old plaid dressing gown, the one that had been her father's.

Her foot sank in the muddy inn yard and she grimaced, knowing this little excursion would put paid to her slippers, which were a lovely pink satin and only six months old, just long enough to break them in comfortably.

Holding both the brass candlestick and her dressing gown hem high, she made her way across the yard and into the stables, then past the ostler she'd seen earlier, who was sleeping with his back against the wall, his feet on an overturned bucket.

Eleanor opened the off-side door of the coach and peered inside. Oh, how marvelous. The coachman was snoring on one of the seats, Walter's largesse not extending to providing a room for the man. No wonder the man was so surly, refusing to unload more than a single portmanteau for each sister. And no wonder the coach reeked of sauerkraut and sweat and, tonight, home-brewed ale.

Holding the candle higher, Eleanor spied the sugarplum tin. The coachie's left foot was braced against it, which wasn't as terrible as having him use it for a pillow, but how on earth was she supposed to move the thing without waking the man?

She stood very still, contemplating her problem, then looked around the stables until she found a riding crop with a dangling loop of leather hanging from one end.

Slowly, carefully, she aimed the riding crop into the coach, then lightly skimmed the leather loop over the coachman's face.

He wrinkled his nose. He swiped at his cheek. And then he shifted his entire body in his deep, ale-induced sleep, his foot sliding off the tin. Withdrawing the whip, Eleanor reached inside the coach once more and quickly lifted out the tin, tucking it under one arm.

So far, so good. Except for the slippers.

She replace the riding crop, then stepped back into the night, looking up at the moon. What time was it? Surely after midnight, not late enough for the gentlemen to retire to their rooms, but much too late for her to be wandering around an inn yard in her dressing gown—not that there would ever be a proper time for her to do that.

Carefully picking her way back to the door of the

inn, she kept her head down and was mightily surprised to be suddenly looking at a pair of very large, buckled, black shoes.

She looked up, a long way up, saw the clerical collar, and gulped.

"Good evening, my child," the giant said, smiling kindly. "Lost your way, have you?"

"Oh. Oh, no, sir. I'm…I'm just fetching something for…for my mistress. Good evening, sir, and, um…bless you, sir," she ended with a quick dip of a curtsy, such as a maid might employ.

"Allow me to hold the door open for you, child," the man offered, and Eleanor quickly slipped into the vestibule, just in time to hear a second male voice say, "Lucky thing she met you, Chester, and not one of the drunken bucks in there."

"Indeed, William," the cleric named Chester replied on a sigh. "Moral tone is so sadly lacking when our fellow man gathers for these mills. A pretty young thing like that? Truly a tragedy waiting to happen. Perhaps I should go back, escort her to her mistress's rooms?"

Eleanor, hearing this, turned toward the stairs with a jerk, and the damn flame on the damn candle damn well sputtered and went out, leaving her totally in the dark unless she wished to ask someone in the common room to relight it.

"Damn," she said succinctly, repeating the word that echoed in her head, and quickly held out a hand to the wall, to help guide herself up the stairs before

Reverend Chester Whoever decided to play Good Samaritan. Francesca would have kittens if she were returned to her room by one of the clergy.

Reaching the top of the stairs, and still very much in the dark—this innkeeper could give Walter lessons in economy—she slowly made her way down the hallway, counting doors as she ran her fingers along the wall.

One. Two. Three.

Three. That had to be it. Their room number was three, wasn't it?

Or was that Number Three, but the fourth door? She'd counted three on her way to the stables. Had she begun her count with their own door, or with the next one?

Bravely resisting the urge to stand in the dark hallway and scream her sister's name, Eleanor finally decided that she was right, the third door was their door.

She put her hand on the latch and it depressed easily. Unlocked. At least Francesca hadn't bolted the door behind her, although she imagined everyone of sense residing in this inn tonight not only bolted their doors, but pressed heavy pieces of furniture in front of them, as well.

"Francesca?" Eleanor whispered the question as she stepped inside, closing the door behind her. "Francesca, wake up, I've got your dratted sugarplums."

Nothing.

Wait.

That had been a snore, hadn't it?

Eleanor rolled her eyes. Wasn't that just like her sister? Sending her out in the middle of the night because she couldn't sleep without shoveling up a few of the sugarplums that had been dancing in her head, and then falling asleep in her absence.

That was gratitude for you.

Placing both the tin and the useless candlestick on the floor, Eleanor held her hands out in front of her and inched her way through the darkness to the bed, guided by the faint moonlight that did its best to poke through the filthy window and the failing light of a miserly fire in the grate.

Her knees collided with the bed and she sighed, kicked off her slippers and slid beneath the covers once more, so exhausted she was asleep almost before her head hit the pillow.

My, she was tired. So very tired that she was dreaming. In her dream, this pillow seemed so soft. And it smelled good, too....

CHAPTER TWO

AT THE NOISE, Nicholas stirred slowly, pulling one of his two pillows from beneath his head and jamming it over his ear.

A moment later he opened one eye, only to close it again as the morning sun stuck into his skull like a pitchfork tine.

That took care of the pitchfork. But the noise wouldn't go away. It was more than a noise, actually, his still-fuzzy brain told him, more like caterwauling.

"Ell-ee! Ell-ee! Ell-ee!"

"Oh, God, make it stop," Nicholas groaned. "I'll never drink again, Lord, I swear it. I won't drink, I won't swear—damn and blast, *shut up!*"

"What?"

Nicholas froze. That sound—that question—had been much closer, hadn't it? And the voice had sounded female.

"Ell-ee! Ell-ee! Help! Help! She's been kidnapped!"

"What in heaven's name—?"

There was that second voice again. And it had definitely been closer. Very much closer. And now the mattress was moving…which wasn't doing wonders for either his headache or his queasy stomach.

"Francesca?" the voice called, and Nicholas was convinced that his ears were simply going to fall off. "Francesca, where are you? I'm here, in bed, you silly widgeon. All the brains of a flea, that's what she's got," the voice continued, even as the covers were thrown back.

"Hey, stop that infernal bouncing, if you please," Nicholas said, turning onto his back to glare at the woman in his bed. He *had* been drunk—hadn't he?—if he couldn't even remember bedding some of the local talent. "Oh, and shut up, unless you're willing to call for Sylvester and a cool rag for my head."

"Who…what…*oh, my God!* Buckland? That is you, isn't it? Buckland? What are you doing in my bed? And where is your nightshirt? Cover up, for God's sake. I don't find your bare chest at all amusing. Oh, my God, what am I saying? Buckland's in my bed?"

"What am I doing in your—what do you mean, my chest isn't amusing? Then again, I don't suppose it should be, should it." Then, giving up any remanant of hope that he could go back to sleep until his head found all its pieces and glued itself back together again, he pushed himself and his bare chest up against the head of the bed—keeping the covers tightly tucked about his waist—and looked at the woman who shared it. "Who are you?"

"Ell-ee! Ell-ee! Somebody! Help me find my sister! Oh, God, she's dead! She must be dead! Help me!"

Nicholas, blinking furiously, and cudgeling his still-sluggish brain, said, "Allow me a guess. You'd be Elly?"

The girl, a rather rumpled-looking little thing with a tangled mop of the deepest black hair and definitely large, brown eyes—and, at last, blessedly mute—nodded.

"And you're somebody's sister?"

Another nod, but she was still gaping at him as if he had two heads and large pointy ears.

"Ah, we progress. However, if you were to tell me that the woman now screeching to bring the roof down is said sister, and that said sister is, in actuality, Mrs. Walter Fiske, I feel I must tell you that I really, really don't wish to hear that."

He didn't wish to hear that, and he highly doubted that this frightened girl wanted to hear that he slept in the buff, which was the only reason he wasn't already out of this curst bed and halfway to London.

The girl looked on the verge of tears, possibly even hysterics. But she seemed to possess some backbone, as well, and summoned it up now. He swore he could actually see her gathering her dignity about her, even though she hadn't moved. "And you think I do? Who told you to crawl into my bed? And how did you get Francesca out of it?"

Nicholas looked around the room. Saw his boots,

his greatcoat, his signet ring lying on the tabletop. "No, sorry, my dear," he said, pointing to his Hessians. "The question is, what are *you* doing in *my* room?"

He watched as the huge eyes grew even larger in her head. "Oh, my stars…it *was* the fourth door."

"Well, wasn't that clear," Nicholas said on a sigh. "But, fascinating as I'm sure your explanation will be, perhaps we should postpone it for the moment."

The screaming had not abated, but had been joined by several male voices, all of them standing outside in the hallway, asking the female what all the fuss was about, who had been murdered, and one voice adding, "Wouldn't you like a chair, madame? In your…condition?"

"Sylvester," Nicholas said, sighing. "Always so solicitous. Next thing, he'll be coming in here, all bright and cheery, asking to take my chair for the woman."

The thought sobered him and he added quickly, "We have got to get you out of here, Miss— What the devil is your name?"

"Miss Eleanor Oglesby, my lord," she said, pulling the covers even more closely beneath her chin, "and there is nothing I would like better. Do you suppose I'll break one or both legs, climbing down from the window? Just a curious question, you understand."

"Happy as I am that you seem *not* to be planning

to go into strong hysterics, Miss Oglesby—you are not in the least amusing. Now, let us figure how to somehow get both of us out of this bed before—oh, damn!''

''Excuse me, my lord,'' Sylvester said, knocking and then immediately walking into the room, leaving the door open behind him. ''But I was hoping to take a chair outside into the hallway and... My lord?''

Nicholas had reached under the covers and unceremoniously grabbed Eleanor by the thigh, roughly pulling her toward the bottom of the bed. At one and the same time, he flung the sheet and blanket over her head, and was now resting his bent arm somewhere in the vicinity of her stomach—he hoped it was her stomach—as he cupped his chin in his hand and smiled at Sylvester. ''Yes, Sylvester?''

''You're...you're looking slightly harrassed this morning, my lord,'' he said, quite obviously staring at something on the floor beside the bed. ''Not that I would ever have to tell you about the evils of strong drink, as you seemed to have learned that particular lesson on your own, and to your regret. Oh, and the other two gentlemen are already downstairs in the private dining room, my lord, partaking of the breakfast I have prepared. Eggs, runny, just the way you prefer them. Ham. *Kippers*. Ah, me, a frown. I wonder why. Perhaps it was the kippers, yes? You are looking a tad green, my lord. Should

I take that frown to mean that you wish to forgo the mill?''

''No. I mean, yes. I mean—am I to be on display this morning, Sylvester? Are you by chance charging admission for all and sundry to see me in the altogether? Would you like me to stand up? Turn around? Anything to please you, Sylvester.''

Sylvester turned to the doorway, but not before Francesca Fiske pushed her way through what could now only be called a curious crowd, to enter the chamber.

''My lord, forgive me,'' Francesca said. She did not so much as glance in his direction, but had covered her eyes even as Sylvester had quickly stepped between her and any sight of the bed under the eaves. ''My sister, my lord. She's gone missing. As a friend of my husband's, as a gentleman, as a caring and compassionate human being presented with the figure of a very fragile woman, please, my lord, help me find my dearest baby sister. I would at least hope for a decent burial before the wolves get to her.''

''Pitiful. Would you listen to that non—'' he heard Eleanor grumble under her breath, so he increased the pressure of his arm, which seemed to silence her, except for a slight, *''Oof!''*

''How terrible for you, madam,'' Nicholas said, frowning in commiseration—which hurt his head, damn it. ''Sylvester? If you would be so kind as to escort Mrs. Fiske to her room…no, much better, downstairs, to my private dining room, for some restorative tea and biscuits. Attend to her, Sylvester, as only you can do. And *keep* her there.''

''That thought had occurred, my lord,'' Sylvester said, pointing toward the floor. What on earth was there? A sign saying She's Right Here—Look!

''Thank you, Sylvester. I'll dress myself and meet with Mrs. Fiske as quickly as possible. I'm sure the girl just arose early and wandered off, perhaps to visit a nearby ruin? Don't you think so, Sylvester?''

''I agree totally, my lord. I'm convinced, actually, that she's really quite close by.''

The valet bowed and ushered Mrs. Fiske out, hastened on his way by Nicholas's frigid glare.

''We're *residing* in a ruin,'' Eleanor said after fighting her way out of the covers and taking a deep breath once the door had closed and Nicholas had released his pressure on her. ''But, I must say, very good, my lord. You think quickly, although another few moments under these covers and you would have been hanged for murder. I could barely breathe. Still, running along on the notion that you have at least half a working brain, perhaps you've already thought up a way to get me out of here?''

''I think I like you better breathless, although, since I don't like you much at all, you probably shouldn't comfort yourself with the notion you've just heard a compliment. And yes, I do have an idea, but cutting you into very small pieces and stuffing you down a drain pipe probably wouldn't appeal to you. Besides, Sylvester knows, not that I know how.''

"Oh, just get out of this bed, would you? Go lock the door.''

"I can't, I'm afraid. I'm not…not dressed.''

"Well, neither am I, not that you should be looking. I'd much rather you—oh.'' He watched, amused, as color ran into her cheeks. "Well, you could have *said* something.''

"True. I could have said, 'Madam, I am buck naked. You, madam, are lying here, sharing this bed, with a totally naked man.' Would that have helped?''

"No," Eleanor admitted in a very small voice. "Let me…I mean, I'll just…just…'' She trailed off, slowly edging away from him, until she was standing on the floor in a voluminous white nightrail, pulling on the most atrocious bit of clothing he'd seen in a lifetime. That had to be what Sylvester had seen when he entered the room.

"What's that?'' he asked.

"My dressing gown," she said, pulling the ugly plaid cloth close to her waist. The hem hung on the floor, the sleeves were at least five inches too long, and she looked as if she'd just been tossed into a Scottish trash bin.

Nicholas felt the corners of his mouth twitching. "Of course it is, my dear. And does Dobbin miss it?''

"You have to be the most insulting man I've ever

met," Eleanor told him, drawing the sash tight. "Now, where are your clothes?"

"I'm sure I haven't the faintest idea," Nicholas said, casting his gaze around the room. "But not to worry. Just turn your back, if you please, and I'm reasonably certain I can locate them. Once I'm decent, or even during the process, you might wish to apply yourself to formulating a plan for getting you out of here and back into your own room."

Eleanor walked over to a corner and all but stuck her head against the plaster. "I already am. My room is right next door, you know. Which is how I came to mistakenly come in here, after I'd fetched Francesca her dratted sugarplums and my candle went out and I had to count the doors and counted three instead of four and if this were a proper inn the numbers on the door would have been in brass, not just chalked on, and I wouldn't be in this problem in the first place, because I could have felt the number and known where I was. No, in the first place, if Francesca wasn't such a total thorn in my side, to demand that I go to the stables to get her dratted sugarplums and tickle the coachman with a riding crop, none of this should have happened. And, my lord, if you had the basic good sense to lock your door, none of this would have happened. In other words, the whole thing is Francesca's fault...and yours. I am no more than the innocent victim."

"Done. You can turn around now, Innocent One,

although you will please disregard my tears at your
sad tale. However, at some later time, curse my curiosity, I would appreciate it if you'd go over that
'tickling a coachman with a riding crop' part of your
story again.''

"Oh, shut— My, you can tie your own cravat? I
thought gentlemen couldn't do that.''

"Yes. At times I amaze even myself with my var-
ied expertise. Now, shall we look outside this window, praying for a convenient ledge you could then
crawl on, to the window in your own room?''

Eleanor laughed. The chit actually laughed.

"What? I hadn't planned to be amusing.''

"Perhaps not, my lord,'' she said, plopping herself down on the side of the bed. "But if you really
think I'm going to go crawling out on a ledge twelve
feet above the ground, you must have either meant
to be funny or you're totally mad.''

"Leery of heights, are you?'' Nicholas asked, his
drink-weary brain beginning to really and truly reg-
ister the direness of their shared predicament.

He was alone in a room with an unmarried
woman of quality, if not of good sense. Said unmarried woman was in her nightclothes—or a con-
verted horse blanket topping a shroud. Said unmarried woman's screech-owl sister had awakened the
countryside, all of whom were now searching for
said unmarried woman…who was in his room. With
him. Alone.

"I'll check in the hallway, to see if you can safely

sneak back into your room,'' he said, already heading for the door, which she hadn't locked, and which was now cursorily knocked on, then quickly opened.

"My Lord Buckland, forgive the intrusion, but Mrs. Fiske is really quite—oh. Oh, my goodness."

Nicholas grinned. Painfully. Pointed toward Eleanor. "Look who I just found, Reverend Thorton. Poor thing. I think she must have wandered off during the night. Perhaps she's hit her head?" He turned to glare at Eleanor. "Or she might be simple?"

"How above everything wonderful. Simple? Am I supposed to drool now?" she asked, stepping up beside him, speaking only loud enough for him to hear.

Cheeky brat!

"No, no, that's not Miss Oglesby, my lord. I met this young child last night. She's a maid."

Nicholas arched a brow, looked at Eleanor.

The cheeky brat smiled. "Only when my silly sister sends me out in the middle of the night to fetch sugarplums," she said, then brushed past Nicholas, heading for the door. "Reverend," she said, dropping a quick curtsy. "If you would be so accommodating as to go downstairs and inform my sister that I am fine? I'll just go get dressed."

Reverend William Thorton, a man who might be pure of heart, but who also hadn't come to earth in the last rain, put out a boney hand and took hold of Eleanor's elbow, neatly trapping her.

"I think not, my dear. My lord Buckland? You do realize that there is only one proper way to rectify what has happened here."

Nicholas put a hand to his throbbing head. "Go on."

"I shouldn't think it necessary, my lord. However, if you insist. This young lady is the sister-in-law of Mr. Walter Fiske, who is the son of Sir George Fiske, a contemporary of mine and a good, good man, rest his soul. We are standing inside an establishment stuffed to the rafters with London gentlemen, all of whom already know that Miss Oglesby has gone missing."

"Ah, but they don't know *where* she's gone missing, Reverend. Only we know that."

Reverend Thorton sighed, shook his head sadly. "I had thought better of you, my lord. It is clear to me that you have seduced this innocent child—"

"He has not!"

"Be quiet," Nicholas warned Eleanor, then faced the Reverend. "I have not!"

"Indeed. She seduced you? Is that your story then, my lord? For *shame,* sir. For *shame.*"

"Oh, for the love of— Reverend. There is an explanation," Nicholas pushed on, heading for the open door before someone else—too late.

"Eleanor! *Elly!* Oh, you pernicious child, what have you *done!*"

Nicholas stood back as he watched Francesca gather the protesting Eleanor in her arms, then slowly closed the door, knowing that, as a man of honor, his fate had already been sealed.

"MY LORD? May I approach?" Eleanor asked, standing at the edge of the small stand of trees where she'd finally located Lord Buckland. She'd watched him for a few minutes, pacing and shaking his head, and seemingly involved in a long conversation with himself. When she could stand it no more, she had spoken.

Which may have been a mistake, because now he wasn't pacing. He wasn't ripping yet another lovely green leaf to shreds between his fingers. No, now he was standing quite still, his arms at his side. *Glaring* at her.

"It is my fault. Entirely my fault," she said, advancing toward him cautiously. "I'd like to think it's Francesca's fault—most everything is—or that it's your fault, which it most definitely isn't. It's my fault. And I cannot begin to tell you how very sorry I am."

"And I cannot begin to tell you how very much I really don't want to hear it."

She stepped back, as if he'd slapped her. "Yes, certainly. You hate me, my lord. You have every right."

"How wonderful, the chit agrees with me. Now there is a grand basis for a marriage. Yes, Miss

Oglesby, I have every right to hate you. I've been stamping about out here for the last hour, adding up the reasons why I should hate you. I've come up with several. Would you care to hear them?''

Eleanor felt like melting into the ground. ''I don't know if they'll hold a candle to the several dozen ways I have destroyed Francesca's reputation, made it impossible for her to look her own husband in the face, and how I'm undoubtedly to be responsible if the Fiske heir is born with the mark of Cain on its forehead—whatever that's supposed to mean. I doubt Francesca knows, either, but she repeated it, twice. Reverend Thorton is with her now, trying to console her. That should give me a few undisturbed hours, at least.''

''Rather volatile, your sister,'' Nicholas said, walking over to a downed tree trunk and motioning for her to approach and sit down. ''Do you often have the urge to choke her?''

Eleanor bit back a smile as she sat down, and he joined her on the log. ''Quite often, yes. I do apologize for her, my lord. She had no right to call you a vile libertine, or a hardened seducer, a debaucher of virgins. I didn't even know she was familiar with the terms.''

''And you are?''

''I read novels, my lord,'' Eleanor said, feeling her cheeks growing hot, for she most definitely did read. And dream. But he wasn't to know that. ''But, all that put by the side for the moment—how are we going to uncoil this mess?''

"Reverend Thorton believes the solution to be a secret marriage this evening, with the bans then announced in London, and a second ceremony.''

"Yes, I know. That seems excessive.''

"Two ceremonies?''

Her head shot up. "No. I mean a marriage at all. After all, we didn't *do* anything.''

"Didn't we? Oh, splendid. I'll just toddle back to the common room and stand on a table, make a general announcement. I, Lord Buckland, being of unsound mind and even more feeble body, had a virgin in my bed last night, and she woke a virgin in the morning. That should do *my* reputation a whacking great lot of good.''

Eleanor hopped to her feet. "No, no, no. We can't say I was ever in your bed. Think, man. We're the only ones who know that. We have to say I got lost in the dark or something, hit my head, fell unconscious, and only woke up and came back to the inn moments before the reverend saw us together. My own door was locked, and so I knocked on yours, asking for your help.''

Nicholas shook his head. "Thought of and discarded.''

"Why?'' Eleanor asked, hands on hips, for she had thought it a splendid idea.

"Because *I* wouldn't believe it, that's why. Besides, the good reverend saw you enter the inn last night, shortly after one in the morning. Remember?''

"I could have gone out again?''

"Or you could have been lured into my den of debauchery and been well and truly ravished, which is much jucier a story, and one that will be all too readily believed in Mayfair."

"Everyone will believe that, anyway, even if we marry," she pointed out, sitting down once more.

"Yes, I know, which is why you and I, Miss Oglesby, are going to crawl on our knees to your sister and confess that, shame on us, oh, shame, shame, shame, we have been meeting secretly this past month. I was to attend the mill, with friends, then follow behind you to Fiske Hall, where I would ask for your hand in marriage from my good friend and your brother-in-law—Walter, is it?—in the absence of your father. Imagine our surprise and delight when we found ourselves putting up at the very same inn. Giving in to our passions, and proximity, we wrongly anticipated our vows, but are now more than overjoyed at the prospect of an immediate nuptials."

"That's truly nauseating. You do know that, don't you?"

"I'll probably never be able to have food pass my lips again, yes," Nicholas said. "Look, Miss Oglesby—Eleanor. We have to make the best of a bad business. Compromise is shabby, injurious to both our reputations. An anticipation of nuptials is to be winked at, and quickly forgotten. By some,'' he ended, looking up into the branches above them.

"By some? Who won't wink?"

"Miss Susan Halstead, I'd imagine. Everyone, including myself, has been assuming that I'd be asking for her hand before the end of the Season. I've all but told her brother of my intentions."

"Oh," Eleanor said, looking down at her toes. She knew of Susan Halstead. Tall. Blond. Blue-eyed. "Do you love her?"

He picked up a two-foot-long twig and began tracing a design in the dirt. "Miss Halstead is well-born, well-respected, very agreeable."

"Tall, blond, blue-eyed," Eleanor snapped, then turned away when he raised his head to glare at her.

"You believe me to be that shallow?"

Eleanor shrugged, still avoiding his gaze.

"You do," he said, getting to his feet. "What else do you believe?"

"I believe you'd very much like it if I were to suddenly choke to death on a fish bone and solve all your problems, but if I don't, you'll actually marry me, just to save your reputation."

"*My* reputation? Have you considered *your* reputation?"

Now Eleanor stood up. "I'm short, dark-haired and totally out of fashion. I've been in London for two months, my lord, and you never noticed me, but that's all right, because nobody else has, either. You men are all too busy making cakes of yourselves by chasing every blonde in Mayfair, as if picking a wife by the color of her hair makes the least bit of sense."

"Not just blond. A marriageable woman would also need good, sound teeth. For the sake of the children, you understand." She heard a trace of humor in his voice, which just made her more angry.

"What an entirely stupid way to choose a wife. And the pity of it is, that's just what happens. However, to get back to our problem. You shouldn't have to worry about me. Being found in your bed chamber can only *help* my reputation. I'd rather be a fallen woman than an old maid tending cats or, worse, stuck at Fiske Hall with Francesca and a half dozen sniveling, sniffling brats."

She glared up at him, as he glared down at her, and then he laughed.

"God, you're an idiot," he said, then turned on his heels and left her where she stood.

Which is where she should have stayed, if she had an ounce of self-preservation in her body. Instead, she ran after him, grabbed his arm.

"I am not an idiot. I just don't want to marry you. Is that so difficult to believe?"

"Not if I imagine you feel as happy about our imminent nuptials as I am, no. Look," he said, taking her elbow and leading her back to the fallen log, waiting until they'd both sat down once more. "You made a mistake, granted an innocent mistake, but even innocent mistakes have very real consequences. I, being a gentleman, have to do my best to rectify your mistake, and I would prefer to do that without facing your brother-in-law or father in the field and honorably holding my pistol at my side while one of them puts a ball through my heart.''

She opened her mouth to say he was being ridiculous again. But he wasn't. She read novels. This sort of thing happened in them all the time. At last, after railing at her fate, shouting and denying and ignoring her fears, Eleanor gave in, gave up, and began to cry. ''I'm so sorry.''

''Don't be,'' he said, handing over his handkerchief so that she could wipe her eyes. ''Just think, Eleanor. You will be the Countess Buckland. Why, you will set the fashion now. Think of all the short, dark-eyed, dark-haired misses who will be forever grateful to you.''

Eleanor sniffed a small laugh, then looked up at him. ''You can be nice, sometimes.''

''Shh, don't let anyone overhear you. I wouldn't want that bruited about, you know.''

''And you really don't love Miss Halstead?''

He didn't even hesitate, and she was being particularly on the lookout for any hesitation. ''No, I don't love Miss Halstead.''

Then, just as she was about to relax a little, he added, ''You will find, Eleanor, that I don't love much of anything at all.''

''JAMIE,'' Nicholas said, waving his friend into the private dining room where he'd been sitting for over an hour, attempting to keep his mind mercifully blank. "Have you been assigned to make sure I don't break out that window over there and scurry off to freedom?"

"Hardly, Nick," Jamie said, pulling out a chair and settling his slightly pudgy frame into it. "I'm here to find out what really happened. I'm with you almost constantly, you know, so I haven't swallowed this business the reverend is singing out, that you and Miss Oglesby have been in love all Season."

"But you'll swear to that lie on your life, won't you, friend?"

"I already have, at least a dozen times. This small village is jammed full of London peers, all men, and if you think women have the corner on gossip you've never heard a bunch of gentlemen nattering on worse than an old biddy's sewing circle."

"How are Eleanor and I faring?"

"Eleanor? That would be Miss Oglesby? About half and half, I'd say. Half swallowing the hum, the other half certain you seduced the poor thing. You notice how men never blame the chit, leaving that to women, who will do everything but draw blood with their whispers about Miss Oglesby."

"They would destroy Miss Oglesby, yes," Nicholas pointed out, "but not my countess. They wouldn't dare, for their husbands won't allow it."

"Not wanting to get on your bad side, yes," Jamie agreed, nodding his head. "I see you've got it all figured out. But what about Miss Halstead? Her brother won't be best pleased to hear the news, especially as he's been quite heavily punting on tick these past two months, telling his creditors he is soon to be related to the great, and endlessly wealthy, Earl of Buckland. I checked and, thank God, Gregory isn't here for the mill. But he'll be calling on you the moment you get back to the city. Or are you going to hide out at one of your estates until the gossip dies down? That might be best."

"And be thought a coward? I think not. No, best to head straight back to London and put a brave face on the thing. Delaying the inevitable will only have the gossips stirring the pot twice. I've already told Eleanor as much, although I'm not quite sure she was listening. She is attempting to be brave, but I've seen a few small cracks around the edges of that bravery."

"You're thinking about Miss Oglesby now, rather than yourself, because you don't care a whit what anyone thinks of you, no matter what you might say about being thought a coward. How very like you, friend, although just the thought would amaze most anyone who thinks they know you," Jamie said, nodding once more. "What is she like?"

Nicholas thought for a moment. "Cheeky brat," he said, then smiled. "She has nearly stumbled, just once, since the start of this, but as I've already said, for the most part she's quite the trooper. And not the least bit afraid of me.''

"Which would make her either very silly and unaware, or highly intelligent and insightful. Tell me, which would it be, Nick?''

"Actually, Jamie, I think she's all of that and perhaps more. Certainly she has spirit. She'll make a presentable countess and a fine mother, I believe, and as that's all a man can reasonably hope for in a wife, perhaps this won't be the disaster it started out to be this morning. It isn't as if my heart would be involved, no matter who I marry.''

"True, Nick. First you'd have to *have* a heart.''

CHAPTER THREE

"I KNOW. I'll tell Walter that the earl took one look at you and was instantly smitten. He paced the floor all the night long, then knocked on our door early this morning, while I was still asleep, and proposed to you, insisted on an immediate ceremony. He's just mad with love for you."

"Francesca, will you stop?"

"No, no, you're right. That won't work. Better to hold fast to the fib the earl is telling. You two met in London and have been mad with love for each other ever since, and then the two of you were naughty last night and anticipated your vows. Oh, Lord, how do I tell Walter *that*? I'd be too embarrassed."

"Francesca, you're married to the man. You've obviously been bedded by him, as you're carrying his child. And you can't tell him the earl and I have been lovers?"

"Then you *have* been lovers! Oh, I knew it, I knew it, I just *knew* it!" Francesca wrapped her arms protectively about her belly. "A shameless wanton! And to think I've asked you to stand as godmother to my poor, innocent baby."

Eleanor finished brushing her hair and put down the brush, which was safer than holding it as she approached her sister, who was all dressed for the wedding, except for her shoes, which she swore wouldn't go on her swollen feet.

"Francesca, think what you like. Let Walter think what he likes. It has been a long day, one way or another, and I really don't care what *anyone* thinks. Now, open your eyes. How do I look? I know it isn't my best gown, considering that all of those are in the portmanteau at the bottom of the coach boot, but it is white, and I was hoping to look…virginal."

Francesca's eyes popped open. "Virginal? Isn't it a bit late to lock the barn door, Elly, now that the horse is so well and truly out? That's what Papa is going to say, you know." She sighed theatrically. "Among other things."

"Thank you, dear sister. I knew I could rely on you to help me through these next hours, be my staunch advocate, my sympathetic and supportive prop in my time of need. And, goodness, how wise of you. Thinking about Papa's reaction was just what I needed to calm my worries."

Eleanor turned back to the dresser, picked up a length of white satin ribbon and slid it through her hair at the nape. But her fingers shook and she couldn't manage the bow. "Oh, drat!"

"Here, let me help you," Francesca said, tying the bow for her. Then she gave her sister's shoulder a small hug. "I am happy for you, you know, even as I wish the circumstances could have been better. Why, you are to be Lady Buckland, Eleanor, walking away with the finest prize of the Season. I should even have to curtsy to you.''

"Not in your present condition, please," Eleanor said, summoning a smile. "We'd need to employ a winch to get you back up again."

Francesca frowned for a moment, then Eleanor giggled and she joined her. Giggling was better than crying, especially with the hour drawing fast on seven and the marriage of the Earl of Buckland and Miss Eleanor Oglesby, whose sole attendant would be standing up next to her in her pink-and-white-sprigged muslin gown…and baby blue slippers.

"MY SINCERE BEST WISHES, my lady," Sir James Donaldson said, bowing over Eleanor's hand, the one with the huge signet ring hanging loosely around the third finger.

"You sound as if I might need them, Sir James," Eleanor said, looking across the private dining room to where her new husband was being soundly clapped on the back by Mr. Beecher Thorndyke.

The wedding feast was even now being carried into the room under the direction of Sylvester, the earl's valet, who had commandeered the inn kitchen for several hours today. The smell of roasted chicken and ham reached Eleanor's nostrils and she fought down a sudden nausea. That wouldn't do! If she were to become ill, the way Francesca had done for several months, not only would she be a compromised bride, it would be whispered everywhere that she was already carrying the heir. People would be openly counting on their fingers when her first child was born and that—

"My lady, excuse me, but you've gone quite pale," Sir James said, taking her hand and leading her over to a chair. "Are you all right?"

Eleanor looked at her sister, her very pregnant sister. As she had said earlier, her sister had gotten that way by—oh, dear God! Surely the earl wouldn't…no, of course he…would he?

She turned to look at the earl again, to see him drinking deep from a glass Mr. Thorndyke had offered him. What was the man doing? Bolstering his courage?

Perhaps there was some ratafia somewhere, as that's all she'd ever tasted in the way of strong spirits. After all, if he could drink, needed to drink, surely she needed at least a barrel of the stuff herself.

"No, no, Sir James, I'm fine," she said, smiling up at the man. Trying to smile up at the man; in truth, she was sure it had come out much more closely resembling a grimace. "It's just that I've only now realized I haven't touched a thing all day, and my hunger is so deep that the aroma of all that food almost overcame me."

"Well, then, I'll tell Nick that your wedding supper must commence right now. Let me move your chair to the table, my lady. You'll take the foot, and Nick will take the head.''

Oh, wonderful. That way, she could see him every time she lifted her gaze from her plate. That should certainly improve her appetite.

As the meal progressed, Eleanor's apprehension grew, as the earl—her husband—seemed to be drinking his dinner, paying scant attention to the food on his plate. With each toast to the newlywed couple, he drained his glass, and when the Reverend Thorton finished his long benediction after the meal, having touched on matters of love and fidelity and fruitfulness and ''cleaving solely one to another alone,'' the dratted man had the audacity to pick up the bottle and drink from it directly.

She remembered Walter telling her that the Prince Regent had fortified himself with cherry brandy or some such thing before meeting his soon-to-be queen for the first time. And then he'd laughed. Just as everyone at this table must be laughing up their sleeves now. Just as all of London would be laughing once the word spread through Mayfair. *The Earl of Buckland and—who? What happened? Did the man lose a wager?*

Eleanor stood up abruptly, causing all the men at the table to likewise stand, a few of them none too steadily. ''Please excuse me, gentlemen. Francesca. I wish to retire now. Francesca? Perhaps you do, too. You have a day's drive ahead of you tomorrow, remember?''

"Yes, I do," Francesca said, getting slowly to her feet. "And isn't it above all things wonderful? The Reverend Thorton has offered to accompany me to Fiske Hall."

Eleanor frowned, realizing that Francesca would be traveling alone, because she, the new Countess Buckland, would be journeying in quite the other direction, back to Mayfair. She wouldn't be accompanying her sister. She would be accompanied by her husband.

Suddenly everything that had happened, everything that could yet happen, was removed from the realm of "silly fairy tale and almost romantic" and placed squarely into "Oh, my God, what am I to do now?"

The urge to scream rocked her to her toes. "Umm, yes, how nice. Thank you, Reverend. If...if you'll excuse us?"

"I'll be up directly, my dear," Nicholas called to her, bowing rather unsteadily.

Eleanor turned on her heels and fled, her sister bringing up the rear with her usual waddle.

"Eleanor?" Francesca asked as they paused at the top of the stairs for Francesca to catch her breath. "I have a small problem you might help me with, my lady."

"Your *lady?* Oh, please, don't *do* that." Eleanor frowned. "What's your problem?"

Francesca sighed, averted her eyes. "It's...it's money, Eleanor. Walter doled out very carefully, but we were to spend but a single night here, not two. I—I have no more money."

"He gave you nothing for emergencies?"

"Is this an emergency?"

"I wouldn't call it a lark, would you?" Eleanor bit her bottom lip as Francesca's face paled. She didn't need the woman turning into a watering pot. She had ample problems as it was. "All right, all right. I'll simply have my—Lord Buckland pay the innkeeper in the morning. All right?"

"Thank you, my lady."

"Would you *stop* that!" Eleanor headed off down the hallway.

"Silly," Francesca said, giggling. "You missed your door again."

Eleanor looked back down the hall, to Number Two, and stiffened. "No," she said, shaking her head. "I'll stay with you tonight, Francesca."

"But you can't. You're married now, and belong with your husband. That nice Sylvester has already moved your bags into the earl's room." She turned her sister about and gave her a slight push. "Go on. You've made your bed, Eleanor, and now it's time to lie in it. *Again.*"

Condemned prisoners walked to the gallows steps with more spring in their step than Eleanor Oglesby Marley, Countess of Buckland, employed as she dragged herself back down the hallway.

"SHE'S IN THERE?" Nicholas asked Sylvester, who merely nodded. Nicholas sighed. "All right. Thank you, Sylvester, for today, for tonight, and most especially for this morning. You saw that atrocious dressing gown on the floor, didn't you? At least you tried to protect me.''

"I was protecting the young lady, my lord," Sylvester corrected punctiliously. "Allow me, my lord," he ended, stepping forward to depress the latch, finding it locked.

"She's locked herself in?" Nicholas said, raising one eyebrow. "Or locked me out? Which do you think it is?''

"I'd rather not say, although I have my suspicions, my lord," Sylvester said, trying to hide his smile. "You are fairly deep in your cups, which might have caused you to forget that we are located in a rather mean little inn, which might not be the most optimum location for a wedding night."

"The devil with a wedding night, Sylvester. I just want to get out of these clothes and sink my head into some pillows. I'm in no mood to bed a virgin."

"And in no condition," Sylvester added, clearly more the older and, if not wiser, at least more sober half brother now than the loyal valet. "However, as this inn is still filled with your compatriots, all of them expecting you to join your bride, passing the night deep in your cups in the common room simply would not be prudent."

"I've had more than enough to drink, thank you. I'll bunk in with you," Nicholas said.

"Oh, I think not, my lord. I'm already sharing with Sir James's valet."

"You're sharing a room? Gad, man, I didn't know. I'm sorry."

"We're not, my lord," Sylvester said, drawing himself up to his full height. "Chester and I have been seeing each other quite frequently for two years now. He may take me home to meet his mother, any day now. I am atingle with delight. I'll knock tomorrow at eight, to shave you?"

Nicholas smiled, shook his head. "Poor Maude," he said, referring to the housekeeper at his seat in Kent, Sylvester's wife of twenty years and mother of their six strapping children. "But you've done what you wanted, Sylvester. I'm much more clear-headed now that you've shocked me sober. And make that seven, if you please. I want to get back to London as quickly as possible. The Countess and I will take the curricle, and you can follow in the coach."

Once Sylvester had bowed and departed, Nicholas faced the door to his room, took a deep breath, then lifted his fist and knocked mightily on the door. "Wife! It is your husband! Open the door, if you please!"

He heard a faint shuffling on the other side of the door and then a voice, low and intense. "Go... away."

Nicholas shook his head, smiled. "I think not, my lady. Now, open the door."

"No. And lower your voice."

"Open…the…door," he said, hearing footsteps on the stairs. This would be all it needed: his peers seeing him standing in the hallway, denied his room, denied his bridal bed. "Eleanor, I'm warning you…"

"What's the trouble, Nick? Your bride lock you out?"

"Very amusing, Thorny," Nicholas said, glaring at his friend, who was advancing down the hallway. "And not at all. As a matter of fact, seeing as how we've anticipated our vows these past months, my naughty Elly has decided she must make this evening more *exciting* for it to be special. Memorable, you understand. If she lives up to her whispered promise at our makeshift altar, she is even now dressing in the marvelous red satin gown I bought for her. Black feathers, black stockings. And, I swear to you, she's even spoken of a small riding crop for—"

The door had opened, an arm had snaked out, and suddenly Nicholas was inside the room, the door already closed, the latch thrown.

"You!" his bride declared, giving him a push in the chest. "You…you…you *rotter!* What were you saying out there?" She gave him another push. "A riding crop?" One more push. "What about a riding crop?"

"I thought it would complement that horse blanket you're wearing, my dear," Nicholas said, stepping back to avoid another jab. The brat was hurting him, damn it. "Now, what were *you* doing, denying your husband entrance to his own room?"

"I am *not* sleeping with you."

"Really?" Nicholas said, already stripping off his neck cloth. "Suit yourself, although I think you'll find the floor rather cold."

He bit the insides of his cheeks to keep from grinning as the girl's eyes grew wide. "You…you'd let me sleep on the floor? Not you?"

"When there's a lovely bed in the room, a bed covered in my own sheets, topped with my own cover, softened by my own pillows? Hardly, my dear." He shrugged out of his jacket, began unbuttoning his waistcoat.

"Put that back on," she commanded, pointing at his jacket.

The waistcoat landed on top of the jacket, which had found its home over the single chair in the room. He looked into the dark corners, locating the boot-jack, knowing that the jack would ruin a perfectly good pair of Hessians, but he wasn't about to summon Sylvester at this stage of the game.

"Don't do that," Eleanor warned him. "Don't use that jack. Oh, for pity's sake, sit down, let me help. Or are you so wealthy you can afford to ruin perfectly good boots?"

"As a matter of fact? Yes, I am," Nicholas said, removing his jacket and waistcoat from the chair and sitting down, holding out his right leg. "I must be more than three parts drunk, me who barely ever imbibes. To let a woman pull off my boots? Shame on me. There. That said—feel free to commence your, um, *services* at any time, madam.''

He watched as she approached, clearly weighing her options as to how to remove his boots and still look like a lady. As if any lady of his acquaintance put her hair in braids and wore plaid horse blankets.

''I believe you'll have to turn around and, um, *straddle* my leg,'' he offered helpfully.

''I know, I know, I've removed my father's boots when he was in his cups,'' Eleanor said, rubbing her hands together. He was surprised she didn't spit in them first. ''Now just sit there, all right? And don't *say* anything.''

He smiled, with his lips firmly closed, and gripped the sides of the chair seat. This was mean of him, terrible of him, but damn it if he didn't deserve some enjoyment after the chit had so firmly corralled him, made him into a married man.

''Good. Stay just like that. Oh, and hold this,'' Eleanor said, handing him his signet ring.

He took it, looked at it. ''What have you done to my ring? What's all this string wrapped around the thing?''

''Don't whine so. I didn't hurt it. I simply wrapped that string around the bottom of it. I couldn't keep it on, otherwise, and didn't want to lose the thing,'' she told him.

He inspected the ring again, amazed at how much

string had been wrapped around it, and how small the opening was now, how slender her fingers must be. Then, because he really did not want to think about her as a female at this moment, he turned his head as she lifted one leg, careful to keep the horse blanket dressing gown around her, and straddled his right leg, her back to him.

Interesting view, even in the near dark of this badly lit room.

She didn't have the finesse Sylvester could lay claim to, didn't cover her hands with white cotton gloves so as to not mar the shiny surface of the leather with her finger smudges the way his valet did, but she did know where to grasp the boot for the best leverage, he'd say that for her.

She did not, however, seem to possess sufficient strength to pull the boot over his heel without assistance. He let her struggle for a few moments, then lifted his left leg, holding tightly to the chair seat, placed his boot sole against her backside…and pushed.

She flew across the room, still holding his boot, and crashed into the wall; the impact, followed by her short shriek of surprise, making a racket that would have Thorny, who had the room beside his, thinking lascivious thoughts for the remainder of the night.

"Why didn't you warn me?" she asked, shaking her head, her dark braids flying out as she did so.

"You told me not to say anything," he reminded her.

"You're not amusing, you know," she said, putting down the boot, then approaching again. "All right. Left leg, my lord. And I warn you, if you push that hard again, my revenge may well terrify you."

"You read that somewhere, didn't you?" he asked as she straddled his left leg. "In one of your novels?"

"And if I did?"

"Nothing. Consider me well and truly terrified." He wiggled his foot slightly, to help her, and the second boot slid off without incident, leaving him in his white hose, his shirt, his breeches, and wondering what in heaven's name he was to do next.

He wasn't going to bed the chit, that was for certain. Not here. He wasn't such a monster.

Still…it might be *amusing* to let her think so.

"Would you care for the right or the left?"

"I beg your pardon?" she asked, lining up the left boot with the right. "You're talking about your boots?"

"Hardly. I'm talking about the bed, wife. Which side do you prefer, if you have a preference?"

"I told you, I'm not sleeping in that bed with you."

"Did I mention sleeping?"

She backed up two steps, picking up the boots and carrying them with her, holding them in front of her, whether as protection, or planning to use them as "revenge that may well terrify" him, he wasn't sure.

But she didn't look frightened, cowed in any way. She looked angry, and belligerent, and ready to give as good as she got. He found himself admiring her and wanting to kick himself for frightening her.

"Oh, put down your weapons, my lady," he said, pushing his fingers through his hair. "I'm not the ogre you think me. However, I'm also no monk. We *are* married, for good or ill. Do you understand what I'm saying?"

"No, thank you," she said, most primly.

"I beg your— Wait a moment? 'No, thank you' to what?"

"To your invitation to share your bed, of course. I've given this some thought, my lord, and there is no reason not to seek an annulment the moment we're back in London. I can go directly to my father's house, you can go to yours, and you can then petition—"

"Are you out of your mind?" he asked, cutting her off. "The whole world and his wife already knows that we've anticipated our vows. We've said so. Reverend Thorton found us here, together. You were in…in *that,* and I didn't have my boots on. An annulment? Impossible. We're bracketed, madam, for good or ill."

"No. I won't have it. I'll…I'll join a nunnery."

"Oh, for the love of—put down those boots!" When she didn't move, he grabbed them from her hands and flung them into a corner, pretty much destroying any hope that his Hessians might have survived this night unscathed.

"My father has a temper, you know. He bellows and throws things all the time. You don't frighten me."

"Good for your father. Riding herd on you and your hysterical sister, I imagine he had frequent reason for aggravation. And good, that I didn't frighten you. I didn't want to frighten you, just to shut you up. Look…Eleanor. We're married. Absolutely, completely, and irrevocably married. I will not divorce you, I will give you no cause to divorce me, and there will be no annulment. I would wait, give you time, be a gentleman—for God's sake be in the comfort of my own bedchamber—but if you think this will remain an unconsummated marriage then you could not be more wrong."

"I'm…I'm not attracted to you," she said, lifting her chin.

Nicholas stared at her for several moments, his jaw dropped, then threw back his head and laughed. "Lord love you, brat, you don't make me go weak in the knees, either. What has *that* got to do with anything?"

NICHOLAS AWOKE reluctantly, with the world still mostly dark, aware that his feet were cold. So were his knees. Where had his covers gone?

He lifted his head. Attempted to lift his head.

He'd raised it up only a few inches before his muscles protested. The muscles in his neck, in his shoulders, in his back.

Slowly, his brain called his attention to the events of the previous evening, and he winced, realizing that the reason he was cold was because the fire in the grate was dying, his greatcoat only stretched so far when used as a blanket, and that he was *lying on the floor.*

What an idiot he'd been. What had he said to her? Oh, yes, he remembered now. Something about not being attracted to his wife. Well, she had insulted him, hadn't she? Wasn't *attracted* to him?

Cheeky brat. He'd thought so, and said so, when they'd first laid eyes on each other, and he thought so now. Not *attracted* to him? Well, she damn well was the only woman in London who could say that.

He was unattractive? He didn't think so. Nobody thought so. He was a handsome man, damn it. Handsome, titled, wealthy. The most eligible, sought-after bachelor in all of London…until seven o'clock last night.

And now what did she want? Some sort of romantic hero? The stuff of marble-backed novels?

Cheeky brat.

Speaking of cheeks…Nicholas raised a hand to his left one, remembering the sting of the slap his bride had delivered as he'd said that business about not being attracted to her, either, not that it mattered *how* they felt about each other.

That probably had been a bit cold, even for him.

Which was why he'd watched her blink back tears, then hop into his bed, move as close to the edge as she could get, pull the covers tightly around herself, and let her win that battle for the night.

But now it was almost morning, and he was freezing, and if he couldn't feel a soft mattress beneath his body for at least a few hours, he'd be damned if he knew the reason why.

He pushed to his feet, looking toward the bed. Yes, his bride was still there, sound asleep, the covers lying lightly on the raised sweep of her hip. Her feet were drawn up slightly, he could see the bend of her knees in the way the covers draped her body, but even if she slept straight out, he doubted her toes would come within a half foot of the bottom of the bed.

So small, and with those ridiculous braids lying dark against the white of the single pillow she had claimed as her own.

She was on her side, as he'd already deduced, with her back to him, her body still on the far side of the bed, as far from him, he imagined, as she could muster without falling off the other side.

And there were the covers. There was an unoccupied pillow. There was more than half of the bed...calling to him, luring him like a siren's song.

He didn't wait for his conscience to awaken and give him any reason why he shouldn't lift those covers and crawl under them. Picking up his pillow from the floor, he tossed it onto the bed, and quickly followed, pulling his share of the covers over him and sighing, deeply, as he sank into the softness.

But his wasn't the only sigh in the room. His wife echoed his sound, slowly stretched, and turned onto her other side, her arm draping across his waist. She sighed again, snuggled closer, as if unconsciously seeking out a source of heat.

Now here was a dilemma to make wise old Solomon himself dash, screaming as he went, to locate the very next ship leaving for the Continent.

Not knowing what to do, Nicholas did nothing. He'd never shared a bed with an innocent. Never.

So he simply lay there, listening to her breathe. Feeling her head against his shoulder. Looking at her hand as it rested just above his waist.

Her skin was so clear, so smooth, fair, but with a hint of pink, as if, convention be damned, she'd go sit in the sun if the spirit took her. Her eyes were huge, even closed, as he could see the outline of her delicate bones, the sweep of her finely arched brows.

She had a bit of a point to her chin, and a small cleft that was…most intriguing.

And she smelled good.

And she fit against him, so very well.

Asleep, she was beautiful, gentle, trusting. Awake, she was a termagant, a fighter, a woman not afraid to give as good as she got. A maddening mix of naive young girl and world-weary woman who had no patience with fools.

She moved closer, sighed once more, and he lifted the covers, tucked them closer to her, tucked *her* closer to him.

He moved slightly, brushing his cheek against her hair, finally giving in to the impulse to lift his free hand and run a finger along the length of one thick braid.

He was married. This was his wife.

It boggled the mind....

CHAPTER FOUR

ELEANOR SAT as primly as possible on the small bench seat that kept her uncomfortably aware that her hip had nowhere else to be but smack up against her husband's hip.

She held one gloved hand in her lap, clutching her reticule, while the other maintained a death grip on her side of the slim, low-backed seat.

She kept her head turned to one side, her intent gaze examining every leaf of every tree they whizzed past in the curricle, just as if she'd never really seen a tree before, or the cultivated fields they'd passed, or the two small villages they'd driven through in the past two hours.

No, she'd never been driven in a curricle before, but it wasn't as if she was afraid of the speed of the sleek bays in the shafts, or was even leery about the driving skills of the person manning the ribbons with understated elegance and masterful expertise.

It wasn't that. It wasn't any of that.

It was remembering how she'd awakened this morning. *Where* she'd awakened this morning.

Eleanor closed her eyes, feeling her face grow hot as, yet again, she remembered opening those eyes and looking up into the smiling face of the Earl of Buckland. Her husband.

"Hello, wife," he'd said with what could only be described as an unholy grin, then pressed a quick kiss on her forehead.

At which point, she remembered, feeling the shame race through her body yet again, she'd squealed like a stuck pig, punched him in the chest, and then most inelegantly *crawled* over him to get out of the bed.

He'd laughed. And he'd laughed some more. And she'd been mortified. And he'd kept on laughing. And she'd picked up one of her slippers and launched it at his head....

"We're coming up to another village in a few moments, wife, and I've planned a stop there," Nicholas said, and she looked forward, reluctantly— hoping the brim of her bonnet would hide her flaming cheeks from view—to see a few chimneys and a single church spire in the distance. "There's a very pleasant inn that serves a tolerable luncheon. Are you hungry?"

She'd never be hungry again. But, blast it all, she had a need to use the facilities, not that she'd say so to him. And did he have to keep calling her "wife"?

"Tolerably," she said, mimicking his own words, then went back to intently inspecting the trees.

It had been bad enough, waking that way, being embarrassed that way. But then she'd had to get dressed, without anyone to help her, and the only clean gown she'd had in the single portmanteau that had been taken from the coach was the same white-and-pink-sprigged muslin gown she'd worn for her wedding.

Except that Francesca had buttoned that gown for her, and unbuttoned it last night, when Eleanor had sneaked down the hallway, knocked on her sister's door, and begged her help.

Someone had brought a rude screen into the earl's room, most likely the very kind Sylvester, and she'd been able to dress herself while standing behind it, even as her new husband got himself into fresh clothes of his own on the other side of that same screen.

He might not have needed help with his cravat, but she'd needed his with her buttons. He'd been so gracious about it that she just *knew* he'd been laughing at her behind her back.

And, thinking of backs…she'd had to stand there and watch—and listen—as his friends, one by one, and in groups, came up to him once they were downstairs, clapping him on the back, offering winks and congratulations, and hinting that his lordship looked "a trifle worn, old fellow…was it a long night?"

Mortifying. Her day thus far had been mortifying, from the moment she'd first opened her eyes this morning. But, other than the way she had awakened, running the gauntlet of his winking, laughing, well-meaning friends had been the worst. The very worst.

He must have sensed her embarrassment, for he'd whisked her into the curricle and out of the court-yard, pushing his horses for at least a mile, to distance themselves from other vehicles also heading back to London.

She could be thankful for that, even grateful, except that she didn't want to be. She wanted to be angry, and to feel put upon and badly used. She wanted, very much, not to like this man, not even a little bit.

"Here we are, wife, the Hoop and Grapes. May I suggest the rabbit stew?" he asked, lightly jumping down from the seat after throwing the reins to an eager lad who'd come running up the moment he'd pulled into the inn yard.

"You may not," Eleanor told him as she reluctantly allowed him to help lift her down from the seat, determined to be contrary. "I've had enough rabbit in the past two days to last me several years. Do you think there will be ham?"

"I think there will be anything the Earl of Buckland asks for, actually," he said, then tossed a coin to the boy, instructing him on the care of his horse-flesh, and leading Eleanor through the doorway of the inn as the landlord himself held the door open, bowing again and again.

A private dining room? Of course, my lord. Ham? It would be my pleasure, my lord. Would you care to freshen up, my lady? I'll send my wife, who will escort you to one of our rooms, my lady.

"This is nice," Eleanor admitted ten minutes later, once the innkeeper's wife had led her to that private room where she'd been able to wash her hands and face…after taking care of other pressing matters. "You cannot imagine the difference between this inn and the one Francesca and I stayed at our first night out of London."

"Oh, I believe I could, considering the inn we just left," Nicholas said, pulling out a chair for her just as the innkeeper and a young maid who looked very much his daughter carried in platters and placed them on the table. "And we won't be spending another night on the road, wife, if you continue to be as stoic and uncomplaining as you've been thus far in our journey. As you may have overheard, I've got a fresh team waiting here, to help us on our way, and Sylvester will gather up my other pair as he drives through the village. Would you mind reaching London by ten this evening?"

"No, I wouldn't mind that at all," Eleanor said, dreams of separate bedchambers dancing in her head. And she could send a note round to Oglesby House, summoning her own maid, Cloris, to tend to her. Protect her.

"Good, then it's settled," Nicholas said, employing a large fork to lift a thick slice of ham from the serving platter and deposit it on her plate. "Eat up, wife, and we'll chase the sun back to London."

NICHOLAS SAT in his own study, the only light coming from the fire in the grate, turning a snifter of brandy between his palms as he lounged in his favorite chair, his feet resting on a footstool, his dog, Archie, snoring on the hearth.

He was home. At last, he was home. Clarke, his majordomo, had made sure he'd eaten well, and taken over the duties Sylvester usually performed, laying out the burgundy dressing gown Nicholas wore now over a clean white shirt, fawn breeches, fresh hose and comfortable slippers.

Clarke had not so much as blinked upon being introduced to the new Countess of Buckland. Clarke wouldn't. Nicholas had a staff that was the envy of his peers; well-trained, loyal and at times even affectionate. Because he, as a master, was such a contrast to his late father? Possibly.

"I'm a good employer," Nicholas told the sleeping Archie. "I'm a good man. I'm…I'm a husband. Good God, I've got a bride upstairs."

"Actually, my lord, you've got a bride down here," Eleanor said, walking into the room.

He turned in his chair, nearly spilling his brandy, to see her approaching, dressed in a soft white dressing gown, a branch of candles held carefully away from her body. Her hair was down, not in braids, and she seemed to be smiling at him.

"Do you talk to yourself often, my lord? I do."

Nicholas got to his feet, sweeping one arm toward the matching leather wing chair in front of the fireplace, so that she sat down, placing the candelabra beside her on the small table. "Thank you. I—I thought we should talk?"

He nodded, although for the life of him he couldn't think what they'd talk *about*. "That's Archie," he said, pointing to the dog, who had roused from his nap and was now nosing against Eleanor's palm. "Are you afraid of dogs?"

"Afraid? No, of course not," Eleanor said, rubbing the dog's head. "I don't think I recognize the breed?"

Nicholas smiled, unreasonably pleased that Eleanor seemed to like Archie and that Archie was behaving himself. "That could be because Archie represents so many of them," he said, looking at the fairly short, squat animal who sported floppy brown ears, a mostly white coat with splotches of brown on it, and a tail that could have belonged to a much larger dog. "I found him in an alley, getting the worst of a tussle with several small boys and a pile of rocks."

"Oh, you poor baby," Eleanor said, lifting Archie's chin—do dogs have chins?—with both hands and going nose to nose with the animal, huge brown eyes looking into huge brown eyes.

Archie put out his tongue and licked her face.

Eleanor laughed and hugged the dog.

Lucky damn dog.

Nicholas blinked. Lucky damn dog? What was he thinking? Was he out of his mind?

"Um, much as I dislike interrupting this mutual display of affection, I believe you said we should talk?"

"Oh," Eleanor said, releasing Archie, who looked as if he might weep as she withdrew her hug—do dogs weep?—then sitting back in the chair, primly clasping her hands together in her lap. "You're right, of course. We should talk."

"*I'm* right?" Nicholas looked into his snifter, knew he'd taken but a single sip. He couldn't be drunk. So what was this about talking being *his* idea?

"Yes, of course," Eleanor told him, nodding her head. That thick dark hair spilled over her shoulders. A lock slipped forward, hanging from her forehead to just past her chin, and she blew at it, shook her head. So natural, so unaffected.

He could look at her for hours.

Stop it, stop it, stop it, he screamed inside his head. "No. No, you don't, wife. I won't be maneuvered. *You* wished to talk to *me*."

"Oh, very well," she said, drawing her legs up onto the chair, so that he could see that, Lord above, her feet were bare.

"Where are your slippers?"

"I left them at the inn. They were ruined anyway. Cloris brought me some things from Oglesby House, like this dressing gown, but I forgot to mention slippers in my note to her," she told him, tucking the edges of her dressing gown over her naked toes...which only made him *really* want to see them. See *toes?* This had to stop!

"I'll send for the remainder of your clothing tomorrow. Is it all here in London?"

"Some here, some at home," she said, shrugging. "None of it suitable for a countess, I'm afraid, although there is plenty of it. Are there family diamonds?"

Ah, wonderful. A failing. The woman was avaricious. "Yes, wife, there are diamonds."

She made a face. "Ah, I was afraid of that. Would you mind terribly if I didn't wear them? I really don't like diamonds."

No, she liked dogs. Not diamonds. And she had a temper. She threw things. He'd heard her say "damn" this afternoon, when he'd been unable to avoid a particularly nasty rut in the roadway as he'd feathered his team past the northbound mail coach. She traipsed about in dressing gowns and bare feet, and didn't seem to be the least bit afraid of him.

And he was intrigued. Damned intrigued.

"All right, you don't have to wear the diamonds. Are you likewise opposed to pearls, rubies, sapphires?"

"No. I like them well enough, thank you," she said, her brown eyes twinkling in the firelight. "I like my wardrobe well enough, as well, but I'm not so silly as to not know a countess must be less...less the debutante, and more the grand dame. Yes?"

"You couldn't be a grand dame if you donned

turbans and carried a quizzing glass,'' Nicholas said, grinning.

She grinned back at him. "Good. We agree. Cloris, that's my maid—she was my mother's maid, years ago—insisted I demand an entire new wardrobe. One with furs, and darker colors, and with lots of shawls. She was most particular about the shawls. I'm so glad you don't agree, my lord. All right then,'' she said, slipping her legs from the chair seat and preparing to stand up, "good night.''

"Sit down,'' Nicholas said, not willing to let her go just yet. He'd been alone in his study almost since they'd arrived back in town, thinking of what tomorrow would bring.

He'd had his man of business write out an announcement to the newspapers, and it was highly possible the notice would appear in the next two days. But gossip moved much faster, and word of his marriage would have spread across Mayfair by breakfast time…all the way to the door of Miss Susan Halstead and her brother, Gregory.

Eleanor had sat back down, and was now looking at him, question in her eyes.

"You…you remember Miss Susan Halstead?''

"Tall, blond, blue-eyed. Good teeth?''

"Cheeky brat,'' Nicholas said, muttering the words under his breath even as he hid his smile behind a cough. "Yes, Miss Halstead. She, and her brother, will not be best pleased by the news of our marriage.''

"And…?" Eleanor prompted when he fell silent.

"And, brat, Miss Halstead is very influential here in Mayfair. A favorite of the Almacks patronesses, among other premier hostesses. She will have great…sympathy."

"Do you think people will throw eggs at my carriage when I go out for a drive?" Eleanor asked, batting those absurdly long-lashed eyelids at him.

He sat back in his chair, rubbed a hand over his mouth. "You don't care, do you? I've never met anyone like you before you barged into my life."

"Perhaps, my lord," Eleanor said, getting to her feet, so that he was forced by good manners to stand up, as well, "that's because you were much too occupied in chasing hotfoot after blond, blue-eyed, *tall* women. Now, once more. Good night, my lord."

He was nearly dumbstruck enough to let her pass, but grabbed at her elbow just before she got beyond his reach. "I'll be coming upstairs later."

"Yes, I know," she said, looking pointedly at his hand, where it gripped her arm. "And Cloris will be sleeping on a pallet beside my bed. I'm frightened more than half out of my wits, my lord, if you have to be told that, and would appreciate it greatly if you gave me some…some time."

He nodded his agreement and let go of her arm. What else could he do? She tried to be so brave, even arrogant, but he'd be a fool if he didn't know this mix of woman and coltish girl deserved the time she'd requested, time to accept what had happened to her.

Then he watched as his wife departed the room, Archie padding after her—did dogs have no loyalty?—while he stood in his study, suddenly very much alone.

"I SAID I WANTED some time, Cloris," Eleanor complained, sitting cross-legged in the middle of her large bed. "I didn't say I wished to be *ignored.*"

"Ignored, my lady?" Cloris asked, sniffing. Cloris had been pleased straight down to the ground to be maid to a countess—just saying "my lady" still gave her shivers. But she'd also taken care of Eleanor since the girl had been in leading strings, and had no compunction in employing a much more informal relationship with said countess than custom dictated. "You've been to four balls in four nights. I hardly call that being ignored. Now, I'm off to press this gown. You leave for the theater in less than an hour, missy—I mean, my lady."

"I know, I know," Eleanor agreed as Cloris left the room, sighing. The earl had been most gracious, really he had. He took her for drives in the park during the Promenade. He introduced her to all and sundry. They attended evening parties and balls together—two routs, one dinner, one ball, but she saw no reason to correct Cloris on that head.

He'd introduced her as his countess, called her "wife," and had danced with her at least three times at the ball before heading into the card room with the majority of the men in attendance.

He'd had his man of business sit her down to go over her quarterly allowance, explain that accounts had been set up for her at the best of the shops in Bond Street. He'd paraded the household staff past her, and encouraged a relationship between his new countess and the able housekeeper, Mrs. Penny.

But he had not touched her since that fairly mocking kiss on her forehead that morning after their wedding. Their first kiss, a cursory peck on her cheek following the ceremony itself, didn't count at all.

In any of the novels she'd read, the dratted man would be madly in love with her by now, courting her relentlessly, perhaps even breaking down her door one night to claim his husbandly rights.

He had knocked at her bedchamber door last evening, that was true, but only to ask if she could please instruct Archie to pay more attention to his master and perhaps even coax him to give up his new favorite spot at the bottom of her bed for the hearth in his bedchamber.

Was she unattractive? Wasn't he attracted?

She was attracted to him, and had been since she'd first seen him at a rout party her first week in London. He simply was something out of her novels. Tall, dark, sinfully handsome. Being rich and titled was nice, but it wasn't what had attracted her.

It had been his smile, full of secret knowledge.

The way he sometimes stood propping up a pillar at a ball, seemingly lost in thought, sometimes not quite happy thought. It was the sound of his voice, the rumble of his laugh. She'd woven fantasies about him for two months, and now the reality had outreached even her fantasies.

He was kind; he was considerate. He was a good master, undoubtedly a fine friend. He could be every inch the earl and he could be silly.

Eleanor had known herself to be infatuated, even when she'd seen him following the herd, romancing all the tall, blond, blue-eyed debutantes while she had sat alone, her estimation of the male of the species dropping a new notch with each dance she sat out, each dinner she was forced to go down to with only Francesca by her side.

But Nicholas—she liked to think of him as Nicholas—hadn't really been a victim of fashion. If anything, Miss Halstead had been the victim, for the man had chosen her at random, because she suited, because, as all men of a certain age and with certain responsibilities to his name, he had needed to marry and set up his nursery.

Eleanor felt rather sorry for Miss Halstead, who had not been present at any of the functions she had attended as the new countess.

But her brother, Gregory Halstead, had been at last night's ball, and had made quite a business out of whispering with his friends, pointing in her direction, and just the once, *leering* at her.

Eleanor wasn't stupid. She had noticed Gregory Halstead. She had also noticed that Mr. Halstead had done none of these things until *after* Nicholas had retired to the card room with Sir James.

She hadn't noticed any lessening of ladies willing to speak with her, and her dance card had remained full. But it had been obvious what Mr. Halstead had been trying to do.

Embarrass her. Embarrass Nicholas.

It wasn't as if all of the *ton* didn't know about the impromptu marriage, and most of them must know that there had been a hasty application for a special license, after which a second ceremony would be performed, privately, hopefully quietly. There was certainly enough fodder for gossip, but the Earl of Buckland had *consequence,* and the whispers would be kept silent while, publicly, everyone would smile and bow and curtsy to the new countess.

Such was the way of Society.

Mr. Halstead was not playing by the rules.

There was a scratching at the door and Eleanor climbed off the bed to let Archie in before he got in trouble with Mrs. Penny for ruining the woodwork. "Shame on you, Archie," she said as she opened the door, only to see that Archie was not alone. The earl was with him.

"I've tried to teach him how to take the latch in his mouth and let himself in and out of rooms, but he's simply too short," Nicholas said, stepping into the bedchamber. "I have the special license, wife. Tuesday next, you become my wife a second time. I thought we'd have the ceremony here, in the drawing room, if that suits?"

Eleanor nodded, watching him walk around the room Mrs. Penny had told her he'd never visited since the death of his mother eight years ago. He had taken over the master chamber on the other side of the now-open door eighteen months ago, upon the death of his father and his own ascension to the earldom, giving away every last stick of furniture and even stripping the Chinese papers off the walls, before redressing the chamber from the walls out.

But he hadn't touched this chamber, a thoroughly feminine room Eleanor had loved at first sight; all rose and pink, and welcoming. To her. Nicholas looked rather out of place, even uncomfortable.

"Jamie, that is, Sir James, told me something this morning that I need to discuss with you, if you don't mind."

Eleanor shook her head. She had nodded, now she had shaken her head. But she hadn't spoken. She couldn't speak. Something was wrong. She could sense it, feel it.

"It concerns Gregory Halstead," Nicholas told her, his back to her. "He's put it about that I have reneged on an offer to marry his sister."

"But you didn't offer," Eleanor said, finding her tongue. "Did you?"

"No, I did not. Not formally. But I will admit

that when Gregory hinted in that direction, I did little to disabuse him of his presumptions. I—I don't think I cared enough to do more than allow myself to be carried along by…events. I am nearly four and thirty, Eleanor. It is time to set up my nursery.''

Eleanor began to nod her head, then stopped herself. ''I don't care what anyone says about me, Nicholas,'' she told him, a small thrill lifting her heart as she used his name. ''But what about your honor? You won't be challenging Mr. Halstead to a duel, will you? Or he, you? If either of you died, the other would be forced to flee England.''

He turned to face her, smiling a one-sided smile. ''Yes, that would be inconvenient, wouldn't it? Dying is acceptable, but being banished? It's unthinkable.''

''Stop it,'' Eleanor warned him, stepping closer. ''This is not amusing. I am not amused. I made the mistake, remember. I opened the wrong door. It is fair if I'm whispered about, and I don't mind. But none of this is your fault. You've been above all things considerate.''

''Yes, I have, haven't I? A true prince, actually,'' he teased, smiling yet again.

She gave serious consideration to shaking him.

''So, what are you going to do?''

''I hesitate to tell you, wife, now that I know I am the figure of your admiration in this matter. However, by the murderous look in those lovely, large brown eyes of yours, I believe I shall hazard the truth. I'm paying him off, gifting him with enough blunt to pay his creditors and cushion his pockets until he hares off to the nearest gaming hell and goes into debt yet again.''

"Paying—? You're giving Mr. Halstead *money?* For his *silence?* Oh. How…how…''

"Unromantic? Even prosaic?'' Nicholas offered.

"Well, yes,'' Eleanor conceded, hanging her head. "I'm sorry. I don't want you to fight a duel. I really don't.''

"But I could have punched him? Horsewhipped him? Blacked his eye, bloodied his lip? You would have approved of that?''

She shrugged. "I suppose not,'' she told him sadly, then looked up at him, grinning. "How do you know me so well, in such a short time?''

"I have no idea, brat, except to believe that, at times, when I look at you, I'm looking in a mirror, seeing myself a few years ago. But much prettier,'' he ended, running a fingertip down her cheek.

"I…you, um, *really?*''

"Really. Young, a little hotheaded, full of thoughts of honor and exploits and feeling…oh, I don't know. Larger than life? Eager for that life?''

"And you don't feel that way now? Why?''

He withdrew his hand, his dark eyes becoming shuttered. "We all grow up, wife. I did, when I became the earl, and you have, in this past week. Haven't you?''

"I—I suppose. Just a little.'' She shook her head.

"No, I haven't. I'm still silly, romantic Eleanor, who lives in her dreams most of the time. I'm sorry."

"Don't be," he said, sighing. "I like the way you look at life. I like the way you look at me."

Eleanor dipped her head once more, then looked up at him through her lashes. "How do I look at you?"

"Like that," he said quietly, then put a finger beneath her chin and tipped up her face. "Like this," he whispered.

And then he kissed her.

Eleanor had been half expecting his kiss, but she had never, not in her wildest dreams, expected her reaction to that kiss.

All strength left her in a rush, turning her weak, turning her bones fluid. Her throat tightened, her arms *ached* until she could raise them, clutch at his shoulders.

She felt his tongue against her lips and, not knowing what to do, followed his lead as he seemed to urge her lips open. When his tongue moved inside her mouth, at first slowly and then plunging, tasting, tasting, she let her pent-up breath go on a sigh and melted against his strength. She felt his palm cup her breast and instantly knew that she wanted more. More.

How long the kiss might have lasted, what might have happened next—she would never know. Cloris took that moment to enter from the dressing room, carrying a freshly pressed gown over her arm, her head down as she fussed with one of the pleats, saying, "Now, see if you can keep this clean until it's time to—uh…uh…*oh, dear.* I'll…I'll be…yes, well…somewhere else."

Eleanor could feel Nicholas's lips curl into a smile, and she pushed herself away from him, still holding on to his shoulders, and glared up at him. "You're laughing? How can you be laughing? That was humiliating!"

"It was? Would that be the kiss, or the interruption?"

"The interruption of cour— Oh! Stop laughing!"

"True, wife, this is no time for laughter. But it will soon be time for something else, won't it?"

She stepped away from him completely, turned her back to him as she hugged her arms around her waist. "I—I suppose so."

"My, aren't you sounding elated. A lesser man, wife, would go into the woods and fall on his sword after a display of enthusiasm such as that."

She whirled around to face him. "I believe you might find one hanging in your study, my lord. Shall I fetch it for you?"

"No need," he told her, sobering. "I believe I have already been cut to the quick."

"Oh, stop it! You've made it more than clear that you don't care who you wed, who you bed. If I were not here, Miss Halstead would be. So please don't try to fob me off now with some farradiddle about knowing me so well or—''

''Just to be clear about the thing, *you* said that, not I.''

''Be quiet! Oh! You spend so much effort trying to be heartless, Nicholas. Why do you do that?''

''I have…a very good reason.'' He looked around the rose-and-pink room, then looked at her once more. ''At least, I did. This past week? I don't know, wife, I'm beginning to think I've wed a witch.''

''You could have had that confirmed if you'd just spoken with Francesca at any length,'' Eleanor said, flushing. ''Now, if you'll excuse me? I have to go settle Cloris, who is doubtless wringing her hands in shame in the dressing room. I shall be downstairs in one hour and we can leave for the theater. Perhaps they're putting on a farce. That, *husband,* would make two in one evening.''

He looked at her for a long, tense moment, then turned on his heels and went back to his own bedchamber.

She locked the door once he was gone, then burst into tears.

CHAPTER FIVE

ELEANOR HAD BEEN to the theater twice in the two months she'd been in London, as Walter had said that the theater could be "too fast" for a simple country girl.

Walter was such a stick.

Eleanor loved the theater. The magic. The world she traveled to by watching the actors, becoming a part of the story, at least for the moment, so that when the intermission arrived, she had to physically shake herself back to the moment, smiling weakly at Nicholas when he said that he and Sir James were off to secure them some refreshments.

Because now she knew a story was a story, fascinating as it could be, and nothing more. She had been smacked into reality, real life, and mere drama could only be a pale and temporary interlude.

"Oh, could that be Lady Imogene? Oh, yes, yes, it is. How utterly famous!" Miss Lucille Simmons trilled, vaguely motioning with her fan to a box down somewhere to the left of theirs. "My lady, would you mind awfully if I just stepped round to speak with her? You can tell Sir James that I'll be back directly."

"Certainly," Eleanor said, happy to be rid of the insipid girl—blond, tall, blue-eyed—Sir James had escorted to the theater. She had talked incessantly throughout the entire first act, and it was only by a firm application of will that Eleanor hadn't picked her up and tossed her over the railing and into the pit.

Eleanor knew she had been, yet again, the center of much attention this evening, and the subject of many whispers. Nicholas had to know that, as well. It was probably why they were here, because Nicholas was not the sort of man to back down from anything. By the sheer power of his will, he was making her a part of Society, establishing her as his wife, his countess.

But he had not taken her as his wife. Not yet. But he would. She knew that. He had said it, almost as if in warning, and now he had kissed her, and that kiss had carried a message of its own. Tonight. Tomorrow. Perhaps next week, when they had said their vows a second, more official time.

Was she ready to be his wife, or was she a child still, living in dreams, making him into some hero out of a novel? She thought she was. Perhaps she was. Maybe she was...

Had he lived up to her hopes for him, when she had first seen him at Almacks, as she had watched him these past months? Yes, he had, and more.

And she had been so nervous all evening that she had been shredding her lovely new lace-edged handkerchief in her lap! Eleanor quickly stuffed the ruined thing into her reticule and sat up very straight, tried to do everything a countess should do.

Looking distant and haughty seemed like a good place to start.

Within seconds, her nose began to itch. Oh, wasn't that above all things wonderful! Did a countess scratch her nose in public? Probably not. Probably even less well-bred to wiggle that nose, trying to get the itch to disappear.

So she picked up her fan, spread it, and began waving it in front of her face, keeping it waving as she turned her head, reached up with her free hand and gave the side of her nose a good rubbing.

"My lady?"

Eleanor jumped in her seat, nearly slicing off her nose with the edge of the fan. "Yes?" she squeaked, then cleared her throat, turned around. "Um, yes?"

"You may not know me, my lady, but I felt it was time I introduced myself. I am Susan Halstead."

Eleanor already knew that. Lord knew, she'd seen the woman enough, crowning over all of Society, or at least all the eligible gentlemen. But this was as near as she'd been to the woman, and she was amazed by just how lovely Miss Halstead was, up this close.

Her skin was peaches and cream. Her eyes the clear light blue of a summer sky. Her blond hair was smooth, heavy and shone like the sun.

No wonder she was so in fashion, had so *set* the fashion.

Eleanor felt short, dark and dull, and decidedly second rate.

"Please, Miss Halstead," she said, waving her fan toward the vacant seat beside her, "do sit down." At least now Eleanor wouldn't get a crick in her neck, looking so far *up* to see the woman.

"We're being watched, my lady," Miss Halstead said, "so I will smile as I say this, and suggest you do the same. I will also be brief, and very much to the point. I would not have had the Earl of Buckland if he had presented himself to me on a silver platter, an apple stuck in his mouth. I just wanted you to know that. You did not *steal* him from me. He's yours, as my gift."

Well, that shut Eleanor's mouth for a few seconds. She even forgot to smile, until Miss Halstead's constant display of fine white teeth reminded her that other eyes were watching.

"Ah, what a pity, Miss Halstead," she said at last when the numbness of shock had drifted away and the anger had surfaced. "And here I thought your poor heart was broken, your reputation in a shambles as the woman who was presented but not taken."

Miss Halstead's eyelids narrowed, and she leaned forward slightly. "I come from a family that can trace its lines back to William the Conqueror, my lady. I come from a family that has never allowed so much as the shadow of a scandal to touch it. My ridiculous brother to one side, that is, but he has been warned that if he says anything else he will feel my mother's wrath, which is considerable.''

"And he's been paid to shut up," Eleanor pointed out meanly. "Your brother is a fine representative of William the Conqueror, I must say."

That took Miss Halstead aback, but only for a moment. "I am not responsible for my brother's actions. But how like Lord Buckland to avoid a confrontation on the field of honor."

"A duel, madam? You wanted a duel? You cannot have it both ways. Either you wouldn't have had my husband on that silver platter, or your honor has been impugned. Which is to be, madam? I vow, I'm confused. In fact, I don't know why you're here at all."

"Really? You don't feel everyone's eyes on us? I'm here, madam, to silence the gossips. In fact, before I leave this box, you and I will cry friends and you will allow me to kiss your cheek, so that I can reenter Society without fear of sniggers behind fans or veiled messages of condolence. I will not be made to suffer because of someone as insignificant as you. Do you understand? And you *will* do this. If not, madam, what I am to tell you now will become public knowledge."

Eleanor, still smiling, cocked her head to one side. "Do you read novels, too, madam? Yes, I would think you do."

"Just listen closely, my lady Compromise, for what I am to tell you is the reason why someone of my background could not possibly ally herself with the Earl of Buckland."

Eleanor supposed scratching the woman's eyes out might be frowned on by some of the *ton,* so she let her sharp tongue loose, to slice where it might. "Allow me to hazard a guess. He has a heart, and you don't?"

Miss Halstead's smile widened. "He has his bastard half brother as his valet, madam. Just one of many bastards his father sprinkled across England."

"Syl—Sylvester?" Eleanor said before she could prudently shut her mouth. "I—I don't believe it."

"*Smile,* my lady, and believe it. I made it my concern to have one of my staff visit the earl's estate, work there for a space, and learn what he could learn. The Buckland bloodline courses willy-nilly through every village within twenty miles. Perhaps this does not bother you, but I would not spend *my* married life running into duplicates of my husband, shining silver, mending fences, cleaning the family chamber pots."

"My goodness," Eleanor said, and finally her smile was real. "You're beautiful, Miss Halstead. You're all the thing, this Season's diamond of the first water, all of that. And you're stupid. You're really, really *stupid.* Oh—and thank you. You may kiss me now."

Eleanor was to be denied that kiss meant to impress the *ton,* as Miss Halstead all but leaped from her chair and raced out of the box, leaving Eleanor to open her fan once more, look out over the facing boxes, nod and smile in real pleasure.

Because now she understood. She understood so many things.

NICHOLAS, carrying a glass of wine and one of lemonade, stepped back as Susan Halstead raced past, one hand to her mouth, her splendid blue eyes brimming with tears.

"I say, Nick, did you see that? The Halstead seemed a trifle overset," Sir James commented, losing some of the lemonade in his companion's glass as he gestured toward Miss Halstead's departing back. "Well, blast, that puts paid to my cuff, don't it? What do you suppose set her off?"

Nicholas looked toward the curtains around his private box. "Not what, Jamie, but *who.* And there's Miss Simmons, talking to Georgie Fox, who seems to have already brought her refreshments. I hate to crush you, but I think the chit has someone other than you in her sights. Better go scoop her up before Fox cuts you out. Just stay away from the box for a while, all right? Excuse me."

"Yes, but if the dratted chit already has got a glass, what am I supposed to do with—she had me bring her here so she could sniff around that buck-toothed Georgie? Oh, the devil with it, I didn't much like her, anyway," he ended, and downed the contents of both glasses, following the lemonade with his glass of wine, then headed back toward the bar.

Nicholas pulled back the curtain and entered the box, to see Eleanor sitting there, facing front, fanning herself with an energy that could have her lifting off the chair at any moment. "Wife? I believe I'm catching a whiff of brimstone in here. What have I missed?"

She turned toward him, her smile so wide it was almost ghastly. "I'm smiling. Sit down, and smile with me."

"I'd rather not," he told her, handing her the glass of lemonade. "You're rather frightening like that, you know."

"Good. Now, if you would be so kind—kiss my hand. Kiss my wrist, kiss my palm, kiss anything at all that makes it look as if you'd like nothing better than to take me home and ravish me the whole night long."

"Well, as a matter of fact, as ideas go, I just might wish to…"

"Just do it. Please?"

She left him with little choice, having extended her hand to him, so that the only alternative would be to let it hang there at the end of her arm.

"My pleasure, lady wife," he said, putting down his own glass and bending over her hand, turning it. He pressed a kiss on the small circle of skin left exposed by the button of her elbow-length gloves, all while he looked at her, looked straight into her eyes.

The fan moved faster, creating quite a breeze.

"More," she said, her voice rather breathless.

"If you'd just tell me what—"

"Just one more time, all right. Then we can leave, before my cheeks simply crack and fall off from all this smiling."

"I think not, wife," Nicholas said, but he did stand up, pulling her with him, and reached for her shawl. "We'll talk at home. Now, keep smiling, and for God's sake, don't wave to everyone before you leave the box. You're not the Prince Regent."

Eleanor's smile disappeared the moment her back was turned to the curious *ton,* and he could feel the tenseness in her shoulders as he laid her wrap around her. He was tempted, so tempted, to bend down and place a kiss on the nape of her neck, but he resisted the impulse. Tongues were wagging enough as it was.

"Jamie?" he called to his friend, who was heading back from the refreshments table carrying two more glasses of wine. "We'll be leaving now."

"We will? But it's only intermission."

"Not you, Jamie. Us. We're leaving."

Sir James blinked. "But...but we came in your carriage, Nick. Oh, wait. I suppose I could fob Miss Simmons off on Georgie. The idiot looks eager enough. All right, toddle off home if you must.

Leave me here. But I'll expect an explanation in the morning, blister me if I won't.''

"And you'll get it," Nicholas promised, ending under his breath, "if we're here." But Jamie couldn't hear that, because it would only start another round of questions he couldn't answer. But something was going on, damn it. Susan Halstead had done something…and he could cheerfully throttle the woman if she'd upset his wife.

My, he was feeling protective these days. He barely recognized himself.

The ride back to the mansion was uncomfortably silent, and as Eleanor seemed to wish to lose herself in thought, Nicholas believed he might be prudent to do the same.

That his thoughts kept straying to how lovely his wife looked in her peach satin gown, how his fingers itched to loose the ribbon holding up her fine dark hair, so that it tumbled over those eager fingers, serious thought was proving difficult, if not impossible.

Still, there was the matter of Susan Halstead and the tears in her eyes.

It didn't take much effort to imagine Susan Halstead dropping in to "visit" with Eleanor in her box, especially since that feather-witted Miss Simmons had actually deserted her, probably to spread more gossip, as if there weren't enough flying about Mayfair like a flock of chattering birds on the wing.

What had Susan said to have Eleanor wishing to

go home—after first putting on a small show for Society?

Even more to the point, what had Eleanor said to make Susan bolt from the box, forgetting that she was the grande dame, and not one to ever show emotion. Most certainly not one to be routed, and let the world know she had been routed.

So Nicholas pondered this as the carriage wended its way through uncrowded streets, and settled on being amused. Amused, and rather delighted, that his wife—gad, his *wife*—was no milk-and-water puss, neither shy nor prone to hysterics.

"Good evening, my lord, my lady," Clarke said, bowing as he all but skidded into the foyer, and without so much as a blink betraying the confusion he must be feeling. After all, his master and mistress had only departed the house two hours ago. He hadn't expected them until at least three.

"Interrupted your game of whist, Clarke? My apologies. Are you winning?"

It was only then that Clarke realized his cuffs had been turned back, and he quickly unfolded them. "I am being thoroughly trounced, your lordship, thank you. By tomorrow at this time, Sylvester may well own my eye teeth."

Nicholas laughed as he handed over his cape and curly brimmed beaver, then escorted his wife upstairs.

And now, the dilemma.

Did he take her into his rooms...into her

rooms…leave her at the door to her rooms, where her dragon of a Cloris awaited?

"Give me a few minutes to shoo Cloris, Nicholas, and then, please, join me?"

He bowed as she stopped in front of her door. "It would be my pleasure, wife."

"Eleanor," she said, tipping up her chin. "My name is Eleanor. My position is your wife."

"Eleanor," Nicholas repeated. "No, I'd rather Elly, if you don't mind. Only in private, you understand."

She shrugged, but her cheeks went rather pink. "I won't argue the point, *Nick.*"

He shook his head and headed down the hallway to his own door, wondering if she'd been spanked much as a child. Probably not. She probably had run the entire household from her cradle.

Sylvester, about as breathless as Clarke, was waiting for him in his bedchamber, already laying out his dressing gown and slippers.

"Thank you, Sylvester, but you needn't linger as I've heard your luck is running high. Best get back, before the tide changes."

"Yes, my lord," Sylvester said, bowing. Then he backed up three paces, turned, and all but ran from the room. His half brother, Nicholas had concluded long ago, had inherited their father's love of the cards but, fortunately, not the man's terrible luck.

He stripped off his neck cloth, opened the top two buttons of his shirt. Rolled up his sleeves, kicked off his evening shoes. Looked at his dressing gown and slippers, and decided against either.

A glance at the mantel clock told him not quite five minutes had passed, so he poured himself a glass of wine at the drinks table and sat himself down to wait.

Would tonight be the night? He had planned to woo her more slowly, then have their wedding night only after this second infernal ceremony. But their kiss tonight had been more than he'd expected, her reaction definitely more than he'd hoped for so soon in their marriage. And then there was that business about kissing her hand—"anything at all"—at the theater. Now *there* was an invitation!

He did not have to be hit over the head with a redbrick to know when a woman was interested, even a virgin. Even a wife.

"So what are you doing, sitting here?" he asked himself as he pushed up from his chair, straightened his shoulders and headed for the door connecting the two rooms.

The door opened even as he approached it, and there was Elly, dressed in her white dressing gown and night rail, her hair loose on her shoulders, her feet bare, although he knew damn well he'd seen slippers on her at least once since they'd come to town.

She probably ran barefoot through the grass at her father's home, and dabbled those feet in a nearby stream. Made crowns out of strung daisies. She hugged dogs. She had no fear. She threw things when she was angry. She colored delightfully when she was embarrassed. And her mouth was so soft, so warm...

"We have to talk," she said, turning her back on him as she headed for the pair of chairs in front of the fireplace.

"That sounds familiar," he said, following after her. "What do I want to talk about now?"

She had the good grace to flush. "Please, I'm being serious. We have to talk about...about your father."

Nicholas dropped heavily into the chair, sat very still. Of all the possibilities he had entertained on the ride home from the theater and while in his rooms, his father had not entered the mix. "My father? What of him?"

"You didn't marry me because you compromised—no, because I compromised myself. You did it for honor, yes, just as you said, but that was only because your own father behaved so dishonorably, not because you didn't want to be involved in a duel. You said it didn't matter who you married, but you also said you would be a faithful husband, that you would give me no reason to divorce you. I should have known something then, because it is the rare *ton* husband who is faithful if he can avoid it. Even Walter, more's the pity, because Francesca really does love the sorry creature."

"My, my, my," Nicholas said, steepling his fingers beneath his chin. "You *have* been doing a lot of thinking, haven't you? What did Susan Halstead say to you?"

She put her head down for a moment, then lifted it again, looking straight into his eyes. "She told me about Sylvester. And...and the others."

Nicholas tried to return her steady gaze, but found he couldn't. "Go on."

"Is there anything else to say? I've spoken to a few people here, not that anyone was divulging secrets, because they all love you and only want your happiness. I already knew that you loved your mother very much, and that you perhaps were not so fond of your father. That you had his chambers completely redecorated upon his death eighteen months ago. And then Miss Halstead...well, she told me the rest. She actually threatened me, telling me that the news of your father's...philandering, would become public knowledge unless I did everything she said. Mostly, all she said was that I was to smile, pretend to be friendly...and let her kiss me on my cheek there at the theater."

"And did you?" Nicholas asked, looking at her again.

"I gave my permission, but she left the box instead."

"Yes, I saw her. Running, and crying. Now, why do you suppose that was?"

Eleanor shrugged. "I don't know. Perhaps it was

when I laughed at her horrible gossip and called her stupid. That…that could be it.''

Nicholas bit on the insides of his cheeks and nodded. ''Yes, that might have done it. I doubt anyone has ever spoken to The Halstead like that. Cheeky brat.''

''This one time, Nick, thank you. I'd like to think so. However, this does not settle our problem.''

''We have a problem? It sounds to me as if you've taken care of it.''

''I don't mean Miss Halstead,'' Eleanor said, dismissing the absent woman with a wave of her hand. ''I'm talking about the reason you married me. It was because your father was such a rotter. Sorry, but, by all indications, he was. And, while I find that very noble of you, now that I know, I believe we could still apply for that annulment. Especially if we don't go through with the second ceremony. The first one was barely legal, don't you think?''

Nicholas stood up, picked up his empty glass, and went into his rooms to refill it. He was getting the headache and he needed a few moments to think.

Eleanor, being Eleanor, didn't give them to him, but merely followed after him, plopping her barefooted self down on one of his fireside chairs.

''Was it difficult, knowing Sylvester is your half brother?''

He poured a second glass, carried it over to her. ''I didn't know. Not until my father died. For ten years, Sylvester was my valet, my companion, my friend. But I was his employer, at least of sorts. His master. When I read the letter from my father, informing me of the truth, I threw up. Sorry, but I find I can't seem to lie to you.''

"Did Sylvester know? He's quite a bit older than you are, isn't he?''

Nicholas sat down, nodded. "He knew. Sylvester is the product of our father's first tumble with a barmaid from the village when he was but fifteen. By my last count, there are at least a dozen more, some older than me, many younger. At least three, besides Sylvester, were employed on our estate, two of them in the house. He flaunted his by-blows. I always wondered why my mother was so perpetually sad.''

"I'm so sorry. But is that any reason to marry a woman who doesn't love you? You must have known that Miss Halstead would only have been marrying your title. She may be stupid, but you're not. I was easily interchangeable with Miss Halstead, one bride being as good as another, to get you heirs, but without your hearts ever being involved, because you'd seen too much pain? Is that it, Nick? Do I understand correctly?''

He looked at her, this time holding her gaze. "I will never do as my father did.''

"So you married a woman you didn't even know, even promised fidelity? That's very...honorable of you, Nick. But I need more than that, fanciful creature that I am. So, no, thank you.''

And she stood up, flung her glass of wine into the fire, and left the room.

HE'LL FOLLOW. He'll follow. He'll follow. Why isn't he following? Did you gamble everything on one roll, just to lose?

Eleanor paced the carpet for some minutes, nervous and baffled and more than a little angry, behind the door she had slammed as she'd stormed back to the chamber, then finally gave up, ripped off her dressing gown and climbed into bed.

She'd leave tomorrow, taking Cloris with her and returning to Oglesby House, here in the city. From there, it would be a simple thing to be driven back to the country.

Why hadn't he come after her?

He didn't love her. Not yet. She wouldn't expect that of him, no matter how many novels she had read during the long winter nights in front of the fire.

She might love him, might have loved him from the first time she'd seen him at Almacks, but that had been the love of a girl. A silly girl, full of dreams.

Somehow, in these past few days, she had become a woman. She didn't know how, she didn't know when, but she did know that what she felt for Nicholas could grow, change, deepen. They just needed time. Time to get to know each other better, so that secrets shared replaced secrets kept, and all the shadows he'd lived with, that shadow she'd seen in his eyes, would be replaced by light.

And that *sounds just like one of your dreams, Eleanor Therese. Shame on you.*

She had almost slipped into a fitful sleep when the door opened, sending a pie-shaped slice of light into the room. She could see Nicholas standing there, outlined by the light.

She quickly closed her eyes once more. Should she feign sleep? Should she pretend not to know he was there? Should she take a breath, because there were little blue lights beginning to dance behind her closed lids…

"Wife?"

Eleanor bit her lips together and remained silent.

She heard him walk toward the bed, walk around the bottom of it. Felt his weight on the mattress as he climbed beneath the covers.

She could still pretend to be asleep. If she was an idiot.

Eleanor turned onto her back and looked at him in the light from the fire. He was lying on his side, his cheek propped on one bent arm, grinning at her.

"Hello, wife," he said in this amused, almost-maddening voice. "This feels familiar, doesn't it?"

She nodded, her tongue fairly well stuck to the roof of her suddenly dry mouth.

"I've never met anyone like you, you know," he told her, and she couldn't move, couldn't breathe. "You don't care about Sylvester. You don't care about Susan Halstead, who should be soundly horse-whipped but will probably find herself a meek and willing male to hop to her bidding for the rest of her days. You don't care about the gossips, the biddies. In fact, all you do seem to care about is rescuing me from what you see as my folly in marrying you. Now, why is that?''

"It wasn't your fault. It was mine."

"True, true," he said, making himself more comfortable on the bed. "I think I shall remind you of that, at least once a year for the next fifty years, just to keep you humble as I spend those fifty years adoring you."

"A-adoring me? I—I don't understand."

And then he smiled. "No? Neither do I, frankly. I think perhaps it was the braids. Or maybe the horse blanket? No, couldn't be that. I know, it was the way you crawled over me, *scrambled,* actually, to get as far from me as you could."

"Don't make fun of me," Eleanor warned, but only because she knew she had to say something. He was looking at her…looking at her as if he couldn't see enough of her, but wanted more… more.

"You're right, I shouldn't tease you. The problem is, Elly—wife—that you have been teasing me since first we met."

"Me?" She pulled the covers closer to her chin. "How?"

His gaze dropped to the covers. "That's one, for

starters, but only one. No, you teased me with your honesty, with your way of saying just what you think. And then, once I was intrigued, you made my life impossible by letting me know that you are a strong woman, stronger than I, I think.''

''Oh, I'm not.'' He was still looking at her that way, and now he was stroking her cheek. Strong? She was melting, her bones dissolving, and she had all the strength of a newborn kitten.

''We'll argue about that once a year, too, all right?'' he moved closer. ''Elly, we've just begun. We've stumbled, but we've moved on. I think...I *know,* we can be happy together. Do you know it, too?''

''I—I had thought...''

''Could we think tomorrow?'' he asked her, cupping the back of her head with one large hand and drawing her toward him, his gaze on her mouth.

''I—I think we could. Yes, please....''

EPILOGUE

BUCKLAND MANOR, one of the earl's lesser estates, but one he was particularly fond of because it was so far removed from its neighbors, welcomed another perfect summer day. The sun shone, the brook bubbled, the blue sky was the perfect background for the fleecy white clouds, and the breeze blew sweet with the smell of wildflowers.

How had he ever been here alone? Perfect, yes, in the ordinary way. But extraordinarily perfect now—now that his son slept in the nursery, and his wife sat on the edge of the brook, laughing and dangling her bare feet into the cool water.

He lay on his side on the bank, his cheek resting on his palm, enjoying the view closest to him, the view he'd never tire of, the view that never failed to fill him with a love that had budded, then blossomed, then grown...and continued to grow.

She wore a daisy chain in her dark, tumbling hair. She wore it because he'd fashioned it for her...fulfilling yet another of his early fantasies about this woman who was his life, his heart, his very soul.

Elly turned to him and laughed. ''Your daisy

chain is slipping over your eye, Nick. Don't you feel it?''

He smiled, close-mouthed, and shook his head. He was *feeling,* definitely. But he hadn't felt the flower ring slipping…just his libido, rising up, ready to break into a gallop.

''You could fix it for me,'' he suggested, then leaned back as she reached for him so that she tumbled against him, her feet splashing in the brook before she grabbed onto him, pulling herself closer.

''Idiot,'' she said, laughing as he pulled her completely on top of him. ''Don't! I'm all wet. I'll get you all—oh, the devil with it.''

''My wife, swearing. I think we'll have to plug Nicky's ears with cotton wool when you're around,'' he told her as she pushed herself up, straddling him. ''I'm sure his Uncle Sylvester could only approve when next he visits from his estate.''

''You and Uncle Sylvester be hanged, husband. Do you think I didn't know what the two of you were planning last month?''

''Cloris,'' Nicholas said, wincing.

''Exactly, my love.'' Bracing her hands on his shoulders, she leaned down, smiled into his face. ''Don't you think a four-month-old child is a little young to be fitted with his own pony?''

''It was going to be a surprise for his first birthday?'' Nicholas offered weakly.

''At the very least. What color is he?''

''Nicky? Goodness, I thought you knew. He's delightfully dark-haired, like his mother, but I believe his green eyes are mine. As for the perpetual roses in his cheeks, I—''

Elly swatted him and he caught her hands, held them tight. "Oh, you mean the *pony?* We haven't yet decided. But I suppose blonde and blue-eyed would be frowned on, love?''

"I'd say so, yes," Elly said as he pulled her closer, let go of her hands so that he could reach up, cup her breasts. "Hmm...that's nice. Am I to believe I'm about to say yes to something else?''

"If, dearest madam, you'd be so kind..." Nicholas said as she melted against him, as he lifted his head, caught her mouth with his own.

The birds chirped, the honey bees buzzed and the sun rose higher in the sky. But Nicholas didn't notice. All the glory in the world was now lying beneath him, and if he noticed the sun at all, it was to admire the way the sunlight filtering through the tree branches made her skin glow, dappled her bare breasts with light and shadow.

"You're the most beautiful woman in the world, wife, and I do believe I love you to distraction."

Elly moved her hips against his, then sighed in pleasure. "Is that what it was?" she asked, "Distraction? Do you think we could go there again? I believe I like it there."

"Cheeky brat," he said, because she always laughed when he called her that...and then he dutifully, and quite pleasurably went about *distracting* her again....

Gentle Reader,

I address you as such in hopes that when you have read my tale, you will indeed be gentle in your condemnation of my shocking actions. I am afraid that those who have made my acquaintance during the past dozen years will have a difficult time reconciling the Emma Stanfield they know with the protagonist of this narrative. There are times when I find it difficult to do so myself.

Of course, I have the advantage in that instance. I remember the Emma who set out for London twelve years ago for her first Season. She was little more than a child, one given to flights of fantasy, who had been told that her future husband would be selected solely by his ability to support her family in the style to which they desired to become accustomed. That admonition did not, as you may guess, keep seventeen-year-old Emma from dreaming of something—and someone—quite different.

This is also her story, you see. A chance meeting with a handsome stranger. A stolen kiss. A snowstorm. One perfect night, which, through the long years, she came to believe must satisfy her thirst for romance for the remainder of her life. Thankfully, that was not to be.

I am no longer that green girl. And yet, when another encounter awakened memories of that long-ago night, I knew I must not let the second chance fate had given me slip through my fingers.

Herein, then, lies the tale of a woman who stood at two distinct crossroads in her life, each separated by a dozen years, and of the choices she made. When you have read it, be kind to her. And if you are not so inclined, she will forgive you, for she is far too happy to do anything else.

Emma

PRISONER OF THE TOWER
Gayle Wilson

For Emily, a heroine in the making.
May you find your own happy ending.

PROLOGUE

1811

THIS WAS QUITE the most daring thing she had ever done in her life. And that was a sad commentary on her seventeen-year existence, Emma Termaine decided as she tiptoed across the gallery, bare feet flinching from the icy coldness of the wooden boards.

When she reached the balustrade, she looked down on the courtyard below. A thick layer of snow blanketed the frozen ground, hiding the ruts arriving coaches had cut into the mud. The old-fashioned galleried inn, which offered the only shelter from the storm on this stretch of road, was filled to overflowing.

Aunt Sophie would never have agreed to spending the night in such a place had their coachman not insisted. Only his dire warnings that they should be overtaken by the blizzard and freeze to death before any rescue could be mounted had finally persuaded her.

As soon as they'd disembarked from the carriage,

she had set the establishment at sixes and sevens with her demands. The inn's servants, carrying buckets of sea coal and warming pans, followed by flagons of mulled wine and the most succulent slices of roast from the spit in the enormous fireplace, had rushed up and down the outer stairway to the room Emma and her aunt had been forced to share.

Not that any of it satisfied Sophie, of course. Neither the food nor the speed of its service nor the dryness of the sheets nor the tightness of the ropes that supported the mattress.

Throughout the resulting turmoil, Emma had bided her time, awaiting her chance to escape. She had listened patiently to her aunt's endless stream of complaints until at last they faded into a low, wine-induced snore. Then she had wrapped Sophie's heavy Norwich wool shawl about her shoulders, managing to cover most of her rail, before she had eased open the door to their chamber.

Despite the fierceness of the afternoon's storm, the night was remarkably clear. The air, washed by the recent snowfall, seemed to sparkle. She took a deep breath, savoring its crispness, and refused to think how long it should be until she would again smell the distinctive freshness of the English countryside.

Mewed about by the rules and conventions of the upcoming Season, for the next few months she would be a prisoner to her family's expectations that she should make a good match. That was all she had heard during the past year until she had memorized it like a litany.

Their hopes rode on her ability to snare some wealthy gentleman who would support them all in the lavish style to which they had become far too accustomed. Feeling the bitterness over the sacrifice they had demanded intruding on her enjoyment of this adventure, Emma determined not to think of what lay ahead.

Not tonight. Tonight was hers. These last few precious hours of freedom.

She leaned over the railing to look up at the sky. The distant stars shimmered like crystals thrown across a spill of black velvet. That brightness was something else she would miss, given the foggy miasma that shrouded the capital.

A solitary snowflake drifted down to land on her cheek. Smiling, she put her hand up to touch the drop of moisture. As she did, out of the corner of her eye she became aware of a movement at the other end of the gallery fronting the bedchambers.

A shape emerged from the shadowed area where the outside staircase led up from the yard. Instinctively Emma drew the shawl more closely about her body. Her high-necked, long-sleeved nightgown was far more modest than the evening gowns she would wear in London. The cold, however, reminded her of its transparency.

"Who's there?" she demanded.

"A fellow traveler. One who is also unable to sleep."

Despite the nonthreatening nature of the reply, its masculine tones produced a thrill of alarm. No gently reared young woman could be unaware of the potential for disaster in such a situation.

"I mean you no harm," he added quickly.

The reassurance had seemed a response to her fear. Which meant, she supposed, that he had *some* notion of the proprieties. A gentleman, perhaps?

As that hopeful thought formed, the stranger stepped out of the shadows and began to move toward her along the gallery. She tried to retreat, but with the railing at her back, there was nowhere to go.

Evidently he realized her dilemma, for his advance halted immediately. In spite of her unease, she felt a momentary disappointment that she could discern nothing about him beyond his height, which was well above the average. There was not enough light there to reveal his features, and the long cloak he wore masked his physique.

"May I be of some service, ma'am?" he asked.

He must be wondering why she was out on the balcony in her rail. She tried to conjure up some credible reason to offer, but she could think of nothing that would explain this excursion. Nothing short of the truth, of course, which she certainly didn't intend to share with a stranger.

"I came out for a breath of air," she said.

If it were not for the night's frigid temperature, the excuse might have served. To claim that she had ventured into this cold for fresh air, however, bordered on the absurd. And they both knew it.

"I'm quite trustworthy, I promise you." His voice had softened conspiratorially, and he took another step forward. The cloak, blacker than the shadows behind it, revealed the broad span of his shoulders. "If you are in trouble…"

Not unless you, too, consider it troubling to be forced to select a husband on his income alone.

She said nothing like that, of course. Whatever her feelings, she had long ago become resigned to her fate. Tonight would be her only rebellion. Until his arrival, it had seemed innocent enough.

"Trouble? Of course not. I'm traveling to London for the Season," she said, trying to imbue her voice with an enthusiasm she could not feel.

"With a trunk full of dresses, no doubt, and another of expectations." The deep voice seemed even more pleasant when touched with amusement.

Emma found that she very much wanted to see his face, if only to judge if it could possibly be as attractive. The stranger was careful to keep his distance, although he seemed more than willing to continue their conversation. And the longer she could prolong it, she realized, the greater the adventure she would have to remember. She tried to think of a witty rejoinder and, failing that, settled for the truth.

"More anxieties than expectations, I'm afraid."

"Ah, but you must never confess to either." The humor she'd heard still lurked in his tone, but his advice held a note of seriousness. "No matter what doubts you feel, you must always present a facade of poise and confidence."

"You have some experience of the Season, I take it."

He laughed, the sound rich despite its softness. And somehow he had made it clear that he, rather than her naiveté, was the target of that amusement.

"I believe I must be acquainted with every hostess in London who has ever had need of a spare bachelor. I assure you I am simply that. Someone to fill up a table or provide escort for a young lady who has not been taken down to supper."

Provincial she might be, but even Emma understood the meaning of the phrase "not taken." And knew it was a fate to be avoided at all costs.

"Then...you are not a catch?"

"A younger son," he said readily. "From a respectable family, I assure you. There are no skeletons rattling about in my closet."

As she watched, he stepped across the narrow gallery and looked out over the balustrade. "It seems we are seeing a break in the weather. This will be completely cleared by morning."

If so, their trunks would be reloaded onto her uncle's post chaise, and they would renew their journey as soon as possible. It would be as if this night had never happened.

He turned his head, looking at her now rather than at the midnight sky. There was enough moonlight reflected from the snow below that finally she could see his face.

His features, regular and pleasant, were centered by an aquiline nose and a square, indented chin. Blue eyes, under a high forehead covered by tumbled black curls, smiled into hers.

Her heart did something very peculiar—stopped or leaped or faltered. And then, as hearts are wont to do, it resumed its steady beating, although a trifle faster than before.

"You still haven't told me why you're out on the balcony at midnight," he said.

It had been a very long time since anyone had really wanted to know her feelings. Emma took a breath and blurted out the truth. "As an alternative to running away, I suppose."

"From the Season?"

"From all of it. From the rules and regulations and expectations. From marriage to someone I shall hardly know."

"Perhaps you'll fall in love."

"Do people do that in London?"

"On occasion."

"But you see, that isn't the primary prerequisite for my husband."

"And what is?" he asked quite seriously, although the blue eyes were still smiling.

"A fortune."

"Ah. You're a fortune hunter. Then undoubtedly you *won't* marry for love."

"Not even, I fear, if I *fall* in love. So tonight…" She hesitated, realizing the delicacy of the situation into which her rashness had embroiled her.

"Tonight?"

"Becomes more important," she confessed softly.

"A last adventure?" he suggested, again seeming to read her mind.

"How did you know that?"

"Because I share the tendency."

"To…seek adventure?"

"The result of an unfortunately romantic nature."

She had not thought of herself in those terms, but perhaps he was right. Perhaps that was at the root of her present melancholia. She should be ecstatic with happiness over the coming round of entertainments. Instead…

"'Unfortunately romantic'?" she repeated, having assimilated fully what he'd said.

"In a society governed by all those 'rules and expectations.'"

"I had not thought men were subject to them."

"Then why ever do you think they would willingly marry fortune hunters?" he teased, smiling at her again.

"I'm sure I don't know. Companionship?" she suggested tentatively.

"*That* they get from their— From other acquaintances," he amended carefully.

She wasn't quite the provincial he believed her to be. After all, Papa had had a mistress, and her mama had still had an honored and necessary place in his life.

"To manage their households," she said, thinking about her mother's many roles. "To keep them running smoothly."

"*And* to bear their children. Very suitable ones with an impeccable lineage."

"I beg your pardon," she said, feeling blood heat her cheeks, despite the cold. She prayed the darkness would hide it, lest he realize how naive she really was.

"I've made you blush," he said, putting that hope to rout. "Forgive me. I had forgotten that tonight is reserved for romantic notions."

"And children are not?"

"Hardly ever," he said. "Children are entails and titles and settlements."

"I think you are very jaded, sir."

"Undoubtedly. And I am charmed that you are not."

Her blush deepened, but she did not deny the charge.

"And is this to be the extent of your last, great adventure?" he asked, waving a gloved hand toward the vista beyond the balustrade.

Her eyes followed the gesture, considering again

the snow-covered ground and the velvet sky lit by stars. Until his arrival she had been quite content with it. Now, seen through his eyes, her rebellion seemed very tame and commonplace.

"I fear it must suffice," she said. "At least the air is clear, and the night—"

She turned to face him and found that he was closer than he had been before. Indeed, it seemed that he was leaning toward her. Before she could object, his lips tilted again, adding the spark of masculine beauty she had noticed earlier to those pleasingly regular features.

Again her heart responded, skipping and then beginning to race as his mouth continued to lower toward hers. Although she was well aware that she should object, put a warning hand against his chest or call for help, she did neither. She simply waited as his lips descended.

They were warm against the chill of hers. Firm and practiced. And very sure of their reception.

She did not disappoint him. Her mouth opened—perhaps in shock, but opened nonetheless—to the invasion of his tongue.

It was not the first time she had been kissed. After all, she had been out in company for almost a year at home. There had been country dances aplenty. And country gentlemen aplenty, too.

None of them had ever kissed her like this. It robbed her breath and then the strength from her knees, so that she swayed, bringing her body into a more intimate alignment with his.

Perhaps he took that as an invitation. His arm came around her waist, pulling her close against his hard masculinity.

She did not resist. His tongue continued to explore, ravaging her senses. Her hands came up, not to push him away, but to slip inside the warmth of his cloak to rest on the broad chest it covered.

After what seemed an eternity, he was the one who broke the kiss. He raised his head, blue eyes luminous in the reflected moonlight as they looked down into hers. No trace of the laughter she had seen there now remained.

"Tell me your name," he demanded softly. He lifted his gloved hand to brush a strand of damp, wind-blown hair away from her cheek.

"Emma. Emma Termaine."

"Don't let them break you, Emma. Rebellion is a good thing. The secret is in knowing when to rebel and when not to."

She nodded as if that made sense, her eyes locked on the mesmerizing intensity of his.

"A distinction I should have learned, I'm afraid." He released her, stepping back as if at the end of a dance set.

Away from the warmth of his embrace, the night felt far colder than it had before he had taken her into his arms.

"Will you be in London?" she asked.

There was no place for false pride in the tumult of emotions she felt. She needed desperately to know if she would see him again.

Even if he were not, as he had assured her, a "catch," he had encouraged her to rebellion. *If* the occasion warranted. Surely, surely, this would.

"For the first time in my existence, I really wish I could be."

"But—"

"Make sure the fortune you find is large enough to make you happy, sweet Emma."

He took another step, widening the distance between them. Unable to resist, she laid her hand on his arm. It was very pale against the fine black wool of his jacket.

He put gloved fingers over hers, lifting them and bringing them to his lips. His eyes above their joined hands watched her.

And then he smiled at her. That same slow tilt of his lips she had noticed before. Again it transformed his face into something extraordinary.

Their eyes held through another eternity. Finally he freed her fingers and almost in the same motion, turned on his heel and crossed the wooden gallery to melt like a phantom into the shadows near the stairs.

She leaned over the balustrade, eyes searching below for a glimpse of him. The snow had begun again, falling like fine powder over the empty courtyard.

There was no sound, just an eerie drift of flakes swirled into motion by a silent wind. No jingle of harness. No hoof beats. Nothing.

She closed her eyes against the sting of tears. After a moment she forced them open again, aware that she was cold and damp and very much alone. Aware also that she could remedy only a limited number of those discomforts.

She looked down, fumbling for the ends of her aunt's shawl to pull it more tightly around her shivering body. As she caught up the fabric, a single snowflake landed on the smooth black wool. For an instant, every detail of its incomparable design was visible, clear and perfect, stark against the darkness of the cloth. And then, almost before she could fully comprehend its beauty, it was gone.

A fleeting perfection, to be cherished more, perhaps, because it could not and had never been intended to last.

CHAPTER ONE

Twelve years later

"BUT SURELY you intend to meet her?"

"If she's your choice, Jamie, I promise you I shall be well satisfied."

There was a small silence. Alex Leighton, the ninth Earl of Greystone, forced his gaze to remain on the printed page before him. He knew his brother was attempting to formulate some plea—one that would not give offense—for his presence when the guests arrived. Through the years, Greystone had become quite adept at rebuffing those, no matter how well intentioned. As Jamie's would be, of course.

"If she is to become my wife..."

His brother's words trailed into silence. This time Greystone looked up, patiently awaiting what he knew was coming.

"And if we are all to live in the same household..."

Again the sentence faltered. Alex decided to take mercy on his sibling, who was really the best of brothers and far more forbearing than he had any right to expect.

"Forgive me. I thought I had told you," he said. "I'm moving to Wyckstead."

"To Wyckstead?" Jamie's voice rose at the end of the name as if his brother had announced he was about to take up residence in a cave. "That's little more than a hunting lodge."

"And will suit me nicely. The stables are fine, and there's plenty of room for my books."

"It won't do. I won't allow it," Jamie said decisively. His fair, handsome face colored as it did when he was upset.

"Forgive me," Greystone said softly, playing a card he seldom used, but one his poor brother could not possibly trump. "I find that I have no wish to live here with you and your beautiful new bride."

Jamie's flush deepened. The finely shaped mouth worked once, but since there was nothing to be said to that very reasonable wish, he wisely said nothing.

"When do they arrive?" the earl asked. Not because he gave a tinker's dam, but simply to break the awkward silence.

"This afternoon," his brother said stiffly. "If I had known that you would object—"

"You mistake me. I have no objection whatsoever to this house party. This is your home, Jamie. You may entertain within it whomever you wish. As long as you don't expect me to play host. Surely you know me better than that."

The silence that answered this equally unforgivable ploy was, thankfully, more sullen than embarrassed.

"I had thought that you might *like* to meet the woman I intend to make my wife."

"I can't imagine why you should," Alex said, smiling at him to take the sting from the rebuke.

"What shall I tell them about your absence?"

It was obvious from the question that Jamie had conceded the point.

"That I've gone to Paris?" Greystone suggested, smiling.

His brother cocked an eyebrow, an I-am-not-amused gesture, one that the earl recognized as a copy of his own mannerism.

"No?" he responded. "Then tell them I am indisposed. If they are ill-bred enough to question that, you might wish to rethink your proposal."

"I wanted your approval."

"You've had it since I put you on your first pony and you very properly failed to fall off. Now, go greet your guests and leave me in peace, if you please."

"I'll look in on you later," Jamie promised, his ready smile restored.

"I believe I shall be in Paris," the Earl of Greystone said, pointedly returning his attention to the book in his lap.

His brother laughed. Then Jamie touched his shoulder in farewell before he crossed to the outer door of the earl's sitting room, which was located in the oldest part of the house.

Alex's eyes remained downcast until his brother's footsteps faded away across the keep's stone floor. Only then did he lay aside his book and lean his head back against his chair.

He was never comfortable when there were outsiders at Leighton. Even without encountering them, he was aware of their presence. Having someone else in the house disturbed the quiet tenor of his days. As would the proposed move to Wyckstead.

He opened his eyes, looking around at the well-beloved objects with which he had filled these rooms. His books and his weapons, the few mementos of friends and places that he had chosen to keep. *His world.* One that he could, had he wished, choose to keep inviolate. The estate and all it encompassed were his and would be until his death.

What he had told Jamie, however, was nothing less than the truth. He had no desire to live here with his brother and his wife. Far better a brief disruption of his environment than a slowly festering envy of the happiness he so sincerely wished for them.

"AND WHATEVER YOU DO, Emma," her brother-in-law said for the tenth time, "don't hover."

"Emma *never* hovers," Georgina denied loyally.

With little more than ten years between them, Georgie had long ago begun calling her by her first name, at least when they were not in public. Much to the annoyance of Charles, of course.

"Your stepmother has your best interests at heart," he said, "but we are here for a private visit. *En famille,* if you please. And since the primary purpose of that visit is to give you two young people an opportunity to become better acquainted, there is no need for her to supervise your every action."

"Of course there isn't," Emma agreed, calmly ignoring the fact that she was only a year or two older than the masculine half of the couple that had just been referred to as "young" people. "Georgina knows very well how to conduct herself."

"The countess will also wish to arrange some time alone with you," Charles continued. "That's customary, I believe."

"To see if I pass muster, do you mean?"

"Georgina," her uncle said repressively.

Emma bit the inside of her lip to keep from answering the quick tilt of Georgie's mouth. Charles need not worry. Although the girl had a lively wit, she was perfectly capable of charming Jamie's mother, at the same time convincing her that in every respect she would be a proper daughter-in-law as well as a proper countess.

She would be, Emma thought in satisfaction, as she surveyed her charge through lowered lashes.

At eighteen, Georgina Stanfield had successfully navigated the treacherous shoals of her first London Season. Her uncle had already received three very respectable offers for her hand. He had answered none of those as yet, in hopes of accepting the one they all believed would result from the journey they were embarked upon today.

"And the earl?" Emma asked.

She couldn't remember hearing Jamie Leighton refer to his father. Nor had Charles referred to him, now that she thought about it, although he was *quite* taken with the title and the long-held nobility of the family.

"I believe he is an invalid," her brother-in-law said. "It is somewhat uncertain, therefore, how long it will be until Mr. Leighton comes into the title. Can't be helped, I suppose."

"I should hope not," Emma said under her breath.

Georgie's laugh was turned into a smothered cough.

"I pray you're not sickening for something," her uncle fretted.

"I am *never* sick. Merely desirous of our arrival."

As if in answer to her wish, the coach began to slow. Three pairs of eyes sought its windows as the coachman pulled the team into the circle in front of their host's country estate, which seemed ablaze with light in the twilight.

The oldest section, a large square tower, appeared to be of Norman construction. Through the generations there had been numerous additions to that original structure, in a hodgepodge of architectural styles. The only guiding principle for those seemed to have been an increase in size and grandeur, which had certainly been achieved.

The footmen made short work of the steps and the carriage door, which opened to reveal Georgina's suitor. Potential suitor, Emma amended, smiling down at him. Providing, of course, that nothing went wrong during the two weeks of their visit.

She watched as Georgina took Jamie Leighton's hand, gracefully allowing him to help her from the chaise. The rush of color one might have expected to find in a young girl's cheeks upon seeing her prospective fiancé bloomed along his instead.

That tendency to blush was one of the most endearing things about the Earl of Greystone's heir. It was an outward sign of what Emma had discovered to be a genuinely sweet and unassuming nature. Jamie might soon inherit what Charles claimed to be one of the oldest and wealthiest titles in England, but one would never guess that from his unaffected manner.

"Welcome to Leighton," he said, as he held out his hand to help her down.

With his words, her gaze naturally rose to again view that imposing, ancient tower. As it did, she caught a flicker of movement in one of the windows on the second story.

Though it had been little more than that, for some reason the hair on the back of her neck lifted. She kept her eyes focused on that particular aperture,

Jenks patted his hand. "It's just an expression, my lord. If it's any consolation, I think Mrs. Mallows has probably learned from past experience to tone down a little on the herbs. Maybe the lady'll only sleep for half a day."

"Inconvenient, nonetheless. I have to go to London. I was hoping to bring her with me."

"But she—"

"Hates London. Yes, I know. Everyone knows. But I haven't given up hope that one of these days, I will change her mind."

"Not tomorrow. But if you go and only stay the one night, there's a chance she'll sleep through the whole thing and not even know that you're gone."

"I suppose you have a good point there, Mrs. Jenks. I could go, conclude my business, and get back without missing much at all around here." And when he came back, he could gift her with her surprise at last. It seemed the perfect solution.

"I would say so. It might be your best time to get away."

"I'll need you to keep close watch over her while I'm gone, Mrs. Jenks. And have Finch send word at the slightest sign of trouble."

She shook her head. "She'll be no trouble at all."

"Then it's settled. I'm going to return to my rooms to ring my valet to arrange my things. You get her comfortable. I'll be back to stay the night in here at her side."

"So it's true what they're saying about your walk this afternoon?" She blushed. "Forgive me, my lord. I shouldn't mention it, but you should know it has been discussed downstairs."

"I've no idea what anyone had to say about our walk, Mrs. Jenks. But I'm every bit in danger of being as besotted with my wife as I ever was."

With that, he left Mrs. Jenks to her business and went off to see to his own.

It didn't take him long. He'd hurried Burns along and left instructions on what to arrange for the next morning's journey. He wouldn't even take a case. Most of what he needed, he had handy at Averford House. The idea was to travel light and make the trip as quickly and as efficiently as he could. More importantly, he wanted to be brief with his valet so that he could get back to his wife's bed.

Mrs. Jenks had left the lights low in Sophia's room. He could only see well enough to strip out of his clothes and get into bed beside her. He had taken to sleeping nude in Italy, due to the heat, and he didn't see why he should change now that he was at home in England. He hoped he could get his wife into the habit, once he convinced her to regularly share a room and a bed. Sophia wasn't likely to wake up and be alarmed at finding him naked in her bed, considering what Jenks had said about the elixir. She would probably sleep straight through the night and into the next day. He would wake early in the morning, dress quietly, and slip back to his room to get ready for the trip to London.

Sophia's sheets were soft, he noted, slipping in beside her and turning off the light on the stand by her bed. Softer than his. Her bed was softer too. His mattress was a little on the firm side. Or perhaps the softness all came from being in bed next to her. The curve of her backside was certainly soft against him. In comparison, he was growing quite hard… He turned to face the other direction. Sleeping next to her was one thing. She had asked him to stay the night with her, and he could only hope that she remembered that when she woke. But he certainly couldn't disturb her with his amorous attentions while she was sleeping, much as he would like to attempt to wake her up enough to join him.

"Another time, my love." He turned back, dropped a light kiss on her shoulder, and attempted to fall asleep.

❧

Sophia woke with a start in the middle of the night. Her mind was a jumble. The last clear memory she had was of Gabriel telling her to sit down while they waited for Finch to bring her water. After that, it all got a bit fuzzy around the edges, like she was looking at the world through a veil. Ah, she recalled Finch bringing her the water and an elixir. Mrs. Mallows's elixir! What was in it?

Gradually, more fragmented memories began to come back to her. Her knees buckling when she tried to stand. Her speech becoming slurred. Gabriel carrying her all the way up the stairs. How she'd wanted to kiss him! Had she? That's when she turned in the bed and saw him sleeping at her side.

She startled. What had she done? Was he…naked? She moved the sheet off his shoulder and peeked beneath it. Even in the near darkness, she could tell that he wasn't wearing anything. But she was. She was in her favorite white nightgown. She had a vague recollection of Jenks pleading with her to turn so that she could unbutton her dress. But if Gabriel was in bed with her, why had Jenks come in to undress her? She remembered asking Gabriel to stay, wanting him to be there. No matter what had happened the night before, she was glad to see him beside her.

Her questions would wait until morning. For now, she remained exhausted and barely able to keep her eyes open. She felt chilled to the bone, and she meant to take full advantage of the warm body in the bed next to her, no matter the circumstances that put him there. She curled up against him and fell back to sleep.

Thirteen

WHEN SOPHIA WOKE AGAIN, IT WAS STILL DARK BUT Gabriel was no longer at her side. She sat up. Had he gone back to his own bed? She felt as if she'd been asleep for days, but it couldn't have been more than a few hours considering the darkness outside. Reaching across the bed, she clicked on the light and squinted to make out the clock on her mantel. Eight in the morning? That couldn't be right, considering the lack of light. Eight at night? Had she slept a whole day? Her clock must be wrong. She rang for Jenks. Jenks would clear up any confusion.

Her maid came not a minute after Sophia rang for her. She must not have been far off. "Lady Averford. Thank goodness."

"Thank goodness? Was there some doubt about my health?"

The last time she had slept for days had been after she'd given birth to a healthy son and slipped into a fever straight afterward. When she woke, she had been greeted with the news that her beautiful boy had died.

The memory made her apprehensive to hear what Jenks had to say.

"No doubt exactly, but Mrs. Mallows is eager to see you. She wants to apologize for the elixir. She might have gotten a bit carried away with the herbs. How are you feeling?"

"The elixir, of course. Was there something wrong with it?" Sophia made a quick evaluation of all her limbs and parts. "I feel perfectly well. No aches or pains. Clear head. Awareness is slowly returning."

Jenks nodded. "As expected. Good. Are you hungry?"

"What time is it, Jenks? Where's Gabriel?"

"It's just after eight in the evening, my lady. You've been asleep for almost a whole day."

"A whole day?" She managed not to gasp. "And my husband?"

"Lord Averford was hoping to return before you woke, but he missed the last train out of London. He's staying the night at Averford House."

"Averford House? What's he doing in London?"

"He had business, urgent. He wanted to bring you with him, but after the elixir had such an extraordinary effect on you, well... He decided it was best to go, tend his affairs, and get back as soon as possible."

Had she only imagined him in bed with her? She looked at the empty space beside her.

"He stayed with you until the morning," Jenks added. "At your request."

"I'm glad. I wish I'd been awake to see him off." Urgent business in London? The divorce! He had gone to file papers, and he would come back and ask her to agree to a divorce. But why would he have shared her bed if he were rushing off to divorce her? She had to admit that it made no sense. Perhaps other business had sent him to London.

"Would you mind terribly if I called for Mrs. Mallows? She has been frantic all day, waiting to make sure you woke up. I know it's unusual, but she would feel much better to see you."

"I suppose it's a little late for me to dress and get down to dinner."

"Aunt Agatha suggested they would all be content with trays in their rooms." Jenks bit her lip and looked down. "But the Dowager Countess has taken the opportunity to step in for you."

"Of course she has. Isn't that sporting of her?" Sophia laughed.

When Sophia didn't take the news badly, Jenks went on. "She's holding court, from what I understand. She invited the Waldens to join in. They're all in the drawing room now. Still time if you wanted to drop in for dinner. Wouldn't she be surprised?"

Sophia waved a hand. "Let her have her fun. I'll take a tray. I could probably do with a leisurely evening. Perhaps I'll catch up on some correspondence and do some reading. Or, is Anna at dinner?"

"Anna requested a tray in her room to be ready in case you needed her. Mr. Kenner is working through dinner and will also take a tray."

"And Mr. Grant?"

"He went to London with Lord Averford."

"Did he? Curious. Gabriel's business must involve Thornbrook Park then, for him to bring his agent along." Protecting the estate in the event of divorce? She wouldn't stand to get any of it, not unless he'd been the unfaithful one. "Or maybe Mr. Grant had some business of his own in London."

"I've no idea. It wasn't my place to ask."

"I suppose we'll find out in due time. Help me get a little more presentable, then let Mrs. Mallows come up if she wishes. Preferably with a tray. I am hungry. After I get something to eat, I'll send for Anna."

Alistair Morris, Gabriel's solicitor, did not like the idea of Gabriel deeding any bit of Thornbrook Park's lands to Lady Averford, not even a small parcel.

"Once it's in her name, entirely hers, who is to say what she might do with it?" the solicitor argued.

"Whatever she bloody well wants. That's the whole idea, Morris."

Morris raised a bushy white brow. "Your father would not approve."

"A good thing he's not here to concern himself in my affairs then, eh?" Gabriel clapped Morris on the back. "I understand your concerns, but I assure you that my wife is a very capable woman."

"Your wife? The same wife you've often lamented was going to spend you into pauper's court?"

Gabriel shrugged. "She has become more responsible since gaining a true understanding of what it takes to run an estate the size of Thornbrook Park. I trust her with my land and my life." And his heart that she held between her two delicate, snow-white hands. He was proud of her accomplishments, he realized. How many women could run an entire estate? Perhaps a good many more than he'd credited.

Morris's vein-riddled nostrils flared out. "Trust her, do you? The same wife who was caught in the arms of the Earl of Ralston in your own house? By you, if I have the story straight."

Mr. Grant, standing off to one side, twisted his lips. He hadn't known? Gabriel wouldn't expect Sophia to have introduced the topic, but that none of the servants had mentioned it to him, the newcomer? Gabriel had to give them points for loyalty. If only Sophia knew how much they esteemed her.

"Alistair." No more Mr. Morris. As far as Gabriel was concerned, the man had swung below the belt. Though he understood that his solicitor was only looking out for his best interests. "Let me be brutally honest with you. What happened that night was between my wife and me, the two of us, and no one else. You have represented my family for forty years, some years longer than I have been alive. But there are new solicitors eager to represent an illustrious estate such as mine, and I wouldn't hesitate to take my business elsewhere should you insult my wife again."

"Forgive me, Lord Averford. Sordid rumors do go around, and one has to question…well, at least try to protect a client from all possible events. Some men, not you certainly but some, are blind to the faults of their beloveds. It is my job to keep a level head and a logical outlook."

"Love is never logical, Morris. I see your point. But I assure you, I am prepared to accept all consequences."

"Your father would never have done the same for your mother."

"There are a great many things my father should have done for my mother, Morris." Keeping his marriage vows would have been a good start. Father had taken more mistresses than Gabriel cared to count. "I mean to leave here with the deed. How quickly can you make it happen?"

Hours later, Gabriel had what he needed, but it was too late to make the train home. "Looks like we'll be staying the night at Averford House, Grant. My apologies. It was under my recommendation that you failed to bring a case."

"I've done worse than wear the same suit two days in a row."

Gabriel laughed. "We all have, my man. Rest assured, we can provide all you'll need at the house. Sutton keeps plenty of supplies on hand for guests under such circumstances. Razors, soap. You've met my brother? I believe he's still in residence with his lovely wife, unless they left earlier today."

"We've met, yes. And you're right. Your brother's wife is a lovely woman. A pity he met her first. I understand she was in residence at Thornbrook Park for some time as a lonely widow. If only I'd come along sooner."

"It wasn't all that long before Marcus became aware of Eve, I assure you." Gabriel still regretted any action he had taken to keep the pair apart. They were perfectly suited for each other. Eve brought out the best in Marcus.

"I would only be surprised if any man failed to be

aware of her. She's…everything a man could want," Mr. Grant said.

"Some men. Petite, curvy blonds hold a certain appeal, I suppose. But I've always been more attracted to a certain willowy, raven-haired woman." Gabriel laughed. He had hated to leave that woman, her raven hair spread across the pillow. Before he left, he'd kissed her cheek and informed her that he was going to London, but she'd offered no indication that she'd heard him. "So you harbor an attraction to my brother's wife? Hide it well. My brother wouldn't hesitate to kill any man who so much as looked at her in a suspicious way."

"I've heard that he was once a prizefighter."

"And a damn good one at that." Gabriel had never seen his brother fight in the ring, but he'd heard stories. And he'd felt the sting of Marcus's left hook firsthand. "He could lay you flat before you even knew what was coming."

"Thank you for the warning. I'll be sure to stay on my guard." Grant held up his hands. "I would never consider making advances on another man's wife, of course."

"Of course." Gabriel smiled. He could tell by the glint in Grant's gray eyes that the man was thinking of what he'd heard from Alistair Morris about Sophia in Lord Ralston's arms.

What if Morris had reason for concern? Sophia had nearly been unfaithful in the past. She'd kissed another man. What would it take for her to turn to someone else should she doubt his love? Gabriel would just have to make sure there was no reason for her to ever question his unbridled passion for her again.

After a long-winded apology from Mrs. Mallows and more information on Chinese medicine than she'd ever wanted to know, Sophia finally had gotten to eat a hearty meal of lamb stew. The others had been served duck, a special request from the Dowager Countess, and Mrs. Mallows had wanted to bring Sophia some too. But she had asked what the servants were eating downstairs and surprised Mrs. Mallows with the request for some of that instead. She'd taken a liking to simple, savory fare, the kinds of things the servants ate. Unfortunately, she didn't get to eat it often, having the responsibility of impressing her guests at formal dinners.

Once she'd eaten, she'd called Anna in to go over her correspondence. There were letters to be answered, one from Alice in Morocco. When had they moved on from India to Morocco? One from her friend Lizzie in London. Sophia should have thought to visit Lizzie while she was in town, but she'd been there so briefly. The Dovedales kept to different social circles than the Earl of Averford, but such things wouldn't stop Sophia from paying a call. Not any longer. Perhaps next time Gabriel went on business, she really would go with him. At the bottom of the stack, there was a letter from her mother-in-law, sent while she was still in Italy. That one didn't require an answer, but at least it provided some proof that Teresa had sent word of her intention to visit. A pity it hadn't arrived sooner. It would have given Sophia some idea that Gabriel had returned too.

"It's a shame your sister won't be back in time for the garden party," Anna said at last.

Sophia looked through the stack of mail. "Garden party? Who's having a garden party? I must have missed that invitation."

"It's to be our party. The Dowager Countess says she has it all worked out and that she will even buy me a new dress. White. Everyone wears white for her famous garden parties. It's going to be so exciting! I wonder if Mr. Kenner is any good at cricket?"

"I can't imagine he's ever played in his life. But when does the Dowager Countess plan to hold this garden party? I've yet to be consulted."

"I'm sure she means to speak with you about it. It was all we talked about at dinner."

"You went to dinner? I thought you had a tray sent up."

"I didn't stay long, but I felt lonesome in my room." Anna shrugged. "You and Lord Averford were right."

"Lord Averford? But he's in London."

Anna waved a hand. "When I first arrived, I was excited to have my own room. You warned that having my own room might not be quite what I expected, and then Lord Averford said much the same, that it could be lonely when you're used to sharing."

"I recall." Sophia reached up to twist her necklace chain around her fingers, then realized she wasn't wearing one. Had Gabriel missed her in Italy as much as she'd hoped?

"The Waldens are eager to see a real English garden party," Anna said, bringing Sophia back to the matter at hand.

"The Waldens? She means to hold an event while the Waldens are still with us? That only gives her a week. She must have been planning all along. Anna, ring for Mrs. Jenks. I must get ready to go down." Sophia leaped to her feet.

"But they'd already moved on to cordials by the time you rang for me. They might be in bed."

"It's not even midnight, much too early for the Dowager Countess to turn in. She likes to keep the party going. I'm sure I can catch her." And if not her, Mrs. Hoyle. Sophia felt certain that if Teresa had hatched a plan, she'd enlisted her favorite ally. "Why don't you go down first to see what they're doing?"

Anna nodded. "I'll see you there."

Jenks had Sophia looking presentable in less than an hour, and she was on her way. Just outside her room, she practically ran into Jane in the hall.

"Lady Averford." Jane seemed surprised to see her. "Are ye well? I'd heard ye were suffering some ill effects from Mrs. Mallows's elixir. I'm so sorry. I couldn't help but feel responsible…"

Sophia waved a hand. "Oh, please don't. I am feeling much better, and it was an accident after all. Not your fault."

"I did deliver it to ye." Jane's fair cheeks colored. "I wish I'd known it was so powerful. I wouldn't have recommended it quite so enthusiastically. And now ye've missed your trip to London."

"Yes, I did. Lord Averford has gone without me. But how did you know I was to accompany him?" She didn't recall mentioning it to anyone. She'd never even given her husband a definitive answer.

"I was bringing another bottle of champagne to the drawing room and I overheard Lord Averford asking ye to go wi' him. I'm sorry. I didn't mean to eavesdrop."

"Some things you can't help overhearing." Sophia shrugged. "I understand. I'll get my chance to go to London another day. As it is, all's well."

"I'm glad to hear it. Excuse me, Lady Averford. I'll be getting back to work."

"Yes. I don't want to get you in trouble with Mrs. Hoyle. Good evening, Jane."

As Sophia approached the drawing room, she could still hear Teresa's voice booming in exclamations. "Capital fun! Let's have another song…"

Sophia suspected her mother-in-law of indulging in more than a few of the cordials, and she was reluctant to breeze on in and make a scene. Instead, she went to the study and rang for Mrs. Hoyle and Mr. Finch, in case Hoyle had already gone to bed.

The pair showed up together to find Sophia seated at the desk. "When were you going to tell me about the garden party? Either one of you might have mentioned it. If we're to have a party, I believe the woman of the house should be the first to know."

Hoyle shook her head. "There will be no party."

Sophia quirked a brow. "Oh? I've heard differently. Perhaps Mr. Finch can set the matter straight. I've warned you, Mrs. Hoyle, that I won't take kindly to your working with the Dowager Countess behind my back."

"But she's not," Finch said, stepping forward. "In fact, it was Mrs. Hoyle who handed me the invitations and instructed me to check with you before putting them in the mail. I was meaning to ask you about it in the morning. I had no idea you were up and about. Forgive me, my lady. The fault was all mine."

"Is this true, Mrs. Hoyle?" Sophia was as surprised as she was remorseful to find that Mrs. Hoyle had been on her side after all.

"As you say, the lady of the house should be the first to know. I wouldn't allow anyone to hold an engagement at Thornbrook Park without hearing from you first." Hoyle pursed her lips, clearly a little put out at Sophia's jumping to conclusions.

"Thank you, Mrs. Hoyle. Please forgive me for making assumptions. I should never have doubted you." But of course, they both knew that Sophia had cause to doubt. "Please, go on about your business. But first, Mr. Finch, could you bring me those invitations?"

Finch bowed and headed out. Hoyle walked off without another word.

"Thank you, Mr. Finch." Finch returned with the invitations and left her again. She opened one to see that Teresa intended to have her party within the next two weeks. Such short notice. Why the rush? She supposed she would have to confront Gabriel's mother and ask.

Fortunately, the gaiety was winding down as she entered the drawing room. Louise Walden barely stifled a yawn as she rose to greet Sophia.

"No need to stay later on my account," she said to the Waldens. "I'm headed to bed myself. I just wanted to take a moment to say hello."

"I'm so glad you're feeling better, Lady Averford," Louise said.

"A party's just not the same without those twinkling

blue eyes watching over us all," Hugh Walden added, eliciting a grimace from Teresa.

"You have my thanks for keeping the Dowager Countess amused in my absence," Sophia said.

"She kept us amused with her delightful songs. Such whimsy! But now I think we need to be getting back. I shouldn't have had that last claret. Puts me right to sleep." Louise Walden and her husband said their good-byes. Anna also went off to bed as soon as she could tell that Sophia didn't need her to stay any longer.

"At last, we're alone," Sophia said, producing the stack of invitations from her pocket. "You've been busy in my absence."

"My invitations! Why hasn't Finch mailed them? It's going to be short notice as it is, but such a grand affair!"

"There will be no affair. At least, not here in the next two weeks. It's too soon, Teresa. Why have a hastily arranged party when you can really go all out?"

Teresa's mouth gaped. Clearly she'd thought that Sophia was going to deny her the fun of throwing a fete. Instead, Sophia surprised her with the suggestion that they could still have a party, only at a later date.

"I wasn't sure you would want anything elaborate." Teresa regained her power of speech.

"Why not? Your garden parties were celebrated affairs. People still speak of them. I wouldn't want you to rush into things and ruin your good reputation. Let's take our time and plan it together."

"You would want to do that? To plan a party with me?"

"To be honest, you have more experience with these things. I'm sure I could learn a lot from you if you let me help." Sophia surprised herself with her diplomacy. She'd meant to be antagonistic, but suddenly inspiration struck. Teresa would always be trying to outdo her or overrule Sophia in her own house. Why not let her think they would be working together? Why not flatter the woman a little for a change?

"I would like that, yes. We have time to do it properly."

Sophia nodded. "Say about six weeks? We can redo the invitations."

Growing animated, Teresa clapped her hands. "We'll have carnival games! And cricket for the men. Perhaps an archery contest for the ladies…"

"I'm too weak to plan now." Sophia held up her hands. "So tired. But perhaps tomorrow…"

"Tomorrow, yes! Of course. You poor dear. Get some rest."

"And we'll have to discuss it with Gabriel before sending any invitations out."

Teresa nodded. "We'll have to make sure he's agreeable to the idea. I'm sure you can be persuasive with him. And how can he say no to his mother?"

"Good night, Teresa. Until tomorrow."

Once back in her room, Sophia found that she wasn't the slightest bit tired. And no wonder, after sleeping for more than a day. She curled up in her armchair with her worn-out copy of *Emma*, her second favorite Austen novel. She'd once thought herself to be quite a bit like the heroine, but she didn't see much resemblance anymore. And Mr. Knightley was no Mr. Darcy. He was a bit too hard on dear Emma. Everyone makes mistakes. Perhaps Sophia had put her biggest mistakes behind her. She was certainly learning to be more agreeable, if her interaction with Teresa was any proof.

The cool night air streamed in through her open window and disturbed her just as she was getting to the part in which Elton proposes, forcing Emma to realize her mistake in interfering with Harriet Smith's romantic life.

"Yes, Emma. You should have seen the danger in it sooner. Alas." Sophia put down the book to close the window. But as she leaned in, she heard a soft mewling outside.

Kittens? Had a barn cat recently given birth? Not that she knew of, but there was definitely something making a soft, needy sound on the ground below. It seemed to be coming from near the service entrance at the back of the house, which her window nearly overlooked. The position of her window over the service entrance had been an inconvenience she had learned to enjoy when she realized she could take note of all deliveries coming to the house. More than once, she had intercepted a new parcel of gowns, bonnets, or perfumes before Gabriel could become aware that she'd ordered them.

The mewling became louder until it was as insistent as a deprived baby's cry. Perhaps it was Agatha's Miss Puss? She laughed at the idea. But she stopped laughing when she realized that the mewling did sound like an actual infant's cry. What was it really?

Curious, Sophia had to know. It was late enough that the guests were most certainly in bed, and most of the servants should be on the way too. She draped a shawl over her shoulders, put on her slippers, and made her way down. She had to access the service entrance by going through the kitchen and up a short flight of stairs to the door. Mr. Finch remained awake in the storeroom off the kitchen. He came out when he heard her approach.

"Lady Averford." His thin mouth opened just the slightest bit to reveal his surprise. "Are you well? Is there something I can do?"

"I'm sorry to disturb you, Mr. Finch. I didn't expect you would still be up."

"Doing a little inventory, Lady Averford. Nothing of concern, just easier to get it done once most of the others are in bed." Unlike the rest of the servants' rooms, Finch's bedroom was not far from the kitchen, the better to keep track of the silver, she supposed, or to take note of anything amiss in the night. He clearly hadn't heard the kitten though.

"There's a noise outside."

"Oh?" His silver caterpillar eyebrows shot up. "What kind of noise?"

"A kitten, I think. Though it sounds quite a bit like a baby's cry. I'm going to have a look."

"Allow me." He reached for his coat from the back of a chair near the storeroom door.

"No, Mr. Finch. I would like to look for myself, if you don't mind."

"I don't mind." The light reflected off the top of his nearly bald head when he shook it. "I can't just let you go out on your own in the middle of the night. I'll come with you."

"If you insist. Bring a candle. We might need some light." The mewling became louder, almost a wail. "There it is. Do you hear?"

"I hear it now. It sounds like a baby, as you said."

"Odd." She gestured for Finch to follow her once he lit the wick of the oil lamp. "Do you think it's a wild animal caught in something?"

"I've no idea what we'll find, but it does sound distressed."

Finch stayed close to her as she went up the stairs and out. The basket was so close to the door that she nearly tripped on it as she stepped away from the door, and the sound was definitely contained within it. Tentatively, she reached out and moved the blanket covering the top.

"Dear God, it is a baby!" Sophia gasped and immediately bent down to pick it up, the little arms reaching out to her. "Someone has left a baby. Call the constable."

Finch held the light aloft and shone it around the yard. "I don't see anyone. Let me help you get it inside and settled. Then I'll make the call."

Instinctively, she cradled the precious weight to her shoulder, protecting the sweet little head, and bounced as she stepped in an attempt to quiet the crying. It worked. The crying dimmed to a gurgle, then became more of a coo before she even made it inside.

Fourteen

"WHO COULD HAVE LEFT YOU, LITTLE ONE?" ONCE inside, she held the baby out from her to have a look at it, her heart racing. A baby. An actual baby, right out her window. And such a beautiful baby, perfectly round head, downy covering of pale yellow hair, chubby cheeks. As she was admiring him, or her, the baby smiled at her. "Look, Finch, a smile."

But as soon as Finch took a look, the smile fell away, as if it had been only for Sophia. At least there wasn't any more crying. Big, dark blue eyes looked all around, taking in new surroundings and pausing on Sophia. In those eyes, she found herself again. She remembered what it was like to be a mother. Those eyes seemed to claim her too. In her heart, she knew instantly. The two of them belonged together.

"He looks very healthy for being abandoned," Finch said.

"Or she. We don't really know yet, do we? What's in the basket? I hope there's a nappy or two, and perhaps a bottle." Someone had given birth to this baby. Had fed him, rocked him, loved him, and abandoned him. How could it be? Who would do such a thing? And why?

"He's a he. There's a note." Finch read the paper aloud. "It's addressed to the Countess of Averford. *Please care for Theodore as you would your own. He's where he belongs now. Love, Teddy's Mum.*"

"You're a Teddy, are you?" Her mother was Theodora. Wouldn't Mother love a little Theodore in the house? Sophia cradled him to her shoulder and rocked him, feeling a calm fall over her as the baby's chest rose and fell in a steady rhythm against hers. Tears formed in her eyes. The peaceful wave of contentment that had come over her as soon as she picked the boy up was exactly what had been denied her for so many years, seven years, since she'd first held her own son, Edward. They might have called him Eddie. And now she had a Teddy.

"Teddy. Yes, it fits you. Did she list a birth date, by chance? By the size of him, I'm guessing he's little more than a month old, maybe two."

"No, but there are nappies in the basket. Two, to be exact. And a bottle. I'll wash it out and see if we have any fresh milk. He's likely to be hungry. We've no idea how long he was out there."

"We'll need more than two nappies. I should check if he needs a change. Will he take a bottle so young? Cow's milk, I suppose. I don't know what else to feed him without a wet nurse in house. Tomorrow I'll contact Eve Thorne to see if she can spare her nurse."

"I'll ring for Mrs. Hoyle, my lady. There's no need for you to be up with the care of an infant. The constable will come for him soon, and that will be that."

"That will not be that indeed, Mr. Finch." She tucked the blanket around Teddy as if to protect his ears from such talk. "You read the note. Someone intends for me to raise this child. We can't allow the constable to take him away. In fact, why don't we wait and call tomorrow?"

"We've found a baby in a basket by the service stairs. Can it wait?"

"Practically under my window. As if somebody knew that I would be the one to hear him and placed him there on purpose. Have we dismissed any servants recently? Female ones especially? Women who might have ended up in a family way?"

She supposed it happened all the time, though she had never thought of it happening at Thornbrook Park. But servants had feelings, and they certainly acted on them at times, inadvisable as it was for a woman to allow a man… Well, who was she to judge? She knew what it was to be lonely and longing and desperate. So desperate.

"I can't believe it could be anyone connected to the house." Still, Finch seemed to be considering. "We haven't lost any maids lately."

"Nine months to a year ago perhaps? Or longer?"

"I'll have to consult the employment records."

"Tomorrow. We'll do it tomorrow. You need your sleep, and so does Teddy. I'm going to bring him up to bed."

"To bed where? You can't mean to take him to your room."

"I mean to do exactly that, Mr. Finch. I've got the space, and he can sleep in his basket tonight.

Don't you think me capable of keeping good watch over him?"

"Of course, my lady. That isn't in question. I just—do you want to be bothered?"

"He's no bother! He's a baby. An adorable baby. Just look at him." She placed him on the table so that they could examine him together. Ten fingers, ten toes. He wore a little green sweater, hand knit, over a plain white shirt, his nappy, and bare legs.

"He is a good-looking boy. Looks quite a bit like the boys when they were young, Lord Averford and his brother." He corrected himself. Sophia couldn't blame him for the moment of nostalgia. Finch had been around when Gabriel was a baby, after all. "Wisps of fair hair, round cheeks."

Lots of babies had fair hair and round cheeks. Certainly, the butler wasn't suggesting a family resemblance, but it struck Sophia suddenly. Could Gabriel have been unfaithful? He'd been so disgusted by the idea of her kissing another man that he had put a great distance between them, both physically and emotionally. Or so she had thought.

But what if he'd really been disgusted with himself, knowing what he'd done to her first? She worked out the timing quickly in her mind. If the child were really his, the infidelity would have happened over a year ago, more or less. Right about the time Gabriel had become distant and disinterested in her, which eventually led to her giving in to Lord Ralston's kiss in the first place… Dear God. It was possible. It was entirely too possible.

She'd always thought him steadfast and loyal,

impossibly stoic. But his father had been quite the adulterer, hadn't he? She remembered Gabriel mentioning it years ago, while trying to soften her opinion of his mother. Like father, like son?

"'He's where he belongs now'? It's what the note said, Mr. Finch?"

He looked it over again. "That's what it says."

"Well, then. Teddy, you're home." She bundled him up again and took him into her arms. "I'll change him upstairs. If you could send up his bottle, warmed. I hope cow's milk will do for the night. I'll look into hiring a nurse. We'll arrange everything in the morning."

"My lady, please." There was a note of tenderness and sympathy in Finch's voice the likes of which she hadn't heard since Edward's death.

"What is it, Mr. Finch?" She would pretend not to have heard it. She didn't need to be handled gently.

"You don't mean to try to keep him?"

"His mother seemed to think that he belongs here, and what if he does? Fate took my most precious gift once, my own baby. Now fate delivers a baby to my doorstep. To make amends? I know it sounds naive, perhaps ridiculous. But I feel that Teddy does belong here with me now. At any rate, he's mine to watch over for tonight, and I mean to do so. I don't want to wake Mrs. Jenks, so if you could do me the great favor of bringing the bottle up when it's ready? Don't bother knocking. We'll let this just be our secret for tonight. The others will find out in the morning."

"As you wish, Lady Averford."

❧

In the morning, Mrs. Jenks found Sophia asleep in the armchair, the baby resting on her chest. At the sight, Jenks dropped her laundry basket in alarm.

"Oh my!"

Sophia cocked one eye open. She had been dozing lightly. "Jenks, good morning. Come meet Teddy."

"Teddy?" Her maid stepped forward. "How on earth did you go to bed alone and wake up with a baby?"

Sophia leaned forward and gently laid Teddy on the ottoman so that Jenks could get a good look at him. Fortunately, he remained asleep. "Someone abandoned him. I heard him mewling out my window last night and assumed it was a cat until the mewling became a cry. He was in that basket."

Jenks looked in the basket, now empty except for the blanket that had been draped over it. "My word. Who could abandon such a precious bundle? A boy, you're sure?"

"I've changed him. Quite sure. Plus, his mother left a note. Mr. Finch has it downstairs. I trust you haven't spoken to him yet."

"I haven't seen anyone. I've been up just long enough to wash and dress and pick up your laundry waiting for me downstairs. I expect the house will be buzzing with the news by the time I get back to the kitchen to pick up your breakfast tray. I assume you're taking breakfast on a tray, considering."

Sophia nodded but couldn't take her eyes off little Teddy, now only in his nappy, his round belly exposed. He had spit-up on his clothes and she had nothing else to dress him in. She stroked his petal-soft baby skin and couldn't contain her sigh when he grasped her finger in his little hand. "You little dumpling."

Mrs. Jenks sighed too, but it wasn't one of contentment. "Don't go getting attached, please, Lady Averford. You have no idea how long he's really here for, or when his mother will turn up. I'm sure she will. She has to regret leaving him."

"You've never been a mother, Mrs. Jenks." Sophia knew she hadn't. Jenks had never even been married. The "Mrs." was a courtesy title to show her advanced position in the house as a lady's maid. "It's easy to warn off attachment but not so easy to avoid. I loved him as soon as I first saw his face. I pulled back that blanket and I knew. He belongs here with me. He simply does."

It didn't matter if he was Gabriel's by-blow or not. She loved Teddy regardless. She might actually love him more if he were Gabriel's, though she would have plenty of emotions regarding Gabriel's infidelity. That Teddy would be a part of the man she loved? No. Truly, it didn't matter. She couldn't possibly love the baby more. Not one second after she'd taken him in her arms, she'd fallen head over heels.

They were all looking out for her, expecting her to be fragile, to fall apart as she had when she lost Edward. The fact remained that as devastating as that had been, possibly the hardest thing she would ever experience in life, she had survived. It had made her stronger. She could survive anything now. She'd been a fool to shun her husband's advances, fearing the worst. The worst and the best happened regardless of one's preparedness. Why live in fear, avoiding experiences? Life was to be lived. Now a woman of twenty-seven years, she was finally wise enough and strong enough to face whatever life had to offer. And she was a countess, after all. In her experience, countesses usually got what they wanted.

"I want you, little Theodore Thorne," she said, trying the name on for size. Not being the earl's legitimate offspring, he could never inherit, but they could give him the family name. Theodore Stanley, after both of her parents? Theodore Gabriel? She was getting ahead of herself. There would be time to think up a name for him later. First, there was the constable to deal with, and then Gabriel would be home. What if he had been drawing up divorce papers? What if he didn't fall in love with Teddy and want to claim him, as she had? What if he recognized Teddy as his own?

At that moment, Theodore gurgled and smiled the biggest baby smile she'd ever seen.

"He smiled, did you see?" she asked Jenks. "Some say that when a baby smiles, it's only because he has gas. I'd better burp him again." She lifted Teddy to her shoulder and lost herself in his sweet baby softness once again.

Gabriel doubted that Sophia had slept through his entire absence, but he hoped that she wouldn't be angry with him for going. Wilkerson had come by to beg him to stay longer and get to a vote, but he was steadfast in his determination to return home to Sophia. As far as he was concerned, he had what he needed to finally convince her of his undying love for her.

"You're deep in thought," his brother accused him from across the breakfast table. "Or ignoring me. With you, it could go either way."

"You can safely assume it is both," Gabriel answered flippantly. He'd been aware that Marcus was talking but had tuned his brother out in favor of his own thoughts.

In recent years, Gabriel had established a good relationship with Marcus, but he had never been happier to see him than he had on arrival at Averford House last night. Gabriel had come up with a plan to rid himself temporarily of most of his houseguests to get more time alone with Sophia, and Marcus had been graciously agreeable.

Marcus and Eve were returning to Yorkshire along with Gabriel and Mr. Grant. Once at Thornbrook Station, they would go their separate ways so that Marcus and Eve could enjoy a brief reunion with the daughters they'd left behind. Then, they would make a quick visit to Thornbrook Park, just long enough to suggest that Mother and Lord Markham go back to Markham House with them.

It was the perfect solution. Marcus and Eve had purchased their estate from Lord Markham and had never changed the name out of respect. Charles would feel at home again, exploring his former residence. Mother would be able to spend some time with the granddaughters she had yet to meet. Gabriel and Sophia would be left with only Aunt Agatha and the hired help, all of whom were capable of functioning without the earl and countess's constant interaction. Gabriel would take Sophia on a picnic to her stretch of land and then hand her the papers and explain the transfer of ownership to her.

"At least Mr. Grant has answered me." Marcus shook his head at his brother. "Apparently, we are all taking the same train. Unless my wife fails to come down to breakfast in time, in which case you'll have to leave without us."

"I'm right here, dear heart." Wearing an angelic smile and a sable-trimmed traveling suit, Eve Thorne appeared and wrapped her arms around her husband's neck. Gabriel had it in mind to wrap his arms around his brother's neck too, but not in such a loving way. "We'll leave on time if I have anything to do with it. I'm eager to see my babies."

"That's how it is when you have children, gents," Marcus addressed them. "You can't decide if you're more excited to leave them behind or to get back home to them."

"I wouldn't know," Gabriel said, emotionless. He hoped he would know soon enough. It had crossed his mind that Sophia could have become pregnant. If not right away, maybe soon enough. He planned on taking ample opportunity to ensure his future generations.

"I'm more excited to get home to them than to have left them," Eve declared. "No offense, Marcus. I've enjoyed our time alone, but I miss my girls so much."

"I miss them too."

"What are we waiting for?" Gabriel rose from the table. "Let's get to the station."

Several hours later, much too long for Gabriel's liking, he was finally home.

"I'll see you at dinner, Mr. Grant." Grant was leaving him to go back to the cottage. Instead of having Kenner move out, the two men had decided to share the estate agent's cottage a short walk from the main house. It was an amicable solution. The cottage had several bedrooms and plenty of room for two men. "Thank you for your assistance in this very important matter. You and Mr. Kenner do make a good team."

"Your wife is very insightful, Lord Averford. I'm glad to continue working for you both."

"Ever the diplomat, Mr. Grant." He tipped his hat to the man as he strode away.

In the house, Gabriel was greeted by a loud commotion. It sounded like a baby's cry, but he was certain that the Thornes' nurse had remained at Markham House with her charges.

"Finch, what's going on?" Even Mr. Finch looked harried, his fringe of silver hair mussed and sticking out on one side. A maid rushed by with a stack of towels in hand. In the main hall? "It's Bedlam in here."

"Not Bedlam, my lord. A baby. It's the baby."

"What baby?"

Finch shook his head. "I'll leave Lady Averford to explain. She's in the drawing room talking to Chief Constable Reilly."

"The constable? Good God. What's going on?" He shrugged out of his coat, handed it and his hat to Finch, and went to greet his wife.

"Sophia?" She too was in glorious disarray, her raven locks trailing about her shoulders and a big dollop of…something on the shoulder of her blouse. He closed the distance. "Is that mustard?"

"No, darling, Teddy has been spitting up. Poor dear. Dr. Pederson is examining him now. I've been talking to the constable about last night."

Gabriel's heart hammered in his chest. "Last night? What happened last night? I knew I should have pushed harder to come home in time. Who's Teddy?"

"The baby." The wrinkled-up, concerned look fell off her face to be replaced with an image of beatific radiance. "Theodore. He was left in a basket under my window, as I was just telling Chief Constable Reilly."

"Good to see you again, Reilly." Gabriel reached out to shake his hand. Tom Reilly, formerly a private investigator in London, was a good friend of Gabriel's brother. "What's this about a baby? Oh dear, there he goes again. He's a loud one, isn't he?"

The cries shot from a low roar up to top volume. "I don't think he likes Dr. Pederson," Sophia said, the worried look returning.

"So far, what we have is that you were interrupted in the middle of *Emma*..." Reilly went over his notes.

"Who's Emma? The baby's mother?" Gabriel was becoming more confused.

"It's a book," Sophia said, seeming less concerned as the cries quieted down again. "I was reading Jane Austen's *Emma*, one of my favorite books, when I felt a chill and went to close the window. But at the window, I heard a soft mewling. I thought perhaps it was a cat. When the mewling sounded more like a cry, I decided to investigate."

"In the middle of the night? On your own?"

Gabriel put his arms around her. "Darling, how could you be so foolish? It could have been a wild animal or a ruffian."

"Ruffians? Not on my watch." Reilly rocked back on his heels, seeming pleased with himself. "We have a safe village, Lord Averford. Small as Thornbrook is, I keep my men on patrol."

"No doubt you do, Reilly. Much appreciated. But how did a baby end up under my wife's window? Was anybody spotted in the vicinity?"

"No," Sophia answered definitively. "Mr. Finch came out to have a look with me, Gabriel. Honestly. Do you think he would let me go out alone? He was awake polishing silver or whatnot. He held the light and I found the basket. Teddy's crying made it hard to miss, of course. The basket was placed right outside the door so that I nearly tripped over it anyway. I looked inside, and there he was. Our baby."

"Our baby?"

She laughed in a brittle way and shook her head. "There's no question about it. He's your son. What's yours is mine, and all that."

"What the devil are you going on about, Sophia?" He really had walked into Bedlam, it seemed. Perhaps she was still under the influence of that elixir. He would have to talk to Mrs. Mallows.

"Later. We'll discuss it more later." Suddenly she wore that polite little smile that she always wore for guests. He didn't like that smile. He wanted to be greeted with the real one. The genuine smile made an appearance not a second later when one of the maids came out carrying a hiccuping infant, flanked by Dr.

Pederson and Aunt Agatha. "You can hand him to me, Jane. Ah, and how is he, Doctor?"

The maid handed the baby to Sophia and went back to her duties.

"Perfect." Agatha clapped her hands. "As I predicted. I couldn't get too close to him without Miss Puss becoming jealous though."

"He's in very good health, Lady Averford," the doctor said, casting a glance at Agatha. "No apparent problems, but he isn't taking well to cow's milk."

"I'm looking for a wet nurse." Sophia looked natural with the child, putting him to her shoulder and patting his back as if she'd been his mother for years. How did that natural affinity for babies come over women so easily? Gabriel was certain he might drop or squish the child should she hand him over to him.

"A good idea," Pederson acknowledged. "I know a woman in the village who could be of service. I'll stop in with her and ask if she can come help you out. He's about two months' old, I would say, give or take a week."

Sophia nodded. "As I suspected."

The infant clung fast to Sophia as certainly as she had taken to the infant. Gabriel felt suddenly unnecessary in his own home.

"Thank you, Dr. Pederson, for your help and for coming out so quickly to have a look," Sophia said.

"I'll come back and have a look at him in two weeks, if he's still with you."

"He will be," Sophia said assuredly. "Mr. Finch will see you out."

"I should be going too," Reilly said. "I think I have

everything I need. No one saw anyone, as far as you know. I'll interview a few of the servants to be sure. I got a good look at the basket. Do you mind if I keep the note? Handwriting sometimes helps in tracking a culprit down."

"The culprit here being the child's actual mother?" Gabriel stroked his chin.

"Exactly." Reilly pointed a finger. "We might find her, we might not. But if we find her, we'll have a better idea of the baby's background. I'll be in touch. I can see myself out." Mr. Reilly waved at Gabriel. Sophia paid no attention.

"I'll walk you out, Mr. Reilly," Agatha offered. "I'm headed that way."

"Just like that, we have a baby?" Gabriel ran a hand through his hair once they were alone. "Someone else's child left in our care."

"Your child, Gabriel. Have a look at him. Is there something you want to tell me?" She turned the infant around her in arms, holding him with a protective arm about his waist. The baby, a chubby-cheeked little fellow, chewed on one of his own fists.

Gabriel looked him over, downy hair, dark blue eyes. "I've no idea what you mean. He looks a bit like Marcus's girls, doesn't he?" That's when he realized what she was getting at. But she couldn't believe he'd been unfaithful. "You couldn't possibly imagine I had anything to do with this baby."

"You're suggesting your brother did instead?" She tapped a foot under her skirts.

"Absolutely not. You know how much he loves

Eve. They must have been having Freddie right around the same time."

Sophia nibbled her lip. "And I know all about your brother's libido when it comes to pregnant women. He doesn't stop loving his wife just because she's enceinte."

"Stop. I don't need to know that." Gabriel recoiled. "Come to think of it, we might have that in common. I also found you very desirable in that condition. But I think we can both agree it's not his child."

"On that, we can agree." She tilted her head. "You found me desirable even then?"

He saw his chance and he wouldn't let it slip by him. He stepped forward so that he was close enough to take her in his arms if there wasn't a baby in between them. "Even then. Now. All the time. You're the only woman I've ever desired, Sophia, ever since I had my first glimpse of you in that ballroom."

"The only one?" She arched a thin, black brow. "There was never anyone else?"

"There's no one else for me in all the world."

"Then why here? Why did the note say that Teddy belonged here?"

"Because we're wealthy, privileged. If a mother was having trouble caring for her own child and had to give him up, wouldn't she choose to leave him at the best house in the area, if not at the church? Admittedly, the church makes more sense. But it's an obvious assumption that we could give the child a good life."

Teresa bounded into the room, interrupting their

discussion. "The cherub is awake and not fussing. Pass him to Nonna."

"Nonna?" Gabriel pulled a face.

"You can't expect me to call myself 'Grandmother.' I'm far too young. I'll use the Italian for grandmother. It's more discreet, plus it's easy to say. Nonna." She took the baby from Sophia, who was surprisingly yielding. "Mind if I take him for a little walk? I won't go far."

"I need to go up and change my clothes anyway," Sophia said. "I won't be long. Thank you, Teresa."

"It's my pleasure." Gabriel's mother bounced off down the hall with a spring in her step and the baby in her arms.

Gabriel shook his head. "And the two of you seem to be getting along. I go away for one night, and the world turns upside down."

"Perhaps it was turning before you even left," Sophia said. "You just didn't notice."

With that, she turned on her heel and headed for the stairs. Was he supposed to follow? He had no idea. He hadn't a clue what to make of her or what to expect next. Just when he thought he had everything under control! He left Sophia alone and went after his mother and the baby instead. If this baby was going to be a part of their lives, he had better try to get to know him.

Fifteen

GABRIEL FOUND MOTHER IN THE CONSERVATORY WITH the baby.

"His name is Teddy, I understand?" he asked, holding his arms out.

"Yes, it is. I brought him in here to see my lemon trees. They're thriving, aren't they?" She handed him the baby. "I took him to try to give you some time alone with Sophia, and here you've followed me instead of your wife. I'm not sure you're making much of a success out of your grand plan to win her back."

"I'm not sure she wants to see me right now. Every time I think I'm making progress, a new obstacle crops up in my way." He cradled the baby under his bottom, so that the child was nearly sitting in the crook of his arm. "He is a handsome one, isn't he?"

"Theodore, it said in the note, actually. And to call him 'Teddy.' Then there was something about him belonging here. In infancy, you were a fair-haired, chubby little fellow too." She twisted her mouth into the moue she made when suspicious.

"Oh, not you too. Sophia asked me if I'd been unfaithful."

Mother shrugged. "There is a resemblance."

"Lots of babies are blond and plump. I would guess quite a number of them."

"Your eyes were that same shade of blue before they turned brown."

"Next, you'll notice that we both have two arms, two legs... He's a baby, Mother. They all look a certain way."

"Hmph." Clearly, she wasn't satisfied. "You're a natural with him."

"I guess I'm more comfortable with a baby in my arms than I imagined I would be. As long as he's in a good mood." The baby still sucked at his own hand. Once he realized there would be more satisfaction in a bottle than his fist, he would probably start fussing again.

Mother sighed and changed the subject. "I know I arrived at an inopportune time. I'm sorry. I couldn't face staying in Italy after all that happened."

"With Conte Miralini?"

"The man was carrying on with my maid behind my back! After having been married to your father, you'd think I would have developed keener senses about such things. It shouldn't have taken me by surprise. With you leaving, it made sense to leave with you. After Paris, I planned to take my time at the London house before moving on, but I ran into Charles and he was speaking of coming here. I've always liked Charles."

"Lord Markham has always liked you too, from

what I understand." Instinctively, Gabriel didn't stand still with the baby in his arms, but rocked gently back and forth.

"He was in love with me once, before your father came along. I probably should have married him. And now we find ourselves at a certain time in our lives, both of us alone. It makes sense, doesn't it?"

"You pursuing Lord Markham? I guess it does. But he's vulnerable after his divorce. Have a care with the man, Mother."

She waved off his concern with a flick of her wrist. "I'm always careful. Of course, it would help if we could ever be alone without that Agatha woman tagging along. Do you know she even has the servants calling her 'Aunt'? She says I have a red aura, whatever that is."

Gabriel could only laugh at that. Mother, careful? It didn't quite fit. "She's eccentric, but I think you'll come to appreciate Agatha. You're about the same age. It would be good for you to have a friend. Marcus has a red aura, too, by the way. Be grateful you're not a beige."

"There are beige auras?" Mother shuddered. "No one would have the nerve to accuse me of being beige."

The baby began to fuss a bit until Gabriel turned him around to face him. A tiny hand reached out to touch Gabriel's face and managed to effect an emotional tug deep in his gut as well. "Hello, little man."

"So much like you." Mother shook her head. "It's not so far-fetched to think you might have strayed. Men do it all the time."

"Conte Miralini might have. Father did. I saw what

it did to you, Mother. How could you even imagine I would hurt the woman I loved?"

"He never thought of it as hurting me." Even after all these years, a teardrop glistened from the corner of Mother's eye. "I never knew you noticed. I tried to shield you and your brother from my pain."

"We were aware of everything, between the two of us. Unintentional or not, Father did hurt you. I'm not like him. Not in that way. Believe me, this baby is not my son. Not by birth, anyway. Sophia seems determined to keep him."

"I'm with her on that. He's a doll. My grandson!"

"How quickly you both became attached to him. I never thought you would be so determined to be a grandmother." Again. He didn't add the "again." But he shouldn't have been surprised by her interest in the baby. When Edward was born, she had practically knocked Gabriel out of the way to try to hold the baby first. And later, she'd insisted Gabriel get some sleep so that she could watch over Edward.

Still, he would have expected her to be focused on legitimacy, a true Thorne. But this baby's birth, though an intriguing mystery, didn't seem to matter to her. She loved him. As Sophia did. Both of them had fallen fast. What would it do to them if they were to lose him now? But perhaps better now than later, after more solid bonds could form.

"A *nonna*," she corrected.

"Still. You didn't exactly rush home to see Marcus's daughters. They're home now, you know. At Markham House. Marcus and Eve came back with me from London."

"What if I don't like her?" Mother bit her lip. "Or she doesn't like me? It's not the little girls I'm avoiding. I'm eager to meet Marcus's babies. I'm just hesitant when it comes to meeting his wife. I haven't been much of a success as a mother-in-law."

"You can work on that. Sophia isn't any more of an ogre than you are a dragon."

"I get to be the dragon? Thank you. That might be one the nicest things you've said to your old mother recently." She smiled and patted his hand, then reached to stroke the baby's forehead. Teddy was falling asleep on Gabriel's shoulder.

"You're not all that old, not that you need reminding." Gabriel rolled his eyes. "Eve is nothing like Sophia. They're friends, but they're very different sorts of women. I think you're worried for nothing. At any rate, you can't put off meeting her much longer. They mean to invite you to spend a few days with them. And Lord Markham too. They thought he might enjoy seeing his house again."

"If he goes, I will go. It would be easier to have him there with me, an ally, not to mention the appeal of getting him away from Agatha."

Gabriel rolled his eyes. "I begin to think you enjoy making enemies, Mother. How would you live without the drama of being dreaded wherever you go?"

"Am I dreaded then? You have a point. I could feel the animosity rolling off Sophia from the second she first saw me. To her credit, she never panics on sight like some women might. She's a most worthy adversary, always up for a challenge. You married well, my dear. But I suppose it's time I try to make peace.

We're both on the same side now, as far as loving this baby and being determined to keep him. Can you imagine the power we'll exude working together after we've been such forces working against each other?"

"I'm not sure the world will bear it." He wasn't sure he would bear it, the two of them both fixed on the same goal.

"Just you wait and see." Mother threw back her head and cackled like a fairy-tale witch, causing Teddy to shift a little in Gabriel's arms. "You get to know your new son. I'm going to go talk with your wife."

"Good luck, Mother." When dealing with Sophia, she was certainly going to need it.

❧

Sophia was at her dressing table, putting the finishing touch, her favorite diamond comb, in her hair when she heard a knock on her door.

"Come in," she called out, expecting it to be Gabriel. Jenks wouldn't knock, and Sophia had already dismissed her to manage on her own. She tried not to show the slightest hint of alarm when her mother-in-law walked in and closed the door quietly behind her.

"I thought we could use a moment together. We haven't spoken much since I've been here, but your idea to throw a party together has emboldened me."

Sophia turned and stood, indicating for Teresa to follow her over to the sitting area. "The party might have to wait."

"I understand."

"I'm not sure we have much else to discuss—besides

Teddy, of course. You seem to have fallen in love with him almost as much as I have."

"Almost? It's always a competition with you, isn't it?" Teresa smiled and took a seat on the pink taffeta divan. "I don't mind. I welcome our unique parlance. I believe I am every bit as much in love with that baby as you are. Amazing how it happens so fast, isn't it?"

Sophia nodded and settled in the armchair. "I'm astonished. It was only last night that I found him out there, and now I can't imagine life without him. It felt like he belonged with me from the moment I first held him."

"It was like that for me with Marcus too. Not so with Gabriel, if I'm being completely honest. The first few weeks, I had no idea how I was going to be a mother. I felt like such a failure. I dreaded the very sight of him every time they brought him in to nurse. It's that look of his, like he's measuring you up and you're about to fall short."

"He's had that look since birth? You didn't have a nursemaid?" Sophia tried not to sound too surprised. She never liked Gabriel's mother to think she'd managed to fluster her.

"Since the moment I first held him." Teresa shook her head. "Having a nurse would have felt too much like admitting defeat. Keep in mind that it was woefully out of style to nurse one's own children back then. But I've always embraced the avant-garde, as you know. I enjoy making people talk."

"I know."

"We're not the kind of women to be wallpaper. What's the point of being in a room if you're not the centerpiece? I know you share my opinion on that. It's one of the reasons we've never gotten along. Neither of us is content to let the other one shine brighter. I've always suspected it's at the heart of your dislike for London as well. A countess has to take a step back when a duchess enters the room."

"It's not like that." Entirely. She knew Teresa had a point. She preferred to be at the heart of their small social circle in Yorkshire instead of fighting for attention in London. "I know you won't believe me, but I'm also shy in new company. And everyone in London feels new to me. They all know each other so well, and there I am at a loss, hardly hearing any names I recognize. It's awkward. I don't like to feel awkward."

"I had no idea." Teresa looked surprised. "I've never imagined you to be shy. You've always stood up to me easily enough, and that takes some backbone."

"Disliking crowds doesn't make me a coward, Teresa. I recognize when it's necessary to be on my guard."

"That you do. But back to me. You see? I can't help but steal the attention. As I was saying, I didn't know what to make of Gabriel as an infant. Then one day, when he was about a month old, he grabbed on to my hair and wouldn't let go. I was nursing him, resentful to be awakened, I suppose, and this little fist grabbed on to my braid and pulled. He would not let go. And when I glanced down, he was laughing. I'll never forget the look in his eyes. It finally looked like I'd won his approval. From that day forward, I was all love for him. With some, it's instant. With others, it takes time."

"It was instant with Teddy."

"For me too. He's a charmer. It runs in the family."

Sophia's eyes widened. "But he's not ours by birth, of course. You're not suggesting…"

"Only that he fits right in. I admit that I did wonder. A baby shows up unexpectedly. The note says he belongs here. But Gabriel swears he has never touched another woman."

"So he says." Sophia nodded.

"You don't believe him?" Teresa cocked a dark blond brow. Sophia wondered if she darkened them somehow? A woman of Teresa's age should have some gray hair, shouldn't she?

"As Gabriel said, we are prominent targets. Deep down, I don't feel that he could have done such a thing. Not the way he reacted to finding me with Lord Ralston."

"I don't believe he could have been unfaithful either," Teresa agreed. "What exactly happened between you and Ralston, by the way?"

Sophia blushed. "I can believe you asked, but I can't imagine you expect me to answer."

Teresa's brow shot up again.

"Very well. You dislike me enough as it is. I kissed him. I did. It's all true. It didn't go any further than a kiss. I was feeling lonely, I suppose. Neglected. My sister had two men fighting over her in my house, and I could barely catch the eye of my own husband. When it turned out that Ralston's only interest in Alice was in getting closer to me, I was flattered. I'm ashamed that I was. I should have been appalled. She's my sister! But on a more visceral level, I was thrilled.

Someone had noticed me. Someone found me worthy of kissing."

"Oh dear. Had it gotten that bad with Gabriel? The clod!"

"He was always working, looking after the finances, and keeping up with his parliamentary duties. When he wasn't working, he was dismissive. I can't blame him entirely. For a while after Edward died, he tried to pay attention. I just kept pushing him away. I suppose he got so used to it that he just gave up on me."

"Both of you gave up."

"No," Sophia said, insistent. "I was afraid. What if we had another baby and he died too? I wasn't sure that I could bear it."

"A reasonable fear after losing a child. And you had such a hard time after Edward's birth. The fever came over you. We were all so worried."

Sophia tried not to flinch.

"Yes, Sophia, even me. I'd always wanted a daughter. You were the closest I had to having one, and then it turned out that I had approached you all wrong. Maybe it's just that you were shy. I thought you were proud. I thought I'd failed to meet your exacting standards, and then the battle was on."

"I thought I was the one who failed in your eyes."

"Don't be ridiculous. You're my favorite daughter-in-law."

"You haven't met the other one yet," Sophia observed.

"I know. I'm scared to do so. What if I botch it up with this one too?"

"Eve is straightforward. You always know exactly

what's on her mind, if that helps to put you at ease. She's more of an open book, while I..."

"Yes, you are a hard one to read," Teresa agreed too easily. "Is that where we went wrong then? We just have to stop making assumptions. From now on, I'll be more honest with you. And you should try to be more open with me."

Sophia nodded. "I'll try."

"Good. Because I have a feeling we're going to need each other in the coming weeks. I want you to know that you have my full support."

A ball of dread formed in Sophia's stomach. Why would she need Teresa's support, exactly? "Thank you. I hope we're not expecting trouble."

Teresa shrugged. "It always pays to be prepared."

⸙

Sophia found Gabriel in the drawing room nearly asleep on the claw-footed sofa, with the baby sleeping on his chest. Her heart expanded with joy. She wished there was room to curl up next to them.

"There you are," she whispered. "He's an angel, isn't he? I think he might have been sent down straight from heaven."

"Except he was abandoned by a mother who might very well be regretting her actions by now." Gabriel looked up at her over the baby's head. "Let's try to put him down to sleep so we can talk."

"But you look so well together. I wish I had a photograph to capture the moment for all time." She smiled, but she could see that he wasn't changing his mind. She rang for a maid. "Jane, could you bring me

Teddy's basket, please? It's in my room. We're going to attempt to put him down for a nap."

"At once, my lady." The maid returned not a minute later, panting from the rush up and down the stairs. "I can keep an eye on him if ye like."

"It's not necessary," Sophia began to say.

"That would be ideal, Jane. Thank you," Gabriel interrupted. "For just a little while."

Sophia lifted the baby and settled him in the basket. He remained asleep and blissfully unaware of the transfer. "But I hate to just leave him."

"Jane, have you cared for children?" Gabriel demanded.

She nodded.

"There you are," Gabriel said to Sophia as he got to his feet. "Jane has experience."

"I do, my lord." She kept her watchful eyes on the baby in the basket instead of making eye contact with her employer, a good sign to Sophia that Jane was skilled at prioritizing.

"We won't go far," Sophia said, somewhat reassured. "Call out if he wakes or seems to need me."

"But of course, Lady Averford. At once."

Gabriel took Sophia by the hand. "To our office."

"As far as that?" She looked back at Teddy, reluctant again.

"It's right around the corner." Gabriel kept walking, tugging her along.

"And some way down the hall."

"We won't be long." He escorted her in and closed the door.

"What is it you wish to discuss, darling?" She took

the seat across from his at the desk. "Is it Teddy? I realize his name is very close to Eddie, as we intended to call Edward. We can change it if it makes you uncomfortable. Though I know Mother would like it. She never got to meet Edward, and Theodore is so close to Theodora, after all. It would satisfy her vanity to think we named our son after her."

"It's not his name that troubles me." Gabriel rubbed his eyes. Sophia would think he was the one who'd been up all night caring for a baby. But perhaps he hadn't slept well in London. He stood over her, took her hand, and met her gaze with a grave expression. "We can never replace our Edward, Sophia. Teddy is not our son."

She shrugged. "Not yet, perhaps. But he was left here with us, Gabriel. He's ours."

"I'm afraid not." He shook his head, adamant. Cold-hearted. "He can never truly be ours. Not until we know where he came from or if his mother intends to come back."

She stood, forcing him to take a step back. "Why would she come back? She made her decision. She abandoned him to our care. As she said in her note, he's where he belongs. With us. At Thornbrook Park."

Gabriel opened his mouth to protest. It wasn't that he was cold, she reminded herself, trying to remain sympathetic. His problem was that he was entirely too reasonable when presented with an obstacle. All head. No heart. Logically, his argument made sense. She hadn't heard his full argument yet, but she knew he had one. He always had one.

"Trust me on this, this once," she said. "We're

wealthy. Powerful. You have a noble name. If we want to keep Teddy, he's ours. You can come up with all sorts of reasons against it, but I'm not going to sit here and listen to them. I want to be there when our son wakes up from his nap."

Sixteen

BEYOND FRUSTRATED, GABRIEL FOLLOWED SOPHIA back down the hall to the drawing room.

"Oh, he's awake." The infant was happily babbling in the arms of the maid, chewing his chubby fist yet again. "Thank you. You may go back to your other duties now, Jane."

The maid stood to place the child back in Sophia's arms. "He's such a good little baby, Lady Averford. Patient and sweet-natured. I'm happy to help out whenever you need it. Until you hire a nurse, of course."

"I'll hire a wet nurse, of course, but I'm not sure I'll be looking for anyone else to help with caring for him. I mean to be a very involved mother." Sophia wore a scarlet tea dress that acted on Gabriel like a red flag to a charging bull.

"If by 'involved' you mean overbearing, by all means." Gabriel knew he would be more successful if he remained calm, but he had been calm since coming home from Italy. He felt a devil of a temper tantrum coming on.

"There's no such thing as an overbearing mother," the maid said quickly in Sophia's defense. "Babies need their mothers. I'm sorry, Lord Averford." As if remembering her station, the maid curtsied quickly and left the room.

"Who is that impudent maid?" Gabriel asked.

"I hired her recently. I guess it has been a month or so now. She came from London, but she grew up in the village and she was eager to return to the area. And I like her."

"You would. She's clearly on your side." Gabriel ignored Sophia's cooing to the baby. "As her champion, you might want to take her aside and suggest she watches what she says to her employer."

"I'm sure she didn't mean to be rude to you, only to stand up for my maternal instincts." Sophia tilted her chin, more thoughtful than defiant. "But you have a point. I'll speak with her later."

"One would think she was a mother herself for all of her nerve." A mother. Gabriel paused to consider. "You say she has been here for about a month?"

"About that, yes. Six weeks at the most. I would have to check. She has been here long enough to make a favorable impression on everyone, even Mrs. Hoyle." Sophia couldn't take her eyes from the baby long enough to look up and make eye contact with Gabriel. If she had, she might have realized what he was thinking.

"But not as long as two months?" he asked.

Sophia looked up at last. "You're not suggesting…"

"She has the same fair hair and rosy cheeks as Teddy. And the timing?"

Sophia glanced down at the baby and back up at Gabriel. "Half of the women in the village have fair hair and rosy cheeks. A good number of the women in all of England do, for that matter."

"But not all of them showed up at our house looking for work just a short time before a baby was left mysteriously under your window."

"We hired a footman at around the same time. Do you suppose he's the father?" She pursed her lips, clearly not convinced.

"I'm merely saying that there could be something to it, a connection between the baby and the housemaid who keeps turning up when I'm trying to be alone with my wife."

"You might have seen her twice in the past week. She seems to be drawn to the child. He's a cherub. She's not the only one enchanted with the new baby in the house."

"No." He tipped his head, considering. "But she does show an interest in him. We haven't many other leads to pursue."

"And we're better off that way. I wouldn't mind if we never discover the identity of the woman who left him for us. The fact is that he's here, and he's ours. Can't we just let it stay a mystery how he got here?"

Gabriel's stomach tightened at the idea. He didn't like mysteries, most especially when they could end up breaking his wife's heart. "For now."

"Besides, I can't imagine how a mother could stand aside and watch someone else caring for her own baby in her place. It would be torture. Jane hardly seems like a tortured soul. I heard her singing in the hall the other day when she was sweeping up."

"I suppose you would know best, darling. Woman's intuition and all that." Still, Gabriel meant to check into Jane's background a little. She probably had family in the village. Constable Reilly had experience doing detective work. He might prove of some service in checking into the maid's activities outside the house.

"I'm sure your mother would agree with me this once." Sophia went back to ignoring Gabriel in favor of studying the baby.

Mother entered the room as if on cue. "Did I hear my name?"

"I was saying that you're as in love with our baby as I am." Sophia shot Gabriel a silencing glare, but he had no intention of filling Mother in on his suspicions.

Fortunately, he didn't have to say a word more on the subject. His brother entered the room with his two-year-old daughter charging her way in front of him. My, she had grown. The last time Gabriel had seen his niece, she had just taken her first steps. Now, there was clearly no stopping her. Her blond curls, barely contained by a pink ribbon, bounced when she ran. She ended up at Gabriel's feet, her tiny arms wrapped tightly around his leg. Her crystalline blue eyes, so like her mother's, gazed up at him.

"There you are, Mina. You've found your Uncle Gabriel," her father said.

"Unca!" Her arms tightened like a vise.

Gabriel bent his knee in an attempt to loosen her grip and restore some circulation. "Mina," he said, "you've got your father's strength."

The girl giggled, making her father laugh along. Her mother came in next, holding their younger daughter cradled against her shoulder. Gabriel had yet to meet Winifred, called "Freddie" by the family, but he never would have dreamed he would be introducing a baby of his own at the same time. A baby of his own? Had he taken to thinking of the boy as theirs, even as he worried about Sophia becoming too attached?

"Where's Mr. Finch hiding that he failed to warn me of your approach?" he said half in jest to his brother.

His brother raised his hands. "I need no formal announcement. I grew up here. And you should be kind to me, since I've come to take Mother off your hands."

"Ahem." Mother, standing back in the corner of the room with Sophia and the baby, stepped forward to make herself known, though no one could have missed her.

"Looking forward to spending some time with you, of course, Mother." Marcus smiled.

"It's good to see you too, Son. And who is this?" She dropped to her knees to inspect her older granddaughter. "Aren't you the pretty one! You look just like your father, except for those blue eyes. You must call me Nonna."

"Nonna," Mina repeated, letting go of Gabriel's leg to hold her hands out to her grandmother, no doubt delighting Mother.

"That's right, dear. And I have presents for you! Come along."

"Ah, not so fast, Mother," Marcus said. "I want you to meet my wife, Eve, and our younger daughter."

Mother got back to her feet as Eve approached her. "Ah. That's where Mina gets her blue eyes. It's lovely to meet you at last, Eve."

"I'm glad to meet you too," Eve said, juggling the infant in her arms as Freddie started to fuss. "I'm sorry. The baby probably needs a nap. She doesn't like riding in cars."

"Oh, the precious girl!" Mother reached out to stroke the baby's cheek. "Two granddaughters! What could have kept me away so long? And now a grandson too."

"A grandson?" Marcus finally looked over at Sophia.

"What on earth?" His wife must have followed her husband's gaze.

"His name is Teddy," Gabriel clarified as Sophia approached with the baby. "He was left on our doorstep."

"Under my window," Sophia added with a glance up at Gabriel. "With a note saying that he belongs here. He's ours."

"You mean to keep him?" Marcus looked at Gabriel. "Just like that?"

"We're keeping him," Sophia said in a tone that did not allow any argument.

"What a surprise!" Eve said, possibly adding more enthusiasm to her tone to please her friend. She and Sophia had always been very close. "Let's meet this new little one. Just as soon as I get Freddie settled."

"Teddy needs a change," Sophia said. "Let's go upstairs and we can let the babies get to know one another. Do you mind, darling?"

"Go on ahead," Gabriel encouraged. It would give him a chance to see what Marcus had to say about the situation. "Take your time. We'll be fine here."

"Yes, go on," Marcus added to Eve. "I'll look after Mina."

"I'll look after Mina," Mother interjected. "My granddaughter and I are going to take a little walk and get to know each other. I promise to bring her back shortly, Marcus."

"As long as Mina has no objections. Do you want to go off with Nonna?" Marcus asked Mina. She nodded, curls bobbing.

As soon as Gabriel was alone with his brother, he shook his head. "I don't know what to say. I came home from London to find that I have a son."

Marcus let a long whistle escape his lips. "Life, ever a wonder. Do you really intend to keep him?"

"Everything happened so suddenly. The boy has a mother somewhere. I can't help thinking she'll return sooner or later. Better sooner, if she does come back, before Sophia has a chance to get too attached."

His brother clapped him on the back. "I saw her with that baby in her arms, Gabriel. I think it might be too late to avoid an attachment."

Gabriel nodded. "You're right, of course. Tom Reilly was here earlier in his official capacity as chief constable. He's going to try to track down the mother."

"If anyone can find her, Tom can." Marcus had

great faith in his friend, as Gabriel knew. His brother's confidence had helped Gabriel to put his trust in the man, but he had his own suspicions.

"Sophia doesn't want her to be found, but I disagree. I prefer to know what we're dealing with, what kind of mother would leave her child and why. Why here with us?"

"There are worse places to abandon an infant, I suppose. Any child would be lucky to grow up at Thornbrook Park." Marcus gestured around the room.

"I'm aware of our good fortune, and yet I'm uneasy. I have my suspicions about one of the maids…" Gabriel started to share his theory on the maid, Jane, but he was interrupted by the return of the women.

"Where are the babies?" Marcus asked.

"They fell asleep together. It was the sweetest thing I've ever seen." Eve placed a hand to her heart.

"So adorable," Sophia agreed. "They got on like siblings."

"Ha, that's not very sweet at all," Mother said, returning with Mina. "My two boys were tiny terrors when left alone. Are you sure it's safe?"

"They're only babies, Teresa. And Jane, our maid, is watching over them. She was happy to do it," Sophia said with a hesitant glance at Gabriel.

"I'm sure she was," Gabriel said. "All too happy."

Marcus changed the subject, to Gabriel's relief. "Well, Mother, it seems you have a new admirer. Mina hasn't let go of your hand. Did you enjoy your walk with Nonna, Mina?"

"We enjoyed our walk very much, didn't we?"

Mother spoke for the girl. Mina nodded but didn't add to the conversation.

"We would like you to consider coming home with us for a few days, Mother," Marcus said.

Eve added, "I would love a chance to get to know you better, and you could see more of the girls. We plan to invite Lord Markham as well."

Mother nodded. "I would like that, I think. I know Charles would like it. Where is he, I wonder. I haven't seen him all day."

"Come to think of it, I haven't seen much of Agatha either," Sophia added. "I'm sure they'll come along at any moment."

"I'll go and have a quick look around, see if I can find them," Gabriel volunteered. "I'll only be a moment."

Before anyone could protest, he left the room. He hated to resort to sneaking around his own house, but what he really wanted was a chance to catch Jane in an unguarded moment with Teddy. Perhaps she would give herself away, or at least set his mind at ease that she had nothing more than a casual interest in the baby.

❧

Sophia prided herself on being a good hostess, but she could hardly focus on the conversation once Gabriel left the room. What was her husband up to now? She didn't think he was hunting down Agatha or Lord Markham as he'd claimed. Ever since he had mentioned that Jane could be Teddy's mother, she hadn't been able to chase the suspicion that Gabriel could be right. It was quite a coincidence, Jane showing up looking for work out of the blue. They hadn't even advertised needing a new maid, Sophia recalled. Jane simply showed up one day asking for work.

"If you'll excuse me a moment?" Sophia interrupted Eve before she could finish her sentence. "I need to check on something."

"Go ahead." Teresa dismissed her with a wave of the hand. "I'm getting to know Eve."

Ah, so Sophia wasn't necessary to the conversation after all. Teresa was interrogating her newest daughter-in-law, and Marcus struggled to help his wife along. Sophia knew it was safe to leave them for now, when she would hardly be missed, but she would have to apologize to Eve later for not warning her ahead of time what to expect from Teresa. As soon as she made it out of the room, Sophia headed upstairs to her sitting room, where she had left Jane watching over the babies.

Before she got to her room, from down the hall, she could see her husband standing in the doorway as if frozen.

"Gabriel," she said quietly, hoping to get his attention, but he did not turn.

Only as she neared did she realize he'd been aware of her presence. He turned at last and gestured for her to join him in the doorway. Once at his side, he placed an arm around her and pulled her in front of him so that she could see for herself.

Sophia couldn't contain her gasp at the scene before her eyes, causing Jane to look up in alarm. The sight of Lord and Lady Averford in the doorway watching her must have scared the young maid half to death, but she remained seated, to her credit, the baby contentedly unaware of his audience as he remained cradled in his mother's lap, suckling from her breast.

"So it's true." Sophia couldn't remain calm, though she struggled to keep her voice down so as not to alarm Teddy or wake baby Freddie asleep in the basket next to Jane. "Lord Averford guessed correctly that you are Teddy's mother."

"No." Jane shook her head, tears in her pretty blue eyes. "Ye are Teddy's mother now, my lady. It's how it must be. The poor babe was hungry, is all. I thought I could help if I still had any o' my milk left."

Yet the child still nursed from Jane's breast. Sophia started to cry as well. Had she lost him? So soon?

"Gabriel, darling." Regaining her composure, Sophia turned. "Send for another maid to come look after the children. We're going to need some time alone with Jane."

"Yes." Gabriel's mouth hung open slightly, revealing his shock at the scene. "At once."

He turned and walked off down the hall, one hand reaching up to run through his hair. Perhaps he hadn't expected to be proven right so irrefutably? At any rate, there was no longer any denying it. They had to find out what had driven Jane to abandon Teddy to them, and whether she truly planned to leave him or take him back. Sophia allowed Jane to finish feeding Teddy and put him down, asleep again, next to Freddie in the basket, careful not to wake either baby. Mrs. Jenks returned with Gabriel and, without a word, took Jane's vacated place on the settee to watch the children. Clearly, Gabriel had given Jenks some idea of what to expect.

Wordlessly, the three of them walked downstairs to the small parlor near the breakfast room.

"Have a seat, Jane." Sophia sat first, on the sofa, gesturing for Jane to take the armchair across from her. Gabriel sat down next to his wife.

Jane took the seat and buried her face in her hands. "I'm so sorry. I didn't mean to cause trouble."

"What did you mean by leaving your child?" Gabriel leaned forward. "By coming here at all?"

Jane took a deep breath, probably to compose herself. At last, she looked Sophia in the eye and then turned her gaze to Gabriel. "Just now, I only wanted to settle 'im down. He woke and started to fuss, and 'e knew me as soon as I picked 'im up."

"Of course. You're his mother."

Jane nodded.

"And now?" Gabriel looked pained, studying the girl for answers. "What are your intentions now? Do you plan to take him back?"

"Take 'im back?" Jane put a hand to her chest. "Heavens, no. I can't care for 'im proper. Coming here was my last hope. I've no husband and my family wanted nowt to do wi' me once my mum figured out I was expecting."

"We can keep him?" Sophia looked at Gabriel, her heart soaring with relief before it came crashing down again. What of poor Jane? She suddenly felt ashamed of herself. What the woman must be going through, faced with the decision to give up her child in order to make ends meet. "Or, perhaps we can help you,

Jane. We only want what's best for Teddy." Which was true. Even if Sophia wanted to think that she was best for the boy, she had to believe that his mother's love could only benefit him.

"Ye've been such a help to me, Lady Averford. Ye've no idea. The first time I saw ye, I knew ye were an angel."

"The first time?" Gabriel asked.

Jane nodded. "When ye first came to Thornbrook Park, Countess. After yer wedding. In the village, ye were all the talk. What would she be like? Did ye see what she was wearing? Everyone was curious. It only grew after the first sighting. Ye're so pretty. We were all in awe."

Sophia felt a blush rising to her cheeks. "Goodness. I knew there must have been talk, but I had no idea I'd caused such a stir. But you're young, Jane."

"Sixteen." Jane straightened up.

"You were a girl of eight or so when my wife came to live with me at Thornbrook Park, then? An impressionable age."

"'Specially fer a girl who has nowt else to look forward to in life," Jane said dismally. "My friends and I all watched yer comings and goings. We would dream out loud of what it was like to be you. One day, I told them, I'm going to live in that fine house. I didn't mean it, of course. Ye know how girls carry on." She rolled her eyes.

"I was a girl once too." Sophia nodded. "I do know. And you do live here now."

"I do." Jane smiled. "Not exactly how I envisioned it. I imagined being a lady, not a maid. But I did accomplish summat; I grew up and worked in the village tavern. My pa was a barkeep, so 'e kept an eye on me and I helped support my family. Papa passed away though, two years ago last month."

"Ah, old Martin Pruitt. You're his daughter?" Gabriel tilted his head as if trying to make out a resemblance. "Yes. I think I remember you. I'm sorry for your loss. Martin was a good man."

"Aye, he was," Jane agreed. "We fell on hard times after Pa's death, the four of us, Mum, my two sisters, and me. I kept working at the tavern to support my family, but one night…"

"Oh dear. My dear girl." Sophia's stomach tensed. She had a feeling that she knew what Jane was about to say.

"Strangers came in, just passing through. Fine men, by the looks o' them. I served them, and they were friendly, tipped well. Mr. Clark, the man who took over fer my pa, liked them too. He usually kept a protective watch over me, but 'e felt at ease with these men. They were an affable bunch, nowt to fear, or so it seemed.

"One of them, a handsome one and the youngest o' the men, flirted with me, and I didn't mind. Not till he followed me to the kitchen and pushed me into the storage closet." Jane looked down at her hands, her cheeks flushed with the memory and probably with the shame of it all.

"You did nothing wrong, Jane. That man took advantage of you." Gabriel's voice sounded tight. Sophia glanced at him to see a vein pulsing at the side of his jaw. Jane's story had upset him as much as it did

Sophia. Her husband was a good man. She laced her hand with his.

"I know." Jane met Gabriel's gaze. "But thank ye fer saying so too. My mum, unfortunately, does not agree wi' ye. Eventually, when it became obvious that I was with child, she confronted me. I hadn't told her what had happened till then. I suppose I hoped it weren't true, that the evidence of what had 'appened to me in that closet would come to nowt."

"I hope he didn't hurt you," Sophia said.

"He took what 'e wanted, but didn't hurt me. Not badly. He did change the course of my life. My mum found me at fault and sent me away to live with her cousin in London. They said I was a widow. I gave birth to Teddy. I hoped I could come back and live with my mum. Somehow, I imagined I would take my job back at the tavern, and Mum and my sisters would help watch over Teddy, and everything would be almost as it had been. Mum didn't agree. She wondered why I came back at all. She wanted nowt to do wi' us. Mr. Clark and his wife took me in."

"Clark is a good man too," Gabriel said. "I've always liked him."

"The Clarks have been very kind, but I can't rely on their generosity much longer. I couldn't manage working at the tavern again either, though I tried. Teddy needed me too often for feedings, and I felt unsettled every time an unfamiliar face entered the bar. I had an idea that I could try to find work here at Thornbrook Park. It always seemed like such a happy, welcoming place to me, not that I knew for certain. Not until I came in looking for a position."

"And I gave you one," Sophia said. "Because I liked you immediately. Something about you inspired my trust." What it was, she couldn't say exactly. Sometimes one just felt a connection with others.

"Ye were as lovely and sweet as I'd always imagined, Lady Averford," Jane gushed. "Ye invited me in and offered me a cup of tea. Ye asked about my health and my family, and it seemed as if ye really cared, when I really needed someone to care. I knew then that ye were the kind o' woman who could be Teddy's mum."

"Because you couldn't keep him and work to earn a living?" Gabriel asked. "Is that why you're giving him up?"

Jane cast her eyes down and shook her head. "It's more than that."

"We need to know, Jane." Gabriel urged her. "Please put your faith in us."

She looked up, her eyes aglow. "I do have faith in ye. In both o' ye. That's why I knew ye would make the best parents fer my boy. I'm not leaving him because o' money."

"Are you sure?" Sophia asked. "Because we can help you. If you want to be a mother to Teddy, we can help you with money."

"Why would ye do such a thing?" Jane looked confused. "I'm nowt but a housemaid."

Sophia shrugged. "I can't even imagine it myself. I want Teddy to be happy and loved. I love him. I love him so much and he's hardly been here for a day. I hate to give him up, but if the best thing for him is growing up with his mother, then that's what I want for him. No matter what it costs."

"But that's not what's best fer 'im." Jane shook her head, adamant. "I get impatient with 'im sometimes. He's such a good baby. I couldn't ask for better. But even so, I look at 'im sometimes and I feel resentful. And angry. And I don't know why. He's innocent. I would never hurt 'im, of course. But I can't imagine 'im growing up wi' me. I'm not ready to be a mum. There's so much I want to do, and I can't do it with the responsibility of a babe in my care."

Sophia smiled. "You remind me a little of my sister, Alice. She also has so much she wants to do."

"And I like working here!" Jane added. "I can 'ardly believe it myself. I wake up every day looking forward to the tasks ahead, as grueling as they can sometimes be. I'm not entirely on my own here at Thornbrook Park, but I feel that I have some independence, something of my very own, my work. The Clarks have been taking care of Teddy, but they're getting on in years, and it's a temporary arrangement. I thought I could leave Teddy here wi' ye. Ye'll be far better parents than I could ever be, and 'e will want for nowt in yer care."

"I'm not sure I understand," Gabriel said. "Did you plan to keep working for us while we raised your son as our own?"

Jane shrugged. "At least I'd get to see how 'e's getting on. But it's not as easy as I imagined. He reaches out for me when 'e sees me. I've been fearing 'e would give me away. And 'e has."

"Are you sure it's what you want, then?" Sophia asked, with hope alive in her heart. "Do you really want to give him into our care? Permanently?"

Jane nodded. "Of that, I am quite certain. I ha' been fer weeks now."

"Even if it means you won't get to see him every day?" Sophia asked. "Does that change anything for you? As much as I hate to send you away, I just can't imagine keeping you on here. It might confuse Teddy."

"I agree." Jane nodded. "I can see that it won't be ideal. I'll seek a position elsewhere. But I still want ye to raise Teddy as yer own. I meant what I said. I feel that 'e belongs here, even if I don't."

Sophia, heart soaring, tried to contain her excitement. "We can give you some money to get started somewhere else. And references, of course, should you decide to remain a housemaid."

"No money." Jane shook her head. "I couldn't. It would feel like I was selling him to ye somehow. I just want the best for 'im."

"And so do we," Gabriel agreed. "We could use you at Averford House, our London residence, for now, if you like, while you look for something else. You'll get the same wages. I can recommend you to some of our friends there, or if you prefer to stay in Yorkshire…"

"No, London would be grand." Jane's eyes lit up. "I was there fer such a short time, and I hardly got to see any o' it, but I liked it there. I accept yer offer, but…"—Jane nibbled her lip—"I need to confess something to ye first. I hope ye won't cast me out."

"What is it, Jane?" Sophia asked without trepidation. She doubted Jane could say anything to spoil her happiness at becoming well and truly a mother to Teddy.

"I added some herbs to your brew the other night. I overheard Lord Averford saying 'e wanted to take ye to London, and it was when I'd planned to leave Teddy. The Clarks have been good to us, but they were growing weary o' caring fer him. Mrs. Mallows said that the herbs would diminish your headache and help you rest, so I doubled the dose when she wasn't looking. I only wanted ye to miss the London trip. I felt summat awful about it as soon as I realized that I had probably given ye far too much. I was so relieved when ye woke up. I'm so sorry."

Was that all? Sophia smiled. "No harm done after all. I forgive you, Jane."

"The offer stands," Gabriel confirmed. "Would you like to work for us at Averford House until we can find you another suitable position somewhere else?"

Jane beamed. "I would. Thank ye. Thank ye both so much."

"We thank you, Jane. You give us a far greater gift than you could ever imagine by entrusting us to raise your son as ours." Gabriel stood, and so did the women.

"I suppose I'll peek in to say good-bye to 'im, if ye don't mind. I do love 'im. Even if I can't keep 'im." Tears brimmed in Jane's eyes.

"Of course, Jane," Sophia said, holding her hand out to Jane. "And after a while, you're welcome to visit him too. I'm not sure yet what we'll tell him about you, but I don't mean to cut you off from him entirely."

Gabriel's brow arched, as if he wasn't quite certain.

"Thank ye both again," Jane said. "Fer everything."

Seventeen

Rocking Teddy in her arms, Sophia stole a glance at the calendar on her desk. She had been a mother for nearly two weeks, and she loved every minute of it. The sleepless nights, Teddy's occasional bouts of seemingly incessant wailing, the mess, all of it brought her inexplicable joy when she looked into Teddy's blue eyes. She was a mother.

And Gabriel was a father. He had seemed so happy when Jane had left the room and they'd found themselves alone to marvel over their good fortune. He'd hugged Sophia tightly and kissed her breathless, and had told her that he'd never been prouder to call her his wife.

"You would have given him back to her," he'd marveled. "After all your talk of being a countess and having the power to keep him if you wanted, you offered him back to his mother. You offered her money to raise him!"

"It only seemed right," Sophia had said, treasuring the feel of his arms around her. They would be a family, the three of them.

"Still." He'd paused to brush a tendril of hair from her cheek, so tenderly. "It's more than I would have done."

"You, with your Labour Exchanges Act vote on the line? It's designed to help women like Jane, isn't it? Mothers and fathers who can't find work to support their families. You can talk, but I know that you have a very large heart in that solid chest of yours, Lord Averford." She'd smiled up at him.

"Which reminds me that I should get back to London soon to make the vote, but I'm not rushing back. Lord Wilkerson can carry on without me. Except..." His voice had trailed off. "If I go to London, I can check with our solicitor and see if we need to do anything to be certain that Teddy is truly ours. I can take Jane there and introduce her to our London staff. It would make her transition easier."

Sophia had agreed. They'd settled it. Gabriel would go to London with Jane, and there they'd gone the very next day. Sophia had expected that he would be home in a few days, and they would celebrate their official parenthood and make up all of their differences, just like that. Everything would fall into place.

But it hadn't happened as she'd supposed, not at all. After a few days, Gabriel had come home, but she had only seen him a handful of times since his return. It was as if he couldn't be bothered with her.

To his credit, Sophia's entire life had become consumed with Teddy. She hadn't gone to any effort to make time for Gabriel alone. But she'd imagined they would be parents together. She'd thought he would return home and be taking care of Teddy at her side.

But he was always busy. Taking care of the estate took time, she knew, and she'd been neglectful of her duties of late, but it didn't take every waking moment. Not like the care of an infant did. When Teresa came back from visiting Marcus and Eve, she would be helpful with the baby, Sophia knew. Sophia would have a chance to confront Gabriel then and demand to know what was keeping him away.

Was it divorce, she wondered? He could have been meeting with his solicitor to plan his own exit from their marriage. Perhaps he didn't really want a baby. They'd talked about having one of their own, but it had been just that, talk. When he was trying to get under her skirts, no less. What wouldn't he have said to encourage her to renew their relations in the heat of the moment? But maybe the reality of Teddy becoming theirs had made him rethink their life together. Sophia tried not to think the worst.

In the meantime, she had her servants to rely on for what little assistance she would accept in caring for Teddy. Mrs. Jenks was her biggest supporter, of course, but Anna had proven helpful as well. She'd hired a nurse for Teddy's feedings. Agatha had gone off with Teresa and Lord Markham to Markham House, surprising everyone. She'd assumed she was invited and no one had had the heart to tell her no. But with Jenks, Anna, the wet nurse, and all of the others, Sophia made do. She managed to bathe every now and then at least.

"Ah, there you are." Gabriel walked into Sophia's room without knocking.

"Where else would I be? It's Teddy's naptime and

I'm trying to get him settled. How good of you to come check on us."

He smiled, deflecting her sarcastic tone. "Mother is coming back later today, along with Agatha and Lord Markham. You'll have more help with Teddy once they're all here."

She pouted. "I don't want more help, darling. I want you. You've been so busy. I hardly see you."

"Is that what's troubling you?" He held his hands out to take the baby from her. "I'm sorry. I've been busy preparing a surprise for you, actually. For you and for our son."

"He's a baby. What could he possibly need besides our love and attention, regular feedings, and frequent changes?" The sight of him cradling their baby to his chest went a long way toward easing her annoyance with Gabriel. She felt her heart beat faster. "And I don't need surprises. I need you."

"Be that as it may, you're getting surprises. And me. Now that I've completed my work, I will be around more to help you with the baby. I promise." His eyes twinkled with a mysterious gleam.

"You mean it, or you wouldn't have promised." Relief flooded her veins. "You don't break promises easily."

"Exactly." He leaned in to kiss her on the tip of her nose. "Now let's go see my first surprise, shall we?"

"I'm a little anxious, to be honest. I usually like surprises, but I don't know what could have kept you so occupied that you hardly had time for your wife and son." She felt a little childish complaining, but she had not been prepared to see so little of him at a time when things were finally going well for them again at last. Unless…they weren't going well for him. Did he mean to divorce her? The fear remained at the back of her mind.

"Come along. Just down the hall." He cradled the baby in the crook of one arm and held her hand with the other. Three doors down from her room, on the opposite side of the hall, he paused outside a door.

"The goldenrod room?" She narrowed her eyes suspiciously. "What could you have to show me there?"

The room was one they avoided unless the house was so full of guests that it became necessary, which fortunately was not often. The walls, the bed linens, the rug…everything was a horrific shade of goldenrod yellow. Sophia liked yellow, but so much of it? It was a room that hadn't been touched since even before Teresa's time. Though every mistress of the house seemed to be about to begin refinishing it, no one ever had.

"Not goldenrod any longer." Gabriel let go of her hand to turn the knob and push the door gently open. "Now it's…well, it's almost every color of the rainbow, but predominantly blue. Have a look."

She met his gaze, then walked through the door. Sunlight streamed through the open windows, along with a light breeze that blew the billowy chiffon curtains. Ivory curtains, no longer goldenrod. A baby's crib along the back wall first drew her gaze, but it was the kites that captured her attention and her imagination. Kites of all colors hung on the walls and from the corners of the ceiling, a whimsical decoration that made the room a lively, happy space, the perfect space for their son.

"Gabriel, it's wondrous!" She looked all around, taking in details. Along with the kites, there were blue walls, no longer yellow. A dressing table, with a low, flat surface topped with a cushion, the perfect place for changing a baby. In the corner by the window was a big, wooden rocking chair topped with patchwork cushions of all colors. "How did you think of it all? The kites! What a delight!"

He shrugged. "They seem boyish, don't they? Fitting, I think, for our son."

"They offer a certain sense of adventure." She held her hands up. "Perfect. How did you manage all this without my knowing? Look, Teddy, a proper place for you to sleep! Place him in the crib. Let's see how he likes it."

Gabriel obliged. Teddy looked up and cooed, his fist in his mouth. He didn't dislike it, but he didn't seem all that impressed.

"Oh, darling!" She flung herself into Gabriel's now-empty arms. "I love my surprise. Thank you."

If she had one complaint, it was that the room seemed so far from her own. How would she get there in time if he needed her?

"I know what you're thinking," he said. "I can see it in your eyes. It's only three doors down and right across the hall. I couldn't put his room right next to yours without you knowing. You would have heard the footmen moving things about and hanging the kites. And besides that, I do want you to myself sometimes, which will be more easily accomplished without our baby and his nanny right next door."

"His nanny? He's to have a nanny now? I'm not

certain I want him to have a nanny, Gabriel. I have the nurse for feedings, and I can manage the rest of his care on my own."

"Of course you can, for the most part. But darling, you've had so little sleep these past few weeks."

She cocked a brow. "Oh? You've barely been around, but you know how much sleep I've been getting?"

"I do sleep too. My room is next to yours, need I remind you again. Admittedly, I've been busy and falling into bed quite late. Far too late to try to do what I've wanted to do with you. But every time it occurs to me to try my luck and turn your doorknob, I hear you up with a fussy baby."

"And yet I haven't heard you knock on my door to offer to take him for a while."

He nodded. "My mistake. You're right. I should have. But…I have no idea what to do with him, Sophia. I know nothing of babies. You'll have to help me, show me what to do for him when he fusses and cries."

"And needs changing? Are you willing to change him?"

"Change him?" Gabriel pulled a face, seemingly horrified. "You're making a strong case for my hiring that nanny."

She rolled her eyes. "He's your own son! I think you can afford to get your hands a little dirty, Lord Averford, when it comes to your child."

"Silly woman. I can afford help so that I never have to dirty my own hands. Or yours."

"I'm happy to care for our baby."

"I'm hiring a nanny anyway."

"Was that to be my next surprise?" She peeked up at him through her lashes. "Have I spoiled it?"

He shook his head. "No. That will come later, once Mother and Agatha return to help with Teddy and I can get you all alone."

"All alone." She felt her breath catch in her throat. The excitement of caring for a baby, and her exhaustion, had cooled her ardor in the past weeks, but her blood began heating up again. Alone with her husband. "Yes, I would like that."

"Good." When he looked at her, his heavy-lidded eyes conveyed exactly what he was thinking of doing with her when they were alone, and she thrilled at the prospect. "Mrs. Jenks should be waiting in your room by now. I've instructed her to run a bath and give you some time to rejuvenate while I catch up with our son."

"Are you sure you're ready to be alone with him?" Sophia asked, suddenly afraid to leave them though she had been dreaming of getting the two of them in one room for days.

"Ready as I'll ever be. And if things go awry, I'm sure you'll hear his wails. Even from the impossible distance of three doors down and across the hall." He flashed her a devastating grin that made it hard for her to leave him for other reasons besides entrusting him with the care of their son. But she managed to leave them anyway. She really did need a long soak in a hot bath.

When she emerged at last, fresh from the bath and having time on her own without grasping little hands, she was dressed in a clean gown. The sound of voices raised in merriment drew her to the stairs. Mrs. Jenks had told her they were assembling in the drawing room, and she headed down.

"They" were Teresa, Lord Markham, and Agatha back from Markham House, along with Marcus, Eve, their nursemaid, and the little ones. And her husband, of course, with their son. The Thornes would probably stay for dinner. The time alone with Gabriel she'd been dreaming of in the bath would have to wait. Again. She supposed that's how it was for parents of young children, never enough time alone together.

She pasted on a smile and made her entrance.

"Darling, you take my breath away," Gabriel greeted her with Teddy in his arms. "I knew some time in the bath would work wonders."

Teresa scoffed. "You make it sound as if she were a ragamuffin in need of a fairy godmother's touch to transform. Your wife is a stunning beauty, even when in need of rest."

"Thank you, Teresa. And I am rested at last." She'd never imagined her mother-in-law would be the one complimenting her, let alone standing up for her. "How was your visit to Markham House?"

"Lovely. We had a grand time! Eve is a delightful hostess. I think she might be my new favorite daughter-in-law."

Sophia suppressed a smile, aware that Teresa wanted to make up for having paid her a compliment. It wouldn't be comfortable for them to be getting along too well. "I'm so glad. Eve is a favorite of mine too."

"I'm right here," Eve said, waving from across the room. "You're making me blush."

"Speaking of inspiring blushes…" Gabriel handed the baby to Teresa. "Mother, I entrust him to your care, as we discussed."

"As you discussed?" Sophia looked from one to the other, confused. Teddy, Teresa, Agatha, Lord Markham, Marcus, Eve, and Gabriel. The girls must have gone up for a nap with their nurse.

"As we discussed." Gabriel approached and held his hand out to her. "I can't take another moment in this crowded room."

"But…" She broke eye contact with her husband to look around. "Our guests?"

"They're not guests." He waved them off. "They're family. And they can appreciate the fact that we need some time alone. Come along."

"Come where? What is going on?" Sophia couldn't fathom what had come over her husband.

"I need to be alone with you at once, or I'm going to go out of my mind. It's all arranged. Mother will watch over Teddy. We're going for a ride, but we'll be back in plenty of time for dinner."

‽

"I don't see why we couldn't have stayed and visited with Marcus and Eve a bit first," Sophia said, wondering what had sparked such a passionate response in her husband that they couldn't have waited to be alone. "Your mother just got back. Are you sure she'll be ready to care for the baby? And I feel like I haven't spoken to Agatha in ages."

"Agatha will be there when we get back. And Mother couldn't wait to be with Teddy again. She missed him."

"You're walking too fast." Sophia stopped dead in her tracks, her own form of rebellion. "And where are we going? I'm not taking another step until you tell me."

"It's time for your next surprise. You don't want to ruin it, do you?" He reached for her hand. She tugged it back.

"Your big surprise, the papers you needed drawn up in London. It explains so much. Just like that?"

"What like that?"

She snapped her fingers. "You'll be rid of me."

"Rid of you? What makes you think I have any desire to be rid of you?" He pulled her into his arms, rough and insistent. She knew he wouldn't hurt her, but the firmness of his embrace said that she had little ability to resist. "God, woman, you are exasperating. I've been dying to get you alone. How does that suggest I wish to be rid of you?"

"I don't know." She leaned away from him, not allowing his kiss until she knew more what he planned. "Lulling me into a false sense of security?"

"Oh." His face inched closer to hers until their noses were nearly touching. "That explains our adventures in the garden shed, does it? If that was part of my grand plan to push you away, I'm a miserable failure."

"I don't understand. What took you so long in London, if not your plan to divorce me?" They'd needed no formal papers drawn up to adopt Teddy, and it was weeks before Parliament would bring the

Labour Exchanges Act up for a vote. So what had he been up to in London, if not planning a divorce?

"Divorce? It never crossed my mind. It's not an option to me. I took you for better, for worse."

"For richer," she said. "I've only made you richer."

"My life is richer because of you. Every waking moment." His brown eyes glowed with tenderness.

"When I'm not driving you out of your mind." She laughed. His hands pressed into the back of her waist, gently easing her into him. She stopped fighting it.

"For better, for worse. We've had our share of struggles, but my every day is better because of you, Sophia. Even at our worst."

"You're trying to seduce me again, is that it? A little flattery and you imagine I'll just lift my skirts…"

"Lifting your skirts isn't good enough, my lady. I'll not make love to you in the middle of the green unless we can really make a show of it. I need to feel your skin against mine." He trailed a finger along her collarbone. "Every beautiful inch."

She nearly lost her ability to breathe. How she wanted it too. "We are, in fact, in the middle of the green. Anyone could look out."

He nuzzled her neck. "Let them look. No, come on. We have somewhere to go. To the stables. We'll need a horse."

"A horse?" She raised a brow. "You expect me to ride a horse. You know I haven't ridden in years."

"That's why you're going to share a saddle with me. You in front, me behind. Your skirts are wide enough. They should allow you to sit astride. Wilmadene is a very gentle mare. And you were a very elegant rider once upon a time."

"Can't we take the car?" She would have worn more proper attire if she'd planned on sitting astride a horse. She had a lovely riding habit just hanging in her closet. Why did men never see the need to explain their intentions in advance so a lady could prepare? There was even a matching hat.

"It won't do. Not where we're headed. Now is not the time to be timid, Lady Averford. My arms will be around you the entire time."

"That brings up another cause for alarm, doesn't it? My backside pressed against you, with the slow, rolling gait of a horse." She almost had to fan herself against the sudden wave of heat that came over her.

"Please. There's something I have to show you. You won't regret it."

She put her hand in his, willing to trust him. The stable master was just leading the mare, saddled, out to the green as they approached.

"Anticipating my demands, Mr. Grady?"

"She needs exercise, my lord. I was about to take her around the grounds. But if you prefer…"

"In fact, I do plan to ride. Thank you, Grady. She might need a good run once I bring her back though. I'll be keeping her to a canter. The countess is riding with me."

"My lady." The stable master bowed.

Sophia tried to maintain her imperious demeanor in case Mr. Grady looked on to bear witness to her attempting to mount the beast. She used to be a skilled rider, she reminded herself, but that was years ago, before her athletic skills dulled with age and lack of use.

Fortunately, Gabriel remained strong. He gave her a healthy boost so that she barely had to drape a leg over the saddle and settle in. His hand lingered on her ankle for longer than a second before he swung up behind her. The stable master had gone back to his duties, paying them no attention.

Her concern about riding in front of him proved valid almost as soon as they started moving. She could feel him against her. Before they'd gone a quarter mile, she wished the horse would move faster to end the torture of being so close to him without being able to turn and look at him.

"We're almost there," he said as she shifted in the seat. "Just through the trees and over the hill."

"She is gentle, as promised," Sophia noted. "But I wouldn't mind if she picked up the pace."

He nudged the horse into a faster gait. "I'm glad to know that Grady has been exercising the horses in my absence. I'll have to make it a point to get out with her more. I would love for you to join me. There's no better way to survey the grounds than on horseback."

"Mr. Grant has been taking care of it. He loves to ride."

"He probably chooses Viking for his jaunts, or Brutus. I have an attachment to old Wilmadene that I can't seem to shake in favor of the more fiery stallions."

"She's very pretty." Sophia reached out to stroke the horse's black mane.

"I took quite a fall from her right at the top of that

ridge when she was just a filly." He pointed over in the distance, past the apple orchards. "I was probably going too fast, not paying attention. The folly of youth."

"I can't believe you were ever foolish, Gabriel. Not even in youth. I think you were born gravely serious."

"I'm sure I was quite serious about going fast. I think we might have been chasing some game, a doe or a rabbit. I can't recall. Whatever it was got away. At least neither of us got hurt, with the exception of a few bruises. Here we are." He led the horse to a clearing.

"We could have walked," she said, once they reached the narrow copse at the edge of the stream. "It's not all that far."

"Over a mile. I don't want to leave them all alone with the baby for too long."

"So you do have some concern for the little angel." Sophia smiled, allowing him to help her down from the horse. Even after her feet were on the ground, his hands stayed around her slender waist. "He's irresistible."

"Not unlike you. Do you recognize the place?" Reluctantly, he let her go and gestured at the surroundings. He led her away from the horse to a patch of grass along the water's edge.

She nodded. "You took me for a picnic here years ago and made me furious at you when you wouldn't stop fishing. I'd thought it was our time to be alone."

"That had been the idea at the time. But the fish were biting, practically jumping up into my lap. You're right though. It was a beautiful day, and you were a vision, sitting on the blanket in the grass, in your light blue dress with the sunlight streaming down on you."

"Until it started to rain." She laughed. "But I'm surprised you remember what I was wearing."

"I remember wanting to throw my fishing pole into the water, to hang with it, and rip your dress off with my teeth. The only reason I started fishing in the first place was so that I wouldn't frighten you off with how badly I wanted you."

"I was easily frightened. It was still so soon after losing Edward. Not that soon, I suppose, but the fear was hard to shake. I'm sorry I created so much tension between us, Gabriel. I wanted to be with you. I needed you. But I just kept pushing you away."

"I wanted you to need me, but you seemed so independent, like you never needed anything from me again as long as you had my title and my estate. I never even knew if you really loved me, or loved what I could provide you. When you could barely stand for me to touch you, I'd thought I'd found my answer."

"Love is so complicated. I think we've had a harder time than most. Maybe I was too young when we married, too naive, too easily influenced. I wish I'd been able to tell you how I felt without feeling ashamed of myself."

"Why would you be ashamed?" He reached for her hand.

She turned red. "My mother put so many ideas into my head. Why do we listen to our parents?"

"You're asking me?"

"Right. Your mother has a few wild ideas of her own. Alice had it easier, I suppose. She has always been rebellious. No matter what Mother told her, she would never have listened. But I've always been more prim, a straight arrow. It took me so long to shake my mother's well-meant advice."

"You've finally grown into your own, Sophia." He stroked her face with the side of his hand. "The woman you were always meant to be. To be honest, I never quite expected it myself. When we married, you were so young and impressionable. But look at you now."

"Yes?" She arched a brow.

"You're magnificent. I can't get enough of you, darling. The woman you are takes my breath away."

"Show me." She suddenly felt very daring, in keeping with his compliments.

"I promised myself that I wouldn't get carried away with you again out-of-doors. You deserve a proper courtship. Dinner, wine, a bed."

She laughed, feeling carefree. "The outdoors seems to be working for us lately. No distractions. We have soft grass."

"You keep on surprising me. A moment." He walked back to the horse, fetched a blanket from a pack at the saddle's side, and returned to spread it on the grass. He reached for her hand. "My lady."

She took his hand and sat down.

"Long gone is the timid young bride." He stretched out next to her. "The woman I married might not have let me do this. Certainly not outside of a bedroom."

With an assured hand, he gripped the hem of her skirt and slid it up, exposing her legs in her short pantalets. When she didn't protest, he positioned himself between her knees and looked up at her with that wicked smile.

What did he mean to do? She might have grown bolder with age, but she still couldn't voice the words to ask. He slipped his hands up her thighs, inside the pantalets, and began dropping light kisses on her delicate flesh, first on one leg, and then the next.

"I love the dimples behind your knees," he said, kissing each one before continuing upward.

Her breath caught in her throat. Did he mean to...

His hand found its way in between the garment's slit. She fell back to the blanket, unable to contain her moan. He caressed her with long, lingering strokes, sliding a finger inside her, out, and in again until he dipped his head and found her taut pearl with his tongue. He kissed her most intimately where she'd never imagined being kissed.

"Gabriel!" She called his name. She might have screamed. She might have called him a god. She couldn't be held accountable for what she did once wave after wave of pleasure began washing over her, a wild tide in a raging storm. At last, as she struggled to regain awareness, she met his gaze. He sat propped up on his elbow at her side.

"Now that is what happens when you embrace your freedom," he said. "Prim no more."

"I've wasted so much time," she said, dazed as she stared up through the leaves of the tree overhead. "We could have been doing that all along?"

He laughed, placing a warm hand on her stomach. "All along. But we've still plenty of time, I hope."

"Make love to me, Gabriel. Let's not stop there.

Your mother can handle Teddy for now. She loves him as much as I do."

"You've forgotten your urgency to rush back?" His hand roamed over her body, pausing to trace a nipple through her clothes.

"I've nearly forgotten my own name, you scoundrel. Don't make me beg. I haven't had nearly enough of you."

"At your service, my lady." He began to undo his trousers. "I won't stop until you're fully satisfied."

Eighteen

"ALLOW ME." SHE REACHED FOR HIM. IT WAS SHE WHO longed to satisfy her husband. There were things she wanted to do to him that she had never been bold enough to attempt, but now was the time. If they were to be together and to be whole again, she had to have the courage to show him what she wanted.

She urged his trousers down his hips and freed him to her perusal.

"Men really are works of art," she mused, taking his hardness in her hand. "You're quite beautiful, did you know?"

"Beauty is in the eye of the beholder," he answered, reaching to tuck a strand of hair behind her ear, the simple intimacy of the gesture stirring a new wave of warmth inside her.

With her finger, she traced the solid length of him. "Spectacularly functional design, the way you grow to fill me. We fit together so perfectly."

"As God intended. Perhaps it is our duty to make more frequent use of our skills."

She laughed. "In that case, I need to improve my

technique. I hope you don't mind my taking some liberties in order to learn more."

He was about to answer when she cupped the precious weight of him. His words turned to a groan low in his throat. She smoothed her hand up his shaft, and down again, before dipping her head to taste him, circling her tongue around the tip. His hands tangled in her hair as she took her time to explore the new sensation of taking him into her mouth, to the back of her throat and forward again, his saline essence on her tongue.

"Mercy, woman, I can't take much more." He pulled away.

"But I'm enjoying myself. Immensely." She smiled up at him.

He shook his head. "Another time, perhaps, we can elaborate on your instruction. I need to be inside you now."

She didn't argue. Her body pulsed with new sensations, a yearning stronger than she'd ever felt for him. He urged them to the blanket, rolling atop her and spreading her legs around him. It wasn't even enough when he buried himself inside her, deep, and they began to move together.

"No." She gripped his wrists. "From behind. Like you tried once before."

He hesitated. "But you stopped me."

"I wasn't ready," she said, turning. "But let's try it now. I have a sudden taste for adventure."

His brown eyes widened, gold flecks glinting. Wordlessly, he pulled her to him, nestling against her backside a moment before filling her so much deeper than ever. He cupped her breasts as they moved in rhythm, each thrust driving her more out of her mind with growing need until she arched against him, overwhelmed with the powerful sensation of her own climax.

"That was…" She lost her words and collapsed to the blanket, struggling to catch her breath. There were no words fit to describe it. She was caught up in awe and wonder.

He fell next to her, stroking the hair from her eyes before nestling against her. "It was, my love. It was."

❧

They lingered for some time longer than intended after making love, resting together under the sweet chestnut tree, the gurgling of the brook lulling them to a near slumber.

"I didn't realize how tired I was," Sophia said. "Though I shouldn't be surprised, after staying up all night with a baby."

"What if we make another child? So soon." He placed his hand on her stomach. "He could be growing even now."

"Or she. I'm prepared for the possibility. He or she will have a lovely big brother to help them along. I always wanted an older brother."

"Talk to Marcus. I'm sure he could relieve you of the notion."

She laughed but sobered almost as quickly. "Teddy is ours, Gabriel. No matter where he comes from, he's ours now."

"All ours. Your strength and compassion in handling the situation with Jane surprised me. I knew you were kind and thoughtful, but I had no idea you could be so generous and strong. You dealt with her fairly, and with so much concern for her welfare as well as Teddy's."

"Never doubt that I'm strong enough to handle anything that comes my way. Anything."

He sat up. "I guess that means it's time for my surprise."

"I'd forgotten there was a surprise." She sat up next to him. "What is it?"

He rose, walked to the saddle to get the papers, and returned. "Sophia, my dearest, I want you to have all that you see around you."

"And here I am." She failed to understand.

He handed her the papers. "It's the deed to this particular parcel of land, in your name. I'm giving you acres of Thornbrook Park to be yours alone, to do with what you wish."

"What I wish?" She looked the documents over. "Dear God, Gabriel, why would you break up the estate? It's already mine as much as it is yours. I don't need a piece with just my name on it."

"You don't understand." He sat back down next to her. "I wanted you to have something special. Other than you, there's nothing dearer to me than Thornbrook Park."

"But it's all ours as it is." She laughed. "I was counting on jewelry."

"I always get you jewelry."

"I know. I thought perhaps another aquamarine? Maybe a ring with a stone as big as a robin's egg? You usually have impeccable taste when it comes to choosing just the right thing."

"But this is land, darling. A part of Thornbrook Park. It's all yours, no matter what happens. You could build a pavilion or a cottage. You could grow flowers. Anything."

"You know I would never choose to break up the estate. It would be madness. And what do you mean, no matter what happens?" She moved an inch away from him. "How cryptic. What do you expect will happen?"

He ran a hand through his hair. "This is why I shouldn't talk. I always get myself in a muddle."

"Is this to be my security should things not work out between us? I'm afraid I am at a loss to comprehend."

"I didn't mean it like that. Please, darling." He reached for her hand. "I wanted to show you that I had respect for your decisions and the way you've handled the estate in my absence."

"By breaking off a chunk?" She shook her head, still not understanding him. "Did it never occur to you that jewelry is security for women? It's dazzling to the eye, yes, but so much more. Should the worst happen, I have millions. All of those gifts you've given me through the years delight me, yes. I love to wear them. But also, I'm financially protected through them. I can sell them to support myself, if need be."

He nodded. "I guess I never thought of it that way."

"Women think of it, believe me. When our guests come and admire my diamonds, they are also admiring the security you've provided me. And they're all gifts from you, given out of love. Should you choose to leave me, I walk away with my gifts."

"But I've no intention of leaving you, Sophia. You

must know that, after all we've been to each other." He laced hands with hers. "You're my whole world."

"Thornbrook Park is your world."

"Exactly. So by giving you a part of it…"

She shook her head. "I don't know what to think. An hour ago, I thought it was love. It's so easy to confuse lust with love. You love my body, but do you really love me?"

"You weren't questioning my love an hour ago."

"I didn't know my name an hour ago. I love what you do to me; that's undeniable. I'm in danger of becoming addicted to you like a drug. But is that love? When you wanted to put a second desk in your office, you made me think that you understood that I'm every bit as capable as you. But perhaps you were placating me. Perhaps you never understood at all. I don't need a piece of Thornbrook Park to call my own. I need all of it, with you."

He stood. He was surprised to find that he didn't keel over, dead on the spot. His world collapsed around him, but he kept breathing, his body going on even while his heart felt like it was drying up and turning to ash in his chest. A day that had started out so promising had gone so terribly wrong, so fast.

"It's what I want as well. It's all I meant to show you by giving you a gift of land. I'm sorry that you misunderstood my intent."

"I'm sorry too. If we still can't make our intentions clear to each other, what does it say about our future?"

"Perhaps it says something serious, or perhaps it's nothing more than that everyone makes mistakes. I can't tell you what to think. I know that much at least by now. Come on, darling. It's time I got you home."

❧

The dynamic between them had shifted so rapidly that she still couldn't figure out how it had happened. One minute, everything was brilliant and clear, a little rosy around the edges. The next, storm clouds rolled in and made her whole world dark. The worst part was that she'd brought the clouds. If only she'd understood his intention when he'd presented her with the land.

She rode in front of him, neither of them saying a word. When they got to the stables, she didn't wait for his hand but got down from the horse on her own and began walking back to the house. His boots crunched the gravel, keeping her aware of his proximity even when they remained so far apart. Worlds apart. After becoming so close. She wanted to take it all back, turn and take his hand, welcome his gift to her, as odd as it had seemed when he presented it.

Lovely, darling! Just what I've always wanted, a piece of the land I already live on and consider my own.

But it wasn't hers, not really. His gift made it all too clear, which is why she didn't understand it, and why he was equally taken aback by her response. He had been so sure of himself, so convinced that he was giving her the most wonderful gift he could give. Why would it occur to him that the gift in itself would just remind her of how little she had on her own, that she wasn't a true owner of Thornbrook Park no matter the efforts she'd poured into keeping it all thriving in his absence? To him, he might as well have been handing her a part of himself, his heart on a plate. And she'd carelessly dropped it and crushed it with her heel. Damn.

To make matters worse, she'd prattled on about jewelry. Jewelry! Why not just let him believe that all she'd wanted was his money and status? That she had never truly cared about him? And he thought he was the one who'd created a muddle? They really were suited after all, both of them unaware of the effects of their words or actions until it was far too late.

If she turned to him now, dropped to her knees and begged forgiveness, would he believe her? Or would he think it was one more attempt to hold on to an earl? As she got closer to the house, she could hear the sound of a child laughing. A second later, Mina came running around the corner, her father chasing after her.

"Ah!" Marcus waved, calling out. "You've returned."

Sophia waved in response. One thing she'd learned as a countess was how to mask her true emotions and act as required. While visitors remained in the house, she would smile like she hadn't a care in the world.

"'She walks in beauty, like the night...'" Marcus quoted as she got closer.

"Save the poetry for your own wife, Lord Byron." Gabriel stepped up to drape an arm around her. He too was skilled at acting, or had he forgiven her?

"Eve prefers nursery rhymes these days. Or at least, that's all we manage to quote to each other. 'Little Bo Peep has lost her sheep'... Not very conducive to romance." Marcus scooped up his daughter and placed her on his shoulders. "Can you see any sheep from up there, Mina?"

"Nope. Just Aunt Soapie." Mina beamed down at Sophia.

"Hello, my sweet." Sophia reached up to touch the girl's hand, momentarily forgetting her troubles.

"Aunt Soapie?" Gabriel regarded her with a bemused expression.

Sophia shrugged her shoulders. "For a child, Sophia is quite a mouthful."

Back inside, they found Eve in quiet conversation with Gabriel's mother while both babies napped. For all of Teresa's fears about meeting Eve, the women seemed to be getting along. Glad as she was to see it, Sophia felt a small pang of envy. Perhaps Eve really was to be Teresa's favorite daughter-in-law.

"He didn't sleep the entire time," Teresa assured her. "Not until moments ago, when he fell asleep after nursing."

"I missed his feeding time." Sophia felt flooded with regret. Perhaps she was going to be a terrible mother after all.

"I had everything under control," Teresa assured her.

"And Agatha," Sophia asked. "Where has Agatha run off to now?" Aunt Agatha had a habit of hovering close when there were guests in the house, perhaps waiting for the opportunity to read fortunes, but Sophia realized that she hadn't seen much of Aunt Agatha, even before Agatha had gone away for the visit to Markham House.

"Haven't seen her for hours, and I don't mind." Teresa made no attempt to hide her dislike. "I had enough of her at Markham House, where she managed to stay at my side all too often. Charles and I could never manage any time alone. "

Eve smiled. "Where is Lord Markham, come to think of it? He too disappeared almost as soon as we arrived."

Teresa shrugged. "He is getting on in years. Perhaps he needed a nap."

"Speaking of naps…" Eve gestured to Mina, who had fallen asleep on a pillow in the corner of the couch. "I suppose we should be getting one in before dinner."

"I think we all need some rest," Sophia said, stifling a sigh. She needed time on her own to think about Gabriel and how to proceed after their afternoon took a turn for the worst. "I'll take Teddy up with me."

"I'll come with you, darling," Gabriel offered, one brow raised as if unsure of her reaction.

He was right to be unsure. She had no idea what to think. "Not now, Gabriel. You men don't look the least bit weary. Why not take the time to catch up with your brother?"

"I've been dying for a game of billiards, old man." Marcus clapped his brother on the back. "What do you say, Gabriel? We finally have a chance to play without the women and children getting in the way."

"All right," Gabriel said resignedly. "I'll be up to check on you and Teddy later, darling."

"Until then." Sophia smiled weakly, scooped her sleeping son into her arms, and headed for the stairs.

❧

By the next morning, she still hadn't made up with Gabriel. Not quite. They'd been polite to each other and their guests at dinner, and they'd warmed up to each other again over cordials. She'd allowed him to sit close and even to embrace her before going up to bed. Teddy had begun to fuss though, so she'd run off to tend the baby and left Gabriel with a quick kiss on the cheek before they could have a chance to talk about how they'd left things between them in the afternoon.

At least she'd had a chance to connect with Aunt Agatha again at dinner, and early in the morning when Teddy had just settled down to sleep and Agatha appeared at the nursery door.

"I had a feeling you needed me," Agatha had said. "I'll look after him while you go prepare yourself for the day ahead."

"Prepare myself? Goodness, you sound cryptic. Am I in for a busy day?" Sophia had asked, but Agatha had remained as vague as she sometimes preferred to be when making her predictions.

"Let's just say that I hope you managed to fit in some sleep last night. You're going to need to be ready for anything." Agatha's green eyes sparkled with mischief.

"I'm ready for a bath anyway," Sophia had said, leaving Teddy in Agatha's capable hands while she went off to bathe and dress.

When she returned, she felt refreshed and ready to face anything that Agatha could possibly imagine. Sophia smiled at the sight of Agatha making faces to entertain Teddy as she rocked him in the rocking chair. "You two seem to be getting along."

"Oh, we're old friends, Teddy and me. He's an old soul, did you know? We knew each other in a previous life." Agatha paused to coo at the baby. "I was captured by pirates and auctioned at the slave trade. Teddy bought me and set me free. I'll be forever grateful. He wasn't called Teddy back then, of course. He was a benevolent trader known as Goldbeard, really an English lord in disguise."

"Oh, of course. What else would he be?" Sophia shook her head at Agatha's imagination. How she loved her dear aunt! "And what was your name in that lifetime?"

"I'll never know. The spirits don't like to reveal such things to protect us from unpleasant recollections. They only show me the very best things that are useful to know."

"How kind of them." Sophia smiled. "But, Agatha, I've been wondering. How did you know where to find Teddy and me this morning? Gabriel had just presented us with the nursery, and I don't recall telling you where it was yet."

"Miss Puss led the way." Agatha nodded. "She stayed behind while I was off to Markham House and watched over the proceedings."

"Did she? And what does she think of it all?"

"We both think Gabriel did a marvelous job of it." Agatha rose with Teddy in her arms. "Who knew he had a skill for decorating? The kites are a wonderful touch."

"Aren't they? I think so too." Sophia took Teddy from Agatha, who held him out for her.

"Now if you excuse me, I'll need some freshening up. We must be ready to meet our challenges when fate comes to call."

"Challenges, oh dear." Sophia believed she'd had enough of those lately, but she knew better than to doubt Agatha entirely.

She was still in the nursery dressing Teddy for the day when Mr. Grant dropped in. "Oh, Mr. Grant. How have you been?"

She felt remorseful that she hadn't even thought of Mr. Grant for at least a week or more. They used to meet every morning to talk over their plans, and yet she had forgotten him so easily.

"I'm well, thank you. I wanted to see what you thought of the nursery. Lord Averford was so exacting about it, determined to get it all just right for you."

"It is. It's lovely. He did get it right. He couldn't have done better."

"I agree." Mr. Grant looked around, though not for the first time apparently. Gabriel must have consulted him as he planned the room. "The kites especially. Well. You can imagine how emotional it was for him."

She met his gaze. "Emotional? The kites? I'm not sure what you mean."

"Oh. You didn't know. I'm sorry. I should let him tell you."

"Tell me what? What the kites mean to him emotionally? If he hasn't revealed it yet, do you think he means to tell me at all? What of it, Mr. Grant? Please tell me."

Grant stared down as if considering. Finally, he looked up. "Every year, when your husband visits the grave of your first son, he brings a kite to leave behind. I'm sorry. I thought you knew."

"I had no idea. Kites, really? I didn't know he visited Edward's grave at all, let alone once a year. I thought perhaps he wanted to forget until I saw him there just a little while ago…" Her voice trailed off. So it wasn't a chance meeting. He had purposefully gone to visit their son, as he had in previous years. He missed their Edward as much as she did. But of course. What did she think? "And these are the kites? How did he manage?"

"Not all of them." Grant walked over to finger the blue tail of one in the corner. "Some of them are the ones he'd left, gathered by Sturridge and tucked away for safekeeping once Lord Averford left them behind. The ones in the corners and a few in the middle. The rest are all new, bought to add to the collection. He means to take them down and fly them all with Teddy eventually, or so he said."

"What a lovely thought. He has honored our past and shown his excitement to move forward all at once, a tribute to both of our boys." She felt the tears gathering. "And I had no idea how much it all meant to him."

Her steadfast, exacting husband was far more tender-hearted than she'd ever known. "Thank you, Mr. Grant. I love the nursery even more than I realized, now that I know the whole story."

"I'll leave you to enjoy it then. Unless there's anything else I can do for you?"

She nodded. "Yes. Please forget what I've said in the past about waiting to cancel the guesthouse reservations. Follow Lord Averford's orders. He does know what's best for Thornbrook Park, and I've been distracted with caring for the baby."

"I'll do that." Grant was agreeable. "But I hope you'll be able to join us again once you hire a nanny for the baby. I find you add a unique outlook to the management of the estate."

"Thank you, Mr. Grant. We'll see." Grant left her with much to consider. She'd almost forgotten how determined she had been to be a part of the decisions made at Thornbrook Park, and she missed it.

Gabriel was quite capable without her, and she had Teddy to think about now. But did it mean that she had to step aside entirely, or could she be a mother and a manager? One thing that was certain to her now but that hadn't been clear enough in the past was that her husband cared deeply—about the estate, about their sons, about her. There was still hope for them, plenty of hope.

With Teddy in her arms, she went off to look for Anna. It was time to see about placing a notice to find a good nanny.

Nineteen

GABRIEL WAITED PATIENTLY FOR SOPHIA TO MAKE HER appearance in the morning. He didn't want to burst in on her and risk waking the baby, but he desperately wanted another chance to get her alone. They needed to talk about what had happened between them. He wanted another chance to set things right with her after his second surprise had failed to make the desired impression.

But when she appeared in the breakfast room at last, a happy baby in her arms, she looked distracted.

"Darling." He rose to greet her, dropping a kiss on her forehead and taking the baby from her arms. "Did you sleep well? Good morning, Teddy."

"Gabriel." For a fleeting second, the worried look left her and she gazed up at him with such a look of love in her eyes that his heart nearly exploded. "I'm so glad to see you. I've been looking for Anna."

"Anna? I haven't seen her."

Her brow creased and the worried look returned. "I can't find her, and I've looked all over the house. I rang for her, and she didn't answer."

"I've got Teddy now. Why don't you have Mrs. Hoyle go look for her in her room? Perhaps she has taken ill."

"I peeked in but didn't see her. I've sent one of the maids up to check again. I have a strange feeling about this, perhaps due to a meeting with Aunt Agatha this morning…"

"Agatha. That explains it." He tried to reassure her. "She's not always right. I'm sure Anna's around here somewhere. Maybe she went for a walk to the farm."

"But she didn't mention it." Sophia paced.

A maid, Lucy, came in. "Forgive me for interrupting. I knew you would want to see this at once."

Sophia took a note from the maid and read aloud. "'By the time you read this, I'll be Mrs. Ethan Nash.' Oh dear Lord." Sophia stopped reading and covered her mouth with her hand.

Gabriel took the note from her and continued reading. "She doesn't say where she has gone, just that the two of them have eloped."

"Eloped?" Teresa came in. "Who has eloped? Foolish decision. What point is there in marrying without any fanfare or new clothes?"

"An elopement? How romantic!" Agatha trailed behind Teresa, with Lord Markham entering the breakfast room after her.

"Between Anna Cooper and Ethan Nash. It's disastrous. What will I tell her mother? And Mrs. Dennehy! They trusted Anna to my care." Sophia pressed a hand to her forehead.

"How could I have read the spirits wrong?" Agatha

wondered. "I knew we would have quite the day ahead, but not like this."

"They're children," Gabriel said. "Without resources, as far as I know. Anna was here last night with us for dinner, and we all went to bed late. They can't have started out long before dawn. We can find them and talk some sense into them. But where would they have gone?"

"Gretna Green!" Agatha volunteered. "It's where I would go to elope."

"Or London," Sophia said. "She lived in London as a child and she has mentioned that she longed to go back."

"They couldn't marry as easily in London, and certainly not quickly, but they could get lost in a crowd," Teresa said.

"Let's divide up then, shall we? I'll go with Agatha to Scotland while you and Lady Averford check London," Lord Markham suggested. "Teresa, you look after things here, just in case they return."

"Why can't Agatha stay? I'll go with you, Charles." Teresa seemed taken aback.

"Agatha has her second sight. It might prove helpful."

"And you can watch Teddy for us," Gabriel suggested, hoping to placate his mother.

"I hate to leave him." Sophia pouted. "Maybe your mother should go with you, Gabriel."

"Out of the question. I need you by my side, Sophia. Anna is our responsibility." He needed time to convince her that he was worthy of her love. What they had was more than lust, if only she could open up to him. It seemed that he wouldn't get the chance if he waited for the time to be right. He had to make his own opportunities.

"True." She tipped her head in that adorable way of hers, considering all options. "We'll have to leave at once."

⚬⚬⚬

"Where do you think she would have gone in London?" Gabriel asked, as the train pulled closer to the station. "He would be eager to please her."

"I'm not sure that's the way it goes. She's younger, more impressionable. He might be leading her along. She would want to show him that she's up for anything."

"No," Gabriel disagreed. "It's always the man willing to do whatever it takes to get a reaction. Look at peacocks. The females are dull, meant to fade in to the background and stay safe. It's the men who strut and show off."

"Ha." She didn't even bother with a genuine laugh. "That's your example? Peacocks? Everyone knows they are the exception, not the rule. What are you wearing? A gray suit. You look very fine in it." She paused to admire him, only for a second. "Meanwhile, I've taken great pains to both match and pleasingly contrast my dress with my shoes, my jewels, right down to the petticoats."

She showed him how one shade of light blue on her trim worked with the darker shade of her bodice and the lace on the sleeves, all set off by the opal and sapphire ear bobs. "My coat is a sapphire blue. Even my corset... Well, never mind. I've made my point."

"Exactly. All I'm thinking about is your corset." His gaze dropped down to her décolletage. "What were we discussing?"

Playfully, she slapped his arm. "Peacocks, of all things. Besides, as you pointed out, the female of that species is meant to blend into the background. The men are flashy to distract predators away from the female and chicks. It's all about survival. With people, it's completely different."

He shook his head. "I would do anything to protect you from predators."

"Ah, but you don't have to spread your tail feathers and put on a show, do you? No. That's the woman's job. Without our female prancing around for your male benefit, humans would become extinct. We need the elaborate costumes."

"Pshaw. Women do all that to show off for each other. Men are always more intrigued to find out what's underneath."

"Is that so? So if women paraded around naked?"

"In a perfect world."

She smacked him again. "No. We would all look much the same. You would become horribly bored with it all. One chest is much the same as the next…"

"Not in my experience." He gestured as if weighing breasts in his hands.

"You're impossible. Where were we? Peacocks. Bad example from the start. Let's look at us, shall we? On our honeymoon, you went deer stalking. Deer stalking!"

"Only for one day. It rained so much that I had to cancel our plans for an outing in the carriage. Deer stalking, on the other hand, occasionally benefits from the rain. You said you wanted to stay in front of the fire with a good book."

"Exactly. Because I knew you wanted to go deer stalking. I wanted to think the idea of me in front of a roaring fire would be enough for you to want to stay in with me. I imagined tossing aside the book in favor of, ahem, other things. Things a lady could not suitably suggest."

"Why not? If you'd said, 'Please stay with me, and we'll swive like bunnies all afternoon,' do you think there's any chance I would have gone off after deer? But no. Men have to do all the guessing. We can't read your minds. You said you were going to catch up on reading. I imagined being horribly bored. Might as well go deer stalking."

"You might benefit from reading more."

He pulled a face. "Marcus was the reader. In fact, if he'd taken you on our honeymoon, the two of you would never have taken your faces out of books to get to it at all."

"Get to it?"

He arched a brow. "*It*. What honeymoons are made for?"

"And yet Eve and Marcus have had two children in three years. I think reading is an aphrodisiac for them. But again, back to the point. I was the one willing to sacrifice in order to make you happy."

"Really? One afternoon? You believe my dream honeymoon involved shopping along the Seine, strolling the Champs-Elysees, and opera? I went to the opera, Sophia! And the ballet. You can't imagine any of that was for me. Our entire trip was built around what would delight you most. And I don't regret a second. Bringing that smile to your face, the genuine one, has always been my greatest enjoyment. You would watch the opera, and I would watch you, while my heart exploded with joy that you were the one at my side."

"Oh." A frisson of happiness danced on her nerves. "That's beautiful, darling. Thank you. I think we've determined that our young runaways will both want to be at their best for each other. And they don't have much money, so that rules out a few things."

"I wouldn't be too sure. I don't think he's quite what he appears to be."

"Not a farmer?"

"Not born and raised. You saw them at dinner. He was subtly coaching her along. He knew his way around a place setting."

"And his clothes. He dressed much finer than I had expected. But why would he be working on a farm if he were from a family of means?"

"It happens. Young men follow their interests. Perhaps he was an agricultural scholar. Or interested in animals, the veterinary sciences? I think he comes from a respectable family, but how well-to-do I couldn't say. Does it change your opinion?"

She bristled at the idea. "Why would it?"

He shrugged. "She's young, but she's not likely to do much better for herself. It's a good match, from her perspective."

"A good match? Perhaps. Does it matter so much now? A woman doesn't need to rely on finding a good match as she had to in the past. Anna can take care of herself. If she stays with me and learns from Mr. Kenner, she can be a good secretary. It will open doors for her. With time and experience, I can recommend her to any position she should choose. What need has she for a man to give her status? She can marry for love when she's ready. As it is, she has no idea what love is. She's experiencing infatuation, probably for the very first time. Once that wears off, what have they?"

"I'm pleased to hear it. And a little surprised. I'm not sure you would have given the same answer in the past. You used to enjoy making a good match. You really have changed."

"I've come to my senses, perhaps. It's no longer enough for me to think that a woman's worth depends on the man she entices."

"Is that what you believe happened between us, Sophia?" He reached out to let his hand linger on her wrist. "That you enticed me and I was helpless to resist you? I can assure you that I decided upon you for myself. It wasn't a matter of bending to your will, but of convincing you to bend to mine. And yet you have a point. I'm not sure I would have been successful if I didn't meet certain criteria of yours in the first place."

"It didn't hurt that you were heir to an earldom. Mother was hoping for a duke." She felt her pulse thrum under his fingertips.

"Would you have married me had I been a mere baron? Or worse, not titled at all."

She shook her head. "I really can't say now. I don't know. I was determined to make a good match. I doubt anyone could fault me for it, considering that a woman is measured by her success at marriage. It will be a beautiful new day when that is no longer the case, but among our set...well, you know it's true. That doesn't mean I loved you any less, but perhaps your title provided incentive to love you more."

"I thought so." With a hurt look in his eyes, he let go of her wrist.

"Don't deny that you held exacting standards of your own. You wouldn't have looked twice at me had I been a housemaid." She pursed her lips.

"I would have looked," he assured her. "I might have acted. As for marrying you, it would have been out of the question. I would have set you up in a lovely house and visited you frequently."

"A lovely, small house. Until you tired of me, or your wife put a stop to it. What makes you think I would have settled for such an offer? To be your escape from real life."

"I would have tried anything to make you mine, no matter your status. At least, I would like to think so. To be fair, I've no idea. We're lucky we never had to consider it. You suited me, and I suited you."

"Are we suited after all these years, Gabriel? Just when I want to think so, everything shifts and makes me wonder. You seem well acquainted with the mechanics of keeping a mistress."

"I know men who do. I'm not one of them. You're going to have to stop questioning and have some faith. I'll prove it to you just as soon as we're done setting these youngsters straight."

"I hope we can find them."

The train stopped all too suddenly, nearly spilling

Sophia out of her seat. Everyone shot to their feet at once and began heading for the doors.

"Come on." Gabriel took her hand. "We're here. Let's start with Mayfair."

"Mayfair?" Breathless, she followed him through the throng. London. Crowds. She hated crowds. She had barely an inch to walk without bumping into someone. She held tightly to his hand until they eased out of the congestion, focused on her breathing. In, out, in, out. There was no reason to panic...

"If he has some money and wants to impress her, he'll take her shopping in Mayfair. She only has her simple clothes. She'll want something more extravagant for the wedding," Gabriel shared his logic.

"Not entirely true." The crowds thinned slightly as they made their way out of the station to the street, where she could breathe easier and begin to think again. She'd been about to say something important... It would have to wait. Their task was at hand. "I had Jenks altering some of my older gowns to fit Anna."

"When you say older, you mean last year's styles." He shook his head. "Perfectly serviceable gowns."

"Serviceable but..." Men thought one year was as good as the next as far as fashion went. They had no idea how much things could change in a year. Shorter hems. Shorter sleeves. Soon enough, they wouldn't even be wearing corsets. Everything changed. "Anna is more petite. Jenks can cut my gowns down to fit her and still manage to make some alterations to suit the more modern styles. She might have finished a gown or two before Anna and Ethan set off."

"Jewelry, then? Perhaps they're buying rings."

"We're going to need to split up to cover more ground." She hated the idea. Alone in London. But she saw the need for it. She could manage.

"No." He clung to her hand. "It's London. I'll not leave you alone."

"Shops are closing. We'll lose our opportunity." She smiled, touched by his instinct to protect her. "We won't stay apart long. I'll check the dress shops and millineries. You look into the jewelry shops. We'll meet back every few blocks."

"Let's start on Bond Street, shall we?" He kissed her hand. "Good luck."

"And to you." She left him at Bloomfield Place.

They met again at Grosvenor Street and again at Brook Street.

"Maybe we'll have better luck on Regent Street," he suggested.

"I spoke with a modiste who thinks she might have discussed a fitting with Anna, but she couldn't be sure. Anna's description fits so many young women in town."

"Ethan doesn't stand out as unique either. Perhaps we'll have a better chance checking lodging houses."

"But where to begin?" It seemed a daunting, if not impossible task. "They might have gone to Gretna Green after all."

"I hope Lord Markham and Agatha have better luck." He removed his hat to run a hand through his hair.

"You mentioned his family. It's possible he comes from London. Where would they live?"

"Brilliant, my dear! If he wants to marry her and

he's an honorable young man, he would bring her home to meet his family. It's the only reason that they would have come to London over Gretna Green in the first place, isn't it? To do things properly?"

"In that case, she should have spoken to her mother." Breaking the news to Prudence Cooper that she had been distracted enough to let Anna slip away was not a conversation Sophia wanted to have.

"But Prudence is a busy woman. And Mrs. Dennehy is an intimidating judge of character." Gabriel shuddered. Anyone would shudder to fall under the scrutiny of Mrs. Dennehy. The woman had a gift for drawing out one's every flaw.

"You're all too right about that. Anna wouldn't want to risk their disapproval. Plus, knowing sixteen-year-old girls, she is carried away by the romance of it all. She's not thinking logically."

"There is no logic in love," Gabriel said, casting a meaningful glance her way. "Let's start in Bloomsbury. With luck, we might stumble onto someone who knows his family name."

⚜

They had no such luck. After a late afternoon and evening of walking London's streets, hoping for a glimpse or a clue, they gave up and headed to Averford House.

"Times have changed, as you've reminded me. As far as we know, Anna Cooper is about to spend the night with a young man without benefit of marriage. Will her reputation be irreparably damaged?" He counted on Sophia to know such things.

"Unfortunately for Anna, I'm not sure times have

changed that much. We can hope that they're prudent. If they're in Scotland, perhaps they are already married, or maybe Agatha's sixth sense has led her to them by now."

"Did she bring Miss Puss? I have faith in that ghost cat. Miss Puss never seems to steer her wrong." He smiled to show that he wasn't entirely serious.

"Anything as long as it helps. If only Anna's aura could glow like a beacon to Aunt Agatha. Let's put in a call to Thornbrook Park to see if they have any news."

They didn't. And yet Gabriel couldn't manage to be all that disappointed. He had a night alone with Sophia, with the exception of a few servants who could be trusted to stay out of the way.

"Not a word from Agatha and Charles," Sophia said, returning to the drawing room after making the call. "I do hope they've been more successful than we have. Your mother says that Teddy has been an absolute angel."

"We're left without any new clues," Gabriel lamented.

"I have no fresh ideas, and I'm exhausted. I think I could sleep for two days without benefit of Mrs. Mallows's elixir." Sophia practically fell into a chair by the fireplace. "But London's not so bad when I'm with you. I suppose I could come more often. I've been meaning to get these chairs redone. And maybe find some paintings to brighten up the place."

"Really?" She surprised him again. "I hadn't realized you'd put so much thought into it."

"I noticed a few things on that night when I was here alone, before Lord Markham arrived and Marcus and Eve came to join us. If I spent more time here, I could really make some improvements."

"Mother hadn't put much into Averford House either, I'm afraid. She always suspected that Father spent time here with his mistresses, though I believe he would have gone to hotels."

"The place needs a woman's touch."

"You're just the woman to make the necessary improvements. Stay there." He stood. "I know just what you need."

He went to the parlor and called for Sutton. "I want our best bottle of wine opened. Pour a glass for Lady Averford and bring it to her, please. Is Mrs. Peele in the kitchen?"

"Certainly, my lord. She's preparing the meal."

"I'll go have a word with her." He left Sutton and found Mrs. Peele rolling a crust for a savory pie.

"Steak and kidney," she affirmed. "For the lot of us. I'm working on a roast duck for you and Lady Averford."

"Lovely as it sounds, I have other ideas." He told her of his plan to make dinner for Lady Averford and made sure they had all the necessary equipment and ingredients. Mrs. Peele only had to get her pie in the oven and arrange for the servants to eat later than usual. Then he could take over the kitchen temporarily. Satisfied, he returned to his wife.

"Lady Averford, are you feeling more relaxed?"

"Yes, I believe so. The wine was delightfully refreshing, thank you." She had clearly only taken a few sips and set the glass down next to her. "Where did you run off to?"

"A surprise. You'll see."

She nibbled her lip. "The last time you surprised me, it didn't go well. I ruined your fun by misunderstanding you."

"You merely reminded me to be more careful in thinking I know what's best. This time, I think I have it right." He pulled the box out of his coat pocket and presented her with it. "Your first surprise of the evening."

"Gabriel." She placed a hand to her chest. "How did you manage it?"

"I was in and out of jewelers' shops half the day. How could I have failed? I think it's what you wanted."

She opened the box. "I'm astounded. It's breathtaking."

It was an aquamarine ring, set in platinum. A single aquamarine larger than a robin's egg, surrounded by tiny diamonds and amethysts. "Do you like it?"

He didn't need an answer. He could tell by the sly smile playing at the corners of her lips, and the fact that it was already on her finger even as she tried to refuse it.

"It's too extravagant." She held out her hand to admire it from afar, and then close up again. "Look how it catches the light!"

"Almost as beautifully as your eyes, but nothing can ever compare."

She smiled at him, then twisted the ring off her finger and handed it back. "If you don't mind, I would like to return the ring and accept your earlier gift. I know that you meant no offense by it. Giving me a parcel of Thornbrook Park is like handing me a piece of your heart. I could want nothing more."

He took her hand and slid the ring back on her finger. "No, you were right. You own all of Thornbrook Park along with me, to manage at my side. I was foolish not to see that sooner. My eagerness to convey how much I value your opinion superseded my best judgment, and I sent the wrong message entirely. All I wanted was to let you know how much you mean to me."

She blushed. "After all we've been through, all I've done."

"And all I failed to do. If I had a chance to do it all again, I wouldn't let you spend one day lacking my full attention. You're the wife of the Earl of Averford. It puts you in a position to be spoiled. All I ask is that you enjoy it. And don't even think about asking me to take the ring back. I can hardly remember which shop I bought it in, and it will take me forever to find it again."

"I really don't deserve it, Gabriel. I have a confession to make. I'm more awful than you can imagine. I went behind your back and told Mr. Grant to keep the guesthouse reservations. I was just so angry with you for excluding me and discounting my opinions. I know the idea of keeping a guesthouse might seem vulgar to you, but it does bring in some income. Your mother is bound to get bored and travel again, and in the meantime… Well, we honestly seem to be getting along. I know you were only thinking of me, and I'm glad of it. I was wrong to undo your plans with Grant."

He reached for her hand. "I was wrong to make plans without you in the first place. I was deliberately attempting to keep you out of my way that morning so that I could start working on moving my mother back to the Dower House. But I shouldn't have forged on without you, even if I thought my plan was for your own good. We're a team. I'll never act without consulting you again."

"Thank you, Gabriel. I suppose that means we can discuss the guesthouse again once we bring Anna safely home. And I don't mind you acting without consulting me when it involves delightful surprises like this ring. But I don't have a gift for you." She pouted, but her eyes held the gleam of a smile. "In all fairness, if I'm going to demand to be treated as your equal, I should probably shower you with gifts and adoration too."

"I'll settle for the adoration. But not now. Later. You can show me your appreciation after I've made you a delicious meal."

"Really? You're going to cook?"

"I told you I could. I've been waiting for the opportunity, but I'm not likely to get it at Thornbrook Park. Come on." He held his hand out to her. "And bring your wine. If things go according to plan, we won't see another servant for the rest of the night."

"Not even to turn down the bed or help me to undress?"

"I think I can manage those things. Consider me at your beck and call."

"A lady's maid and a cook all in one? This doesn't bode well for the staff. Aren't you the one always preaching that it's our responsibility to provide?"

"Believe me, I won't do either job well enough to

replace anyone. Besides, I'm counting on the kitchen maids to clean up for me once I'm done. And if anything, our household is about to expand now that we have a baby. We'll be home to Teddy soon enough. For now, it's finally time that I got you alone."

She followed him to the kitchen. "I couldn't agree with you more."

Twenty

FASCINATED, SOPHIA SAT ON A CHAIR AT THE EDGE OF the room and watched Gabriel's hands deftly roll out the dough. He had mixed mashed potatoes, flour, eggs, and seasoning into a dough and rolled it all out like he was making a pie. It soon became apparent that this was no pie. He made the dough into ropes, cut them into pieces, and shaped them into tiny moons. The whole process had taken some time, long enough for her to finish her wine and for him to refill her glass and get one for himself.

"You learned to do all this in Italy? And you remembered the recipe without consulting any notes?" She got up to stand closer to him, the better to watch his skilled hands as he worked and imagine them on her again.

"It's all up here," he said, tapping his temple and leaving a white burst of flour behind. She didn't bother to point it out. It softened him somehow, reminded her that he was as human as the rest of them, far from the perfection he radiated. "Signora Gugino was an excellent teacher."

"She was old, I hope. Ancient. White-haired, with a carbuncle on her chin. Enormously fat?" Sophia could hope. She found that the idea of him working in the kitchen with a potentially vivacious Signora Gugino left her a bit concerned.

"Would you prefer to believe it?"

She nodded.

"Then I won't tell you that she was barely thirty, a widow, with luscious curves that had only benefited from having given birth to four strapping young sons."

"Don't tell me!" She laughed, took a small handful of the flour, and tossed it at him.

"Is that the way it's going to be? Throwing flour? I might have to remove you from the kitchen or seek revenge." He tossed a small handful at her. It hit her on the nose, and she struggled not to breathe it in and sneeze all over their dinner. But she left it where it was, on her nose. Better that they matched. "How do you think I felt to come home and discover that you spent hours in my office holed up with your Mr. Grant?"

"I suppose some women might find him handsome. He never really appealed much to me in that way. I do admire his business sense, but that's not enough to tempt me." She sipped her wine.

"Signora Gugino was old," he admitted. "And she would be ashamed of me for relying on Mrs. Peele to provide me with mashed potatoes for the gnocchi. When I told the cook what I needed, she said she would have plenty left over after making her pie and offered to prepare them for me."

"Is that what I smell cooking? The pie? Lamb?"

"Steak and kidney, and thank you for reminding me. I promised I would take it out of the oven for her when it was time." Wrapping his hands in two tea towels, he opened the oven, pulled out the pie, and set it on the counter. "Looks perfect and smells delicious. The servants might have a better meal than we do. Should we switch with them?"

"Not on your life. I intend to try this gnocchi that you've made me with your own two hands. I'm very impressed watching your technique. You seem to really know what you're doing."

"And I haven't started the sage butter sauce yet. Just you wait."

When the dumplings were rolled, he dumped them in boiling water and sifted them out minutes later. Then he sautéed butter and sage in a pan, added some lemon, and tossed the cooked gnocchi in the sauce.

"It smells heavenly. Even better than the pie."

"We don't have the right cheese," he said. "But I think we can make do. I didn't learn how to make Signora Gugino's special cheese."

"And a good thing. If you added cheese-maker to your list of skills, I might have to give up on ever being good enough for you."

"You're more than good enough, Sophia. You're perfection."

"Why?" she asked, the wine making her bold. "I don't have many skills, when it comes down to it. Or I've only recently discovered the few that I have."

"You're wrong. When I met you, you were the most graceful dancer in the room. You had the ability to melt my heart with a smile, and you still do. When we were courting, I learned that you could embroider, paint, and play the piano with such skill as to rival the masters. You've a remarkable knack for knowing how to set people at ease, and you can make the most fascinating conversation with the dullest partner in a room. You've made me want to be stronger, better, smarter every day since I've met you. And I can't fathom my life without you."

Her mouth fell open. For all her supposed conversational skills, she found herself utterly speechless. She knew that he'd loved her once. But that he still thought of her in such a way? It was beyond anything she could hope for.

"Dinner's getting cold," he said. "Let's get our plates to the dining room, and I'll open another bottle of wine."

❧

Sophia put her fork down at the side of her plate. "I couldn't eat another bite. It was delectable, all of it. It surprised me enough that you know how to cook, but that you know how to cook like *that*?"

"I'm glad you enjoyed your meal. I didn't find it all that bad myself. Signora Gugino would be proud. Ah, but I meant to sing to you while I cooked. I'm supposed to be delighting all of your senses, not just one at a time."

She laughed. "A man can only do so much. I'll happily spend more time in London if you promise to cook for me like that now and then."

"I will do whatever it takes to keep you by my side." He looked at her and hoped he could make her understand how seriously he meant it.

"I haven't had a chance to tell you things I think you need to hear," she said. "I'm glad we have this night alone to finally talk."

"What things?" he asked, dread churning in his gut. Would she tell him that she'd never loved him, but she was happy to be his wife anyway? Or that he satisfied her and provided for her, and that was good enough, now that they had a baby?

"Excuse me, sir." Sutton came from the hall to interrupt them, despite his strict instructions that they were not to be interrupted unless there was important news. "You have a visitor. Lord Wilkerson has come to call. I tried to send him away, but he says it's urgent."

"Urgent. Everything is urgent to Wilkerson. I assure you that it's not as urgent as me being alone with my wife."

"Darling, perhaps you should see him. He can have his say and you can send him off again. How long could it take for a man to impart urgent news?"

"You don't know Wilkie. The man could blather on all night."

Sophia shrugged. "We simply won't let him."

Gabriel sighed. "I suppose there's no polite way to avoid him. Where is he, Sutton?"

"I've had him wait in the parlor, my lord."

"We'll join him there." He held a hand out to Sophia. "Come. Perhaps he'll be quicker if he sees I have my wife with me."

"Or he may not be wearing his spectacles and he will mistake me for your mother and attempt to make passionate love to me."

"I'll never allow it." Gabriel laughed. "I wish I'd never mentioned her to him."

"And you thought I was the busybody always making matches."

"I should know better." Gabriel kept his arm around her as he escorted her to the parlor. "Wilkerson, what brings you here so late?"

"Late? The evening's barely getting started. I came with news. Ah, Lady Averford. Good to see you again." The man blushed, clearly remembering his earlier blunder. "We've got more support for the vote."

"For the Labour Exchanges Act? Wonderful. As you can see, I'm with my wife."

"Yes, I won't keep you. But I wanted you to know. Lord Tavisham is with us. I've been working with him on the Child Welfare measures, and he's all in. With his support, I believe we have all we need to bring it to a vote."

"Excellent news, Wilkie. Lord Tavisham, you say?" He hadn't considered Tavisham at all, but a thought had just occurred to him "Nash is his family name, isn't it?"

"Yes, it is."

"Do you happen to know the family well?" Sophia asked.

"Not very. I knew Tavisham's younger brother well at one time. We were mates at Harrow. Fell into some disgrace, he did. Sharp fellow though. Made lots of money importing Lord knows what. He has an office over by the East India Docks. Leamouth Road."

"The East India Docks?" Gabriel shot Sophia a look.

"Matthew Nash." Wilkerson nodded. "I haven't looked him up in a while, but I suppose he's still there. I could ask Lord Tavisham, but I don't think he likes to be reminded. His brother was quite a rebellious sort."

"Ah, well then." Gabriel rubbed his hands together, eager to head over to check out the Nash connection. It was late to be out at the docks, but it might be their best chance to find Anna. "Thank you for the news."

"I'm hoping you will remain in London for the vote."

"Ever hopeful, Wilkie." He clapped the man on the back and steered him to the door. "You can count on me to do my best."

Once Lord Wilkerson left them, Gabriel turned to Sophia. "I think I should go alone. It's a rough neighborhood at night."

"That's more reason for us to stick together."

Gabriel sighed. "I thought you might say so. You must stay very close to me then."

"I think I can manage it." She smiled.

"And let me do all of the talking."

"Agreed."

"All right. Let's arrange for a car. There's no time to waste."

∽≫

A while later, they found themselves at a tavern on Leamouth Road, near Nash's warehouses. "We'll need to go in and ask questions. It's not the sort of place I want to bring you, but we've no choice. I won't leave you outside on your own. I'll warn you though, you might see things that unsettle you."

She shook her head. "Gabriel, I'm a grown woman. I understand what might go on in rough, old taverns."

"You do?" He cocked a brow.

She shrugged. "Drinking. Whores. Maybe a fist-fight or two. I think we'll manage. I'm not likely to be mistaken for a whore, and you've got a strong left hook. Or so your brother seems to think."

"Did he say so?" Gabriel curled his fist and looked down at it with apparent appreciation.

She rolled her eyes. "Let's go in."

The place was dark, fortunately, lit only by the candles on some pitted, round tables and a gas lamp behind the bar. She wouldn't want to see the place in broad daylight, considering that it looked filthy and in grave disrepair in the dimness. When something, a mouse or rat, scurried along the floor at the edge of the room, she managed to contain a shriek. Gabriel led them straight to the bartender.

"I'm looking for Matthew Nash. Any idea where I might find him at this hour?"

The bartender, a portly lout, wiped a grimy glass and looked up but didn't say a word. His dark eyes looked Sophia over from head to toe before he turned his attention back to Gabriel. Gabriel held out a pound note or two. Sophia couldn't be certain how much, but she wasn't surprised they had to resort to bribery. They were dressed too well to fit in with the regular crowd, which was one couple off in a corner and a single ruffian in rags at the end of the bar.

"Nash is a popular man today. 'Nother couple came

in looking for him earlier. They didn't belong here any more'n you lot do."

Sophia's heart soared. Anna and Ethan, it had to have been them. They were going to find them! Sophia only hoped it wasn't too late. There was no chance they were married yet, but that might not stop them from sharing a bed. Especially if they were low on funds and forced to share a room.

"And where did you direct them?" Gabriel offered more pound notes.

The bartender took them, nodding. "Nash is out of town for the week. He keeps a house in Bloomsbury, but he ain't there. I sent them to a guesthouse my sister runs."

"And where is that?"

The bartender put down one glass and picked up another, not answering until Gabriel held out more pound notes. "Farrington Lane. Not far from Nash's house."

Sophia was glad to hear it. The man's sister kept her house in a considerably better neighborhood.

"Thank you. You've been most helpful."

Gabriel directed her back out the door. Their car waited at the end of the street.

"To Bloomsbury," he informed the driver. "Farrington Lane."

"Do you think his sister will require as many bribes to be forthcoming with information?" Sophia asked him.

"In the first place, she's probably not his sister. Perhaps a past partner in crime. And I'm not optimistic. Money gets answers."

As luck would have it, Ethan Nash was walking out the door as they arrived. Gabriel hastily paid the driver and leaped out after him.

"Mr. Nash, a word."

The boy turned, his eyes wide. "Lord Averford. A surprise to see you here."

"Oh, is it? I should think you would be expecting us after running off with Anna Cooper. Where is she?"

Ethan sighed. "She's in her room. I came out to find us something to eat."

"Her room?" Sophia breathed a sigh of relief. "You're not sharing."

"She wouldn't. Not until we're legally wed. Though I tried to tell her it didn't matter what people thought. They would think it anyway, and we could have saved some money by sharing."

"I can assure you, Mr. Nash, that it very much matters what people think. Anna has her family's reputation to consider as well as her own. As, I assume, do you. The Duke of Tavisham is your relation?" Sophia tapped her foot.

Ethan startled. "Yes. My father. How did you know?"

"Your father?" Gabriel, like Sophia, had clearly assumed that the elder Nash might have been an uncle or something else. "So Matthew is your uncle?"

Ethan nodded. "I'm the youngest of three sons and a great disappointment to my father. I left school to work on a farm when he wouldn't let me choose my own course of study at Cambridge. Mr. Higgins has no idea. I was hoping my uncle would welcome us."

"Due to his estrangement with your father? You

fancy yourself in the same lot as your uncle, who previously separated from your family?" Gabriel asked.

"That's about right. I never imagined you would find us so fast."

"I'm as surprised as you are," Gabriel said. "Dumb luck."

"I still intend to marry Anna. Just as soon as we can." Ethan pulled himself up to full height, which was equal to Gabriel's.

"I'm sure you do, but you're both young. I believe this all happened rather fast. I would like to speak with Anna and hear what she has to say," Sophia said.

"I'll take you to her. She'll tell you that we want to marry as soon as possible. When love happens, you don't need time to figure things out. You just know. Anna and I belong together."

Gabriel shared a glance with Sophia. "I can agree on that. Once upon a time, I was young too. I looked across the room and saw my future bride. I just knew. But I also knew that I had to make things right for her. Are you sure running away is right for Anna?"

Ethan hesitated. The moment's hesitation was all it took to prove to Sophia that they weren't too late. The young people could still be talked out of making a hasty decision that could affect them, for better or worse, for their entire lives.

～

"Lady Averford!" Anna's eyes were wide as saucers when she opened the door to find Sophia standing there. Gabriel had taken Ethan for a drink at a tavern so that she would have some time alone with Anna.

"You were expecting Ethan? I'm sorry. I've come to find out why you've run off. Your family will be very worried."

"Then they don't know yet?" She nibbled her lip.

"How could I tell them? They left you in my care. Your mother will never forgive me."

Anna nodded. "By the time they all find out, perhaps I'll be able to sign my name as Mrs. Ethan Nash."

Sophia quirked an eyebrow. "And do you think that will make things right? Knowing you eloped and lived alone with a young man before marriage?"

Anna waved her hands. "Times have changed. Ethan says that no one will pay much attention to what happened before the wedding as long as we do wed."

"Times haven't changed that much, Anna. It could ruin any chance for your younger sister to marry properly. Have you considered that? Not to mention how it will break your mother's heart to miss your wedding. And your older brother? Imagine if he were the one to have found out and come after you."

"He might have killed Ethan." She shuddered at the idea. "They're friends, but Brandon is so protective of me, and he has a bit of a temper. As for Mother, she has so much to do around the farm and with the extra baking. She never would have missed me. She'll be glad to welcome Ethan to the family. As will Brandon, once we're wed."

"Oh, my dear." Sophia hugged her. "You're so wrong. You have no idea how much a mother dreams and waits for her daughter's wedding. I think it might be a way for them to relive their own. With your father gone especially, your mother would love to be there to help you when you're getting married. And think of Mrs. Dennehy. If you consider that your brother would be hard to face, imagine Mrs. Dennehy feeling her trust had been betrayed. She's formidable."

"You might be right."

"I am. Is losing your family a chance you want to take for a boy you hardly know? It will take some weeks to publish the banns. Have the two of you money to last that long?"

"I love him, Lady Averford. He said when his uncle gets back, he will take us in. He'll give Ethan a job on one of his ships."

"On a ship? Ethan will be away a lot of the time and you'll be on your own. Are you prepared for that?"

Anna stopped pacing and turned to face Sophia. "I hadn't thought of it. We can deal with it when the time comes."

"You. You will be the one to deal with it while he's off working on his uncle's ship. What then? You could have a child, maybe more than one. What if you don't even like his uncle's family? Ethan barely knows the man, from what I understand. It's possible that he won't take you in and he won't give Ethan a job. You're both supposing an awful lot."

"But Ethan is so handsome. And he kisses so…" She broke off in a sigh.

"Kissing can be wonderful." Sophia understood how a girl could be swayed by a kiss.

"He knows how to kiss. And I like him. I do. He's sweet, and he's funny, and he's very protective of me. He wouldn't let anything bad happen to us."

"Unfortunately, sometimes things happen whether we want them to or not. Though I'm sure he has every intention of doing his best. And who knows, maybe his father will welcome him back as long as Ethan's willing to do as he says."

She grimaced. "Ethan will never do what his father wants. His father wants him to study theology and take a living in the church. We should have gone to Gretna Green. He said we couldn't get married in London, and I said that I knew. But I'd always wanted to come back to London, and it would give us more time to get to know one another. If we'd gone to Gretna Green, we would be married by now."

"A good point, to get to know one another," Sophia said. "I notice that you said you like him. You didn't mention love. You should know each other as well as you could possibly imagine to get married. What if you find out more about each other and decide that you jumped into things too quickly? Marriage is a commitment that you make for life. It's not always easy. There's no harm in a long courtship. Or a slightly longer one."

She paused a moment to consider. A girl growing up on a farm couldn't do much better than to marry the son of a duke. In the past, she might have encouraged Anna. Now she knew better. In the end, the girl would have to make up her own mind. Sophia only hoped to provide sound advice and encouragement.

"No. Ethan wants to start our lives together now. He doesn't like work on the farm and he wants to see the world, and he thinks he can make a lot of money working for his uncle. His uncle has made a successful business all on his own, with no help from his family. It has inspired Ethan to do the same."

"I imagine it takes hard work and a long time to build a successful business, especially without much help. And taking care of a wife and family requires some sacrifice. What if Ethan comes to resent you? He won't see much of the world if he has to keep coming back for you."

Tears glimmered in Anna's eyes. "It all seemed so clear when he laid out his plans, but now—"

"Isn't it better that he has a chance to develop his business without encumbrances? Then one day you can find each other again. Once you're both mature and ready. You know how much work it is to take care of a family and run a household. You've been such a big help to your mother on the farm. But I had the impression that it wasn't the life you wanted, taking care of people. When I hired you, I thought you wanted independence and the chance to learn."

"I do. The last thing I wanted was to be cooking and cleaning and putting breakfast on the table every morning. I imagined that Ethan would go to work, and I would go to work, and we would come home to enjoy each other's company every night. But if he's away on a ship and I'm the one left to work and keep house…"

"You'll have a hard time finding work in London without experience."

"I don't know what to do." Anna sighed. "Ethan loves me. I know he does. I see it in his eyes, and I feel it. He says it has to be now, but…I wanted to wait. I've been trying to imagine what my life will be like with Ethan, and I have no idea what to expect. It frightens me. It excited me at first, when we were only planning to get away. But once we did…"

"Let me tell you my concern, Anna." Sophia kept her voice gentle, trying not alarm the girl. "You're a young woman, and you've run away with a man. No matter what happened between you, and I don't need to know, people will make assumptions about you. If you come home with me now, I think we can put any rumors to rest by assuring everyone that we found you before it was too late. And we did, didn't we?"

"I need to speak to Ethan. We'll figure this out together."

"I think you need to know your own mind first. I would be more comfortable knowing that you made such a big decision on your own without any influence from him or from me. Think about your family. Think about your future. Decide what you really want. I'm going to leave you alone just long enough to go get Ethan and Gabriel. Then I think you should come back to Averford House with me. It will give you time to make a responsible decision. You don't need to rush into anything."

Sophia had known that feeling of indecision all too well. On her wedding day, halfway down the aisle, she'd thought her knees would buckle and she wouldn't make it. When she did make it all the way down, before she'd had to speak any words, she'd thought about running the other way. She'd looked at Gabriel and suddenly hadn't been sure. Until that gold gleam lit up his eyes and reassured her. This was the man she wanted to be with for her entire life.

"Thank you, Lady Averford. You've been so kind. I'm sorry to have been such a disappointment."

"Not at all. I would only be disappointed if you went ahead and got married to a man when you weren't sure. I want you to feel confident about your decision, whatever it will be."

Twenty-one

"Are you certain they aren't running out a back way? Attempting to make it to Gretna Green after all?" Gabriel asked. They waited outside the guesthouse for Ethan and Anna to talk and come to a decision.

"I doubt it. I think I gave Anna plenty of things to consider."

"I'm sure you did." He slipped his arm around her waist.

"She might decide to marry him after all, but at least I'll know that she took time to consider. We'll have to help them out, of course. I'll stay with Anna at Averford House until we can get her family here. We can at least make sure they keep up appearances before the wedding. No living alone with the boy in a guesthouse."

"I think we have to call him a man, darling. He has made the decision to take a wife."

She laughed. "Oh, is that all it takes to make a man, a good woman at his side?"

"It worked for me." He dropped a kiss on her head. "But we'll have to see about Ethan Nash."

With tearstained cheeks, Anna made her appearance in the doorway, followed by Ethan holding a bag. "I'm coming with you, Lady Averford. Please help me to get back home. There will be no wedding."

"No wedding. I see," Sophia said. Ethan Nash shot her a dark look. Clearly, she had become the villain in all this, in his mind anyway. "Of course you can spend the night with us and we'll return you home tomorrow."

"You're making a mistake, Anna," Ethan said, handing her bag to Gabriel. "We could have a fine life together."

"We still can. I just need more time," Anna said. "If it's really right between us, why the sneaking off? Why can't we take the time to do things right?"

"You mean to follow convention? You know how I feel. I refuse to bend to society's demands." Ethan puffed his chest out, full of the pride and ignorance of youth. So he fancied himself a rebel then? Anna seemed to be making the right choice. Sophia didn't imagine that the girl had the stamina or desire to be a rebel's wife.

"But what about my feelings? You're not even considering me. I have a family that I do care about, and all I want is some time to allow them to accept us together."

"Time is what I don't have. As soon as my uncle comes back, I'll be starting my new life. I'd hoped it would be with you, but it will be alone. So be it. I'll always love you, Anna."

"I'm sorry." Anna reached out to take his hand. "I'm just not ready."

"I trust you'll take good care of her, Lord Averford." Ethan turned to Gabriel but ignored Sophia. "My biggest regret is that you found us. Things might have turned out differently if only we'd been left alone."

❧

Gabriel was in the drawing room sipping a brandy when Sophia returned from showing Anna her room at Averford House. The brandy heated his blood and perhaps loosened his tongue a little. It was his second glass.

"How is she?" he asked.

"She's stronger than she knows. Thankfully, she realized that she was making a mistake in time. She spent some time alone with the young man, but not enough for anyone to call her into question as long as she returns with us before much is discovered about her disappearance. She doesn't even want her mother to know."

"Can we keep it from her?" he asked. "Shouldn't we mention it?"

"I think we have to leave it up to Anna. As long as she's safe and back home with us, I think we've done our part."

"I see. All's well for her now, I suppose. She can go back home and no one will be any the wiser, or not much the wiser. Will she stay on as your secretary?"

Sophia shrugged. "We'll give her a chance to figure it all out. I wish we knew where Lord Markham and Aunt Agatha ended up, so that we could tell them to give up the search and come home."

"I'm guessing Agatha already knows." He spread

his fingers and waved them in the air. "The spirits are active."

Sophia laughed and became serious again. She went to stand next to Gabriel, where he leaned against the mantel. "Earlier, I was about to tell you something."

He shook his head. "I think I would rather not hear it. Sophia, I've loved you from the moment I first saw you. I gave you reason to doubt me, and I'm so sorry for it. We've lost so much time due to my own foolishness. I went to Italy because I couldn't simply tell you how I felt. That I was torn apart to see you in the arms of Ralston, but I knew that it was my fault. I stopped letting you know how much I loved you."

"Gabriel, please. I—"

"Let me finish. I thought that I could become a better man, a man that you would love. I learned to play the guitar. I perfected my singing. I painted landscapes."

"You paint?" It was the first she'd heard of it, and she was obviously surprised at the news.

He nodded. "I'm terrible at painting portraits, but my landscapes are passable. It's about layering textures with the paint. Suddenly, I understood that it's what I needed to do to win you back as well, to layer textures. To present a more well-rounded man with an understanding of the arts and artists and love. I wanted to be a better lover."

"So that I wouldn't turn to other men? I never did, Gabriel. Not really. It was one minute of foolishness, followed by a world of regret. I'm so sorry that you had to see me in another man's arms. It should never have happened, and I have only myself to blame. Not you. Not really. I know that now."

"I've tried to change for you, Sophia. I've done all that I can. I know I'm not perfect, far from it, but I hope that you can find some comfort with me, enough to stay with me and raise our son, and be together no matter what comes."

"So cryptic again." She shook her head. "'Find some comfort'? And still so sure of yourself. You've never wanted for confidence, Lord Averford."

"What do you mean?" He sought her gaze, desperate to see some glimmer of understanding in her eyes, some hope that she could stay with him even if she didn't love him beyond sharing a familiar warmth in each other. Anything just to be with her. "I'm humbling myself before you."

She laughed. Laughed! And smiled a genuine smile. He did not understand. She placed a hand on his cheek. "You're so sure you know what I'm feeling or what I'm about to say that you've prepared this whole speech. I know you love me, Gabriel. Deep down, I've always known. Before we even married, you swore a love to me so complete that it would never die. And it hasn't. If anything, it has flourished, no matter how vain or insensitive or hopeless I can be."

"You're not any of those things."

She tipped her head in the way that made his heart turn to lava.

"But I did you the great disservice of not declaring myself in the same way. I've loved you from the start in a way that frightened me with how overwhelming it felt. Better not to express it then. To keep it hidden. To play it safe. Well, I'm done with all that. I love you with every fiber of my being, Gabriel Thorne.

I always have, and I always will. You pretend to be humble, but you're truly self-assured. So self-assured that you have ignored every sign that I'm honestly, quite desperately in love with you."

"You love me?" He couldn't help but smile. "You truly do." She loved him. His heart raced. His nerves danced. For a second, he felt every aching bit of joy that it was possible for any man to ever feel, building up in his veins until he feared he would explode.

In his profound happiness, he must have looked addlepated, because she took his face in her delicate hands and forced him to look at her. "Do you understand, Gabriel? You never had to change, not one thing, for me to fall in love with you. I love the man you are, the man you've always been. I've loved you all along."

He couldn't hold off any longer. He kissed her madly, deeply, as long as he possibly could before both of them were in danger of losing consciousness for lack of oxygen.

"Then let's go to bed, my love," he said. "Together. It has been an impossibly long and torturous day."

Twenty-two

LADY AVERFORD WOKE UP IN A BED BESIDE HER husband. In his arms, she'd slept more soundly than she'd ever thought possible, certainly better than she had ever slept before. The only thing that could convince her to open her eyes and prepare to get out of bed the next morning was the memory of the little face that she had waiting for her back home—their son, Theodore. Theodore Neville.

"It has to be Neville." She sat up suddenly, looking back at her husband, sprawled naked across the bed. She laughed. "Darling, aren't you cold without even a bedsheet over you?"

He didn't look cold. He looked magnificent, his body tanned and hard and rippled with muscle in all the right places. Her eyes were drawn to the golden thatch of hair that ran in a thin line down his abdomen, and spread to a thicker patch just over his... Well, well. She'd thought that part of him had certainly gotten enough attention last night, but there it stood tall and thick and ready for her this morning.

Suddenly, he gripped her around the waist and

pulled her back down to the bed with him. "You took all the sheets. I don't mind entirely, but let's pretend that I'm about to make you pay for it." He kissed her behind the ear and lower, on the tender spot on her neck that made her toes curl. And lower. His hands slid over her breasts, catching a nipple between his fingers.

"What's that you were saying about Neville?"

She took a minute to catch her breath. She'd nearly forgotten. "Teddy's full name. For his christening. We'll need to give him a middle name. Neville."

"But that's Mother's family name. Before she married Father, she was Lady Teresa Neville."

"I know. That's why it has to be Neville. Teddy will be named after both of our mothers. Theodore, for my mother, Theodora. And Neville for yours."

"Theodore Neville Thorne. I like it. Now can we stop talking about our mothers? This is hardly an appropriate time."

"I like it when you're inappropriate," she said.

For the next hour, he proceeded to show her just how inappropriate he could be.

Back at Thornbrook Park, Sophia was all too happy to hold her son in her arms again.

"Teddy! How I've missed you. Mummie missed you." She dropped kisses all over his chubby cheeks and tiny nose until he laughed out loud, the most adorable sound she'd ever heard in her life. "Thank you, Teresa. You've done a wonderful job with him."

"It was only one night. Try letting me have him for a week next time. He's a complete joy."

"We'll have to hire a nanny. Someone who can help out with him occasionally, as needed."

"I suppose so," Teresa said. "The Waldens have left the Dower House, and Mr. Grant tells me that I'm free to move back in. All of the other reservations canceled. You must have developed a reputation of being inhospitable."

She knew Teresa was being deliberately antagonistic to show that they were in no danger of becoming too comfortably close. She was happy to play along. "Or it's the poltergeist. Perhaps word has gotten out. Aunt Agatha swears there's a mischievous spirit in the house who occasionally steals her gowns. The spirit of George."

"George?"

Sophia nodded. "You know the one, the great-great-uncle who allegedly drowned in a vat of wine. He's come back as a poltergeist who inhabits the Dower House and steals gowns."

"Why would he steal ladies' gowns?" Teresa's brows knit in her confusion.

"Agatha says he probably likes to dress up in them. She has known men who like to dress up as women. She claims it's hardly all that unusual."

"To be the ghost of a boy who drowned in a wine vat and has come back to steal and try on women's gowns?" Gabriel asked. "Not unusual at all."

"Nothing surprises me from that woman Agatha. Except that she isn't back yet."

"Still not back? I suppose they had a long way to go. And no idea that we've already brought Anna back home to the farm where she belongs, until she decides if she wants to come back and work for me. She's always welcome."

Teresa sighed. "I don't like the idea of Charles out all night with that woman. I have a bad feeling when it comes to those two. They're getting entirely too close for my liking. When I'm around them, I'm starting to feel like a third wheel."

"Mother thinks that Lord Markham should be in love with her," Gabriel explained, drawing a pained look from his mother. "He was in love with her once when they were young, and she thinks that maybe they could have something together again."

"Gabriel, a woman needs her secrets," his mother admonished.

"I have no secrets from my wife." He kissed Sophia on the top of her head.

"But I do!" Teresa exclaimed.

"Isn't Lord Markham a little old for you, Teresa?" Sophia asked in effort to placate her mother-in-law. "I pictured you more with someone like Mr. Grant."

"Mr. Grant?" Teresa began to laugh.

"What's wrong with Mr. Grant? I thought you liked him. He's handsome, in a way that some women respond to. Not me, of course. I have my own golden god."

"You two are starting to make me ill," Teresa said. "But there's nothing wrong with Mr. Grant. Not really."

"But why did you laugh?" Sophia was intrigued. She believed that Teresa was too grandmotherly to appeal to a man like Grant, but she didn't expect Teresa to find it funny for Sophia to suggest a romantic interest.

"Did you ever wonder why he decided to share the cottage with Cornelius Kenner? Or why Kenner accepted the idea of the two of them living together?"

"You don't think…" Sophia couldn't finish the thought. "But there are two bedrooms. It doesn't mean…"

Teresa shrugged.

"I can't believe it," Gabriel said. "Mr. Grant expressed an appreciation for Marcus's wife, Eve."

"I like her too. The man has taste. But he was simply distracting you from the truth. He couldn't very well claim an interest in your wife, and there aren't many other women around here. He deemed it safe to pretend to have an interest in your brother's wife. She's married. She's very pretty. But not for him, trust me." Teresa waved a hand dismissively. "Six years in Italy. I've seen it all."

Gabriel and Sophia locked gazes, and she knew they were thinking the same thing. How she had missed that most of all—being such a part of someone that you knew what they were thinking just in a shared glance.

Teddy began to fuss. "I think Theodore Neville needs his nurse. When was the last feeding, Teresa?"

"What did you call him just then?"

Sophia smiled. She knew her mother-in-law wouldn't miss the reference. "We've decided to name him Theodore Neville Thorne, after both of his grandmothers. Do you like it?"

Teresa beamed. "Other than the fact that my name should come first, yes. I like it very much. It will do well for him."

❧

Several hours after they'd arrived home, just after they'd gotten Teddy bathed and ready for bed with a maid in his room to look after him in case he woke, they were preparing for a quiet, early dinner when Agatha and Lord Markham finally arrived back from Scotland.

"No luck at Gretna Green," Lord Markham said. "At least, not in finding the young people."

"Charles, please." Aunt Agatha was resplendent in a subdued peach-and-ivory ensemble with only half the usual number of feathers pluming from her hat. She giggled like a girl and elbowed Lord Markham. "Be serious. I knew the young people had probably gone off to London. You found Anna just as she had her change of heart?"

"Yes, how did you know?" Sophia asked out of courtesy. After all their years together, Sophia knew that Agatha preferred for people to marvel over her skills instead of taking them for granted.

"The spirits!" Agatha said. "The spirits know all! And sometimes, when I'm blessed, they reveal a little of their vast knowledge to me. Unfortunately, my skills did not get passed on to you, dear. If Alice were here, she might guess. Alice has a bit of a gift, though she hasn't embraced it yet. It must be the green eyes. I've always said they mark her as special. Green eyes."

"Agatha, you're getting carried away again," Charles reminded her. Oddly, they suddenly reminded Sophia of an old married couple.

"Aunt Agatha! You didn't."

Agatha brought her hands to her face. "Oh my

word, you did guess! Charles, she guessed. She has the second sight after all! My dear Sophia. I'm so proud."

"What are you all blathering on about?" Teresa couldn't stand it any longer. "Anna was found, of course, after coming to her senses and not marrying the boy. And she has been back home at the farm for hours now. We've all been waiting for the two of you to return. And here you are. I suppose that wraps up every lingering mystery. Well, would you look at me! I must have the second sight too."

Sophia should have warned her mother-in-law never to make fun of Agatha's gifts. At least not directly to Agatha. She didn't like it. Sophia only half feared that her aunt might have the ability to cast spells along with reading auras, tarot cards, and tea leaves, and getting messages directly from the spirit world. Sophia had accused Teresa of being a dragon often enough, but that didn't mean she wanted to see her mother-in-law suddenly covered in scales and sporting a tail.

Fortunately, Agatha wasn't angry. But of course, newlyweds seldom were. And Agatha had all the power over Teresa she wanted, now that she had won something Teresa had fancied for herself: the love of Charles, Lord Markham.

"I hate to admit it freely, but I am also confused. What did or didn't Agatha do? And how does it prove that my wife is gifted, or cursed, with this second sight you speak of? What am I missing?" Gabriel remained close to Sophia. He could hardly stand to be more than a few feet from her at any given moment, or so it had seemed since they'd come home.

"Charles and I went off to Gretna Green," Agatha explained. "Not really to find Anna Cooper. I knew she was in London all along…"

"But to get married!" Charles announced, unable to wait a second longer to make their announcement. "I loved this woman from the moment I first met her, well, first met her again, after meeting her a few times in the past. Coming back to Thornbrook Park and meeting Agatha again, I fell instantly in love with her. And I wasn't about to let her get away. Pursuing the runaways to Gretna Green provided the perfect excuse. Meet the new Lady Markham, my wife."

"Agatha." Teresa shook her head in disbelief. "You married Agatha?"

"I'm a wife!" Agatha shouted excitedly, holding out her ring for all to see, a lovely square-cut emerald.

"Congratulations to you, Lord Markham. And best wishes to you both. May I still call you Aunt Agatha? It feels odd to think of you as anything else." Sophia hugged Agatha tightly.

She couldn't wait to tell Alice! Alice would be so surprised. She desperately missed her globe-trotting sister. And Mother! Mother would be in shock to learn that her free-spirited sister had married at long last.

"Are you sure it's not a spell or potion?" Teresa asked, unable to accept the news. "Did you get into some of Mrs. Mallows's Chinese herbs?"

"I hope you can be happy for me, Teresa," Lord Markham said. "I've found someone who delights me as much as my first wife did. We were never really suited for each other, you and me. You knew it when you chose Edward, and I learned it when I chose

Sarabeth. You're a dear friend, but it never would have worked between us."

Teresa shrugged. "I suppose you're right. You're too old for me anyway."

"I guess this calls for champagne," Gabriel said. "I'll call Finch to bring the glasses."

Over dinner, Teresa explained that she would be spending the next few weeks with Marcus and Eve at Markham House, starting the next day. Agatha and Charles announced their intention to go to London for a honeymoon. And Miss Puss?

"Miss Puss has left me for the afterlife," Agatha declared over cordials after dinner. "It was time, I suppose. She made her peace with whatever was keeping her here and drifted off to the next world, where she belongs. I'll meet her again one day."

"Not for a very long time, Agatha dear," Agatha's husband announced. "We've got plans to see Egypt. The pyramids!"

"Egypt?" It was the last place Sophia expected her Aunt Agatha to go. "Why Egypt?"

"Alice is on her way home from there. She wrote a few weeks ago. Didn't I tell you?" Agatha said.

"It must have slipped your mind." Alice was coming home! Sophia couldn't wait for Teddy to meet his aunt Alice. They had so much catching up to do. "What about Mother? How will you tell her that you got married? How will I tell her about Teddy? It might be too much good news for her to bear at once."

"I predict she will get through it. But she will be so surprised! The woman has absolutely no ability to see the future. She can barely cope with the present. Perhaps we will stop in to see her on our way to London. Yes! I'll need to see the look on her face when I tell her. Theodora will have to stop being so high and mighty with me at last, now that we're both married to earls. Oh, this will be fun." Agatha clapped her hands.

"I still can't believe it," Gabriel said. "I never saw it coming, the two of you. But I'm very happy for you both."

He was, in fact, happiest for himself. For the past year, Gabriel had had only one thing on his mind: showing his wife how much he loved her. They had the rest of their lives to bask in the glow of that love with no more struggle, no more doubt.

Gabriel raised his glass. "To love!"

Without hesitation, the rest of them raised their glasses in agreement. Sophia slipped her hand into his and glanced up at him with that same dazzling smile she'd flashed him from across the ballroom some eleven years earlier. "To love!"

Read on for an excerpt from

An Affair Downstairs

Thornbrook Park
November 1907

LADY ALICE EMERSON KNEW EXACTLY WHAT SHE wanted, and it wasn't a husband. She had a whole list of things she longed to accomplish in life, all on her own with no one to hold her back or tie her down.

Her plan had been years in the making, the first step being to get out from under her parents' control. Once Alice's maiden aunt, Agatha, and her father had found themselves more frequently at odds, it had been child's play to convince Mother that accompanying Agatha on an extended visit to Thornbrook Park would be best for everyone, saving Father's health before being around Agatha could make him apoplectic. Had it been anywhere else, Mother might have hesitated, but she had full confidence in placing Agatha and Alice in the capable hands of Alice's older sister Sophia, the Countess of Averford.

Alice knew that her mother expected Sophia to find her a husband, and her sister had been more than up to the task. In her nearly two years at Thornbrook Park, Alice had dissuaded two of her sister's candidates from proposing, and she had faith that she could survive a few more attempts before Agatha was comfortably settled, all Sophia's responsibility, and Alice could announce her intention to depart. Who could stop her once she turned five and twenty, when she would come into the money her grandmother had left her? Just three more years.

On her great list of things to accomplish, Alice had lofty dreams: to travel the world, to climb a mountain, to ride a camel, to captain a pirate ship. And she had simpler goals that she could start on right away, like cornering the fox in a hunt, getting drunk on whiskey, and having a wild affair. She should know love at least once, even if she never planned on marrying. And she had just the man in mind, the same man who could teach her to hunt and to shoot, and who enjoyed a good whiskey—her brother-in-law's estate manager, Mr. Logan Winthrop.

Mr. Winthrop would be no easy conquest. To begin with, he didn't seem to really *like* people, choosing to keep to himself as much as possible. When he did find himself in company, he maintained a cool, all-business demeanor. *Most of the time.* Alice had managed to break through his icy exterior once or twice, enough to fuel her hope that she could manage a seduction.

There were rumors that he'd killed a man, a rival for a woman's affections, and had come to Thornbrook Park to escape his dangerous past. Rumors didn't deter Alice. All men had pasts, and rumors were often far from fact. What made him the perfect candidate, besides his soulful eyes and god-like physique, was precisely that he was not the sort to form emotional attachments. There would be no pining after her or rushing into a commitment.

An estate manager's income wouldn't come close to supporting an earl's daughter in the style to which she'd become accustomed, or so he would believe. He would never expect her to marry him, even if she managed to seduce him. Once she could convince Logan Winthrop to let his guard down again, she would take the opportunity to kiss him.

She'd hoped to run into him that morning when she left the Dower House to breakfast with her sister at Thornbrook Park. The gardeners were preparing the grounds for winter, and it was rare that Winthrop wouldn't be out with the groundskeeper overseeing the efforts. Unfortunately, Winthrop hadn't been in sight. She stood outside the breakfast room, hand poised to turn the beveled-glass knob, when she heard his voice inside.

"Lemon trees? So many of them?" His voice had that raspy edge that signaled his displeasure. Alice knew it from the many times he had told her to stop asking questions and leave him to his work. She smiled. "I don't know much about the care of exotic fruit trees, but I will research the subject."

"Four trees. I can't imagine what the woman was thinking, as usual." Her sister wasn't delighted by the prospect either, apparently. "It's practically an orchard."

Sophia had a tendency toward exaggeration.

"Mother means well. Likely she feared a few might

not make the journey safely. She wants you to have lemonade, not exactly a sinister sentiment behind the gift. You could try to be more grateful." The rumpling of a newspaper followed Lord Averford's explanation. Typical. He tended to hide behind the news once he'd had his fill of morning pleasantries, or unpleasantries, as it were.

"It's not that I'm ungrateful. I'll send her a letter as soon as they arrive, of course."

The old Dowager Countess was sending lemon trees to Thornbrook Park from Italy, where she had taken up residence these last few years? Alice, thinking of the hours she could spend in the warm conservatory with Mr. Winthrop, couldn't muster any disappointment. There were roses, sweet peas, and lemon trees on the way. What an ideal setting for a kiss!

"You know who has some experience with lemon trees?" Lord Averford asked, not really expecting an answer. "The Marquess of Brumley. I remember his wife had several trees, oranges and lemons. Perhaps I should invite him to come offer you a hand, Winthrop."

"I wouldn't mind some advice." Winthrop seemed to be none too sure. He might have meant the opposite, that he would mind very much indeed.

"Brumley?" The sound of her sister's teacup clinking in the saucer made Alice jump. "The *widower* Brumley? Your brother's former classmate, the one with the ancient wife who recently passed away?"

"The very one. Eleanor died last year, though, not so recent. He's—"

"Out of mourning." Alice could picture her sister

clasping her hands in glee. "And a marquess. I'm sure he's lonely. We should invite him. For an extended stay."

Alice felt the sinking feeling in the pit of her stomach. A widower. Her sister's next candidate to win Alice over to the idea of marriage. Not again. If the aroma of cinnamon toast had tempted her to enter the room, the idea of a marquess being pushed at her changed her mind. She backed slowly away from the door. Perhaps she would break her fast with Aunt Agatha in the Dower House after all. She turned and had begun to walk quietly down the hall when the housekeeper, Mrs. Hoyle, sprung on her from out of nowhere.

"Good morning, Lady Alice. Have you come for breakfast?"

"I thought I left a pair of gloves behind last night. I just had a quick look in the drawing room. No gloves. I'll be on my way."

"But I've just come from the drawing room. I didn't see you come in." The infernal woman cocked an accusing brow. "Perhaps one of the maids picked them up. Come along to the kitchen and we'll have a look."

Alice couldn't imagine a way to decline gracefully, and at least the kitchen wasn't the breakfast room. She would manage to avoid her sister's attempts to present the Marquess of Brumley, undoubtedly a toad, as a charming fairy-tale prince. "Thank you, Mrs. Hoyle."

She followed the old hen to the kitchen, where the few maids at the table jumped to attention to greet her, causing Alice to blush and mutter an apology for interrupting them. The three maids all ran off to attend to duties elsewhere in the house despite Alice's protestations to stay put, and Mrs. Hoyle excused herself to ask Mr. Finch about the gloves, leaving Alice to stand alone next to the great table where the servants took their meals.

Off in the adjoining room, she could see Mrs. Mallows covered in flour as she rolled out dough and occasionally cursed at Sally, the kitchen maid. A footman rushed right by Alice with a tray, not even noticing her in his haste to fetch what he was after and get back to the breakfast room. Glad to go unnoticed, Alice stepped into a shadowy corner to wait for Mrs. Hoyle's inevitable return with the news that her gloves were not to be found.

"Looking for your next victim, Lady Alice?"

"Mr. Winthrop." He hadn't failed to notice her. His voice ran over her like one of the velvet gloves she claimed to be missing, causing her heart to beat faster. She turned and stepped back into the light. "I'm not sure I know what you mean. I'm waiting for Mrs. Hoyle to confirm if she could find something I've lost."

"Oh, is that the ruse? You've *lost* something. Meanwhile, you're deciding which of the servants to trail after all day asking questions to the point of vexation." He laughed. Laughed! What a rare occasion. Never mind that he was laughing at her, she was entranced by the way his eyes lightened ever so slightly from black to cobalt with his mirth. So dark were his eyes, so normally inscrutable, that she'd had no idea that they were actually a very deep blue and not brown at all. Or maybe they simply appeared cobalt in the light, drawing from the dark blue of his coat.

Forgetting herself, she took a step closer to examine them. He seemed to hesitate an extra second, staring back at her, but he didn't move away. "Naturally, Mrs. Hoyle will come along any moment now to report that she was unable to find the item, for you've lost nothing at all. What really brings you to Thornbrook Park?"

"*Why, you, Logan. I've come to deliver this, just for you,*" was what she said in her mind, as she placed a hand to the silk plum waistcoat covering his solid chest and leaned in. In actuality, she stammered like a fool and clenched her hands at her sides. "Wh—why on earth would you suspect me of having an ulterior motive?"

She *had* lost something after all. She'd lost her nerve. She'd had the perfect opportunity to completely surprise him with a kiss, and she hadn't been able to manage it.

"Why do you do anything, my lady? Because you can. Forgive my impertinence." He cleared his throat. "I've come to fetch a set of keys from Mr. Finch. I'll leave you to your search."

He stepped back, obviously deciding that whatever course he'd been taking with her was the wrong one to follow. Flirting? Could she conclude that he'd been flirting with her? And if so, what had she done to frighten him away? He turned on his heel.

Quick! She had to say something to bring him back. "Mr. Winthrop?"

"Yes?" He turned to face her again. She released the breath that she'd been holding.

"Do I really vex you?" She didn't attempt to hide the concern in her voice.

He sighed. "No, Lady Alice. You do not. I'm sorry to have upset you."

"Oh, I'm not upset." She hazarded a step closer to him, and another one. "I was simply making sure before I tell you that I actually know a little about the care of citrus trees. Mother kept oranges in our conservatory back home. I might be of some assistance to you when they arrive, if you'll allow me."

He quirked a dark brow. "Oranges? Lady Averford didn't mention it."

Alice nibbled her lip. She knew very little about trees, citrus or otherwise. Certainly she would have time to read up on the subject and try to appear knowledgeable. "She wouldn't. She didn't notice. My sister is so often in her own world."

"I see." He stroked his jaw as if considering. "And how do you know about the fruit trees, seeing as the news only came at breakfast and I don't recall you at the table when Lord Averford opened the letter in front of me?"

"You've got me there." Alice blushed. "I was listening at the door. Eavesdropping, can you imagine? What a terrible habit. I didn't mean to, of course. I was about to join my sister for breakfast and then I heard—"

"The mention of Lord Brumley?" He nodded, and his lips curved up in a smile. "The countess enjoys a bit of matchmaking. Before you came along, she tried to pair me with her maid."

"Mrs. Jenks?" She wrinkled her nose at the idea. Jenks was a mousy slip of a woman, no match for a robust, vigorous man like Winthrop.

"No, the one before her. Mrs. Bowles."

"Dear, no." Worse than Jenks, Bowles was a snip-nosed shrew and certainly far too old for Mr. Winthrop. "I'm sorry. Sophia clearly has no talent for making matches."

"Perhaps not. You were wise to run away instead of sitting through another conversation about yet another bachelor. I don't blame you a bit."

"You—you don't?" Ah, a man of sense. She knew she could rely on his sound judgment, at least. And she appreciated it, though it would make seducing him more of a challenge.

"Any pretty girl in her right mind dreams of a dashing suitor to sweep her away, doesn't she? Alas, Lady Averford's only suitable choice for you so far had eyes for another."

"Captain Thorne." Alice rolled her eyes. "He's better off with Eve Kendal. They're perfectly suited. I didn't care for him much myself, if you must know."

"I mustn't." He shrugged. "It's none of my affair."

Alice bit the inside of her cheek. How she *wanted* it to be his affair. "There isn't a suitable choice. I'll never marry."

"Don't despair, Lady Alice. There's someone out there for you. Your sister simply hasn't found him yet."

Acknowledgments

Thank you, my Sourcebooks team, for all that you do: Valerie Pierce, Jenna Quatraro, Sean Murray, William Preston, Heidi Weiland, Amelia Narigon, Rachel Gilmer, Susie Benton, Eliza Smith, Deb Werksman, and the ever-inspiring Dominique Raccah. You're my heroes! Hilary Doda, thank you for sharing your insights. And a very special thanks to my best friend, Laura Sieben Jerry, for fueling my late-night writing sessions with coffee.

About the Author

Sherri Browning writes historical and contemporary romance fiction, sometimes with a paranormal twist. A graduate of Mount Holyoke College, Sherri has lived in western Massachusetts and greater Detroit, Michigan, but is now settled with her family in Simsbury, Connecticut. For more information, visit www.sherribrowningerwin.com.

part of a large oriel, for several long heartbeats, trying to fathom what she had just seen and why it should have disturbed her.

"Is something wrong?" Jamie asked.

She forced her eyes back down to his face, feeling foolish. One of the servants had probably been taking a peek at the arriving guests.

"Someone was looking down on us from the tower."

Jamie's eyes darted up to the exact window where she had seen the movement, despite the fact that she had given him no indication of which it had been. When they returned, his smile seemed strained, the color along his cheekbones deeper.

"No one there now," he said brightly.

A little too brightly, Emma thought, now even more curious. At that moment, however, the second coach in their caravan arrived, carrying their luggage, the abigail she and Georgie would share during their visit, and her brother-in-law's valet.

Amid the resulting flurry of footmen and baggage and welcoming chatter, her eyes again lifted to search that dark glass. Then Georgina took her hand to ascend the steps, and she lost sight of it as they were swept into the Earl of Greystone's ancestral hall.

HE FINALLY REMEMBERED to breathe. When he did, the air ratcheted into empty lungs in a series of shuddering gasps.

He had moved away from the glass as soon as she'd lifted her eyes to the window, but he knew he had not been mistaken. Not unless his solitude had finally resulted in the loss of sanity his mother frequently predicted.

He had thought about that night too often to have ever forgotten her features. Despite the many attempts he'd made through the years to rationalize away the importance that encounter had attained within his heart, he had failed.

Emma Termaine had been his last sweet taste of England and home before he had sailed for Spain. Her face might have lived within his memory if for no other reason than that, but of course there had been other factors, equally valid.

He could never have imagined, however, that he would see her again. That she would one day come to the only place on earth where that might be possible.

He had never even asked the name of Jamie's sweetheart, he realized. Not that it would have meant anything if he had.

Twelve years ago Emma Termaine had been on her way to London to find a suitable husband. The ritual of the so-called marriage mart was repeated every spring. Even if she had not been successful that first year, she would have been eventually. The classic beauty of that heart-shaped face surrounded by softly curling chestnut hair would have ensured it.

Although his disbelieving eyes had locked immediately on Emma, he had been peripherally aware of the grouping around her. His brother and the girl who must be his intended. And behind them...

Emma's fortune? Stout and ruddy, balding and old.

Was that supposed to be a comfort? he wondered bitterly.

There was little comfort to be found in any of this. Emma was in his home, and if this house party followed the usual pattern, she might be here for several weeks. He took another breath, trying to stem the welling tide of remembrance.

And found it impossible.

"THE TOWER is the oldest part of the house," Jamie said, setting down the candelabra he carried. "It was the original keep. This level was undoubtedly the solar."

"Your lineage must indeed be ancient," Georgina said, running long, elegant fingers along the edge of one of a pair of parquetry tables that graced the high-ceilinged stone room.

"Positively decrepit," Jamie said, feigning a limp. "Like this place. I can't imagine why my ancestors didn't tear it down and start over instead of making additions."

"A sense of history, perhaps," Emma suggested with a smile.

She was the one who had asked for a tour of the

tower. She had actually thought for a moment that Jamie would refuse. She had already been racking her brain for a graceful way to rescind her request when he had acquiesced.

"What's above?" Georgina asked, pointing to a narrow staircase in the corner.

"The battlements," Jamie said. "Open to the sky."

"Then this really *was* a fortress," Emma said.

"According to family legend, there was even a siege of Leighton. I assume, stubborn lot that we are, we successfully withstood it."

"Is it haunted?" Georgina asked, looking around the stone structure as if expecting a specter to appear in their midst.

"Not that I'm aware of," Jamie said. "Unless, of course, as our honored guests you would prefer that."

"And what if I should, Mr. Leighton?" Georgie said, smiling in response to his teasing.

"I could probably arrange an artistic moan or two and some clanking of chains for your entertainment."

"Please don't bother on my account," Emma said. "I prefer a more traditional musical evening myself."

Both Jamie and Georgina had insisted she accompany them on this after-dinner excursion. She had welcomed the chance to see something of the house.

Far better than staying downstairs with her brother-in-law or retiring early to her chamber.

Other than the servants and the countess, who had appeared frail but welcoming at dinner, they had seen no one else. She wasn't sure, and did not wish to ask, whether there would be other guests joining their party. Charles had said it was to be a private visit, but she had never anticipated their numbers would be so few.

Perhaps that was because of their host's health. They had been told before the evening meal that the earl was indisposed and unable to welcome them personally. Although no other information had been forthcoming, she had at least learned from the conversation that the present holder of the title was not Jamie's father, as she had believed, but his brother.

"Clanking and moaning sound more interesting to me," Georgina said, "but then I have just endured an entire season of musicales."

"Including one very bad Italian soprano," Jamie said.

"At Lady Eldridge's. Yes, I had forgotten that," Georgina answered, laughing.

"*I* have not. How could I? That's where I first saw you."

Georgina had been very open about her determination not to be disappointed if the offer they all expected did not materialize. It was obvious by her quick blush, however, that she was pleased Jamie remembered their first meeting.

What girl would not be? Emma thought. Especially since the compliment had been offered with such obvious sincerity.

As the two gazed into one another's eyes, she averted her own, pretending to examine the architecture. It was obvious that if this had indeed once been a keep, it had at some point undergone extensive renovations.

Although still connected to the lower and upper stories by spiral stone stairways, the central area of this particular floor, which in medieval times would have been open except for the crosswall, had at some point been divided into rooms. The door to those was firmly closed, but there was light coming from beneath it, where the massive oak did not fit with absolute precision against the hand-hewn stones of the floor.

She glanced back at the couple, who were engaged in laughing conversation about the events of the Season. Feeling for the first time as if she might be superfluous, Emma turned her back on them to cross to one of the windows that looked down on the entryway. That meant the window where she had seen movement must be...

Her eyes again considered the closed door. Perhaps the housekeeper's rooms? If so, her interest in the arriving guests would have been natural.

These isolated rooms might have been chosen to provide a haven from the normal commotion in a household of this size. Her own Mrs. Hardy might well find such solitude highly attractive at times.

"Shall we go?" Jamie said. "There's really nothing else of interest up here."

Startled from her speculation about the tower's occupant, Emma smiled at him. "I was wondering if those are the housekeeper's rooms."

Jamie's gaze touched on the closed door, that betraying tinge of color staining his cheeks. "Mrs. Dobbs's rooms are near my mother's. In the east wing. They find it more convenient."

Emma waited for the explanation that never came.

"Of course," she said when the pause stretched. "I quite agree. Georgina, did you noticed this tapestry? It is really very fine."

She was thankful there was something near at hand to provide a bridge to a less uncomfortable topic. After a short discussion of the hanging, they made their way down to the more modern sections of the house.

As she prepared for bed later that night, the incident continued to nag at her. It was not so much that whoever was in the tower had been interested in their arrival, but that the normally outgoing Jamie had made no attempt to explain who lived there.

Given the opulence of the rest of the Leighton Hall, that anyone should choose to inhabit that damp, drear keep seemed a puzzle. More puzzling still was Jamie's obvious reluctance to explain who had chosen to do so and why.

CHAPTER TWO

EMMA'S SLEEP had been restless, but that was hardly surprising since it was the first night she'd spent in an unfamiliar house. She lay in the high bed, watching dawn creep into the room. After a few minutes, she rose and, slipping on her *robe de chambre*, walked over to the windows.

They had arrived late enough yesterday that the countryside around the estate had been masked by dusk. Now, bathed in the purity of the morning sun, it should show to its best advantage.

She sat on the window seat, and then leaned forward, propping her elbows on the sill and her chin on her hands. A panorama of lush lawns and elaborately landscaped gardens, all shaded by stately oaks, spread out below her.

Invalid or not, the current earl seemed well served by his estate managers. Hopefully they would feel the same loyalty to his brother. She had begun to turn, intending to ring for her maid, when something caught her eye, stopping that motion.

A black horse flew along the crest of the nearest hillock, hooves scattering the morning mist. Even from this distance, it was obvious that mount and rider had achieved that rare perfect union of man and beast. As she watched, the horseman directed the animal down the slope and across the grounds toward the estate. Jamie Leighton? Out for a morning gallop?

Last night he had invited Georgina and her uncle on an excursion around the property. Although possible, it seemed unlikely he should wish to ride the grounds twice.

Not Mr. Leighton, she decided as the rider neared the house. She had relied more on instinct to arrive at that conclusion than on an ability to discern distinguishing characteristics about the horseman.

The bare-headed man astride the black was tall and broad of shoulder. Jamie was slighter. And fairer, she added to her assessment as the rider drew close enough for her to see the raven's-wing gloss of his long hair.

She had hoped for a glimpse of his face, but in that she was disappointed. Before he reached the drive, he turned the black, directing the animal around the hall toward what she assumed were the stables at the back.

As he disappeared, she felt a strange emptiness. That might be explained by the beauty of the moment. The union of horse and rider. The mist along the hilltop. The contrast of green fields and open sky.

But there had also been something about the rider

himself that compelled the eye. Some element of power or command or character.

Far too fanciful an explanation, she thought in amusement. Especially for someone not given to flights of whimsy.

This one could undoubtedly be blamed on being in the company of two young people who were discovering they got on very well together indeed, despite the outside pressures urging them to a "suitable" marriage. The growing attraction between Jamie Leighton and Georgina should please everyone involved. It certainly pleased her.

Still, she was aware of a gnawing, inexplicable feeling of loss. Because she was about to lose Georgie?

When she had married Robert Stanfield, Georgina was only six, a shy, lonely child who had spent far too much time in the company of servants. Although Emma's brief marriage could not, by her standards, be considered a romantic success, she was enormously proud of what she'd been able to accomplish in healing the heart of that lost little girl.

The whole point of which, she reminded herself, had been to help Georgina become what she was today—a poised and elegant young woman, capable of taking her rightful place in society. She would be an exceptional countess, and the fact that she seemed to be falling in love with a future earl and he with her was what Emma had prayed for. Why then was she experiencing this unsettling sense of bereavement?

Unconsciously her eyes returned to the vista beyond the window, tracing along the ridge where the rider had swept the fog away before him. It was empty now, as tranquil as if that magnificent display of horsemanship had never taken place.

Perhaps that was Jamie's ghost, his appearance arranged for her entertainment, she thought smiling.

She would be sure to thank him for it at breakfast and see what he said. He might avoid an explanation, just as he had avoided any identification of the tower's occupant, but at least she would have given him the opportunity.

Still smiling, she turned and rang the bell for her tea, preparing to begin this day in exactly the same prosaic fashion she had all the others for the last dozen years.

"BECAUSE Miss Stanfield's stepmother saw you, damn it," Jamie said, the words clearly an accusation.

"Her *stepmother?*"

Alex had known Emma couldn't possibly be the girl's mother, but perhaps his question would prompt Jamie to supply additional information without his having to ask for it directly.

"Lady Barrington. She asked me at breakfast who was riding a black horse at breakneck speed over the hills this morning."

"And what did you tell her?" Greystone asked, more amused than alarmed.

"That it was I, of course. I don't think she believed me, but...I wish you'd warned me you intended to ride. I might have been better prepared for her questions."

"I'm sorry if my appearance inconvenienced you," Alex said. "Had I any idea your London guests would be up at dawn, I assure you I should never have ventured outside."

"I didn't mean *that,* and you know it. *You're* the one who insisted you didn't want to meet them. It makes it deuced awkward then to have to explain who the hell you are."

"Why explain anything? It seems to me the woman's damned impertinent for a guest."

She would be, he thought with a ridiculous surge of satisfaction. Apparently no one had managed to stifle that youthful rebellious streak, although her pudding-faced husband looked as if he would delight in trying. Poor Emma.

"On the tour of the tower last night, she asked about your rooms. She wanted to know if they belonged to the housekeeper."

"Good God, Jamie. You aren't obligated to explain the arrangements of the household to her."

"I know that, damn it. She does it in such a way that it seems a perfectly natural question. It isn't until later that I wonder at her cheek."

"And she is Miss Stanfield's stepmother, you say?"

"For a dozen years. She married the viscount shortly after her mother died. Georgina's very fond of her. So am I, of course, but she's too sharp to be put off with lies and evasions. Eventually she'll catch me out."

"What can it matter if she does? I hardly think it's her place to question how we do things at Leighton, no matter how they appear to outsiders."

"And what if she becomes convinced there's something peculiar going on here? What if they pack Miss Stanfield up and leave?"

Greystone laughed, although he could see that his brother was actually concerned about the possibility.

"You're a catch, my dearest Jamie. An absolutely brilliant one for a viscount's daughter with very little to bring to the table. It's unlikely, I assure you, that *they* are going anywhere. Not until they have what they came here for."

"I'm afraid I can't take the chance."

Jamie's jaw was set in a way that indicated he'd said all he intended to say about the subject. It seemed his heart was engaged, which was exactly what Alex should have wished for, of course. Except in this case…

He put his arm around Jamie's shoulder, pulling him into a quick, brotherly embrace. "I shall do my best to stay out of the path of true love, I promise you. No more rides. Unless the woman lays siege to the tower, I should be safe enough.''

''There *is* another solution,'' Jamie suggested, his eyes suddenly serious. Almost pleading.

Alex might even have been moved to consider the plea had it not been for that brief encounter more than dozen years ago.

''Far better to let them wonder if there's something strange afoot than to provide them with proof,'' he said, smiling.

At the refusal Jamie had lowered his eyes, but not before Alex had seen what was within them. When they came up again, thankfully the emotion had been cleared, deliberately replaced by a teasing light.

''I think perhaps I should take Sultan out for a short run tomorrow, just to add teeth to the assertion that I was the one she saw this morning.''

''Try that,'' the earl said laughing, ''and *he's* likely to add teeth to your backside, you feckless child.''

HE HAD KNOWN this morning's ride was a mistake even before Jamie's warning. It seemed he'd known it even as he had mounted the black. Yet he had been unable to prevent himself from making that run. The despair of knowing Emma was under his own roof and the understanding that her presence there could make no difference in his life had driven him from this refuge to that.

Only when he was astride Sultan, riding over the

vast acreage that comprised the estate, could he be completely free. After last night's realization of how much a prisoner to his own dread he was, he had desperately needed the sense of control, as well as the heady release, riding gave him.

That desire for freedom was part of the reason he was now climbing the winding stairs to the top of the tower. After enduring an interminable day confined to his rooms, wondering far too often what Emma Stanfield might be doing, he had finally given in to this urge.

Pushing the estate books away, he had blown out the candles and thrown his cloak around his shoulders. Then he had stood in the darkness a moment listening for the presence of any intruder into his territory. Hearing nothing, he'd stepped out of the sitting room, closing the door soundlessly behind him.

As he neared the top of the stairs, he tried to will his tension away by drawing the fresh, rain-scented air into his lungs. This staircase to the roof was one of the reasons that, despite the obvious disadvantages of age, chill and dampness, he had chosen to inhabit the keep.

He was safe here from the inquisitive eyes of both the servants and his family's occasional guests, of course, but that might have been accomplished in any of the lesser-used wings of the hall. The easy access to the ancient battlements offered by the tower had been a lure he could not resist.

He stepped out onto the roof, automatically raising his eyes to the sky. There were no stars tonight. The clouds that had been building all day obscured both them and the new moon. It was as dark as even he could wish. He began to cross to the wall walk, boot heels echoing loudly against the stones.

"Who's there?" The voice, clearly feminine and coming from above him, stopped him in his tracks.

None of the servants, other than the footman who saw to his personal needs, ever came up here, although he had never been sure what stories were told about him that prevented them from venturing into the tower. Once a housemaid, either lost or acting on a dare, had come face-to-face with him on the stairs. She had crossed herself as if she'd encountered the devil and then she had run.

His mother would never brave the climb, especially not up to that narrow walk that ran inside the parapet wall. And the only other feminine occupants of the house—

"Forgive me," he said calmly, despite the increased pulse of blood through his veins. "I had no idea anyone was here."

His first instinct had been to flee without answering the challenge. Despite his many failings, he had never been a coward. Besides, she had obviously heard him. Jamie was hardly creative enough to continue to devise plausible explanations for his unexpected appearances.

"I believe I'm the one who should beg forgiveness," Emma said. "Wandering guests are surely an anathema to any civilized household."

Her voice had deepened slightly with maturity, but there could be no doubt with whom he was conversing. As Alex acknowledged that, she moved, the paleness of her gown drawing his eye to her location. She was standing very near one of the sets of steps that led up to the narrow wall walk, almost halfway across the tower from his own position on the roof.

"I confess I've been curious about the view from up here since Mr. Leighton showed us the stairs last night," she went on. "I hope you don't mind my trespassing."

It was obviously a trap. If he granted her permission to roam, she would have confirmation of his authority to do so. A very clever way to verify his identity.

If he continued to make a mystery of it, however, she might, as Jamie feared, convince the girl's father that Leighton harbored a madman. They would have the chit packed up and headed back to London on the morrow. While he trying to decide whether to sacrifice his privacy or his brother's happiness, she spoke again.

"I assume the rooms on the floor below are yours."

Since the stairs leading up from the second level were the only access to the roof, by necessity she had passed his suite on her way up, he realized. He hadn't heard her as he had heard Jamie the night before. Of course, his brother's chatter had been intended to give him fair warning that his domain was being invaded. He had foolishly thought at the time that would be the end of such excursions.

"Obviously, you are wishing me to the devil," she said into his continuing silence. "The only thing worse than wandering guests are inquisitive ones."

Her voice was touched with humor rather than the petulance another woman might have used to get her way. And her method was far more effective. After all, he could hardly stand here like a dolt, refusing to answer her.

"I'm Greystone," he said. "The rooms below are mine."

Her stillness after his pronouncement seemed to last as long as had his before it. When she spoke, the laughter had disappeared from her voice. Perversely, he found he missed it.

"I'm afraid I have been making a mystery of you."

"I beg your pardon."

"We understood that you were…indisposed."

He examined the words, searching them for mockery, and found none. There was concern. A scintilla of contrition. Which made him wonder exactly what Jamie had told his guests.

"A bout of fever," he lied.

"A recurring one? How inconvenient. I am so glad you are presently recovered."

It sounded sincere. Jamie was right. She made it extremely difficult to be rude.

He wondered if she even remembered their long-ago encounter. And why would she? he mocked his own delusion. A girl on her way to the pleasures of her first Season. Their meeting would have been far less memorable than dozens of others she had enjoyed that spring.

Indeed, he had always known its significance to him had been far out of proportion to its reality. That was an argument he had made more than once during the interminable hours of last night. It had no more impact then than now.

"I'm Emma Stanfield. Georgina, as you must already know, is my stepdaughter."

She had begun to move, coming down the steps, perhaps to offer her hand. In spite of the darkness that hid him, his stomach tightened.

"Please stay," he said hurriedly, again fighting that ridiculous urge to turn and run. "I didn't intend to disturb your reverie."

She laughed, the sound low and pleasant. Almost musical. A small frisson of emotion coiled warmly within his stomach.

"Hardly a reverie. I confess that I'm escaping from too much time *en famille*," she said, amusement still underlying the words. Her forward progress had stopped, thank God.

"Mine or yours?" Somehow, despite his long absence from society, he had fallen back into the effortless repartee it demanded.

"The children are playing Jackstraws, your mother is engaged with her needlework, and Charles is reading the *Gazette*. I believe the issue is days old, but he doesn't seem to mind."

There was a hint of indulgent criticism in that, as, to be fair, there had been in her descriptions of the others. She didn't seem enamored of her husband's every action, which should probably please him. Of course, as someone who had been very open about her need to marry for money, Emma could hardly be expected to pretend hers had been a love match.

"The *children?*" Only when he had repeated it did he realize how apt the word might be when applied to Jamie. Not quite nine years separated them, but he often felt as old as Methuselah in comparison.

"My brother-in-law prefers the term 'young people.' To me they seem *very* young, especially tonight. And very much in love. I do hope you have no objections to that."

The frankness bordered on impudence. Since he had come to the same conclusion about Jamie's feelings, he could hardly fault her for having presented him with the fait accompli.

"That decision is Jamie's."

"To be made with your approval surely," she said, sounding surprised that it might be any other way.

"Did you require Georgina to seek yours?"

"She has it. Not that I believe it would have dissuaded her had I been unable to approve her choice. Luckily I can, and with a whole heart. I like Mr. Leighton very much."

"Thank you. So do I."

"And my brother-in-law is quite as enamored of him as is Georgina, though that might have something to do with his prospects." The lilt of laughter was back in her voice.

That was the second reference she had made to her brother-in-law, and this one finally had an impact. As he considered its possibilities, that unfamiliar emotion fluttered again.

"Your...brother-in-law?"

"Charles. The Viscount Barrington."

"Is your *brother-in-law?*"

There was no reason for the sudden increase in his heart rate. It was absurd. And undeniable.

"Georgina's father died almost eight years ago. In one fell swoop Charles inherited the title and the responsibility for the two of us. I'm sure he'll be delighted to get us off his hands."

Could that imply she intended to live with her stepdaughter? Here at Leighton?

He had planned to exile himself when Jamie wed, but he had never intended to cut all ties to his family. Only now, faced with the prospect that he might be forced to do just that, did he understand the long years of loneliness that loomed before him.

"Oh, dear," she said. "I have only now realized

what that must have sounded like. I *don't* propose to invade Leighton, I assure you.''

He should say something to the effect that the decision must be between herself and the ''children,'' as she had called them. Instead, he found himself once more at a loss for words.

''My governess has a cottage, you see...'' The words faded. ''I have not yet told Georgina. May I ask that you will respect my confidence, at least until I can tell her personally.''

''Of course,'' he said. ''But...a governess's cottage?''

''It will suit me quite well, I assure you.''

It sounded very much like his disclaimer to Jamie concerning Wyckstead. He wondered if she viewed the coming disruption of her life with the same unease he felt.

''But...away from society.'' That had not been framed as a question, but she answered it.

''Both my husband and my brother-in-law have entertained extensively. I confess it will be a relief not to have to play hostess.''

''Still...''

''Is that choice so different from yours?'' she asked.

''Choice?'' He repeated the word with an edge of bitterness and realized she had trapped him again.

''Then...it is not from choice that you occupy the tower?''

''Are you imagining I'm here as a prisoner?''

"Are you?" Again, she sounded almost amused.

"I think of it as my retreat."

There was a small silence, much like those that had punctuated the earlier portion of their conversation.

"And I have intruded upon it," she said. "Once more, I beg your forgiveness."

The social niceties demanded that he give it. And if he did? Would she take that to mean she was welcome to again intrude?

"They must be wondering by now where I've got off to," she said. "If I don't return to them soon, you shall have the entire household prying through your 'retreat' in search of me."

There was little danger of that, but he didn't demur. It seemed an acceptable excuse to end this encounter. She was probably as relieved as he.

"Of course," he said. He stepped away from the stairs, moving toward the opposite side of the square.

He had taken only a few paces when she said, "Will you not join us? Now that you've recovered from your...fever."

"You are my brother's guests, Lady Barrington. And I believe others will be joining the party in a day or two. I have no wish to intrude."

"Of course. I understand completely. Nor did I wish to intrude, I assure you," Emma said. "Good night, Lord Greystone. It has been a pleasure to meet you."

He bowed, despite the fact she would not be able to see the gesture. And then, as she made her way across the tower to the spiral stairs that would take her away from the confines of his world, he deliberately turned his back on her, climbing the second set of steps that led up to the wall walk, where she had stood during the entire encounter.

Once there, he stared out over the parapet into the darkness. And it was a very long time before he moved again.

CHAPTER THREE

"THE BLUE SILK, then?"

It was only with the waiting silence that Emma became aware she didn't have the least idea what her stepdaughter had just asked. "I do beg your pardon. Woolgathering, I'm afraid."

"You seem to be doing a great deal of that lately," Georgina said, tossing the dinner gown she had been holding for Emma's approval onto the counterpane of her bed.

"As your stepmama there *are* a great many things I have to think about now," Emma said, putting out her hand. "I do believe your Mr. Leighton will make an offer."

She was rewarded by Georgina's smile as her finger clasped 'round hers.

"Do you truly think so?"

"I don't see how there can be any doubt of it. He looks at you in such a way…"

"He does, doesn't he? Sometimes I glance up and find his eyes on me, and it takes my breath."

"Do you love him, Georgie? It isn't too late if you don't, you know. No matter what your uncle says."

"I can *imagine* what he'd say if the future Earl of Greystone made an offer and I tried to refuse it. I believe he would have apoplexy."

They laughed together, picturing Charles's already florid face flushed with indignation if she balked at this point. His temper was a phenomenon they had seen on more than one occasion during the past few years.

"No," Georgina continued, "it isn't any doubt on my part I'm worried about."

"Then whose? Obviously not your uncle's. Nor mine, of course. That the two of you would form such a mutual attachment is all I have wished for."

"And Jamie's family? What of their wishes?"

"The countess adores you," Emma said, squeezing her stepdaughter's fingers. "Surely you're aware of that."

"And the earl? We have been here three days and have yet to see hide or hair of him. What if that is because he opposes the match?"

"But he doesn't," Emma said quickly, pleased to be able to reassure that anxiety.

Georgina's eyes widened. "How can you possibly know that?"

"Because I met him last night," Emma said.

"The earl? Why in the world didn't you tell me?"

"It was an accidental meeting. Something neither of us had planned."

"But...I don't understand. I thought he was an invalid."

That was something Emma had considered during the sleepless hours after their meeting. Neither indisposed nor invalid seemed to fit the man she had encountered on the battlements. Besides, she was convinced, based on nothing more than his height and the width of his shoulders, that he was the rider she had seen yesterday morning.

Where the rumors Charles had heard originated, especially about a man who was so obviously vigorous, she couldn't imagine. Any more than she could explain why someone who owned a property like Leighton would choose to sequester himself in the most unappealing part of it. Yet that message had been very clear last night. Greystone had no intention of leaving his tower to play host to this house party.

"At least not to the extent that would prevent his climbing to the top of the tower or riding," she said. "Quite recklessly, too."

"Jamie says he's bookish."

"Bookish?" Emma repeated in disbelief.

That schoolboy description didn't fit with the display of horsemanship she had watched. Nor did it jibe with the impression she had formed of the earl last night.

"Actually, what he said was that his brother was quite the scholar. He didn't exactly call him a recluse, but he did say he is more attuned to the intellectual than the social realm."

Obviously those were Jamie's exact words. They

were not ones Georgie would use to describe someone. Although Emma had no reason to doubt the earl's intellect or his reluctance to mingle with his brother's guests, she found them at odds with her impression.

Or perhaps she had enjoyed the hint of mystery about Greystone too much to be willing to give it up. Her notorious propensity for romantic notions. Jamie certainly knew his brother better than she did.

"Ah," she said aloud. "That explains his nonappearance, I suppose. Perhaps his reluctance to be social resulted in the rumors Charles heard."

"But he *did* tell you he had no objections to the match?"

"He said it was Jamie's decision. I questioned him very pointedly on that, I assure you," Emma said, lips curving a little as she remembered.

"If he doesn't care whom Jamie weds, then perhaps he doesn't mean to make him his heir after all."

That wasn't a possibility Emma had considered, although it did seem strange that the earl would have so little interest in his brother's future wife.

"The estate is surely entailed. I doubt that particular decision is his to make."

"I'm not certain that will matter. Uncle's conviction that the earl doesn't intend to marry and produce an heir is based upon his belief that he is very near death's door."

She was right, Emma realized with a sinking feeling.

The information Charles had been counting on was obviously erroneous. And if there were no title or inheritance coming to Jamie, Charles would undoubtedly accept one of the other offers Georgina had received. It was clear from the girl's eyes that she had been following that same frightening train of thought to its inevitable conclusion.

This courtship had gone too far to be dismissed so easily. Georgina's heart was engaged. If anything were to happen to prevent the match at this juncture, she would be devastated.

"In the marriage settlements Uncle will ask for some assurance that Jamie is to be the earl's heir," Georgina said. "If his man of business is unable to make one—"

"Let's not borrow trouble," Emma soothed. "After all, the earl has not married. There must be *some* reason for that."

"What if he has simply not yet found the right woman? Uncle will *never* consider the match without more assurance."

He wouldn't, Emma admitted. At least one of the other offers Georgina had received was very respectable. A young man with a title and a fortune, neither of which could compare to those of Greystone's, of course. If there was any doubt Jamie would be his brother's heir, however, Charles was quite capable of grabbing the bird in hand.

And the longer they were here, the more enamored her stepdaughter would become of a man who was both handsome and charming and flatteringly attentive. Jamie Leighton seemed the epitome of every young girl's dreams.

"I have allowed myself to put too much hope into this prospect." Georgina's wide blue eyes suddenly glazed with tears. "I do not think I can bear it if nothing comes of it."

They had all encouraged her to hope. Emma herself had tried to do so with her reassurances tonight.

"Perhaps you could ask Mr. Leighton—" she began, only to be quickly cut off.

"What should he think if I did? That I am only interested in him *if* he is to become the earl?"

That would be true for Charles, but never for Georgina. Simply asking the question might, however, introduce doubt into Jamie's mind about her motives.

"Besides, this is his brother," Georgina went on. "It would be very awkward to question whether or not the earl intends to marry. Perhaps Jamie doesn't know. He says very little about him and only in response to a direct question."

Which was another mystery, Emma thought. Neither the countess nor his brother had mentioned Greystone, not since Jamie's initial explanation of his absence. That seemed no more normal than that the owner of Leighton Hall should live such a solitary existence in the most primitive part of it.

Because they had been so delighted with Mr. Leighton in London, both as a person and as a prospective bridegroom, they had accepted his explanation of the earl's nonappearance. Now it seemed there were far too many unanswered questions about this entire situation.

Questions Charles could not legitimately ask until a proposal was made. Questions Georgina was reluctant to pose for fear of creating doubt in Jamie's mind. Questions to which only one person could provide answers.

"Then perhaps," Emma said, "we should ask Greystone."

"If he intends to marry?" Georgie's shock was clear.

"Why not? He is, after all, the only person who can tell us that for sure."

APPROACHING GREYSTONE had seemed like a good idea until she was actually climbing the stairs that led to his rooms. She had been positively eager for dinner to end, although their company had been enlivened tonight by the addition of more guests.

Throughout the meal there had been an almost desperate gaiety to Georgina's manner, surely the result of their conversation and the concerns it had raised. As soon as she could, Emma had pled the headache, pretending to retreat to her rooms. Instead she had made her way straight to the tower.

Now she stood before the massive oak door, gathering her courage for the coming confrontation. Taking a deep breath, she knocked and then waited through a long silence. There was no response, not even to her more forceful pounding, although that telltale thread of light was clearly visible along the bottom of the door.

If the earl were not in his rooms, she believed she knew where he might be found. Gathering the skirt of her dinner gown in one hand, she crossed the stone floor to the far corner where the spiral stairs ascended to the roof.

She climbed slowly, her trepidation over the coming meeting increasing. Her first intrusion on his privacy had been quite by accident. This, however, was a deliberate assault, and she knew he would welcome neither her presence nor her questions.

As she reached the top of the stairs, it took a moment for her eyes to adjust. There was a little more light than there had been last night.

Looking up, she realized that the clouds were drifting intermittently across a sliver of moon, which rode high in the heavens. As she had anticipated, outlined against the sky was that arrogantly held head set atop a pair of impossibly wide shoulders.

The earl was on the wall walk where she had been last night, looking out over the battlements. As she hesitated, wondering how to present the purpose of her mission, he turned abruptly, looking down on her.

"Forgive me," she said.

"I believe we've *had* this conversation, Lady Barrington."

"Then I shall endeavor to break new ground."

"How kind. I assume I may be of some service to you."

Although the words themselves were courteous enough, his tone was filled with ice. Emma took a breath, trying to think how to phrase an explanation of her mission to give the least offense. And was forced to acknowledge there was probably no way to do that.

"I would like to tell you a story," she said, employing a flanking tactic rather than the frontal assault that was much more in her nature.

There was an unforgivably long silence in response.

"I shall be brief, I promise you," she added when it seemed he might really say no.

Intellectual rather than social indeed.

"Then how can I refuse?" he said finally, his voice resigned.

"It's about a girl on her way to her first Season."

She was aware there had been a reaction from the man standing above her. Some subtle movement. Perhaps a straightening of his body. Or an added tension.

"It isn't about Georgie," she clarified, using the nickname unthinkingly because she was concentrating so fiercely on making him understand. "Although the situations are somewhat similar, I think."

She was making a mull of this. Drawing it out until he would surely stop listening from sheer boredom.

"You see, the girl met a man. *Before* she arrived in London. There was only one night. A brief conversation. One kiss. It should all have been meaningless. The kind of flirtation every young girl indulges in at one time or another."

She paused, inviting comment. Agreement or understanding, she hoped. He gave neither. He simply stood, silhouetted against the sky, as still as if he were hanging on her every word. Giving her no choice, she realized, but to continue.

"She never knew his name, but for her, he was the essence of... Of what falling in love should be," she admitted, knowing that was exactly what that man had been to her. "The adventure. The excitement of it. She experienced them for only a few brief minutes, but they changed her life forever."

"And they both lived happily ever after."

She had thought his voice was cold before, but that had been nothing to the contempt she heard in it now.

"No, of course not. I told you. One night. A kiss. She never saw him again, but she never forgot him. Meeting him colored the rest of her life."

Silence. Which was better than his mockery, she supposed. She had not realized how painful it would be to expose her most cherished memory to someone who would scoff at it.

"If there is a parable or lesson, I'm afraid I have missed its meaning," he said after what seemed a very long time.

"I'm not certain it has one," she said truthfully. "She fell in love, perhaps with the moment rather than the man. One could make an argument for that, and believe me, she has. But whatever *really* happened that night, the encounter came to represent for her what being in love should be. And when she never again felt that way...she never again fell in love."

Another interminable silence. Because she wasn't sure what else to say to him, she allowed it to stretch until he broke it.

"Why are you telling me this, Lady Barrington?"

"Because I'm concerned about Georgina."

"You said she wasn't the girl in your story?"

"No, but like that girl, she has, I'm afraid, developed a great fondness for your brother. Because she is young, you may feel it is a harmless infatuation that will quickly fade. She does not give her affection lightly, however. I believe that she truly loves him."

"Yet you *fear* it? I thought that to be the purpose of this entire visit."

"What I fear is that her heart will be broken."

"My brother's intentions are honorable, I assure you," he said, the ice back in his tone.

"I have no doubt. And I am pleased to think that he is as taken with Georgina as she is with him."

"Then… Forgive me, madam. I have no idea what your concern could be."

"You asked if they lived happily ever after. The girl and the man in my story. They didn't, of course. She was not free to marry the man she had fallen in love with. She had an obligation to marry well. An obligation to her family."

"She was a fortune hunter."

They were the same words the man who had kissed her at the inn that night had used. His voice had been full of teasing warmth, while this one…

"She had no choice," she said, defending the child she had been. "She was seventeen and under the thumb of her guardian."

"I am beginning to see the parallel. You fear Jamie's fortune is not sufficient to satisfy your family's wants."

It was the cruelest possible interpretation, but one she could not completely deny. "Charles was willing to sanction the match based on what he believed about Jamie's prospects."

"And you, inveterate busybody that you are, have now discovered that, inconveniently, I am not at the point of turning up my toes. How disappointing for you all."

"You quite mistake me, sir, if you believe I desire your death."

"But you will admit it would hasten Charles's approval of the *children's* plans."

Cold, mocking and cruel. And true as well.

"They are in love. I had thought that if you understood the situation, for your brother's sake you might—"

"Of course," he broke in, as if he had just realized her purpose. "What do you suggest, Lady Barrington? A plunge off the parapet? A tincture of poison? Or did you come prepared?"

"No one desires your death," she said, her temper beginning to flare. He was being deliberately obtuse, and they both knew it. "You have quite mistaken the matter."

"I think not, but I would not deprive you of the opportunity of explaining it to me for the world. What is it that you want so much you have come here with your pretty story and your not-so-subtle request?"

"Before he'll agree to the engagement, Charles will need some assurance that your brother is indeed to be your heir," she said evenly.

If she allowed herself to be driven to anger, she would lose. And this was too important.

"Then my man of business will see to it," the earl said. "Was there anything else?"

Capitulation. It was time to thank him politely, turn and leave. Being Emma, she did neither. The opening he had given her was too hard to resist.

"A reason, if you please."

"I beg your pardon?"

"You're a young, vigorous man. How can you be so sure you'll never want a son of your own?"

"My social contacts are, by choice, rather limited. Unless, of course, you are volunteering your services." The sentence rose in inquiry at the end.

Services. There was only one possible interpretation of that.

"How dare you?" Emma sputtered angrily. "I assure you I have no wish…"

The words faltered. Even she, noted for her outspokenness, could not bring herself to state out loud what she believed he had just suggested.

"Or perhaps I, too, had a brief encounter in a snowstorm."

"And fell in love?" The mockery this time was hers.

"Would you accept that as reason enough?"

"For shutting yourself away from the world?"

"How is this any different from your governess's cottage, Lady Barrington?"

"I won't be in *hiding*," she said, stung that he would use something she had told him in confidence against her.

"We all hide. Now if you'll excuse me, I should like to get back to mine. I've grown accustomed to my solitude and guard it jealously. Your brother-in-law will have his guarantee about Jamie's future, and Georgie will have her romance. Is there anything else I may do for you before you leave?"

"That will be quite sufficient, thank you," she said, fighting such a surge of fury it frightened her.

"It seemed the least I could do for a guest who

has been so cavalierly neglected. I'm sorry you are bored.''

''I assure you, sir, I am not. There are far too many things at Leighton to puzzle out. I should warn you that I'm very good at riddles.''

It had the effect she had wanted. There was no quick rejoinder. And again it seemed that his body had stiffened.

''Let it go,'' he warned softly. ''You will only do harm to those who don't deserve it.''

The deep voice was filled with something she had not heard there before. Neither amusement nor contempt nor coldness. It seemed instead to resonate with regret.

You will only do harm to those who don't deserve it. Georgie or Jamie? His mother? Or was it possible he was speaking of himself?

''You should not throw down the gauntlet to a busybody, Lord Greystone. We can never resist a challenge.''

She turned and walked back to the head of the spiral stairs. It was not until she was halfway down them that she realized she was trembling.

Infuriating, despicable man. She could not remember the last time she had felt this alive.

CHAPTER FOUR

"MY LORD, you must understand that such a statement has no legal force," the earl's man of business protested. "It cannot be considered binding on the disposition of the estate or the title. The entitlement was created in such a way that even if you and your brother agreed to such a stipulation, you could not change the terms of the inheritance."

"I understand perfectly," Greystone said. "I am only trying to put the Viscount Barrington at ease concerning the marriage settlements."

"I wish you would not do this," Jamie said.

"I have been informed by a reliable source that such an assurance is necessary before Barrington agrees to the match. Or am I wrong in assuming you want him to agree, Jamie?"

"You know I do."

"Then it's settled. This is much ado about nothing, Mr. Shackleton. If you will include in the settlements language that assures my determination not to marry—"

"I must protest, my lord." Shackleton's interruption was much more forceful than before. "It simply isn't wise, even if it doesn't have force of law."

"A gentleman's agreement, if you will," Alex said. "Put it in."

In the silence that followed the command, one unconsciously given in the tone he had used often on the battlefield and rarely since, the earl walked across to the window. The same one from which he had watched the arrival of Emma's coach.

A little less than a week ago, he realized. It seemed he had been aware of the passage of every hour they had spent under the same roof. And the topic of today's meeting was not, of course, making her presence in his house any easier to forget.

"I must urge you to reconsider, my lord," Shackleton said, carefully modifying his tone to something more conciliatory. "You are still a young man. There is no reason—"

The argument he had been about to make was cut off abruptly. Far too abruptly.

"Exactly," Greystone said softly. He clasped his hands behind his back to still their idiotic trembling and kept his eyes fastened on the pane of glass before him.

"This is ridiculous," Jamie said. "I don't give a damn what Barrington wants. To hell with him. Miss Stanfield doesn't give two figs about the title. She is the only one who matters in this."

"How childishly romantic," Alex said. "That sentiment, however, bears no resemblance to the way the world works. Women of our class marry at the direction of their male relatives, Jamie. You must know that.''

Marry at the direction of their male relatives. As she had done.

Again, as he had each night since Emma had been here, he put from his mind the image of her lying sated in the arms of another man.

''We could elope.''

Greystone finally turned his head at that bit of bravado, looking directly at Jamie for the first time. His brother's mouth was set stubbornly in a manner he recognized. Jamie might be very easygoing, but once he made up his mind, he was nearly impervious to argument.

''Elope?'' he said, raising one dark brow. ''And thereby ruin Miss Stanfield? Is that what you're suggesting?''

''Eventually—''

''Oh yes, of course. *Eventually*. Since she seems to be as great a romantic as you, she might actually be willing to suffer those months or years of censure and isolation. The question is—Are you willing to watch her suffer them?''

As he had intended, that put a stop to any further suggestion of such a solution. Jamie could never bear to see anyone hurt, especially someone he loved. There would be no more talk of a run to the Border, thank God.

''Perhaps if we solicit Georgina's stepmama to speak on our behalf...''

"It might interest you to know that she is the one who urged this declaration," Alex said.

"Lady Barrington?"

"She is convinced her brother-in-law will never give his consent to the marriage without some assurance that you will be my heir."

"Then assure him you have no intent to marry, my lord," Shackleton offered.

"I *believe* that is what I have just instructed you to do," Greystone said with a nearly forgotten arrogance.

"Saying that you will *never* marry and that you have no *intent* to marry are two very different things, my lord."

Normally they were, Alex acknowledged. Just not in his case. "I'm not sure that wording will satisfy Miss Stanfield's uncle."

"And I am *very* sure that any other would not satisfy a court, my lord. Besides," Shackleton went on quickly, "you may well change your mind at some time in the future." He ignored Greystone's laughter to continue with his point. "In that case, I should not wish you to feel honor-bound by such a pledge. Especially when it is unnecessary to achieve your ends."

"And if he balks?"

"Then we may be forced to consider other language. Not until, if you please. As your advisor, of course, my lord," the man of business added respectfully.

There was another silence, this one clearly waiting. During it, Alex again pretended to contemplate the falling rain, picturing instead the face of the woman who had looked up at him as he had watched her from this very window. He forced his eyes to follow the slow downward glide of a drop that landed on the top of the pane before he spoke again.

"Jamie?"

"If this must be addressed, then it should be in that language," his brother said readily. "That's the only way I'll accept the addition of that stipulation."

The pause after his brother's pronouncement lengthened until Alex turned from the window to face him.

"Who can know what will happen in the future?" Jamie added, his chin lifted in challenge. "Whatever you may intend now—"

"Do it, Mr. Shackleton," Alex instructed, breaking in before his brother could finish that assertion. "If you please," he finished, careful to modulate his tone.

"Of course," the barrister said, sounding relieved that this had been resolved to his satisfaction as well as the law's. He shuffled through the papers before him, then stacked them together with a showy efficiency. "If there is nothing else, my lord..."

"That's all. If you could have the settlements drawn up by the first of next week, I should be grateful."

"I shall put the clerks to it immediately after I return to the city."

"Then I shall bid you good day, sir."

"My lord," Shackleton rose, bowing slightly in his direction. "Mr. Leighton."

"Thank you, Shackleton," Jamie said. "I'm sure you'll make a capital job of it."

"We shall try, sir."

"I'll see you out," Jamie offered.

"No need. I know my way." After he had opened the door of the sitting room, he turned to add, "You've made the right decision, my lord. One you won't have cause to regret later on. That's always the wisest course."

Greystone continued his pretended contemplation of the rain. He could almost feel the look the two of them exchanged behind his back.

Let them celebrate, he thought. The victory they had achieved was meaningless, which Jamie at least should understand. And if the wording of the agreement added force to the legality of it, well, that was exactly what he paid Shackleton to ensure.

When the door closed behind the older man, again he waited, this time for what he knew would be Jamie's continuation of Shackleton's argument. It was one his brother had made a number of times through the years.

"Thank you," Jamie said instead.

Alex turned to find his brother eyeing him with

something that looked suspiciously like compassion. An emotion he refused to acknowledge.

"There's no need for your gratitude. What I've added to those documents is nothing but the truth."

"I didn't mean that, although I shall be very grateful if it wins over Georgina's uncle."

"Then for what do you thank me?"

"For freedom from guilt."

"I beg your pardon."

He had a sickening suspicion that Jamie might be referring to guilt over having found someone with whom to share his life when it was obvious his brother would not. Although he was aware that the thought must have crossed the boy's mind at some time—indeed, he had employed it himself in his announcement of his move to Wyckstead—Alex didn't want to hear him express it.

"Freedom from guilt if *you* fall in love at some future date. I would not want to be responsible for forcing you to have to choose between your honor and the woman you loved."

"You're as ridiculous as Shackleton."

Jamie's responding laugh was low and free of mockery. When he spoke, however, his voice was deadly serious. "It wouldn't matter to a woman who loved you, you know."

"You *do* have absurdly romantic notions of the world, don't you? Mother's influence, I suppose."

"And you have a remarkably cynical one," his brother rejoined.

"I believe the appropriate word is realistic. Let it go, Jamie. Nothing has changed."

"Except I understand better now what you are missing."

Alex turned at that, fighting the ridiculous anger the comment had inexplicably evoked. This was something he had made peace with long ago. Or so he had thought.

"Should I thank you for that reminder?"

"It is my dearest wish that one day you will."

"I've told you—"

"Yes, I know. You've made up your mind that it's quite impossible. You are, however, the only one who believes that. Please allow the rest of the world, like Shackleton and I, who are not fools by the way, to disagree."

He held Jamie's eyes, expecting his brother to back down as he always did when faced with his displeasure. Instead the blue gaze remained calm and steady.

He was the one who finally broke, turning again to the window. To the entrance below. And to the memories.

You are, however, the only one who believes that. And for the first time in more than a decade, he wondered if that could possibly be true.

"JUST THINK, Georgie, one day *you* shall be hanging here. Perhaps looking every bit as pleased with yourself as she is."

Emma was staring up at the life-size portrait of a woman in a wide, lace-edged Elizabethan ruff. The ornate frame that surrounded the picture was an appropriate setting for the richness of her velvet gown and the rubies and pearls that adorned it.

"Shh," Georgina cautioned her, trying not to laugh. "The countess will hear you."

"Oh, she'll quite approve of your addition. Perhaps she will have you and Jamie painted side by side."

Georgina's ready smile tilted the corners of her lips, but her eyes remained dutifully on their hostess's back. Leaning on a gold-topped cane, Lady Greystone was leading the procession of her female guests along the house's portrait gallery, understandably famous in the district. Generation after generation of the Leighton family lined the walls of the central corridor of the great west wing, peering down upon them as they strolled along at the snail's pace the countess's infirmity demanded.

"I wonder if Jamie has already been painted," Georgina said, her eyes examining the young cavalier under whose portrait they were now passing. "That one looks to be barely out of the schoolroom. He's surely younger than Jamie."

"They died very young in those days," Emma said sotto voce. "It was necessary to have them painted early."

"Emma," Georgina protested, trying not to laugh.

They were far enough back in the group that they had missed most of the countess's commentary, which bothered neither of them. At least the stroll along the gallery was a form of exercise. Today's rain had denied them any other. Not only were they accustomed to long country walks, but this afternoon in particular, they had desperately needed something to occupy their minds.

According to Charles, Jamie was meeting with the earl and his man of business, which seemed to portend something important was afoot. That information had only added to the tension Georgina had been feeling the last few days.

Her obvious nervousness was one reason for Emma's silliness about the portraits. Despite her repeated assurances that the earl had promised to make the stipulation they believed Charles would require, Georgina was terrified something would go wrong with the negotiations.

"We seem to be coming into the more modern section," Emma said as they approached the current generations of Leightons.

The first portraits were of the countess and her husband, the late earl. In her youth Jamie's mother had borne a remarkable resemblance to her youngest son. His delicate coloring was hers, as well as the slight statue. His father was a far more imposing figure, wide-shouldered and dark, with striking blue eyes.

Emma could hardly tear her gaze away from his

picture. And she knew why, of course. If the current earl had taken after him in facial features as well as in build and coloring, he would be a very handsome man.

"It's Jamie," Georgina said, her sweetheart's name uttered in a voice that was almost reverent.

Her stepdaughter had continued down the gallery while Emma had been lost in contemplation of the late earl. Now Georgina was standing several feet away, looking up in love-struck awe.

Emma hurriedly closed the distance between them. As her gaze followed Georgina's, she found the expected portrait of the youngest Leighton. The expression Jamie had assumed for the portrait was too solemn to capture the sweet charm that was such an attractive part of his nature. Still, it was a very good likeness, even to a hint of color along his fair cheeks.

"And those must be his brothers," Georgie said, turning her attention to the massive oils hanging between the one of Jamie and those of his parents.

"Brothers?" Emma questioned while her eyes eagerly examined the first of them.

This then was the earl. After their clandestine meetings, he had become almost as much an object of her fantasies as the young man she had met so long ago at the inn.

"That must be Simon," Georgina said, indicating the picture Emma was staring at. "He was the first born, but he died shortly after attaining the title. A weakness of the heart. Jamie says he was always sickly, even as a child. Because of his ill health, there was some talk within the family of not purchasing the commission for Alexander—"

The narrative halted abruptly. Of course, Emma had only been aware of the sound of the words and little of their sense for several seconds now. As soon as Georgie said the words "he died," her gaze had shifted to the next portrait.

A cone of silence had descended over her, blocking everything from her consciousness except the likeness of the second Leighton son. He had been painted in uniform. As dashing as the gold-laced red jacket, white breeches and high boots were, however, they were not what had held her eye.

It was his smile. The one she had thought transformed his face into something extraordinary. As it did now.

"Why, Emma," Georgina exclaimed, putting a steadying hand under her elbow. "You look as though you'd seen a ghost."

A ghost. That was exactly what she had thought the night he'd disappeared into the shadows. That he had faded away like a phantom. Or a figment of her imagination.

"Alexander?" She whispered the question.

"The Earl of Greystone. Jamie calls him Alex."

Emma shook her head, closing her mouth and pressing her lips together. There was a sting at the back of her eyes, but she ignored it, concentrating on the handsome features she had never forgotten.

The world they both inhabited by virtue of their births was incredibly small. Everyone in the *ton* knew everyone else, as well as their family connections. After all, they frequented the same clubs and resorts and stately homes at virtually the same times every year.

She had always looked for him, no matter where she was. Even after she'd married Robert, her gaze would sweep across any room she entered, searching for tumbled black curls. Then they would focus on the face below, praying to find that particular smile and those blue eyes. She had always been disappointed.

It was only much later that she had allowed herself to think the unthinkable, and her search for him had become more and more desperate. And more hopeless.

Sometime in the course of those long empty years, she had come to accept that she would never see him again. She could not even be certain when that had happened. She had never consciously thought of him as dead, but the place he had held in her memory, once so strong and vibrant, had become little more than a hallowed shrine. An empty one.

"Emma?" Georgina said, "What is it? What's wrong?"

"I met him."

"The earl?"

She nodded, unable to tear her eyes away from the portrait.

"Of course you did," Georgina said. "You talked to him about the title. About giving his assurance to Uncle Charles."

Emma turned to face her. "Before. I met him *before* we came."

Her stepdaughter's eyes lifted to the portrait and then came quickly back to hers. "But…Jamie says he never leaves the estate."

"Long before. Even… It was before I married your father."

There was a telltale hesitation.

"Then… You didn't know? Before we came, you didn't know it was he?"

"I never knew his name. We met, and he went away. Then here… It was dark. I never saw his face. I had no idea."

Georgina glanced down the long corridor at the group of women still looking up at the portraits. She was concerned, of course, that someone might notice they were no longer with them.

If so, Emma thought, there was nothing she could do about it. Perhaps the houseguests would put their concentration on this grouping down to Mr. Leighton's quite obvious infatuation with Georgina. After all, his portrait hung right beside his brother's.

His brother. Alexander. Alex.

"I take it," Georgina said carefully, "this was not a casual meeting."

"Do you remember the first time you saw Jamie?"

"But if it were that way…" Georgina allowed the question to trail.

"I thought I'd never see him again. After all these years I'd given up hope."

"You couldn't have," Georgina said with the simple conviction of youth. "Not if you loved him."

It had not yet occurred to Georgie that Emma's clinging to that hope would have been a betrayal of her own father, an emotional if not a physical one.

"I finally decided he must be dead."

"And now that you know he isn't?"

She had no idea, Emma realized. She had barely had time to assimilate the shock. Certainly not enough to consider the ramifications of it.

The first of which, she realized, was that if the earl had been the watcher at the window the day they arrived, then he had known all along who she was. Even if he hadn't recognized her with the passage of those long years, he could have had no doubt of her identity after the story she'd told him.

No doubt. And still he had said nothing about their first meeting. Because it had meant nothing? Because it had been only her fantasy? Her delusion alone that the kiss they'd shared had affected him as much as it had her?

By his own admission he had been a popular

young man about town. He had probably kissed a hundred girls, few of them so green as she.

Or perhaps he had said nothing because he feared what she would do if she knew. Something he would find a far more annoying invasion than her repeated intrusions on his solitude.

CHAPTER FIVE

"I SHOULD HAVE REMEMBERED how she feels about showing off the gallery. I had been too concerned with the logistics of the house party to even think about her fondness for organizing tours of Leighton."

"I shouldn't worry," Alex said absently. His eyes strayed longingly back to the ledgers spread out before him. "After all, it's an excellent likeness."

He had been immersed in the estate accounts when Jamie arrived. And he still wasn't sure of the purpose of this late-night visit. His brother's conversation to this point had been vague and slightly disjointed. The latest topic seemed an attempt to garner sympathy for their mother's display of his portrait to the female guests this afternoon.

"You flatter me," Jamie said, his voice subdued enough to bring the earl's gaze back up to his face.

"I'm sure Miss Stanfield was enchanted," Alex said, trying to feign interest out of a sense of brotherly duty. "She's probably busy considering what color her gown should be when she sits for its companion piece."

"Her comments were extremely kind," Jamie said. "Of course, that is her nature."

There was an awkward pause. Uncertain the conversation was over, but quite willing to prod his brother to leave him to his work if it were, Alex moved one of the account books nearer and ran his finger along a line of figures as if to verify them.

"She expressed pleasure in viewing the rest of the family, as well."

"Good," Alex said, his attention rather obviously fixed on the ledgers.

"She mentioned that they had especially enjoyed the portraits of the current generation."

There was something about Jamie's tone that brought Alex's gaze up. That bloom of color, which always stained his brother's cheeks when he was upset or embarrassed, was there now. The blue eyes met his steadily, but Jamie's expression was far more serious than this discussion should warrant.

Alex mentally reviewed the tail end of the conversation, to which he had admittedly been giving only half his attention. When he reached the last phrase his brother had uttered, a chill prickled along his spine, causing the hair on the back of his neck to lift.

She mentioned that they had especially enjoyed the portraits of the current generation, which could only mean...

He didn't bother to put the question into words because he could see the answer in Jamie's open countenance. He pushed back his chair instead, standing to face his brother.

"I ordered that it should be taken down," he said, forcing himself to calmness through a Herculean effort.

"It was. As soon as you asked, but... Mother told me some time ago that she didn't like the empty space. I should have had something moved there to replace the portrait before the guests arrived. Of course, a substitution would have thrown the groupings off, which would have upset her even more."

"What has she done, Jamie?"

"Nothing so terrible. And it's already been taken care of. I shouldn't have known anything about it, except at dinner tonight Georgina...that is, Miss Stanfield—"

"I asked you a question, damn it. What has she done?"

Another pause, briefer but more telling.

"She had them rehang it yesterday morning."

"Damn her," Alex gritted out.

"I know that you're sensitive to the—"

"I *knew* something like this would happen. If you had to have guests, why the hell—"

"There's no harm done," his brother broke in soothingly. "Actually, it's entirely possible that *not* having your portrait there might have caused even more—"

"Was Lady Barrington with Miss Stanfield?"

Alex demanded before his brother could complete his attempt to excuse this disaster.

"I don't know." Jamie almost stuttered in response to the sharpness of the question. "Georgina didn't mention her, but I would assume so, since the ladies of the party were all invited. You know how Mother enjoys leading guests along that—"

"Damn it," the earl said again, slamming both fists down onto the desk in front of him. "Bloody hell."

"No one had any reason—"

Before Jamie could get any more of that ridiculous appeasement out of his mouth, with one motion Alex shoved the stack of ledgers forward. They and everything else on the surface of his desk flew off to land at his brother's feet.

Shocked into silence, Jamie had watched them fall. Then, his mouth still open at that uncharacteristic display of rage, his eyes lifted to his brother's face.

"What is it? What's wrong?"

"Get out."

The fury that filled him made him want to pummel someone. Since Jamie was the only one within striking distance and had, besides, confessed to being at least partially responsible for this fiasco, the odds were excellent it might be he.

"It can't possibly matter—" Jamie foolishly began.

Only when Alex started around the desk did his

brother retreat. He stalked him across the room, slamming the door in his face as soon as Jamie had stepped out into the hall.

Then, his hand still on the knob, the Earl of Greystone bowed his head, closing his eyes against the unwanted images that bombarded him. That portrait, which had been painted shortly before his departure for Spain, was exactly how Emma would remember him. And it was how she would expect to find him now. The same man who had kissed her that night.

Before she'd come to Leighton, he had prayed that if she thought of him at all, she would believe him dead. Now she knew that he was not.

And there could be no doubt in her mind after she had told him the story of their stolen kiss that he had to know who she was. Being Emma, she would eventually show up here demanding to know why he had remained silent about his identity.

Her memory of that brief interlude had remained inviolate all these years. As had his. For both of them it seemed to have attained far more importance than it should.

The encounter came to represent for her what falling in love should be. And when she never again felt that way…she never again fell in love.

That knowledge was a burden no man should have to bear. Rather than creating an even greater burden, however, this time one for her to bear, he had kept silent.

Every dream he had ever had of finding love, of

marrying a woman who loved him, of having children, had long ago been shattered. It seemed possible that Emma's capacity to dream had survived the slow passage of the years. And now, if she forced another meeting between them, hers, too, would turn to dust.

"Damn you," he whispered, his head still bent. He was unsure, even as he spoke the words, to whom or to what they were addressed.

AFTER SHE'D UNDRESSED for bed, Emma had gone to the window of her room and watched twilight deepen to dusk and then to deepest night. Still she stood there, remembering what had happened in that country inn. And everything that had happened in the intervening years.

Then she had carefully examined each word she'd exchanged with the Earl of Greystone since her arrival at Leighton. Trying to understand why he had not acknowledged that he was the man in the story she'd told him. Wondering what she would have done if he had.

After hours, during which she had found no satisfactory solution to either of those questions, she had decided her only course of action was to do what she had done once before. She had gone to find the one person who *could* answer them.

WHEN SHE HAD ASCENDED the flight of stairs, she discovered that tonight there was no light at all on the second floor of the keep, not even the thread along the bottom of the door. The single candle she carried cast little illumination in the cavernous space, barely dispelling the shadows in front of her as she crossed the stone floor.

For some reason she felt the same disquiet she had experienced while staring up at the tower window the evening of their arrival. Although the sensation was vague and undefined, she knew that it portended that something was very wrong.

If she had been of a less stalwart nature or less determined to get to the bottom of Greystone's behavior, she might have fled, assigning the unease she felt to Jamie's imaginary ghosts. Instead, being who she was, as soon as she reached the door to the earl's rooms, she raised her hand and knocked.

The noise, echoing off stone walls, seemed unnaturally loud in the predawn stillness. She waited, holding her breath in anticipation. Although she strained to hear above the pounding of her heart, there was no response. Perhaps he was a sound sleeper, or perhaps...

She glanced across the tower to the corner where the spiral staircase led to the roof. Clutching her shawl more closely around her, she walked over to them.

Despite their configuration, standing at the bottom, she could see the sky, far lighter than it had been on her previous visits. She set the candle down on one of the lower steps and began to climb, still uncertain after all those hours what she would say to him.

It was obvious as soon as she stepped off the top step, however, that he wasn't here. The battlements, revealed in the half light of impending dawn, were empty, each merlon and crenel outlined like dragon's teeth against the sky.

What do you suggest, Lady Barrington? A plunge off the parapet?

She fought the strongest inclination to climb the steps to the wall walk and look down. A patently ridiculous notion, born of anxiety, not logic.

There was no earthly reason to be frightened because she couldn't find him. He was asleep. He hadn't heard her knock. Or, more likely, he had chosen to ignore it. No matter what she told herself, that unsettling feeling that something was wrong, which she'd felt since she had entered the keep, persisted.

The sky was beginning to lighten perceptibly now. The servants would be rising in a few minutes to begin the numerous tasks involved in seeing to the well-being of the earl's guests. If she didn't get back to her room soon, she would be caught wandering the house in her nightgown.

Taking one last look around the roof, she hurriedly descended into the darkness of the lower level. She stooped to pick up the still-burning candle, intending to light her way to the other set of stairs.

Halfway across, however, the temptation proved too great. She stopped before the oaken door, raising her fist to knock again. She changed the motion in midair, her hand closing around the latch instead, seemingly without her conscious volition.

She slowly pushed the massive door inward and stepped inside. Even with the faint illumination provided by the single candle, it was immediately clear that she had entered a totally masculine domain.

Leather-bound volumes neatly arrayed on shelves lined two of the walls. The gold lettering on their spines glowed dully in the dim candlelight. On the third wall, arranged above the fireplace, was a display of weapons, including both firearms and swords, most of them antique.

Two chairs had been placed invitingly before the hearth, but the ashes inside it were cold and gray. Beside one of the chairs was a small table, which held an empty glass and a half-full decanter.

The other side of the room was dominated by a massive rosewood desk. It had been positioned in front of the oriel window, now touched with a first pale ray of the rising sun.

It was not until she had walked to the center of the room and nearly stumbled over them that she discovered the objects in front of the desk. Books and papers were scattered haphazardly over the stones. A broken inkwell lay there as well, the pool of black liquid around it reflecting the flame of her candle.

Unthinkingly, she bent to pick up the book nearest the well before its pages could be ruined. Only when she had the volume in her hands did she realize that what she held was an account book. She closed it, feeling like a voyeur, and laid it carefully on the desk.

This destruction could not have been the result of an accident. It was obvious someone had deliberately pushed everything from the surface of the desk onto the floor.

What emotion had precipitated that action? she wondered. And where was the man who had performed it?

The door to the remaining rooms of the apartment stood open. Emboldened by the continuing silence and the growing sense that she was quite alone here, she walked across the cold floor to peer inside.

In the growing light, she could see it was as deserted as the sitting room and the roof had been. The bed had not even been slept in.

The feeling of dread that had haunted her since her arrival swelled to a sickening flood of anxiety. It was nearly dawn, and it was obvious the earl had spent the night elsewhere. With someone else?

Was that why he had kept silent after her maudlin confession? Had he been embarrassed, or even worse, disgusted, by her too obvious infatuation with a man she had met for a few minutes more than a dozen years ago?

That didn't explain why he had made a mystery

of his existence since their arrival. And he had. Since the moment she had looked up and discovered that he was watching them—

Remembering, her eyes lifted to the bedroom windows, searching the terrain beyond the drive and formal gardens. There, just as on that first dawn, was the black horse and its rider. Although it hardly seemed possible, the speed at which they were racing along the crest of the hill was even more reckless than it had been then.

That day she had tried desperately to catch a glimpse of his face. She had failed because she had continued to watch from her vantage point as he had directed his mount toward the stables.

Eventually, he would arrive at that same destination today, she realized, turning quickly away from the window. This time she would be waiting for him.

SHORTLY AFTER Jamie's departure, the Earl of Greystone, still dressed in his shirtsleeves and waistcoat, had thrown his cloak around his shoulders and left the tower. On each step he descended, he had expected to find Emma making her way up. Thank God, it hadn't happened.

He understood that by fleeing his rooms, he was only postponing the inevitable confrontation between them. He had decided, however, it would be on his time and in a manner of his choosing. After all, he had little choice about anything else.

He had spent the remainder of the night amid the comforting scents of hay, horses and well-oiled leather. Wrapped in his cloak, he hadn't attempted to sleep. Instead he had allowed the emotions he'd fought so long full expression.

Rage and despair. Dread. Even self-pity, which he despised. Tonight he had denied none of them.

At the first streak of light below the horizon, he had arisen, found one of the grooms asleep by the tack room fire and nudged him awake with the toe of his boot. Sleepy and disoriented, the boy had staggered up willingly enough from his pallet.

Sensing the earl's mood, perhaps, he had asked no questions. He had simply brought Sultan around, saddled and bridled, in less than five minutes.

Deprived of his dawn gallop for almost a week, the gelding was far too fresh to ride out into the near-darkness, but neither of them hesitated. Alex had dug in his heels, sending Sultan out of the paddock at a dead run.

That had been almost an hour ago. Now they were back, both drenched in sweat. The horse, ill-used in an attempt to exorcize his master's demons, trembled with exhaustion.

Greystone had never before in his life abused an animal, and the mindless race he had set this one on had been not only dangerous, but fruitless. He had escaped nothing from which he'd been fleeing.

There had been a point in that wild ride at which he had pulled his mount up, controlling the eager gelding through force of will while he contemplated a fork in the lane. If he had nursed Sultan along, taking frequent breaks and walking part of the distance, he could have been at Wyckstead in a few hours.

The temptation had been great enough to cause him to actually spur the horse in that direction before he'd pulled him up again, admitting what his heart had known all along. It was too late. He owed Emma an explanation. One that was overdue by more than ten years.

After he'd handed the gelding over to the stable boy, who was clearly shocked by the state the two of them were in, he discarded the cloak, throwing it over his arm as he made his way toward the back of the house. As he walked, his fingers worked at the knot of his cravat until it was loose enough to allow him to rip it off.

He turned his head slowly from side to side, trying to ease the tension that had tightened the muscles of his neck and shoulders. As he neared the entrance to the kitchens, almost oblivious to his surroundings, someone stepped out of the shadows beside the doorway.

In less time than it took his heart to stop and then resume beating again, he had recognized the figure. Emma was dressed in a thin cotton nightgown, over which she had thrown a wool shawl. Except for its color, white like her rail, it looked identical to the one she had worn that night.

Her hair was confined in a long braid, which lay over her shoulder. It was the only touch of color about the slender figure. That and the blue eyes, which had widened as he approached.

If the lighting had been more subdued, he might have convinced himself she was a fantasy. A figment of his disordered thinking, which had envisioned her exactly like this.

Dressed for bed and waiting for him to come to her.

As soon as he'd recognized her, his forward progress slowed. There was nothing to be gained, however, by delay. What must be done should be accomplished quickly and cleanly, like a surgery intended to excise a festering wound.

He took a breath, forcing his feet to move. One step at a time, taking him closer and closer to the woman who had not seen him in a dozen years.

He had thought her pale before, but as he neared, the blood literally drained from her face, leaving it the same parchment-white as the nightgown she wore. Her eyes were no longer blue. The pupils had dilated, eating up the surrounding rim of color.

When fewer than five feet separated them, he stopped. Neither of them said a word as her eyes continued to search his face, examining each feature as if she had never seen them before. And she hadn't, of course. Not like this.

He had no idea what he expected her to do or to say. Perhaps nothing. Perhaps, like the maid, she would simply cross herself and flee. Or perhaps she would scream.

That had been the worst of the variations that had played out in his imagination last night. It seemed that in the morning stillness he could hear the sound, echoing again and again within the stone walls of his self-appointed prison.

She did none of the things he had dreaded. And nothing he could have anticipated. As he forced his gaze to hold on her face, her eyes filled with moisture. Watching them, his own burned.

She blinked, trying to contain the tears, but one escaped, sliding down the curve of her cheek to catch at the corner of parted, trembling lips. Her shoulders lifted with the depth of the breath she took. It shuddered inward, just as his had the day he had first seen her being helped down from the coach.

After a soundless eternity, she closed her mouth, again blinking against the tears. She took one step forward. And then another. Moving closer and closer in the unforgiving sunlight. When she stopped, she was so near that the faint, sweet aroma of rosewater engulfed him.

She was tall for a woman, but his height forced her to tilt her head. And again her eyes searched his face.

Although there were, by design, no mirrors in his rooms, he was intimately familiar with every centimeter of the damage, the image seared in his memory from the first time he had made the mistake of looking into a glass. The saber had slashed down his face, laying it open from forehead to chin. Battle-field dressed, the scar pulled at the skin, distorting the line of his lip and the lid that should have covered the now-blind eye.

As her examination continued, Alex forced himself not to flinch from it. Not to indicate in any way how painful it was to be exposed like this.

Again she surprised him. She raised her hand, reaching toward his face as if to touch the evidence of the deformity. With the lightning reflexes that had served him in combat, his fingers closed 'round her wrist before she could.

"No," he said softly.

It was as if the word broke a spell. Her eyes refocused on his, avoiding the ravaged countenance. She shook her head, the motion tight and small, and her lips parted as if she were about to speak.

He waited a long time, some part of him hoping she would find the right words to say. Since he was unsure what those might possibly be, he wasn't surprised when she was unable to form them.

He released her wrist and stepped around her, striding quickly toward the back entrance to the hall, driven again by the same need that had caused him to spur Sultan past the gelding's endurance. And although he listened, foolishly hoping, Emma never called to him.

CHAPTER SIX

"LADY BARRINGTON, I have no intention of discussing my brother with you," Jamie Leighton said. "It simply isn't possible. Not only would it be an invasion of his privacy, but his friendship and support are far too valuable to me to risk—"

"Do you remember the first time you saw Georgina?" Emma interrupted calmly.

The only outward sign of her nervousness was that the fingers of her left hand worried the lace edging of the handkerchief she held in her right. As soon as she became aware of it, the movement stopped.

She had taken almost the entire morning to decide what she should do to rectify the unforgivable error in judgment she had made. The first part of the campaign she'd settled on had been to request a meeting with the earl's younger brother, which Jamie had readily granted. If he had known the subject she planned to broach, he would probably have refused.

"Of course I remember," he said.

The color in his cheeks had been high since her first mention of the earl. It increased suddenly.

She realized that Jamie was dealing with his own

anxieties. If this hadn't been so important, Emma might have felt sorry for him, caught between her determination and his brother's equally strong intention to isolate himself from the world.

"I, too, had such an encounter," she said. "Long before I married Georgina's father."

"Indeed," Jamie said faintly. He was probably wondering why she imagined he might care about her romantic adventures.

"Although I never knew his name, that brief meeting made such an impression on me that I never forgot it. Or him." Then she added, her voice deliberately softened for the greatest impact, "That man was your brother, Mr. Leighton. That encounter took place more than a dozen years ago."

She watched as the significance of the time span dawned on her audience.

"Before he went to Spain," Jamie said.

Spain, she thought. Along with the evidence provided by the portrait, that explained a great deal.

"And then I met him here," she said.

The silence this time was more prolonged. The obvious result of his having no idea of what to say to her.

"I must confess I was not totally unprepared to see him again," she went on, since she seemed to have rendered him speechless. "Actually, I was the instigator of that meeting. I had noticed his portrait in the gallery—"

There was an unexpected reaction to that. Jamie

straightened away from the mantel against which he'd been leaning, his mouth opening and then closing. Whatever he'd been about to say, he had apparently thought better of it.

"However, since that must have been painted prior to the earl's departure for Spain..."

She hesitated, her throat closing with the emotion she had fought all morning. An emotion she had known instinctively Greystone would hate above any other she might harbor for him.

"I was *not* prepared," she forced herself to continue, "for the changes that had occurred in the interim. I reacted badly."

She refused to let her eyes fall before the flare of anger in Jamie's.

"How badly?" he asked, his voice hard.

"I cried," she admitted. "I am quite ashamed of that, I assure you. I had cherished an image of him for so long, you see, and I was...caught unawares."

The stern line of Jamie's lip softened. "How did Alex respond?"

Alex. Alexander.

He would never have used his brother's given name if not for the stress of the moment. Although Emma had whispered it like a schoolgirl since she'd learned it, she could not bring herself to repeat it now.

"Not well," she said, remembering what had been in his eyes as he'd caught her wrist and held it, obviously waiting for her to say something to him. It was only *after* he'd disappeared, however, that she had realized that. She had told herself it might be better she had *not* tried to express herself at that moment. She had needed time to sort through her feelings, and she couldn't do that with him so near.

"You wish me to offer him your apologies?"

"Of course not," she said sharply.

"Then…forgive me, Lady Barrington. I'm unsure why you wanted to speak to me."

"I want to know what happened to him."

"You shall have to address that inquiry to my brother. I have told you that I do not discuss him with…"

"Strangers?" she finished for him when he hesitated.

"With anyone."

"I believe you must make an exception," she said softly.

"I have no intention—"

"I'm in love with him, Mr. Leighton. I have been for years."

She had caught him off guard. And, if the truth be told, herself as well. Now that she had made the confession aloud, it did not seem so peculiar to her as it would to someone who knew of their single, very brief encounter.

"In *love* with him," Jamie repeated in disbelief.

As well he might. "For years," she said. "And still."

"Forgive me, Lady Barrington. I don't mean to be unkind, but...had my brother cherished a *tendre* for you, I believe I should have been aware of it."

"I did *not* say he was in love with me, Mr. Leighton."

She wanted to believe he might be, of course, but Greystone had given her little cause. The only thing that suggested such a possibility was something she had not caught at the time. Only during last night's attempts to reconstruct their conversations had she realized its significance and felt very foolish that she'd missed it.

Or perhaps I, too, had a brief encounter in a snowstorm, he had said, mocking the story she'd told him. She was certain she'd never mentioned the storm. That he had remembered it was snowing was a slender thread on which to hang such high-flung hopes, but it was all she had. And so she clung to it.

"He *could* be." She amended her denial, faltering for the first time under the intensity of Jamie's gaze. "That is something I must yet discover. But first... Won't you tell me, please, what happened to him?"

Jamie's reluctance to discuss his brother had been so strong only a moment ago, it had been almost palpable. She could tell from his eyes that he was now wavering, and once he began, the story came out in a rush.

"My brother was a soldier, as you know since you saw the portrait. He received that slash across his face saving the life of his commanding officer. He will never tell you that. He didn't tell me, but the incident was mentioned in the dispatches.''

When it seemed Jamie had run down, Emma began to rise. "Thank you for your time, Mr. Leighton. And for the information.''

"Shortly after they removed the bandages,'' Jamie continued as if she hadn't spoken, "the child of the woman with whom the wounded had been housed saw his face. She ran away screaming. Unfortunately, Alex had enough Spanish by then to understand what she was saying.''

Again her throat closed, but Emma rigidly controlled any outward reaction. Tears were a mistake she would not make again. As horrifying as the tale was, it at least explained what she had seen in his eyes this morning. A watching despair, like a dog that knows it is about to be beaten.

"Thank you for that, too,'' she said sincerely. "I trust you will not betray my confidence to your brother. You may be right in your suspicion that what I feel is not reciprocated. I should, however, like a chance to confirm that on my own.''

"Then… You'd better hurry, Lady Barrington. He's leaving for Wyckstead.''

"Today?''

"I shouldn't be surprised,'' Jamie said, not unkindly. "The servants have been packing his things most of the morning.''

As she once more climbed the tower stairs, she acknowledged the debt of gratitude she owed poor Jamie. If he had not taken pity on her, she would almost certainly have waited until after dark to confront Greystone.

And it would have been too late. This way she would have some answer, even if it was not the one she wanted.

"Beg pardon, my lady."

Startled, she looked up to find a footman coming down the stairs, burdened with a portmanteau and a large box tied up with heavy string. Although he had flattened himself against the wall, the staircase was narrow enough that it would still be difficult for her to pass.

"Is the earl above?" she asked.

His eyes widened. Before he answered, they flicked to the top of the stairs. When they return to meet hers, he leaned forward, lowering his voice like a conspirator.

"In 'is rooms, 'e is," he said. "The door be open."

She slipped past the man, mouthing a heartfelt, "Thank you." When she reached the top of the stairs, she discovered that the door of the earl's rooms was indeed standing wide. Ridiculously, she almost tiptoed across the stone floor. Then she paused, taking a breath before she stepped into the doorway.

The sitting room seemed far less depressing with

the full light of the afternoon sun pouring in through the oriel window. Someone had picked up the books that had been scattered in front of the desk. The broken inkwell was nowhere in sight, but the stain its contents had left was visible on the light gray stone.

The ledger she had laid on the corner of the desk was still there, although many of the volumes that had filled the shelves were missing. Packed in boxes tied with string, perhaps?

Unthinkingly, she walked over to the desk and touched the account book. Perhaps it was the sound of her footsteps or perhaps, long attuned to an atmosphere of solitude, he had simply sensed he was no longer alone here. As she did now.

She turned, the tips of her fingers still resting on the ledger, and found him standing in the doorway to the bedroom. Watching her.

The slant of afternoon sunlight was crueler to the scarred visage than pale dawn's had been, but it also revealed that the undamaged blue eye, meeting hers unwaveringly, had not changed. Nor had the finely shaped nose, almost out of place now in that ravaged face. The cleft in the center of his chin had been bisected and almost obliterated by the ragged tear.

Neither of them said anything for a moment, their eyes holding. Because she was the one who had sought this meeting, she finally broke the silence.

"I searched for you."

His head tilted slightly. Questioning.

"Everywhere I went. For a very long time. Even after I married, God forgive me, I looked for you."

"Emma," he said, and then nothing else.

"I kept thinking that one day I would glance across a ballroom or a dinner table, and you'd be there. Or I'd round the corner or idly stare into a passing carriage, and I'd see you. And then, after a long time, years and years, I stopped looking. Stopped expecting. Stopped hoping."

He said nothing, his eyes falling to the box he held in both hands.

"This morning..." Her throat closed over the words.

"Don't." The word this time was not a command, but an imploration.

"I know I behaved badly, but it wasn't—" She hesitated and then forced herself to begin again. "It was the shock of finding you after all this time. In the last place I might have expected."

"My brother told me you'd seen the portrait."

Damn you, Jamie.

"Because of that," he went on, his voice perfectly steady, "I thought that you might have puzzled it out. This morning I knew you hadn't."

"My powers of deduction are not, apparently, so great as I had supposed," she said, trying for something lighter than the near tragic tones they had been using.

Surprisingly, there was a small upward slant at

the corners of his mouth. Encouraged, she smiled at him.

The effort was slightly tremulous, and seeing that, his lips pursed. Then he stepped forward, setting the box he held down on the table that flanked the door.

"Are you going somewhere?" she asked, allowing her eyes to touch on the empty shelves.

"Since it seems Jamie's proposal is to be accepted, I decided it was time to turn the estate over to him."

"I didn't know he had offered," she said truthfully.

She had been aware of almost nothing except her own hopes and memories and fears for the last twenty-four hours. Poor Georgina, left without her support at such a propitious time in her life.

"He hasn't. Not officially. I believe that's planned for this afternoon. If she accepts, the announcement of their engagement is to be made at dinner tonight. It seems Miss Stanfield has succeeded in her quest. My congratulations."

He was regaining his equilibrium, she realized. The last comment had been as sardonic as their previous exchanges.

"If we are acknowledging Georgina's success in something, I believe it should be in falling in love with a man who returns her love," Emma said. "We are not all so fortunate."

There was a small silence.

"Was he very like his brother?"

He meant Robert. In her mind's eye she pictured him and Charles together. *As alike as peas in the same pod.*

"Very," she said. "Except he was ill for most of our marriage. A terrible wasting sickness."

"Then why did he marry?"

"He wanted a son."

He waited, and she added the rest. Still painful.

"In that I failed him."

"Or he failed you."

That would be comforting to believe. She had often wondered if she, a young and healthy woman, hadn't conceived because she hadn't loved him. A punishment for not completely wiping the memory of this man's kiss from her heart?

Instead of grieving over what she couldn't have, she had lavished all her love on Georgina. And now...

"Do you believe in fate?" she asked.

"Some force that predetermines what will happen to us?"

"Yes."

"I knew men who did. They believed they would die, and so they did. Others believed they were charmed against death and acted as if they were."

"Were they? Charmed, I mean?"

"They died with the same frequency as those who thought they were fated."

A heartbeat of silence.

"Is that what you believe, Emma? That we were fated to meet here?"

"Here and now," she said. "At this time and place."

"For what end?" He sounded almost amused by the idea.

Poor, fanciful Emma.

"Because we are at another crossroads."

"Another?"

"When we met before, our lives were about to change. I was off to London and the Season, and you—" She stopped abruptly.

"I was bound for Spain."

Spain and war and all it had cost him. Far more than the slow death of her dreams that her marriage had cost her.

"Our lives changed forever that night," she said. "What we had known before was no more. Now again we face the ending of the lives we have known for the last dozen years. And incredibly, at this particular crossroads, we meet once more."

"A highly romantic notion, Emma." The deep voice was still touched with amusement, but it was not mocking.

"Perhaps. You will concede, however, that we *are* both here, and that we are both about to embark on a different phase of our lives."

"And you think fate has therefore thrown us together again?"

"Although you may prefer another term, I cannot but believe there is some purpose in this."

"And you believe you know what that purpose is."

It was not a question. The thread of gentle raillery she had heard before had disappeared. His face was as serious as it had been when she had turned and found him watching her.

This was the critical moment, and she knew it. Her mouth had gone dry, and her hands had begun to tremble, although she had unconsciously clasped them together at some time during the conversation.

She reminded herself that she had nothing to lose because she had nothing. Only a poor, faded dream. If she did not find the courage to tell him what she wanted, that is what it would always remain. A dream. When she wanted so much more.

"Take me with you," she said. "Take me to Wyckstead instead of going there alone."

CHAPTER SEVEN

SHE WASN'T SURE what reaction she had expected. Shock. Disbelief. Perhaps even ridicule.

After all, she had made no conditions and no demands. Only the one she might more properly have made twelve years ago when she had been a fanciful child. *Take me with you.*

"As what?" He had cut straight to the heart of what she had offered him.

"Whatever you will," she said simply.

"My mistress?" he mocked. "Is that what you want?"

"I want what I've never had. To be with the man I love. Is that so wrong?"

"The man you *love?* We met once for a few minutes years ago and little more than that here."

"I wasn't aware that the length of one's acquaintance had anything to do with falling in love."

"You aren't in love with me, Emma. You admitted as much. You're in love with the memory of that night. And with the memory of the man you met then."

"And now," she insisted stubbornly.

"Except that man no longer exists," he continued

ruthlessly, ignoring her disclaimer. "We are no longer those same two people."

"We could be."

"Beyond my powers of self-deception, I'm afraid."

"And what of me?"

She could see that he was thinking, as she was, about what she'd told him of her plans. Only a few days ago that seemed a future to be cherished. Comforting and serene. And now...

"I can't be what you want," he said.

"How do you know what I want?"

"You want the man who kissed you that night. I've told you. He doesn't exist."

"He does to me."

"Emma—"

"I may be the only person in the world to whom he still *does* exist. Doesn't that mean something to you?"

She wasn't sure that argument would convince him or drive him away, but she could tell she was losing. And she could not bear it.

"I'm not asking you for anything," she went on. "Nothing but a chance. Isn't it worth a chance?"

He said nothing for a long time. She held her breath, hardly daring to hope. And then he crossed the room with the same decisive stride with which he'd left her that night.

He stopped before her, searching her face as intently as she had examined his this morning. She did not allow her own to waver, determined not to look at that brutal scar.

Eventually the line into which his lips had been set relaxed. He took the remaining step that would close the distance between them and put his arm around her waist, drawing her to him with a pressure she could easily have resisted.

She never even thought about it. As she looked up at him, her lips parted, just as they had the first time he'd kissed her. Waiting. Wanting.

He gave her time to protest. She didn't, of course. There was not a single thought in her head that concerned objecting.

When his head began to lower, tilting to facilitate the kiss, her relief was so great that her knees went weak with it. Her hands found his shoulders, clinging to their solid strength as his mouth claimed hers. The first sweet touch of his lips, as warm and as experienced as she remembered them, made the support she had sought a necessity.

Her tongue answered his, a slow, primitive dance of advance and retreat. Nothing had changed about this. Nothing except the depth of her need.

His initial embrace had been tentative. With her response, he pulled her ruthlessly against the hard wall of his chest, and for the first time she became intimately aware of *his* needs.

Whatever doubts he had expressed about the wisdom of this, his body denied them. He wanted her. At least physically.

She was no innocent as she had been then. She knew how to assuage that need and to give him pleasure. Those were lessons she had learned in a hard school, but worth it all if she succeeded in convincing him not to leave her behind.

Her hand found the back of his head, fingers tangling in the long, silken strands. He deepened the kiss, his palm cupping possessively beneath the fullness of her breast while his thumb teased back and forth over the tip. Despite the double layers of fabric, gown and chemise, that covered it, the nipple tautened with pleasure.

Within her body, anticipation stirred—hot and sweet and hungry. A hunger she knew was strong enough to match his growing arousal. And to answer it.

His lips left hers, trailing slow, wet heat down her throat. She moaned, only a breath of sound, when they reached the curve of her breast, exposed by the low neckline of her dress. His fingers pushed aside the thin fabric of its bodice to allow him greater access, as his tongue delved into the shadowed hollow.

"Emma?"

The sound of her name was faint. Distant. Troubling. She was so caught up in what was happening between them, however, that for a few seconds she didn't want to think who could be calling her.

"Emma? Are you up here?"

Greystone was the first to react. His hands closed

around her shoulders, holding her away from him. Mouth open, the moisture of his kisses still on her lips and throat and breasts, she stared up at him in shock, questioning his desertion.

"Emma?"

Georgie. And the sound of her voice seemed much nearer now. Almost as if she were in the same room.

"Go to her," he ordered harshly.

She shook her head, her eyes on his.

"Do it now. Before she comes in here."

Surely she had as much right to happiness as Georgina. And he as much as Jamie.

"It doesn't matter—" she began.

"It matters to me, damn it. Now go."

"I don't care if she finds us together."

"*I* care."

"If it's because of this—" She reached out to touch the marred profile.

He jerked his head back, avoiding her fingers. Then, using her shoulders, he turned her and shoved her toward the door that led out of his suite. Still drugged by the sensual spell of the kiss, she staggered under the force with which he had pushed her away from him.

As soon as she regained her balance, she turned, bewildered by the suddenness of what had just happened. The door to the bedroom slammed shut between them with a ferocity that made her jump.

"Emma? I have something wonderful to tell you."

The betrothal. She had completely forgotten about the betrothal.

She put the backs of her fingers against her lips, as if she could wipe away the evidence of his kiss. For someone who knew her as well as Georgie did, it would surely be obvious that *something* had happened.

She would never be able to imagine, however, that her stepmother had just boldly offered herself to a man she had seen only a few times in the course of the last dozen years. No one who knew her could imagine that.

"Emma?"

"Coming," she called.

Her voice sounded strange to her own ears, but that was the least of her concerns. She glanced down, smoothing her hands over the disarrayed bodice.

Then she took a final look toward the bedroom where Alex had disappeared. When she turned back again, Georgina was standing in the open doorway to the sitting room.

"Whatever are you doing up here?" A small furrow formed between the smooth winged brows as she examined the room.

"Books," Emma said, a trifle breathlessly. "Jamie told me I might borrow some."

Georgie scanned the half-emptied shelves. "It

seems someone else has had the same idea. What is this place?''

''The earl's library. Jamie *did* say he was scholarly.''

''It looks as if someone has been packing them.'' Georgina walked over to a box on the floor partially filled with books.

''I believe he's planning to move to another of his properties. After the wedding, of course.''

''You know,'' Georgina accused. She crossed the room, holding out both hands, which Emma quickly took in hers. ''Did Jamie tell you? I wanted you to be the first to hear, but I couldn't find you. I looked all over the house.''

''I take it then, it's official,'' Emma said, pulling her close to press a kiss against her cheek.

She had been afraid Georgie would somehow discern her emotional upheaval. Lost in the euphoria of the moment, her stepdaughter seemed oblivious to anything other than her own happiness.

Which was only right. Nothing should be allowed to dim her joy in this day.

''It's to be announced at dinner. Jamie says there will be a more formal entertainment in the near future to inform the people of the district, but yes, it's official.''

''I could not be more delighted.''

''Then come downstairs and help me choose what to wear. I want to look my best. Do you think, since it is his own brother's engagement, that the earl might join us?''

"I shouldn't expect it," Emma said. "He's given his approval to the match, and presumably his blessing. That's probably all you can count on."

All you can count on. The words seemed prophetic, although for one brief moment...

One brief moment. It seemed as if those were all they were to have. Two kisses separated by a dozen years of loneliness. And all that lay ahead for either of them—

"I'm thinking it must be the silver gauze," Georgina said, pulling her toward the door by their joined hands, "although Jamie has seen it at least three times."

"He'll remember nothing about it except how beautifully it becomes you," Emma said, throwing a last, longing look at the closed bedroom door.

"Is something wrong? You aren't sad to be losing me, are you? You know that I want you to live here with us. The countess would welcome your company, as you know I would."

"Dear goose," Emma said, squeezing her fingers. "My plans are quite firm. You know I'm not sad, especially since Jamie seems head over heels in love with you and you with him. What more could any mother ask?"

"Then wish me happy?" Georgina teased with a smile.

"With all my heart," Emma said truthfully as she

closed the door to the earl's sitting room behind them.

She could not begrudge Georgie's happiness, even if she envied it. And in acknowledging that, she understood more than ever Greystone's decision to remove to Wyckstead.

ISN'T IT WORTH a chance?

For a moment at least he had believed it might be. And then the world, in the form of Georgina Stanfield, had invaded that ridiculous fantasy.

Fantasy? Emma offered herself without condition. She melted into your arms, her mouth eager to accept your kiss. Why then was the chance she had talked about a fantasy?

Because they barely knew one another. And he was too long accustomed to his solitude. To his isolation. Where he was safe from screaming children and maids who crossed themselves.

She did neither. She kissed you. Not as if you were a monster, but a man.

I may be the only person in the world to whom that man still exists. Emma's words. Except he knew, if she didn't, how far removed he now was from being that man.

And you can go on being exactly who you are now. An outcast from society by your own design, or…

Or what? A man who wasn't forced to face a

lonely future, one that was a reflection of an equally lonely past? Was that possible?

Isn't it worth a chance?

The very idea was ridiculous, he reminded himself as he turned to retrace his path across the bedroom. That's all he had done since she'd left. From the armoire on one side to the wide, bowed window on the other. Back and forth, as the memories and the promises warred in his brain.

They hardly knew one another.

I wasn't aware that the length of one's acquaintance had anything to do with falling in love.

What kind of life could she have with him? A prisoner to his dread. It was one thing for him to choose isolation, but what kind of life would that be for Emma?

My governess has a cottage, you see…

Anything would be better than that for someone as alive as Emma. As sexual. Even as his brain formed the word, his groin tightened with desire for her.

Isn't it worth a chance?

Why not? She could always leave. No commitments for either of them. If it didn't work out—

Then she would be ruined. Her good name and reputation left in tatters. That was not a role he could condemn her to.

Nor himself, he realized. He had been reared in a tradition of honor. Of protecting women. Of guarding their reputations rather than destroying them.

He could not make Emma his mistress, no matter what she offered. Neither could he make her his wife and condemn her to a lifetime of hiding.

And that *was* what he had done all these years, he acknowledged. He had hidden.

Because a child reacted as a child? Or because, deep inside, you're a coward?

Far easier to charge into battle than to face the revulsion in a stranger's eyes. Far easier to bury himself in a book. Philosophy. History. Something besides life. Something not nearly so painful.

Except apparently it didn't have to be. Not with Emma.

Isn't it worth a chance?

Was it? Could it be?

There were no mirrors in his rooms. There was, however, an alternative to them. One he normally avoided.

Now he took the two steps that would bring him to the window overlooking the entrance to Leighton Hall. When he had stood beside it before, watching his brother's guests arrive, it had been the result of an idle curiosity. This was a deliberate and calculated action. And a necessary one.

The drive and the steps below were deserted, although the servants, anticipating the arrival of those who had been invited to join the engagement celebration, had placed torches in the sconces on either side of the entryway. Beyond their light, night had fallen with summer's swiftness after the long twilight.

The windowpanes would be dark enough for his purposes. Slowly he raised his eyes until they were focused on his own reflection. *Through a glass, darkly.* The image was far from clear, but it sufficed.

An unruly mass of long, untrimmed hair. An empty eye socket. The scar's distortion of muscle and skin. A monster and not a man.

You want the man who kissed you that night, he had said. *I told you. He doesn't exist.*

The reflection he was staring at made that painfully obvious.

I may be the only person in the world to whom he still does exist. Doesn't that mean something to you?

Only that the present reality could never live up to the memory she'd cherished all these years.

Forgive me, Emma.

There was no way they could go back. And even if they could, would it be wise?

They had been two strangers seeking shelter from a storm, and they had found instead one brief, perfect moment together. Now they were the lonely survivors of other kinds of storms, seeking not perfection or romantic fantasy, but safety.

Long before Emma had arrived at Leighton, they had both decided where that lay. It wasn't in being together.

Isn't it worth a chance?

The Earl of Greystone leaned forward, putting his forehead against the cold glass of the windowpane, as the phrase that had haunted him all afternoon repeated over and over in his head.

CHAPTER EIGHT

IN THE END, Georgina had decided on the silver gauze. Emma thought she had never been more beautiful.

She would make a magnificent countess. More importantly—at least from Emma's perspective, which was heightened by her own situation—Georgie had made a love match.

"To the bride and groom," Charles boomed. He was obviously very pleased with himself.

Their number at dinner had been increased by invitations sent to a select few in the local society. Glasses were raised around the table as Charles's toast was echoed by a chorus of voices. The bride-to-be's blush this time was as pronounced as her betrothed's.

The assembly had begun to sip the wine with which the toast had been made when the double doors of the dining room were flung open. Although there were myriad wax candles in the chandelier, as well along the wall and on the table itself, it took a few seconds for the presence of the newcomer to be noted all down the long table.

As it was, silence followed, moving among the

chattering guests like frost through a garden. In less than a minute there was not a breath of sound in the room. Every eye was fastened on the man who stood in the doorway.

"Ladies and gentlemen," Jamie said, rising from his place at the head of the table, "may I present my brother, the Earl of Greystone."

Alex was impeccably dressed, but not in attire suited for a dinner party. A coat of navy superfine stretched across the shoulders Emma had admired the first time she'd seen them. Fawn pantaloons fit closely over the flat belly and emphasized muscled horseman's thighs. The white cravat at his throat, elegantly yet simply tied, set off his dark coloring. Even the thick, black hair had been neatly trimmed.

He looked every inch the English lord. Except for the scar and the midnight patch he wore over the damaged eye. They gave him a rakish, buccaneering air. From the soft stirrings around the table, that was not lost on the feminine half of the company.

"We were toasting the engagement of these fine young people," Charles instructed as if *he* were the host. "Join us, Greystone."

Emma wondered if her brother-in-law had yet realized the implications of the earl's appearance for his carefully negotiated marriage settlements. It must surely be obvious to him by now that, despite what he had been led to believe, Greystone was quite capable of siring children of his own.

The thought sent a shiver of excitement through her body.

"Thank you, no," Alex said, his gaze never leaving Emma's face. "My brother knows that I wish him every happiness."

Her heart had begun to behave in a most extraordinary way. She had come to the conclusion, the only one that seemed to fit the parameters of the situation, that he might have come here for her.

"Miss Stanfield," the earl went on, releasing Emma from the intensity of his gaze long enough to incline his head in Georgina's direction. "To your happiness."

"Thank you, sir." Georgie's voice was perfectly modulated, though her eyes had widened. "Coming from Jamie's brother, that means a great deal."

"Please join us," her fiancé urged, indicating the chair he had been sitting in at the head of the table. "The place is rightfully yours."

The corners of the Alex's mouth slanted upward as he looked at his brother. He put his hand on the younger man's shoulder.

"I wish you every happiness, Jamie. I'm afraid that tonight, however, I have pressing business of my own. I beg you will forgive me for not joining your celebration."

"Of course," Jamie stammered.

"Mother, ladies and gentlemen, I beg pardon for intruding on your dinner. I have come for Lady Barrington."

The fascinated gazes that had been locked on Alex since his arrival now turned, with the precision of mechanical toys, toward her.

"If she is still willing to come with me," he added.

"What the devil is this? Emma?" Charles demanded. Receiving no answer, he turned back to the earl. "Go with you?" he repeated as if he had just realized the significance of that. "Go with you where?"

"To Scotland. If she will."

Although her knees felt as weak as they had this afternoon, Emma forced herself to her feet, her eyes still locked on his.

"To Scotland? You can't mean— Look here, Greystone—"

"Yes," Emma said.

The word betrayed nothing of what she felt. It seemed as calm and as steady as any agreement she had ever made in her life. As ordinary.

"To Scotland?" Jamie echoed, sounding as flummoxed by the turn of events as her brother-in-law did. "You can't mean—"

"Exactly," Alex said decisively. "We are at a crossroads, you see. Choices must be made."

"You're mad," Charles blustered.

"Quite," Alex agreed calmly.

"Emma, I forbid you to go with this man."

"I'm sorry, Charles," she said, making her way along the side of the table before Greystone could change his mind. She stopped long enough to bend and kiss Georgie on the cheek. "Promise me you will be incredibly happy."

"Only if you will promise me the same," Georgina said.

"You can't do this," Charles said again.

"I can't do anything else," Emma assured him as she passed behind his chair.

She held out her hand to Alex. He took it in his, strong fingers fastening around hers with a reassuring firmness. For an instant she feared that he intended to pull her into his arms in front of the entire company. Luckily, he seemed to come to his senses, simply grasping her hand tightly as he bowed to his mother and then to her brother-in-law.

"Forgive me, but it was meant to be, you see. I have it on the best authority that we are fated to be together. I shall take very good care of her, I promise you."

"The devil you say—" Charles began again.

By that time Alex had swept her out through the double doors and into the hallway. Her feet barely touched the marble floor as, still holding hands, they ran across it like children released from lessons.

He didn't stop until they were outside, the rain-washed air so fresh it seemed to glisten in the light from the torches on either side of the entryway. A carriage with a team of four matched bays stood in the drive below.

Instead of leading her down the steps to the waiting coach, Alex gathered her into his arms, putting his cheek against hers as he held her. Whether by design or accident, it was the unmarred profile. Although he was freshly shaven, there was a slight masculine abrasiveness that was both sensual and exciting.

After a moment he lifted his head, looking down into her eyes. "I am a damned poor excuse for a Lochinvar."

"It's all right. I wasn't the bride."

"You will be."

"Yes, I know," she said, standing on tiptoe to touch her lips to his. "But…it's a very long way to the Border. A journey that might more safely be made in the daylight. And since I'm fairly certain Charles doesn't intend to pack up his pistols and follow us…"

"Just what are you suggesting, my darling, managing Emma?"

"You have a house, I believe."

"Wyckstead. It hardly suited to a—" He stopped abruptly, apparently unwilling to employ any of the current terminology for what she was suggesting.

"To a honeymoon?" she supplied instead.

"Actually, it's ideally suited for a honeymoon. Small, isolated, and empty, except for the caretaker, who lives in a cottage on the grounds."

"Perfect," Emma said.

She knew it would be. After all, it was fated.

WHATEVER DOUBTS Alex had once had seemed to have disappeared. He had made the decision to come back to Leighton and offer for her. Not only that, he had put whatever soul-searching that required behind him. Even her suggestion that they spend the night at Wyckstead had evoked no arguments.

In for a penny, in for a pound, Emma thought, following him through the darkness of the small house. That must have become her motto as well, since she had left Leighton with nothing but the clothes on her back and a few dusty dreams.

"In here," Alex said. "Mind your step."

In the moonlit dimness she could see the hand he held out to her, but little else. His fingers closed 'round hers, trustingly offered, to guide her past the obstacles in their path. As soon as they were inside the room, he released her. She waited, following his movements by sound alone, as he lit candles.

Provided with illumination, she had her first glimpse of her new home. It would have been obvious, even had she not known, that he was still in the process of moving in.

Boxes were stacked haphazardly along the four walls of the room, but its dominant feature, a huge bed with old-fashioned crimson hangings, was invitingly empty. The small, awkward silence after he had finished lighting the candles was almost certainly the result of their mutual awareness of it.

"Are you sure—" he began.

Emma cut him off before his doubts could resurface.

"Completely. And even if you are not, it's far too late to back out now. You have proposed in front of a score of people. You have no choice but to make an honest woman of me. Just not tonight, if you please."

"If not marriage, then what *did* you have in mind for tonight?"

The amusement that had once delighted her was back in the deep voice. And she vowed that as long as he would let her, she would keep it there.

"To make up for all those other nights," she said bravely.

Years of empty nights. Although she had not had the courage to speculate before, she wondered now if his had been equally lonely.

"I can't believe you're here," he said. "I keep thinking I'll wake up and this will all be a dream."

Smiling, she held out her hand to him. "Flesh and blood. Quite substantial. And I have no intention of going anywhere."

He closed the distance between them, taking her fingers into his once more. He brought them to his lips, his eyes holding hers above their joined hands.

"The entire time I was dressing tonight, I tried to imagine what I would do if you said no."

"I should far rather you concentrate on what you will do now that I've said yes."

"There was *never,*" he said softly, "any question about that."

HE HAD UNDRESSED HER by candlelight, amused to discover he had not forgotten the intricacies of female attire. And more than a little surprised to find the hooks and ribbon fastenings hadn't changed appreciably during the last dozen years.

And it was still a miracle to him that, although he had been vigilant to detect the slightest reluctance on her part, Emma didn't find his touch repugnant. Quite the opposite, actually.

One snowy night, he had fallen in love with a seventeen-year-old virgin. For some reason he had expected Emma's responses to be the same as if she still were that green girl. He had been delighted to find they were not.

After all, she had been married for several years. There would be no unpleasant revelations as to what was about to happen between them. Only pleasant ones, he prayed.

At last he knelt to remove her stockings, holding the second narrow, high-arched foot in his hand a moment after he'd stripped away the wisp of silk that had covered it. Then his gaze traveled unhurriedly upward. The flames of the candles gilded the smooth, white skin, painting it with luminescence as they emphasized slender curves and darkened mysteriously the shadowed places of her body.

In their soft light, she looked like Botticelli's

Venus, stepping from the sea at dawn, naked and perfect. It seemed a sacrilege that she should belong to someone like him.

"You are *so* beautiful," he whispered, his throat aching with emotion.

"Beauty is in the eye of the beholder. You look at me with love, and that makes you *think* me beautiful."

"*Not* up to your usual standards, Emma."

"I beg your pardon?"

"That homily is hardly subtle enough for you."

"Would you believe me if I had said *you* are beautiful?"

He laughed at the assertion, releasing her foot and rising to face her.

"You are to me." Her eyes, blue-black in the half light, did not echo his laughter. "This," she said, putting the fingers of her left hand against the undamaged half of his face. "*And* this." Her other hand touched the scarred cheek, cupping his chin between them.

He forced himself not to flinch away, but after a moment, sensing his discomfort, she released him. She put her arms around his neck, leaning her cheek against his chest. Unable to resist, he gathered her to him, holding her next to his heart.

"It doesn't matter if you believe me," she said. "I have years to convince you. Eventually—"

Before she could complete the promise, he bent, slipping his arm under her knees to lift her off her feet. And when he laid her in the center of the high bed, he never even thought about pulling the crimson hangings to hide himself from the light.

SHE KNEW from the first that this would be no hurried coupling like those she had once endured. With his hands and lips and tongue, Alex had worshiped her body, exploring every sensitive, secret hollow. Claiming them for his own.

"Here." His breath, warm and moist, teased against her throat. "And now," he said, positioning his knee between hers.

As if they possessed a will of her own, her legs fell apart wantonly. Overwhelmed by feelings she had never before experienced, she was beyond resistance. Beyond all thought of denying him anything.

Not that she wanted to. His hands, hard and masculine, had caressed her skin knowingly as his mouth trailed wet heat over the most intimate parts of her body. And she had uttered not one word of protest. Nor did she now.

Building within her had been something for which she had no name. Nor any frame of reference.

Pure sensation, it had grown more demanding as he continued to touch her. Each stroke of his fingers, each deliberate flick of his tongue, had increased the pressure for a release she could not yet imagine but knew she wanted.

"Yes," she begged softly, without any understanding of what it was she asked. She knew only that he alone could provide it.

As he moved over her body in the candlelit darkness, she looked up into his face. For an instant the profile that bore the scar was shadowed, hidden by an accident of the lighting, so that he seemed again the dashing young soldier she had met long ago.

With his first downward thrust, unerring and powerful, all she had experienced between that night and this fell away. She was again the girl who had stood on the snow-swept balcony and dreamed. Of this. Of him.

Then, in response to the rhythmic motion of his hips, the sensation that had trembled inside her lower body began to spread. Like molten gold it ran, burning along newly awakened nerves, searing muscle and bone.

Her hips began to move in answer to his. Trying to bring him closer. To hold him to her.

As her body responded, her mind spiraled away into the darkness. Incapable of coherent thought. Incapable of anything beyond reacting to the relentless demands he was making.

"Now," he said again, the words hoarse and gasping.

He closed his eyes and put his forehead against hers, supporting the weight of his upper body on his elbows. The motion of his hips never slowed. Driving. Demanding. Until it seemed as if he were pounding for entrance against the very walls of her soul.

For a fraction of a second she was frightened by what was happening. And then, as if a dam had broken apart, the force that had been building inside released in a white-hot flood.

It washed over her in wave after wave of feeling, as relentless, as inexorable, as the thrusts that had created them. Her mouth opened, but she didn't recognize the wordless cry that emerged as coming from her lips.

In the very midst of her extremity, his body seemed to explode inside hers. Convulsion after convulsion shivered through his frame. Caught in her own maelstrom of sensation, she was powerless to do anything but hold him, nails digging into the broad shoulders that strained above her.

His answering cry, when it came, was sheer exaltation. He raised his head, throwing it back so that the tendons in his neck were exposed.

By then, the emotion that had gripped her, making her mindless, had already begun to ease. She could breathe again. And she could think.

Her hand found the back of his head, fingers tangling in the newly cropped hair. Urging it downward.

He obeyed, his mouth closing over hers with a frenzied possession. The kiss ravaged, claiming her lips as he had just claimed her body. Branding them as he had branded it.

Gradually the intensity lessened, becoming finally a series of feather-light touches. Eyelids. Temples. The hollow in her throat, pulsing with the aftermath of what they had shared.

The last of those kisses was placed gently on the tip of her nose. He pushed himself up, once more looking down into her eyes. She smiled at him, knowing that whatever argument he might have made about their being together was forever moot.

What had just happened between them was so right, so perfect, it had to have erased any doubts he harbored about her feelings for him. Or his for her.

"I think I prefer you as a wanton."

"As opposed to an honest woman?" she asked, her smile widening.

"As opposed to a girl on the way to her first Season."

"A hundred years ago."

"Hardly that. Only a lifetime."

"Or two."

"It's all right. In *this* lifetime we can be sure at last we've made the right choices."

"Do you remember what you called me that night?"

"At the inn?" A crease formed between his brows.

She smoothed it with her finger and then boldly traced along the ribbon that held the patch in place.

"You said I was a fortune hunter."

He laughed. "And I had none to offer you. A penniless soldier on the way to war."

"Penniless?" she mocked.

"Virtually. A younger son. I believe I confessed as much."

"And now you have the fortune I needed then."

"It's yours," he said promptly.

"I already have my fortune, thank you. One that has nothing to do with titles or estates, and very much to do with a man brave enough to face down a dinner party in order to elope with an elderly widow."

His shout of laughter was unrestrained. And she smiled to hear it. This was the way he should always be. The way he had been that night. Young and carefree and unmarked by all that was to come.

"Poor Charles," she said. "He'll be so disappointed, he may go into a decline."

"Charles? Why should Charles be disappointed?"

"He believed he had secured an earldom for Georgina. And now, I'm afraid…" She paused delicately.

"And now?" he prompted, smiling.

"I do believe the Earl of Greystone has a plan to produce a successor to his title on his own."

"How *very* well you know me," Alex said. "And on such short acquaintance."

"The length of one's acquaintance—"

"Has nothing to do with falling in love," he finished for her.

Then his lips descended, covering hers. And even the redoubtable Lady Barrington was left with nothing to say.

Dear Friend,

As a prelude to this letter, I share with you the words of Miss Elizabeth Shelley, sister of the renowned Percy Bysshe. As I am certain you will agree, our wise Elizabeth has the right of things.

> When Hope, gay deceiver, in pleasure is drest,
> How oft comes a stroke that may rob us of rest.
> When we think ourselves safe, and the goal near at hand,
> Like a vessel just landing, we're wrecked on the strand.

You will doubtless consider me wildly impulsive when you begin to read this account of my actions to avoid such a wrecking. However, before you judge me heedless, I urge you to recall the time when you were a shy girl not yet in long skirts and first discovering a fascination for the opposite gender. Was there not a certain young gent who stirred your youthful heart with his merry laughter? A teasing gesture here or a fleeting look of interest there might well have prompted you to wish away the years between that day and your age of choosing a mate. Come now, you know it is so! Such were my early encounters with the young lord, Hugh Richfield.

I would ask you to imagine yourself in a quandary such as mine. Would you surrender, hand to head, and faint into the arms of a blackguard bent upon stealing your virtue and your fortune? I should think not! Well, neither shall I, my friend, you may count upon that. I figure I can do no worse choosing for myself than in having a husband thrust himself upon me by force. And since I must select quite swiftly to avoid disaster, what better candidate than the fellow I once admired above all? As you know, the *Word of a Gentleman* is his bond and Richfield may be trusted if he gives his. At least, I think he can.

Come, let us see how I fare in my first great adventure. Who knows? There might come a day when you suffer a like dilemma and must pluck up your courage and assert yourself. If nothing else, I would wish to entertain you for a while with these scribblings of my most unusual behavior, and I do have hope that you shall enjoy them.

Yr. Servant,
Miss Clarissa Fortesque

P.S. If you desire to remark on my wisdom or folly, please post your reply to me upon the Guestbook of my mentor, Lyn Stone. Her direction is as follows: http://www.eclectics.com/lynstone/.

WORD OF A GENTLEMAN
Lyn Stone

For Allen, who traveled to Gretna Green with me
and stood over the anvil. Here's to our adventure,
elopement and hasty wedding! I could not have chosen better.

CHAPTER ONE

London—September 1815

"SURRENDER," he taunted, laughing at her, "or scream the house down. Either way, you're mine." His bruising fingers bit into her upper arms. His cigar-fouled breath rushed in and out against her face as she struggled. "Rather be mastered, eh?" he growled.

Clarissa beat against his broad chest, twisting violently to avoid his kiss, gritting her teeth against the urge to cry for help. No one must hear. No one must come outside now or she was lost. That was his plan, of course.

In desperation, she kicked at his shins and only succeeded in hurting her toes. He felt hard against her through the supple sarcenet of her skirt. Instinctively, she jerked up her knee and connected with that most sensitive part of him.

Trenton yelped, released her and doubled forward, groaning pitifully.

Clarissa dashed across the short expanse of flagstones, praying she could make it into the house without being seen.

Hair askew, gown in disarray, she flew past the open doors leading out from the lesser ballroom, hoping against hope no one in there would be looking out. It was early yet. Not all the guests had arrived and, hopefully, those who had would be focused on the entrance to greet the others. Why in the name of heaven had she thought to await Richfield on the terrace?

She reached a small door that led to the servants' stair and ducked inside, not daring to slow her steps or look over her shoulder. Breathless, gasping, she hurried up to the bedroom the Dicksons had so kindly provided her, rushed inside and twisted the key in the lock.

For a long moment she braced her back against the door, palms flat against it, her chest heaving like a bellows. But she couldn't tarry here. She couldn't hide all evening, or even for very long. She would be missed.

Quickly, Clarissa gathered her wits and pushed away from the door. She made hasty repairs to her appearance with shaking hands, sucked in deep breaths to calm herself as best she could. Hopefully, Trenton would be gone when she rejoined the party in progress. No one must know. And if the plan she had formed yesterday to prevent a disastrous union with her black-hearted cousin ran its proper course, no one ever would.

Someone knocked. Clarissa glanced about in desperation for a way out. The window was entirely too high off the ground for her to jump out. There was no door connecting to another room. Trapped. The door handle turned, then rattled frantically.

"Clarissa Fortesque, open this door immediately! Why is it locked? Are you ill?"

Phyllis. Thank God. Clarissa pressed a hand against her pounding heart and exhaled with sharp relief. Phyllis Dickson was the best friend in the world, but not even she could know what had nearly happened. *Nearly* would be quite enough to dash the plan. "Just a moment," Clarissa called out to her friend, made a quick final appraisal of her looks in the mirror and went to unlock her door.

"Where were you?" Phyllis demanded. "I looked around and you were nowhere to be found. And neither did I see your cousin, Trenton. Mother should not have invited him tonight. Not to mention that he gave you such a fright at your uncle's, the man's a pretentious bore."

Worse than a bore, Clarissa thought. And no, he should never have received an invitation. But Lady Dickson had insisted upon including the only relative Clarissa had left who was able to attend. She readjusted a hairpin, tugged on her half-gloves and plundered the clutter of the dressing table for her fan. "Shall we go?"

"Are you certain you're all right, dear? You look rather pale." Phyllis took her arm as they traversed the upper hallway to the wide staircase.

Clarissa forced a smile. "I'm perfectly well. I

merely went up to find other slippers. The blue ones pinch my toes. Could we forget my boorish relative and join the others now?'' she asked brightly and smiled at Phyllis as though nothing untoward had happened. ''As you know, I have important business to conduct.'' Her knees trembled so, she had to focus her full attention on the treads beneath her feet and grip the banister with one hand.

''Confess, Clarissa. Did your cousin speak with you tonight?'' Phyllis persisted, the look of concern still clouding her pretty features. ''Did he threaten you or something? We could tell Father.''

Clarissa took her time answering as they approached the door to the ballroom where the guests were gathered. ''No need. Trenton simply insisted that I change my mind about his proposal.''

''You won't, will you?''

Clarissa laughed and shot Phyllis a wry look.

''I thought not. Still and all, you had best stay visible and not allow him to get you alone. Heaven knows what he might try.''

''Has Richfield arrived yet?'' Clarissa asked, changing the subject lest she be tempted to confide and ask for comfort.

''Yes. See? There he is with Harry and the boys. But I wish he hadn't come. You cannot really mean to propose marriage to him, Clarissa. Doing something this outrageous is so unlike you.''

''I have decided it is much better to be the hammer than the nail.''

Oh, God, and there he was! She had not seen him for years. Her loss, she thought with a rueful smile as she appraised him.

He stood across the room conversing with his companions, the lot resplendent in their evening clothes, all handsome as sin and almost surely guilty of committing a few.

"A lofty thought, but it *is* too bold a move, even for you," Phyllis declared with a sharp shake of her head.

"I admit I had rather not resort to such a drastic measure, but I have little choice. The moment Uncle James gives up the ghost, I shall become Trenton's ward. That could happen any day now and I must act before it does."

That sounded uncaring of her, Clarissa realized, and regretted being so forthright about it. But it was not as if she knew her uncle well. He had spent most of his adult life in seclusion. She had only met the man twice, and briefly then. She was, however, extremely grateful to him for not exercising his power over her these last ten years since she had been orphaned and legally, if not actually, under his supervision.

If so inclined, he could have arranged her life however he wanted before she was old enough to protest, but he had not. Instead he had left her there at school. She felt almost certain Uncle James had completely forgotten she existed. Thank goodness.

Unfortunately, the Hopewell Female Academy,

where she had remained after finishing her studies and accepted a teaching position, had closed down this past month due to lack of funds. Now here she was with no employment, no home, and with the man currently holding her wardship likely to die at any moment.

She would not see a farthing of the inheritance her parents had left her unless she married someone who would claim and manage it for her. Her cousin Trenton had made it very clear who that someone was to be.

"I understand your rush." Phyllis sighed. "But should you marry *him?*" She inclined her head toward the man in question. "You know Harry says Richfield's become nothing short of a madman with no thought of caution. He thrives upon danger. They say he'll do anything on a dare and attempt any feat to win a bet. If you must do this thing, at least choose an adult."

Clarissa smiled, brushing the edge of her lace-trimmed fan against her chin as she surveyed the room. She felt much calmer now. Apparently, Trenton had left the party. "Ah, but that is the beauty of it, Phyllis. Richfield will be more concerned with seeking excitement than with managing investments, wouldn't you think? Tending the wife's business affairs would be deadly dull for a fellow like him."

Phyllis looked doubtful. "Harry has worlds of admiration for the man's courage, very nearly idolizes the fellow. However, he did caution me roundly about him several times. You will have noticed Harry's not invited him to our house until this evening. Though he has always liked Richfield enormously, I suspect Harry argued with Mother over that invitation.''

Clarissa shrugged. ''I wish *we* had argued with her over the issuance of Trenton's.''

''I did, but she said it was only proper to ask him. You made me vow not to tell anyone what he was up to.''

''Hmm. No harm done.'' But there almost had been tonight. If anyone had seen them on the terrace... She shook off the thought and picked up the issue of Richfield's welcome or lack of it. ''I can see Harry's point, Phyllis. Richfield would never do as a suitor for you. However, he is precisely what I require.''

Phyllis shrugged. ''I fail to see how you would be any better served with Richfield running through your inheritance than if Trenton acquired the power to do so.''

''At least Hugh Richfield will be *my* choice. If my fortune is to buy me a husband, then I shall do the shopping, thank you very much.''

''If you believe he can be purchased like a hunter at Tattersalls, how on earth can you ever trust him? I doubt he has much, if any, income since he left the army. Rumor has it his elder brother squandered the family wealth.''

Clarissa nodded. ''Common knowledge. So Richfield should leap at the opportunity to gain a wealthy wife. So long as I hold my own purse strings, I can accept his motive for marrying me. No other man I know might allow me to conduct my own affairs, but *he* will." She could not take her eyes off the man.

"Wild and foolish he may be," she admitted to Phyllis, "but he is a gentleman for all that. I overheard him say once that his word is his bond, that honor is everything, the only commodity that matters for a man. Before we marry, I shall extract his promise that what is mine shall remain mine, save for the amount I shall settle on him for his loss of bachelorhood. He will keep his word."

Phyllis scoffed. "You have not even seen him since you were fifteen. And what was he then? Not quite twenty? He's a man now, no longer some callow youth full of lofty ideals. How can you know he will stand by a promise even if he gives it?"

"I *do* know," Clarissa assured her, sounding a great deal more confident than she felt. She tamped down the frisson of doubt that chilled her. "Now how shall I get him alone to do this deed? It must be tonight or else I shall lose my courage." Or her only chance, if Trenton had his way. "You will help?"

Phyllis groaned softly. "If you insist, I suppose I have no choice. Come along."

"No," Clarissa said, pulling back, shy of approaching him directly when the others were around to hear. "I shall wait here. You tell him I need to speak with him in private."

The gathering Phyllis's parents were hosting at Dickson House tonight was relatively small. Only twenty guests and family attended the impromptu celebration of Harry's coming safely home after the victory at Waterloo.

So many were lost. Thousands dead. She wondered whether anyone had celebrated Hugh Richfield's miraculous return. He did not seem to mind if they had not. That casual elegance he had exhibited even as a boy had not changed. Nor had his indolent grin. If anything, the years had enhanced both.

Clarissa knew, on the other hand, that she was much different now. A great deal more confident than she had used to be. She musn't allow her shyness to return after working so hard to overcome it.

She waited impatiently as her friend went forward to set the plan in motion. Phyllis paused briefly to speak to other guests, then excused herself and continued on to where Hugh Richfield stood with his friends.

John Bernard drifted away from the group, obviously trailing after Lady Hermoine, the Menchard heiress who was also a good friend to Phyllis. Hugh leaned forward and muttered some aside to Cole Fletcher who promptly laughed aloud. Harry Dickson turned aside, comically rolling his eyes in mock horror.

Phyllis's brother Harry was a good fellow by anyone's standards, though not the sort Clarissa wanted to wed. He was too responsible, too in-charge. Besides, he only saw her as another sister.

And Cole Fletcher was no candidate, either. He had suffered an obvious tendre for Phyllis when they were much younger and apparently still did. That left only Richfield if she was to choose a man she knew anything at all about. Not that she knew much of him, either, but she had decided what she did know would have to suffice.

The plain truth remained that she had met very few men in her life. There had been no coming out in society for her. No balls, no royal introductions, no courting. No social life at all save for what Phyllis had provided with her kind invitations over the years.

How merry the lads looked tonight, not a care in the world, it seemed. Soldiers fresh from their victory over the French at Waterloo, happy to be alive, brimming with the knowledge that they were being noticed by every female in attendance and admired by every man.

Clarissa envied their carefree state. She wondered briefly if Hugh Richfield would be willing to give that up to marry a solemn old maid of twenty-two for any price. Well, she would soon know.

Phyllis reached the men just then, smiling sweetly as Hugh, then Cole, bowed over her hand with exaggerated courtesy. Harry leaned forward with some sally that set them laughing again. Phyllis giggled and tapped her brother on the shoulder lightly with her fan.

They were a pretty pair, through and through, the Dickson offspring, fair as May with bright dispositions to match. One could not help but love them. All their friends were much the same except for Richfield and herself. Oh, he was golden, too, that one, but there was also an element of mystery to him that set him apart.

Perhaps that was what drew her to him, that difference. But her own dark looks—brown eyes and hair the color of coal, skin that tended to darken in the sun—made her the true anomaly when she was seen among them. She had never fit in.

Clarissa did admit she'd developed an infatuation for Hugh Richfield she was not certain she had shaken off even now. That was one reason she had chosen him to wed, but certainly not the most crucial one. She knew better than to choose with her heart.

No, she had deliberately selected Hugh for his honor, but more so for his devil-may-care ways and total disregard for impressing those around him. Given his current reputation, he would not be overly fond of responsibility and therefore would not wrest it from her.

Hugh was extremely handsome, even more so than when he was nineteen and the object of her every fantasy, so she must be on her guard. Simply looking at him made her want to sigh as she used to do when she was a girl and smitten with him. She wished she were close enough to see those amber eyes of his as she recalled the way they had always sparkled with humor.

As if he were attuned to her very thoughts, he turned and looked her straight in the eye from across the room. Her heart pounded like an urgent fist against a door.

Phyllis had been whispering to him, no doubt on Clarissa's behalf. His expression, the slight tilt of his head, indicated interest. Or at least curiosity.

She pasted on a smile though her face felt stiff with trepidation. Clarissa was about to attempt something no woman of quality should even think of doing. What would he think of her then?

With an infinitesimal nod in her direction and a pointed look toward the door leading out of the ballroom, he abruptly deserted Phyllis, Harry and Cole. Clarissa waited a few seconds, then followed him.

When she reached the foyer, she looked both ways to see whether he was leaving the house or had gone up the stairs. She saw him immediately, waiting at the far end of the hallway, well beyond the staircase, half inside the doorway to the library. The moment she spied him, he disappeared from view as if challenging her to join him.

Glancing around her, carefully ensuring that she was not observed, she sidled down to the dimly lit end of the corridor and slipped into the room where he waited.

The library, being somewhat out of the way, generally remained closed when the Dicksons entertained. Good. They should not be interrupted.

She sucked in a deep breath, smoothed the fabric of her new blue gown and raked her teeth over her lips to heighten their color.

How she dreaded change of any sort, but now she must face it squarely. School had been safe, familiar and had offered the stability she had lacked before she'd been orphaned. She would sorely miss that comfortable cocoon. There was no choice now but to play the butterfly whether she looked the part or not.

Well, this was it. She was here, to meet in secret with the man she had selected. It was a sight more preferable than being alone with the man who had selected *her*, Clarissa reminded herself.

Her palms felt damp inside her half-gloves and her heart beat so frantically, she feared she might swoon. But she had no time for fear or for swooning.

He was waiting.

CHAPTER TWO

"MISS FORTESQUE," Hugh greeted her softly as she entered. He raked her up and down with a bold gaze before settling it on her face. "My, how you have grown."

"Mr. Richfield," she replied. "So have you." She felt uncertain how to proceed now that they were alone. Even in the low light she could see on closer inspection that his eyes gleamed a shade too bright, his smile appeared too fixed. Did he resent her summoning him this way instead of approaching him directly?

"Our Miss Dickson said you wished me to attend you on some matter of greatest importance," he remarked, his expression unchanged. "Phyllis was so secretive, I confess I am highly intrigued."

She stood well away from him, some six feet or so, trying not to twist her hands together and duck her head. How best to do this? she wondered with a heavy sigh. "May I ask you a few questions?"

"If you like." He shrugged. His stance remained contraposto, like some Greek god aware he was being admired by a mere mortal and thoroughly amused by the idea.

"Is honor important to you? Have your views upon it changed since we knew one another?"

His answering laugh was more of a small, surprised cough. "I shouldn't think it has. Honor is quite necessary in my opinion. Perhaps the most important—"

"Yes, yes, so it is," she interrupted, satisfied she was right, impatient to be done with this so they could get down to business. "Now would you please answer me this? What goals have you, Mr. Richfield? What ambitions?"

He looked very curious now and perhaps a bit disbelieving she would ask him such personal things. "I'm not certain I have any at the moment. Are you perhaps trying to reform me, Miss Fortesque?" Then he rolled his eyes and scoffed. "Has Harry put you up to this? He *has*, hasn't he?"

"Not at all. I understand that you have mustered out, sold your commission, or whatever it is one does when one leaves the army?"

"Indeed, I have embraced civilian life, such as it is," he admitted. With one hand propped on the back of an armchair, he gestured idly with the other. "So there you have it, your questions answered, impertinent as they were. You may tell our esteemed Dickson that I am doomed to an aimless existence with honor as my only redeeming quality. Does that end your interrogation?"

He looked perfectly at ease, that all-knowing smile unwavering, which for some reason angered her no end. Her presence obviously had no effect on him whatsoever, while she stood here suffering a high state of agitation. The childish urge to shock him out of that comfortable pose of his simply overtook her.

"No. No further questions. However..." She screwed up her courage, raised her chin a notch and met his assessing gaze with one every bit as bold. "Since you are without employment and probably in need of funds, I have decided to marry you."

That did the trick. He straightened immediately, his casual stance stiffened, the smile turned upside down. He blinked hard, as if she were an apparition he thought might attack. Apparently she had rendered him quite speechless for once in his life. Amazing feat.

Clarissa suppressed a nervous giggle while a feeling of power shot through her, boosting her confidence. She pressed on before it could flag. "For the sum of ten thousand pounds, you must agree to elope and then ask no more of me than the amount I have mentioned. For the remainder of your life," she added for good measure so there would be no misunderstanding. "I will have your solemn word on that before the ceremony. Have we a bargain, sir?"

He stared at her as if she had lost her reason. Perhaps she had, Clarissa thought. In any event, he was not jumping for joy at her proposal. She raised a hand to rake an errant curl behind her ear, realized the mannerism would betray her lack of composure and ceased immediately.

"Well?" Locking her trembling hands together in front of her, she waited.

The silence mounted for what seemed an eternity. Then he cleared his throat, blinked and looked away. "May I ask why, Clarissa? Are you in some sort of trouble?"

"That is none of your concern," she snapped, uneasy because he had not immediately leaped at her offer. He should have leaped.

He studied her for a moment, his eyes narrowed with speculation. "If you are…in an interesting way, then it definitely *would* be my concern. Are you?"

Her mouth dropped open and her own eyes flew wide. "How *dare* you suggest such a thing!" She stepped closer and lowered her voice to a vehement whisper. "I am certainly *not* with child, if that is what you imply!" She wished she dared slap him.

"It is a legitimate query in light of your proposition," he argued, though by the immediate relaxing of his shoulders, he seemed vastly relieved. Small wonder.

Clarissa was not certain she wished to marry him now if he thought so little of her as to believe she would attempt to foist another man's offspring on him. "In light of your insult, I should rescind my offer immediately."

"But you are not inclined to do that, are you?"

he guessed correctly. He cleared his throat again. "Well, do you mean to elope immediately? To-night?" he asked, his voice husky, though it had regained its former note of dry humor.

He was making sport of her now, she knew. Still she did not task him for it. Time was of the essence. Tonight was a bit sooner than she had thought to do this, but there was little point in delaying the deed and every reason in the world not to put it off.

"Yes. Tonight. Why not?"

"The license for one thing," he informed her. "Unless you are prepared to wait three weeks, we would need a special license in lieu of the regular one. And that we cannot get until midmorning at the earliest."

"No, I prefer not to wait." She cast about for another alternative. Word would spread like a house afire if they applied for a license of either sort. Trenton would find out. He would do something to stop her. "Scotland then. We shall go there and we shan't need one. Isn't that so?"

"Gretna Green? Is *that* what you have in mind?" he asked, disbelief coloring his tone.

"Is there a closer destination where it would be legal?"

He issued a short laugh, more of a scoff, really. "Legal? Well, I suppose it is legal enough *there*. I hear all a pair must do is declare themselves, before several witnesses of course, and the marriage is taken as fact. Many have done it, though I know no one personally who has dared. For the most part, I believe it is to avoid the Marriage Law here in England. But as luck would have it, Clarissa, we are not Scots and would have to return here to live.'' He paused. ''Confess. This is some jest Harry put you up to, isn't it?''

''Absolutely not. We could reside in Scotland. Though I have not traveled greatly across the border, I am familiar with the city of Edinburgh. I went there once as a child.''

He quirked an eyebrow. ''I've been there, too.'' Now he was beginning to look not only scornful, but highly entertained. ''And I must tell you, I should rather starve in a ditch than live in Auld Reekie.''

''Then you are refusing me outright?''

He took a deep breath and released it slowly. ''A quick wedding over the anvil, as it were, would call for a real wedding as soon as may be, or you would be forever ruined. You'd still suffer a scandal, I expect. Willing to face that, Clarissa?''

''Yes. Are you?''

When he did not answer immediately, she prompted him a little. ''Be frank, sir. This is a business arrangement, not a plea for everlasting devotion. Will you or won't you?''

''I have to ask this, Clarissa. Why go about it in such a way? If you are that determined to have me, I could approach your uncle and ask for your hand, as is proper. Have the banns called, dress to the teeth, marry in style, celebrate for days." His eyes sparkled, catching the lamplight like polished amber agates.

She realized he still didn't believe she was serious. Not at all. However, she continued. "And you would be promptly refused permission to pay me court. My cousin Trenton would persuade my uncle that a match between us would be highly inappropriate. Impossible, in fact."

"Oh? Why would he do that?"

"Because Trenton wants to wed me, of course. And even if that were not so, you are a younger son with no title, property or means. Even though your brother is a peer, you would not be considered suitable."

He inclined his head and grimaced. "Correct. Nothing at all to trade, have I?"

"Your name will do. And your solemn vow that you will not gamble," Clarissa said. "Ten thousand pounds, sir. Your freedom to continue doing precisely as you like. Within reason, that is. No gambling, as I said. And I would require utmost discretion in any clandestine matters...of the heart."

"I much doubt my *heart* would be what concerned you, Clarissa." His nostrils flared and his eyes went a bit cold. "I, of course, would require absolute fidelity from any woman I marry."

Clarissa shrugged. "Naturally."

"And I would want heirs," he added, rather

pointedly, as if he thought she was proposing a marriage in name only.

He probably would be astounded to know that avoiding intimacy with him had never even occurred to her. Quite the contrary.

"Naturally," she repeated, nodding, meeting his gaze, assuring him that she fully understood.

He looked away, sighed heavily, then faced her again.

For a long moment they stood there looking at one another, both at a loss when it came to the next move.

Then he closed the distance between them and took her hands in his. "Clarissa, think. You would likely be cut from your circle of friends for such an infamous act. Your family would be furious."

"That is entirely the point. And they—Trenton in particular—would be powerless to refute the marriage."

"This *is* a mad thing you plan to do, Clarissa. I would not have expected it of you." He gently squeezed her fingers as he said it. Though he sounded earnest, she could swear there was a touch of laughter in those eyes. This amused attitude of his was wearing exceedingly thin.

She jerked her hands from his. "If you wish to decline, Richfield, simply say so. Do not pretend it is the loss of my reputation that would trouble you. If you had rather not marry me, I shall choose someone else straightaway and we shall pretend this conversation never took place!''

"Who?'' he asked, his taunting grin suddenly absent.

Clarissa tossed her head and flicked an errant curl off her cheek. "Oh, perhaps John Bernard. He seems to be fishing at the moment.''

"So *any* man of dire circumstance would do, eh?''

"Not any man,'' she argued hotly. "That is an affront, sir!''

"I beg your pardon.'' But he did not do so sincerely. He clasped his hands behind his back and glanced idly around the room, pretending nonchalance. He was pretending, she knew. That muscle jumping in his strong, square jaw indicated his teeth were clenched fair to cracking. He could not be piqued by this. What on earth did he have to be piqued about?

He drew in a harsh, deep breath as if to brace himself before pursuing the matter. "May I ask why you favored *me* as first choice?''

Too polite. Oh, he was entirely too polite. Butter wouldn't melt…

Clarissa forced her sweetest smile and countered. "Who said you *were* first choice?''

A flash of anger crossed his features, so instantaneous she almost missed it altogether. Then he matched her expression with one every whit as false. "Then surely you will understand if I decline.''

"You are a beastly oaf, Richfield!" she almost shouted, flinging up her hands in frustration. "No gentleman at all! Oh, why did I ever think—"

"So find yourself a gentleman, Clarissa," he said angrily. "One who will not mind chucking his self-respect to feed at your little trough of generosity!" With that he stalked past her and reached for the door.

Clarissa rushed after him and clutched at his sleeve. "Wait! Please!"

He stopped, his back still to her, his hand on the door handle. The rigidity of his stance spoke his fury as clearly as his words had done.

What should she say? Could she persuade him after speaking so recklessly? She simply had to. Despite what she had told him, she did not think she could bring herself to put her case to another candidate. Any man she wed would expect her to fully honor her vows. At least with Hugh, she could not view the intimate aspect of marriage as an onerous condition or a sacrifice. In fact, quite the opposite.

Images of sharing his bed flooded her mind and she ruthlessly shoved them aside. They had been intruding like clockwork for the past two days since she had formed this plan.

There would be no other chance. She could not let him go. "Please," she said again and hurriedly insinuated herself between him and the still-closed door. Before she lost her courage, Clarissa stood on tiptoe, grasped his face in her hands, pulled it down so she could reach his lips and kissed him.

His lips were open—to speak, she supposed—and she pressed her own against them, parting hers. The gesture felt far more intimate than she had expected a kiss to feel.

To her surprise, he slid his arms around her and angled his head, deepening the meeting of their mouths. He pressed her back against the door, his body flush against hers, hard and demanding...and wonderful.

A truly heady rush of sensation radiated through her like a sudden fever. The skin of his face glowed hot beneath her fingertips. She wished she had doffed her half-gloves. His scent surrounded her, a hint of spicy fragrance and brandy. He tasted of that, as well, intoxicating her senses as if she'd consumed an entire bottle.

He groaned, a deep, pleasurable sound that rose from the depths of him and invaded her from without and within. He could do this forever, she thought. If they were wed, it would be frequently done. Oh, she could not let him go. Not ever.

Slowly, as if very reluctant, he parted from her and held her by her shoulders, looking down into her eyes. His breath almost shuddered out. Then he dragged his gaze away and gave his head a small shake, perhaps to clear it if it felt as muddled as hers.

She lowered her voice to a whisper. "My temper

is not usually so high, but I find myself in dire straits. Could we discuss this further? Please?''

He looked down at her, then backed away, putting her at arm's length. ''Only if you tell me what has forced you to flout convention this way.''

Clarissa sighed and lowered her gaze to the turkey carpet beneath their feet. Perhaps if he knew the truth, he would agree to help her. ''My cousin is determined to compromise me. If he happens to succeed, I should have no choice but to marry him in the event someone observed us. Or if there were, heaven forbid, results.''

Suddenly there occurred a stillness about Hugh that seemed ominous. ''What has he done?'' His voice was deadly quiet and without inflection as if he deliberately controlled what might have been outrage.

Clarissa sighed and looked away.

''Tell me,'' he insisted, giving her a gentle shake.

Though he need not know of the incident on the terrace, she had to tell him of Trenton's plan. So she began at the beginning. ''The Dicksons invited him here when we first arrived in town. Trenton was charming to our hosts, but behaved with me as though we knew one another much better than we actually did. I had only met him a few times at family gatherings before my parents died. He frightened me even then, he was always such a bully.''

She sighed at a particularly unpleasant memory of Trenton as a boy, then continued. ''Two days ago,

I went to visit our uncle who is not at all well. There at Uncle James's house, Trenton stated quite baldly that he intended to marry me, that he always had done so. He said now I had no other option whatsoever and that I would be wise not to protest. Or else.''

"Or else *what?*" Hugh demanded, fists clenched, his control visibly slipping a bit.

Clarissa frowned. "That he would see to it I had no choice." She pressed a trembling hand to her chest. "I assure you I am not easily terrified, but his expression of determination gave me chills. He left no doubt in my mind that he means to force me into marriage with him."

"Has he tried?" The amber eyes had darkened and his lips were firm with anger.

Clarissa shrugged and looked away, even now unwilling to admit how near Trenton had come to doing what he threatened.

"So he *has,* damn his eyes! I'll call him out! No, wait. That won't do," Hugh muttered, worrying his chin with his thumb. "You would be ruined for certain if the reason became known."

"And you would be arrested. Dueling is not legal," she reminded him with a mirthless laugh.

He scoffed as if that did not signify. "Has he…has he hurt you, Clarissa?"

"Not yet," she assured him, and wondered if she had perhaps said too much.

She had heard that gentlemen frequently settled

matters with dueling despite the law against it. Given Hugh's impetuous nature and daring ways, she sincerely hoped he was not one of them. But she should not risk giving him further impetus.

"Let me think," he said shortly, pressing his fingers to his brow and beginning to pace.

"I *have* thought it out," Clarissa declared. "And you can see my quandary. I must do something, and do it quickly, to prevent his pressing the issue."

"Indeed." Hugh stopped pacing and stepped closer, slid one hand under her elbow and his other hand beneath her chin, causing her to look up at him. "Clarissa, please tell me the truth. He has not actually…?"

"No, I swear it." His concern warmed her as nothing had in a while. Clarissa added, "It is not really my person he wants, you see. How can it be when I am nothing but a plain and aging teacher?"

"Balderdash. You are quite beautiful and not above twenty if you are a day." The way he assessed her with those golden eyes of his, she could almost think he believed it.

"Twenty-two," she admitted. "But I have no doubt it is my inheritance he's after. I will be damned to perdition before I let him have it."

Hugh paced again for a moment, obviously giving all she had told him due consideration. Surely he would agree. He *had* to agree.

Then he stopped and shook his finger at her. "You chose me for this because I have soldiered and you want me to kill him for you.'' His voice sounded flat. ''You never had any real intention of marrying me, did you?''

''No! Yes!'' she exclaimed.

''Which, Miss Fortesque? No or yes?'' Oh, now he looked angry. Well, so was she!

''I am aghast you should think this of me. I merely want the protection of your name and I'm perfectly willing to pay you for it! I certainly do not require you to cause anyone's death. Never did I think of such a thing!''

''Then why *me* in particular?'' he demanded.

Clarissa cast about for a reason. Any reason that would convince him. Other than the real one, of course. She could scarcely admit she wanted him for his immature inclinations to go sporting through life instead of settling down to manage a wife and her money.

So she ducked her head again, looked up coyly from beneath her lashes and mumbled, ''Because I have always found you handsome?'' To her dismay, it emerged more question than statement.

He all but snorted with disbelief. Then he tipped up her chin again. ''Now how could I refuse such forthright honesty?''

''Then you will do it?'' she asked hopefully.

He shook his head and ran a hand through his hair. ''Sacrifice and profit our substitutes for love. I daresay we should suit quite admirably, you and I, the desperate and the greedy locked in unholy wedlock.''

For a long moment Clarissa looked up at him, bemused by his ridicule and the fact that he caressed her chin with his thumb as if he already owned her face. After that kiss of theirs, he probably thought he did. So much the better. ''I allowed you to kiss me quite thoroughly, as a fiancé might do. You're not going to be a cad about this, are you?''

He sighed. ''If I am, at least I'm a more amenable cad than your cousin. You should know me well enough to realize I would never frighten you or force you to my will.''

''Yes, that I know or I should not have permitted you such familiarity. And I certainly never would have asked you to be my husband,'' she declared, watching him intently.

He paused, stared at her for another moment, then answered. ''In serious answer to your proposal, yes, Miss Fortesque, I would be honored to marry you.''

When he looked as if he might say something else, Clarissa backed up a step and offered her hand. He took it, but when he would have raised it to his lips, she resisted and shook hands the way a man might do to seal a bargain. ''Thank you. I consider your word our contract, both for the betrothal and the financial terms agreed upon,'' she said calmly. ''Now if you will excuse me, I must go and arrange for a coach.''

How she was to complete that particular chore,

she had no notion. Where did one come by a conveyance to transport them the length of England at
near midnight?

"No." He clasped her wrist, loosened his hold on
it, then carefully placed her hand through the crook
of his arm. "I will see to that detail. I know someone
to hire. Watch your clock closely. I shall arrive precisely at three and it will not do for me to hang about
with horses stomping and awaking the household
while you stuff your valise with last-minute items."

Now he sounded as if the whole thing were a
terrible inconvenience to be borne. Perhaps she
should have kissed him again and put him off balance. But then, she, too, would have been affected
and they needed their wits about them at the moment.

Suddenly he reached for the door handle, slowly
opened the door and looked out.

"What is it?" she whispered, clutching the edge
of the door frame and peering into the semidarkness
of the deserted corridor.

"Thought I heard something," he murmured as
he turned to her. "Hmm. No one there."

"Someone was listening?" she gasped.

"More likely my conscience kicking up a fuss."
He took out his timepiece, glanced at it, snapped it
shut and returned it to the pocket of his waistcoat.
"For the moment, we should join the others. When
everyone is abed, bring your things and meet me at
the back gate. We should be able to travel some

distance by daybreak or before they discover you are missing. In any case, too far for anyone to interrupt our journey and prevent the marriage. Be sure to leave a note so no one will worry.''

Oh, so now he was to become all business-minded, was he? Giving orders as if she were one of his soldiers. Clarissa highly resented his taking over the venture and bidding her about the way he was doing. His commanding manner did not bode well and she must set him straight immediately if she planned to remain in charge.

''I shall leave no note,'' she declared, asserting herself. He need not know that Phyllis would immediately guess her plans and reassure everyone that Clarissa had not been kidnapped. Though she and Phyllis had never discussed the possibility of the marriage taking place in Scotland, the Dicksons would surely deduce that fact when no issuance of a license was discovered.

So long as Trenton was not notified, no one would trouble to follow them, anyway. Who was there to mind whom she wed? No one but her dratted cousin and he would find out too late to do anything about it.

''As you wish,'' he said with a shrug as he gestured for her to precede him. ''But I think you should.''

They marched along the dark hallway, Clarissa lengthening her steps to match his.

''I will allow you to arrange transportation,'' she

said, granting the necessary compromise in a near whisper. "But you are to be at the outer gate of the garden at precisely *two* o'clock, no later." Though she did not raise her voice, she demanded that in her most imperious way, in a tone she used to control unruly students. "If you are one instant late, Richfield, my offer is null. Are we understood?"

He nodded, his eyes narrowed and his lips quirked to one side. "Two, it is then."

Clarissa almost heaved a sigh of relief. She had done it. The unthinkable. She had proposed and been accepted. As soon as she reached the border of Scotland and spoke the necessary words, neither her uncle nor Trenton would have any right whatsoever to interfere with her life. And the man beside her would be too occupied with his own flighty pursuits to present her any problems. She was safe, or soon would be.

They reached the ballroom and he paused. "Mind now, you should act as though there is nothing out of the ordinary when we go in. If we are to carry off this enterprise without a hitch, no one must suspect what we're up to until the deed's accomplished."

"Will you please stop giving me orders?" she argued, teeth clenched, shoving her elbow into his ribs. Either he was quite solidly built or encased in a corset for it had absolutely no effect on him. His body felt as impervious as the rocks at Stonehenge. "That is precisely what I'm trying to avoid, Richfield! Someone directing my life, my very existence. Can you not understand that? You must promise to stop it!''

He looked down at her, his head cocked slightly to one side, one eyebrow raised in a mocking manner. ''Then come with me or not, as you like. Only please, *please* do not forfeit our agreement, I beseech you. It truly is the best offer I've had all evening.''

''I abhor sarcasm, Richfield. I won't have it,'' she stated firmly. He might as well come to heel now as later.

''Duly noted. Stay here by yourself, then, if that's what you want.'' He disengaged his arm while glaring quite directly.

''I believe I shall come with you. After all,'' she said archly, grasping his arm again and putting on a smile, ''who could ask for better company?''

''Oh, and I must embrace *your* sarcasm. I expect it is another requirement of the match, eh?''

''We should both refrain,'' she told him with a succinct nod. ''It is rather a common indulgence and I do apologize. So should you,'' she added.

''Your pardon,'' he said idly with no attempt at sincerity. ''You're quite enjoying all this, aren't you?''

''Certainly not.''

With no further comment, he led her to rejoin Phyllis, Cole and Harry. John was back with the group, as well, with the simpering Miss Hermoine on his arm. Harry had somehow acquired Blanche Nesbitt, so they were eight altogether, paired off like gloves.

"Shall we stroll about the gardens?" Harry was asking as they arrived. "I cannot hear myself speak for all this noise."

"That is *music*, Harry!" Phyllis teased with a wide-eyed glance toward the musicians. "You have such a poor ear, 'tis a wonder you ever learned to dance. Not that you manage more than a leap and hop at your best."

Harry winked, then frowned at his sister. "Be aware I am attempting to gain Miss Nesbitt's regard and you are sorely hampering my effort, sister." Blanche Nesbitt blushed as Harry shot a sly look at Hugh and Clarissa. "Well, Rich, old son. Where did you get off to? Clarissa, you really must cheer up this fellow. He's a casualty of war, y'know."

She swung her gaze to meet Hugh's. "You were wounded?"

"Pay no attention to him. Harry embroiders everything to such an extent, you could outfit a bed with the result."

His attempt to imbue the response with levity failed miserably. The words sounded almost bitter. Obviously the very reminder of his injury made him feel ill. For the first time Clarissa noted that fine lines of worry or perhaps even pain had etched themselves on his features.

"Were you badly hurt?" she questioned, leaning closer, observing him even more closely.

"I've heard tell he gave much worse than he got!" Harry answered for him as they exited the ballroom through the open doors that led out to the terrace.

Cole joined in eagerly. "Righto! I wish we could have seen ol' Rich in the thick of it at Waterloo. Astride that surly black beast of his, they say he charged into the fray slashing left and right, his sword a bloody scythe, mowing a path right through 'em! Gave ol' Boney's lads a run for it before going down. Ain't that right, Harry?"

They nattered on, relating tales of Hugh's ferocity with gory details and horrid scenarios of battle unfit for a lady's ears or imagination.

"Hugh, tell me, is that true?" she asked, pressing him.

"Hearsay, all of it," he snapped.

"Hearsay? They were not there with you? Where were they?"

"Assigned elsewhere, obviously. Ask *them* if you want to know."

Clarissa stared up at Hugh, who fell silent and grew increasingly grim. He quickly caused them to drop behind the others and guided her along a graveled path that branched off the main one.

Harry and others continued on, apparently so caught up in the grisly war tales they did not even notice the departure. Over the drone of the men's deep dramatizations she heard the high-pitched, horrified gasps, moans and exclamations of Phyllis, Hermoine and Blanche.

The idle thought occurred to Clarissa that Harry was perfectly willing for Hugh Richfield to attach himself to *her*. He seemed to be pushing for it, in fact, probably relieved beyond imagining that Phyllis had escaped becoming the object of Richfield's attentions.

Clarissa admitted feeling envious of the brotherly concern Harry offered Phyllis. At the moment there was not a soul alive who would bat an eye at anything she did that might precipitate her downfall. Except for her cousin, and even then, Trenton would not care a whit about that so long as he got his hands on her money.

Thank goodness she had found a way around that and in so doing, had chosen better than she imagined. Apparently, Hugh was a hero, not the sort another man would dare cross. He did not seem to be suffering a wound as Harry had indicated. Perhaps Harry exaggerated. Or perhaps the wound was not physical.

"I daresay it was an awful time. The memory of it troubles you still, doesn't it?" she demanded softly as she clung to Hugh's arm.

"Harry and Cole have drunk too deep and their tongues are loose. The war is over and I neither wish to hear of it or to speak of it again." The muscles of the arm she grasped had turned to cold steel. His voice was every bit as cool and rigid. "That is my one condition to our getting on well together. Surely you can manage that."

"Of course," she whispered, feeling the waves of pain that emanated from him. Was she wrong? Was he hurt somewhere and not yet healed? "Where were you wounded, Hugh?"

"Oh, for God's sake, I said leave *off!*" he snapped. Before she knew what had happened, he roughly disengaged his arm from her hands and disappeared into the darkness.

Clarissa stood alone among the carefully sculpted topiaries decorating the Dicksons's formal garden and wondered whether her concerned curiosity had just caused Hugh to cry off their agreement.

Would he still meet her at two o'clock as planned?

She looked upward and formed a small wordless prayer that her persistent questioning had not foiled her plans. That he would be there when she came down to meet him and would carry through with their elopement.

Clarissa worried even more because she knew she wasn't praying for herself altogether. The insistent notion occurred that Hugh might possibly need her even more than she needed him and for reasons far more critical than her avoiding an undesirable marriage to her avaricious cousin.

She knew one thing for certain. She did not need to become deeply involved with Hugh Richfield even if they were to become man and wife. His problems were his own and he obviously wished them to remain so.

But what was he really? she could not help but wonder. A daredevil with no thought for anything but his next breakneck adventure? Or a heroic figure attempting to outrun the events that had made him so? Whatever the case, Clarissa knew she must take him as he was.

The wise thing would be to ignore the past, both his, hers and theirs together. It would be devilishly hard enough not to love him knowing as little about him as she did now. And Clarissa had determined not to love him. Any fool could see that was a path to disaster, and she was no one's fool.

But for whatever reason—hands clasped firmly beneath her chin as she stared up at the stars—Clarissa still prayed Hugh would hold to their bargain. He simply had to.

CHAPTER THREE

THE NIGHT WAS CLEAR of fog, excellent for travel. Hugh saw Clarissa waiting beside the gate. She stood half hidden by a large wisteria vine.

She looked so young and so delicate in her high-waisted pelisse and neat little capote confining her wild, dark curls. Like a proper schoolgirl abandoning her classes for a lark.

He cursed under his breath, thinking he should have brushed off her proposal as a joke. But he could no more have done that than he could have struck her down. Heaven knew whom she would have approached next, and she might have done even worse than that cousin of hers if left to her own devices. At least, this way, Hugh could make certain she came to no harm.

Not that he didn't find Clarissa attractive enough to marry. Not that he would mind having her as a wife. In fact, if he had ever found himself in any position to contemplate marriage, she probably would have occurred to him first. He had always admired her, unapproachable as she had been.

But Clarissa had changed since he had known her as a graceful, intelligent girl who rarely spoke and who exuded a quiet sensuality. He could scarcely credit the forthright woman she had become.

She was still graceful, of course. And sensual— much more so now that she had blossomed fully— but she was no longer quiet, or at all shy about speaking her mind. In fact, she had become a regular little termagant. That quick temper of hers had certainly surprised him, almost as much as her kiss. Kitten turned tigress, apparently.

He alighted from the post chaise and approached her. "Ready?" he asked, reaching for her tapestry case. He hefted it, wondering how she had managed to lug it so far alone.

She glanced back toward the house before answering. "Yes, quite."

He experienced a sudden urge to wrap his arms around her and kiss her again, to assure her that all would be well, that he would protect her. Amazing how she stirred these ridiculously powerful longings in him without even trying.

Even more astonishing, Clarissa had been able to prick his anger. No one else had done that in a while.

She had caused a veritable rage in him when telling of her cousin's machinations. Also, Hugh admitted to feeling a moment or two of shame when she had asked about his ambition. Life had wrung that out of him completely and he was not proud of it. Now that she'd reminded him so pointedly, the lack of it plagued him like a sore tooth. He needed a direction and knew it. She had given him one with this nodcock scheme of hers.

"There," he said as he plunked her case inside and turned to assist her into the post chaise. He took her arm, remarking to himself how small it was in relation to his, how fragile she seemed. Merely touching her sparked thoughts he should not be having. Thoughts he had fought like mad seven years ago and had all but forgotten in the interim.

His swift reaction to Clarissa's softness, her sweet, intriguing scent, those dark, fawnlike eyes and tremulous lips, had given him quite a turn, then and last night in the Dicksons's library. Now he had to keep telling himself repeatedly that the longing was allowed, no longer forbidden. She was a woman, not the girl he had tried so hard to ignore when she was but fifteen and he a good four years her senior.

Arousal was a natural occurrence, he told himself. His body was not what had failed him these past two months. He could still bed a woman and had frequently done so, though he had not experienced any overpowering need to perform. It was simply a regular hunger to be assuaged.

No, the body had never shut down. The feelings were the thing. The bloody feelings. And Clarissa was bringing them back. How could he resist that? How could he resist her? He couldn't, of course, and he didn't mean to try.

He had to wonder, though, if he was not taking

blatant advantage of Clarissa's conundrum. Was this fair to her? Despite his qualms, he could not in all conscience leave her to the mercy of others. What else could he do but this?

"We should hurry," he said. He grasped her by her waist and all but shoved her inside. "All we need is to be caught in the midst of this farce. Harry would have a damned fit."

To his surprise, she had not mentioned the fact that he had arrived ten minutes late. With all the preparation required, he would have welcomed another hour. As it was, he'd barely had time to change his clothes and pack a bag after hiring the coach.

She huffed as she settled herself into the conveyance on the seat facing the back. "Try not to trouble yourself with basic courtesy!" she grumbled.

He could not see her face for he had extinguished the interior lamps as well as those outside of the coach. In the faint light of the quarter moon, they should not be observed by anyone who happened to be looking out the back windows of Dickson House.

The driver he had hired—a former sergeant he knew who had purchased himself a natty post chaise of the new and light variety—had padded the team's hooves so they would make as little noise as possible. The man's two young sons rode post astride, while Sergeant Devlin sat atop the thing to mind the reins and supervise his lads.

Though Hugh knew Clarissa was set on this course, he gave her a chance to change her mind.

"I still wish you'd consider going about this properly, Clarissa. If I were your uncle I would have my head for this."

"Uncle James would need to come looking for you in order to accomplish that. He's not been out of his suite of rooms for heaven knows how many years and is not able now, even if he wished to," she declared. "You needn't worry about him. However, I believe my cousin might be another matter altogether. Have you a weapon?"

"I always have a weapon," he replied. "I thought you said you didn't want me to kill him."

"If he should cause trouble, the fact that you are armed should be enough to dissuade him. I've told you he's nothing but a bully."

He could hear the nervous rustle of her skirts as she arranged them around her and the scuffle of her tiny boots as she searched for a place to rest her feet. Apparently her legs were too short for her feet to reach the floor. He snatched his leather satchel from the seat beside him and dropped it between them. "Use that as a footrest, else your legs—pardon my crudity, your *limbs*—will grow numb within the hour."

"You are so kind," she snapped.

Then he heard her soft sigh. This could not be easy for her, abandoning the rules she had lived by all her life, fleeing into the night with a man she knew little about, worrying about the possible consequences of her hasty actions.

Hugh wished he could somehow assure her everything would go well, but this escapade was as likely to turn disastrous as not. Even if they accomplished what they were setting out to do, the aftermath would pose problems she probably could not yet comprehend.

"Clarissa?"

"Yes?"

"Shall we call a truce? We have a long way to go. Would you come sit beside me? If you lean on my shoulder, perhaps you can sleep."

"No, thank you," she replied, sounding so prim he almost laughed.

She was such a curious mixture of seemliness and impropriety, he never knew quite what to expect from her. One moment, as now, she would insist on observing the strictest decorum. The next she might very well suggest something totally beyond the pale, such as when she had proposed to him. And kissed him. He could scarcely credit she had done that. And could hardly wait for her to do it again, he readily admitted.

He could kiss her, of course, but he wouldn't. Not just yet. If he did, he would not be inclined to stop at that and a rattling, poorly sprung post chaise was no place to initiate a woman to the joys of intimacy.

"Come," he insisted, despite his resolve not to begin what he could not finish here. "It's dark as a tomb and no one can see. Pretend you are five and I am your nanny."

She scoffed.

"There's a good lass, Clary dear," he added, raising his tone an octave and sounding a bit like Miss Meldrum, his own former governess. "Have a wee lie down."

He heard Clarissa stifle a laugh, though she tried to turn it into a cough.

"I dare you," he enticed her with a deep growling whisper.

"Stop. This is no time to jest."

"Well, be sensible, then," he admonished. "When we reach the main road and speed up, you'll be tumbling this way with the first bump anyhow. This wretched thing has no springs under it to speak of and we'll be flying along at nearly ten miles to the hour."

"Oh, all right," she said with mock irritation. At least he thought it was mock. "Move over."

He slid to one side, heard the swishing of her skirts and immediately caught her as she plopped firmly down upon his lap.

She shrieked. "Oh! Oh, I thought you…"

"Quite all right," he assured her, his arms clasped firmly around her waist to prevent her falling between the seats. The contours of her bottom nestled snugly against him and he had not the slightest wish to give up the contact. "Sit still."

"I will *not!*" she cried, struggling madly to slide off onto the seat beside him.

He released her and helped her arrange herself at

his right, not minding at all the very provocative tangle of limbs and accidental touches that ensued. "There you are," he said finally. "All set."

She exhaled sharply. "You behave entirely too familiar, sir! Do not presume simply because I allowed you one kiss."

"Two strangers riding through the night, anticipating connubial bliss," he drawled. "Ah, what a pair we are, Clary. Do you regret it already?"

"I—I am not quite certain," she said, and he felt her shiver against his arm. "Do you?"

"Not yet," he answered honestly. "However, I do think the more well-acquainted we become, the easier this will be. Are you game?"

"Not yet," she murmured, repeating his truthfulness so faintly that he could barely hear her over the clatter and squeak of the coach. "To tell the truth, at the moment I feel somewhat...undone."

He granted she had good reason to doubt the wisdom of this harebrained scheme of hers. "Not too late, y'know. We could easily reverse our direction and have you back inside Dickson House in less than half an hour. No one but us would ever be the wiser."

For a long moment she remained silent. Then she asked, "What of our agreement?"

He smiled to himself. "Oh, I'll demand you honor your word no matter what you decide about the elopement."

Even the darkness could not conceal her disbelief.

"You will still insist on the ten thousand even if we do not marry?"

"Actually I shall insist on the marriage. A fellow has his pride, you see. A breach of promise suit sounds rather more scandalous than an elopement, don't you think?"

"Yes. Yes, it does," she muttered.

"So, it is off to say our vows in secret or I shall have to remove the obstacles to them so we can do this publicly. I leave that to your discretion, of course. This *was* your idea."

Again she sighed. "I suppose we should get on with it since we've come this far."

"How you bolster my hopes for a happy union, my dear girl. I can hardly wait to become one with you."

"Droll, aren't you? Do try to restrain your eagerness," she replied in a wry voice.

The irony was, he wished he could look forward to it with his whole heart. But he had no heart.

Clarissa was quite beautiful, highly spirited and, discounting this undertaking, very practical in some ways, all things a man might seek in a wife. If only he were the man he once had been. If only he thought he could really make her happy.

The best he could offer her now was a caricature. He had no inner self left, no depth of feeling whatsoever. Battle and the ensuing horror had burned away the core of him and left nothing but a husk that was proving rather indestructible no matter what he subjected it to.

However, if Clarissa could use the empty shell for her protection and surface pleasures, he might as well provide both. Why not? Besides, he did think—for old times' sake if nothing else—he was obliged to save the poor dear from herself. It was the least he could do.

The only thing he really dreaded about this was how cheated Clarissa might feel when she discovered he had no soul. Perhaps she would not look so deep or even care, in which case he still could do a bit of good with what remained of himself.

It was not much, but it was more than he'd had to look forward to yesterday.

CLARISSA WOKE with a start. The coach had stopped. A faint streak of light peeked around the sturdy velvet curtain. She brushed the fabric aside, squinting. "Where are we?"

"A post stop," he replied. "Here we'll change teams and take a short respite. Best take full advantage. The next leg of our journey will be somewhat longer."

Hugh exited the chaise, looked around for a moment, then turned and assisted her out. After he spoke with the coachman, he guided her into a small two-story structure where a cheerful barrel-chested innkeeper greeted them with a smile and a word of welcome.

Good as his word, they were back on the road within the quarter hour. The hurriedly consumed scone and cup of dark chocolate sat heavily on Clarissa's stomach.

This was proving a strange journey, riding in a hired chaise, alone with a gentleman. Whenever she had traveled from the school, she had always been accompanied by Phyllis and one of the Dicksons or a maid. Their private coach had been considerably larger and much more well appointed than this one. And there had never been this uncomfortable silence that simply screamed to be filled.

Hugh seemed perfectly content to let it go on as he sat across from her and studied her with those tawny tiger's eyes. His features looked pensive.

She had to say something to relieve the tension. "I hope you were able to sleep before we stopped, and that supporting me earlier while I did so was not too tiring."

Hugh inclined his head, still pinning her with that gauging look that confounded her so. "Not to worry. I require little sleep."

"Oh. Wakeful habits acquired in the army, I expect. I guess it would be difficult to rest well if you were anticipating the call to serve at any moment." She shook her head. "That cannot be conducive to good health."

He stared out the window that he'd left uncovered after their last stop. "*Nothing* about the army was conducive to good health."

"Will you tell me about it?"

"No," he said simply.

Clarissa threw up her hands and rolled her eyes heavenward. "Well, I suppose we could rattle along for the duration this way. *Or* we could make some attempt to get to know one another as adults. What do you think?"

He smiled and turned his gaze back to her. "I believe I suggested something of the sort a while ago. Tell me about yourself."

She smiled back, pleased that he was at least trying to be agreeable. Bracing her half-boots on his satchel and sitting up a bit straighter as if for a recitation, she clasped her hands in her lap and asked, "What would you care to know?"

He folded his arms over his chest and stretched his long legs out to one side, crossing his ankles. His chin resting on his foulard, he peered at her from beneath his lashes. "I've already observed that you are impulsive, painfully direct and determined to govern with an iron fist. You seem to have changed quite radically from when you were younger. Why is that?"

Clarissa gaped, rendered speechless. She trembled with indignation.

However, once the first shock had passed, she granted he might have come to his conclusions with some reason. She swallowed hard and formed her reply carefully. "I fear you mistake me dreadfully, sir. I assure you I am not—"

"Not impulsive?" he interrupted, and gestured with one hand. "Look where we are, my dear, and where we are bound. Not direct?" he continued without pausing. "You proposed marriage and never quibbled about stating why. And even you must admit you've made very clear at every opportunity that I am to provide little, if any, contribution to this marriage of ours. Or do you deny you mean to command?"

Now it was her turn to escape the gaze that pinned her. Fair was fair. He had her on every count. "It is self-preservation that has moved me to act so out of character, I assure you," she confessed. "Usually I am quite retiring."

He laughed aloud, his entire body shaking with mirth. "Ah, Clarissa!"

She couldn't help but grin. "Well, I *am*. You have a nice laugh, Richfield. I have always admired it."

He sobered a bit, but a small smile remained. "Always? Confess it, you never even noticed me before last night except in passing."

"But you are wrong there. Though I will not admit to any silly infatuation with you in particular, I did notice you from the start of our acquaintance. You, Harry and Cole were forever laughing when we were all together at the Dicksons. Phyllis, too. I promise you, such capacity for merriment is definite cause for envy in a plain stick such as myself."

"Now who told you that you were a plain stick? How can you not know how lovely you are? Impossible." He shook his head and laughed again. This time it was more scoffing than not, but she didn't mind.

"That's kind of you to say, but you needn't lie." She brushed her face with her gloved fingers, wishing to hide her blush. Then she promptly changed the course of the conversation. "I am so glad you are merry still, even after the dreadful time spent fighting Napoleon. It must have been quite horrible for you, and yet you—"

"Back to that again? I wish you would give it up, Clarissa." He sounded angry now, as he had before when she had brought up the war.

Well, damned if she planned to spend the entire trip with him pouting across the way. But if he wanted a different topic, she could oblige. "The school where I was teaching is closed now for lack of funding." She sounded bitter and she wished she did not. "My *commanding* nature seeking an outlet through instructing others, I suppose. Be that as it may, my plans had to change."

"Unfortunate for your students."

"More so for me. Uncle is ill—not long for this world, says his physician—so I returned to London with the intention of tending him. Unfortunately, Cousin Trenton was already in residence, and of course I could not stay there."

"So Phyllis invited you to Dickson House?" he guessed.

"Yes, thank heavens she was with me when I

went to Uncle's. She suggested immediately that I remain with her. Else I would have had no place to turn.''

''Your cousin did not object when you accepted her offer?'' Hugh asked, seeming very interested in her reply.

Clarissa shrugged. ''Of course he did, but he thought it was temporary. He assured me he would speak with Uncle and settle the matter of our marriage within the week.''

''Had he insulted you with his unwanted attentions at that point?''

''Phyllis excused herself for a few moments shortly before we were to leave. He approached me and I fear I all but ran from him. In fact, I collided with Phyllis in the hallway and we departed immediately.''

''Good thing she was there. But what prompted you to reject your cousin's idea at first, before he showed his true colors?''

She thought that should be rather obvious. ''I refused because I do not like Trenton, much less love him.''

''I thought you said you hardly knew him.''

''We were not so well acquainted, but I knew him well enough not to want him for a husband! He was vile as a boy and worse as a man!'' Clarissa replied with vigor. ''It took no genius on my part to realize what he really wanted was not me, but my inheritance. Uncle's not poor, but neither is he that well off, despite his title.''

''And you *are* well off, as you say?''

''I shall be once I marry. Until then, Uncle controls what my mother's family left to me. It is in government funds, so I was told.''

''When was that?''

''Years ago,'' she admitted, ''but I've been informed of no change.''

''I see.'' He sounded concerned.

''You fear I'll not have enough to pay you what we agreed?'' she asked.

''Have I said that?'' he asked, his expression closed.

''Well, you needn't worry,'' Clarissa said. ''You will have your ten thousand and I shall have quite enough left to form and draw upon an annuity and live quite comfortably for life. I have done the figures myself, applying the amounts that were quoted to me when I received news of my parents' accident.''

''But you were hardly more than a child,'' he said.

She nodded. ''A child indeed, but one with an eye to the future. There was no one else to mind except my uncle and he seems oblivious to my very existence.''

With a tight smile she added, ''And I shan't expect you to trouble yourself with finances, either, except for managing what will be yours alone. The ten thousand.''

His eyes narrowed and his gaze grew keen. ''How generous you are. I could have been had for much less, you know.''

Was that true? Had she made a poor bargain? What did she know of such things? Well, it was done now and she had promised the amount. ''Then consider yourself fortunate I am so naive and enjoy your bounty.''

''I plan to do just that,'' he retorted.

''Fine.''

Strange how the very mention of the money upset him so, Clarissa thought. One would imagine a man with no prospects at all would delight in acquiring the ample income she was to provide him.

His brother had run through his own family's wealth, so it was said. The reclusive Nigel, Lord Hartcastle, lived in a crumbling heap of a manor house far to the north in the wilds of Cumberland. As second son, Hugh had been obliged to go out and seek his own way in life.

On that thought she commented, ''I have always wondered why you did not go into law, or the church.''

''Did you?'' He raised one eyebrow, obviously startled from his own thoughts, which appeared to be particularly dark at the moment. ''I might have. My education was such that law was a possibility, even a probability,'' he admitted. ''I read law for two years. When I left school, my brother suggested a commission in the horse guards.''

She smiled. ''You always were horse mad, as I recall.''

He frowned and continued as if she had not commented, almost as if he were talking to himself. ''But the cost was too dear for the Guards, so I bought into the regular cavalry.''

''And Harry and Cole followed where you led, as usual.''

His nod was slow and introspective. ''Yes. For a while. As did John. And Terrance. And Elton Younger.'' His voice was a near whisper, almost lost in the clatter of the coach noise. She knew he had not meant her to hear. It was doubtful he even realized he had spoken aloud.

Clarissa frowned, observing him closely now, noting the pallor that had risen beneath his sun-kissed skin, the lines that formed at the corners of his eyes and in between.

She did not know the other men he had mentioned by name—perhaps John, if he was the same boy she had met once at the Dicksons—but it was obvious that the fellows he spoke about other than Harry and Cole must not have survived the war. He was reflecting on it now, she thought. And she knew she was entirely forgotten for the moment. Grief and self-blame were his current companions.

Clarissa bit her lips together to keep from intruding. He would neither thank her for suggesting he absolve himself, nor would he forgive her again for initiating any more talk of the war.

She rested her head against the wall behind it and closed her eyes, pretending she had heard nothing and feigning sleep. Her heart went out to poor Hugh. His friends had died and he felt responsible somehow. Or perhaps just terribly sad at remembering them.

How she wished she felt free to move and sit beside him again, that she could hold him close as she used to do the students in her care who were distraught, and give him comfort. But it was not her place to console him. He was merely a partner in an enterprise to protect her and enrich himself.

Except for responding to her kiss as any man might have done, Hugh had not indicated in any way that he wished more from her than she had offered: ten thousand pounds, perhaps a child or two in the years to come and free rein to do exactly as he pleased. That was all he required of her and all she was prepared to give him. In return, she would be securing her future against the laws that prevented women from taking full responsibility for themselves and their own assets.

It was a fair trade all around, she thought. But she could not help wishing for something more. How sweet it would be to have someone who truly cared whether she were happy or not, someone to kiss away sadness when it occurred and to celebrate the joys. Someone to hold.

She peered again at Hugh Richfield through the veil of her lashes as she pretended to sleep.

Was it possible he might wish for the same thing at times? It was simply too soon to know, but a faint little hope began to take root inside her heart. A hope she had never dared put voice to even in the privacy of her thoughts.

CHAPTER FOUR

HUGH RUTHLESSLY SHOVED aside his dark thoughts. This would not do. He must not inflict his darkness on Clarissa, for she had done nothing to deserve it.

The more he thought about her proposal, the more flattering he found it to be. He wasn't happy about her offering money, of course. What man would like to consider himself bought and paid for? Well, some wouldn't mind, he supposed.

He grew more and more fascinated by her as the day wore on. True, it remained but a surface fascination. Sadly, nothing moved him very deeply anymore, but if anything could have, it would have been her. Even so, she was a wonderful distraction, every whit as effective as the curricle races, boxing matches and games of hazard he frequently engaged in to fill his empty nights and days. And his pockets.

She changed like the weather. First quiet and a bit moody, her every thought readable as a newspaper. Then all of a sudden, she would pretend a vivacity he saw right through. He could see that she wanted him to like her. Little did she know how hard he'd been pressed to fight his attraction to her when she was but a girl and out of reach. The sort of attention he *could* offer would probably only offend her. Despite that kiss in the library—more to the point, because of it—he knew Clarissa was still an innocent. Perhaps too innocent for her own good.

He admired her courage. He thought she was beautiful. She aroused him without even trying. But Hugh wanted more. He longed to burn hot for her in his heart as well as his loins. He wanted to suffer in the throes of desperation, feel the angst a man endured when uncertain whether a woman would ever return his love. He wished to reach the ultimate heights a man experienced when discovering the woman he loved shared his feelings. But alas, he had precious few of those for her to return, now did he? God, she deserved more.

She never complained when only allowed a quarter hour to refresh herself while the teams were changed every dozen miles or so. Instead, now past her first misgivings, she seemed to embrace the entire trip as a grand adventure. He supposed it was, for her. His ennui disgusted him. He despaired of it.

Whether her jaunty attitude consisted of pretense or not, he appreciated the fact that she did not bedevil him or whine about the inconvenience of it all as some people would. The constant bouncing of the chaise, the squeak of the springs, the endless dust were tiring nonetheless, even for him.

He hated travel, always had. But one could not shy from it if there was no alternative. Secretly, he wished for a home where he might put down roots and grow old, perhaps breed horses and hounds, forget the past. But it was not to be. His brother had inherited that life.

"Have you given any thought to where we shall live?" he asked her when there came a lapse in conversation.

She turned from the window, eyes wide with surprise and lips pursed in an enticing moue. "You...you mean you plan to live with me?" she asked, her gloved hand fiddling with the cameo at the neck of her pelisse.

Hugh shrugged. "I assumed you would live with *me,* since you haven't a place of your own. What, precisely, did you have in mind?"

Distress marred her lovely features. "I had not thought that far ahead, to be perfectly truthful."

"Well, you must think," he advised. "You certainly cannot expect the Dicksons to entertain you as their guest for life, now can you? And I seriously doubt you would wish us to live under your uncle's roof, given the circumstances."

"Good heavens, no! On both counts," she assured him. Her nose wrinkled prettily as she winced. "Where *do* you live?"

Hugh smiled just thinking about Clarissa sharing his rooms in Gilmorton Street. The entire section was packed with unemployed former officers and bachelor sons of the nobility, none with any other than the most modest of means. His lodgings were hardly better than his old rooms at school. But what *was* he to do with her?

"Could we impose upon your brother until we decide what to do?" she asked tentatively. "I daresay I should meet him, don't you think?"

Well, his marriage to Clarissa would give him the perfect excuse he needed to visit his brother again. How could Nigel turn him away if Hugh had a weary little bride in tow?

They could marry at Hartcastle and dispense with this ridiculous junket to the Scottish border. Then recalling his last visit with Nigel, he reconsidered. It might be better if he arrived home already wed to her.

"The family's old heap of stones is far from what you are used to, Clarissa."

"I understand. But I wouldn't mind."

"Nigel is not what you are used to, either," he warned.

"I will be glad to meet him in any event. Will he object to our marriage, do you think?"

"With Nigel, one can never tell," Hugh told her truthfully. His older brother was an enigma, even to him.

"Is he married?"

"No, there is no countess," Hugh said simply. "In fact, I am currently his heir. Not that inheriting would change much other than my name. There's nothing left of his estate but the building and that's hardly worth having."

"Tragic," Clarissa muttered, shaking her head in sympathy.

Little did she know. But Hugh did not expound on it.

THOUGH THE SPEED of the chaise continually surprised Clarissa, the hours crawled by, their journey broken only by the requisite change in teams every ten or fifteen miles. She would climb out of the coach, assisted by Hugh, and return to it when the fresh team was hitched and ready to go. The novelty had quickly subsided into monotony with the repetition. It seemed they would go on forever this way.

Hugh had coaxed her to sleep, but Clarissa was awake when night fell.

The chaise halted in the courtyard of the large inn that surrounded it on three sides. "Ah, at last," Hugh said with a weary exhalation. He stretched his arms wide and yawned. "This is Trelawny. A nice enough village and quite safe," he informed her.

"You are famliar with it?"

"I had a school friend from hereabout whom I used to visit often as a lad. I know several others from here who served with me. We'll rest, then resume our journey in a few hours' time."

"We could go on," Clarissa suggested.

"Not possible," he argued, then patted her gloved hand. "You needn't be afraid. I don't see how anyone could be following us, but even if they are, they will have to stop and rest, as well."

Clarissa nodded. "I suppose you're right."

Hugh smiled, his gaze gone soft. "We should be well ahead of anyone who might have guessed where we're off to. Besides, who would ever believe us bound for Scotland?"

She shrugged. "The Dicksons might. But even if they did and informed my uncle or Trenton, it wouldn't have been immediately done."

When they entered the inn, Hugh seated her in the dining room, made arrangements for their overnight stay and then joined her at the table. "I hope you won't mind, but I have sealed your fate. There is no way out of this now."

"What do you mean?" she asked warily as she folded her gloves into her reticule.

"Push has come to shove, my girl," he told her with a helpless shrug. "Tonight we must share a room."

"No!" she cried, then clamped her lips closed, glancing around to see whether anyone had heard her. She leaned forward and dropped her voice to a whisper. "Are you daft? I am *not* sharing a bed with you now!"

"Of course you won't. But the only thing available was their best accommodation, which contains a large four-poster and a servant's cot. Guess where you'll be sleeping."

"The bed," she announced. "If I am paying for this, then I should—"

''But you are not paying,'' he said with an arch look.

Clarissa gasped, clapping a hand to her face. ''Oh. Oh, I am so sorry. I haven't given you any money. I simply forgot! But how did you pay for the chaise? Our food? The teams? I simply wasn't thinking!''

She quickly pulled open her reticule, but he closed his hand over both of hers and smiled at her. ''Save what you brought until we need it.''

''But—''

He shook his head. ''I was only teasing about the bed, Clarissa. You may have it and welcome. God knows I've slept on worse than a cot before, though I doubt you have.''

''That's unfair. I slept on a cot for years!''

''I *am* a cad, remember?'' he said with a short laugh. ''I needn't be fair unless the mood strikes me.''

She couldn't help laughing with him. ''You are the most absurd man I have ever met, Richfield.''

''Could you call me Hugh, do you think? No one has in a long while and I find I like it when you do.''

''Hugh,'' she said with a nod for emphasis. ''But only if you cease calling me Clary. You've done that a time or two. I despise nicknames.''

''Heartfelt apologies for the offense. *Clarissa* it shall be.''

Just then a man approached their table. Not the publican, Clarissa noted, but a large, dark fellow dressed all in black save for his linen. And there was blood in his eye.

"I know you," he growled at Hugh.

Hugh pushed back his chair and stood, meeting the stranger's look with one just as fierce.

Clarissa wondered what had raised the man's ire, for neither she nor Hugh had noticed or spoken to him. She rose, too, looking from one man to the other.

"You have me at a disadvantage, sir," Hugh said evenly.

"You knew my brother well enough, I reckon. Trod these meadows together as lads along with his lordship's whelp and the Elmore boy. Then all the fools had the misfortune to call you commander in the field." He spat angrily to one side. "The field where Will died, I might add. Had you known what you were about over there, he'd be home now where he belongs."

Hugh's eyes closed and his lips drew tight. "Tasker Oldham. I should have noted the resemblance. I can't tell you how sorry I am about William. Did your family receive my letter?"

"Aye, and here's my answer to it," Oldham rumbled as he reached for the weapon tucked into his belt.

Clarissa quickly threw herself between the men and laid both hands on top of Oldham's right one, stalling it on the butt of his gun. "Stop! I know you are heart-stricken for your brother, but there is no call for violence!''

She felt Hugh grasp her arms from behind, but she stood firm, clasping her fingers even more securely around the stranger's.

Oldham glared down at her, but left the gun in place for the moment. ''Get out of my way, lady. Who are you to interfere with this?''

''It hardly matters who I am. What does matter is that you are not thinking, Mr. Oldham. How can you blame Mr. Richfield for your brother's demise? He fought beside, not against your William. Mr. Richfield has suffered greatly, too, I assure you. You said yourself that your brother was his childhood friend. Think how you would feel in his place!''

''What the hell would you know about—''

Clarissa pinned him with a look of sympathy and tightened her grip on his hand even further. ''Listen to me, please. If you must lay blame, lay it to the French, but not to this brave man. Surely you have heard how valiantly he fought. His fellow officers and men will tell you of it if you have not.''

Oldham gritted his teeth and shot Hugh a look over her shoulder, then faced her again. ''He did not protect my brother as a commanding officer should have done! I ought to kill him for it now I have the chance!''

''Reason with your grief, sir,'' she said with a bittersweet smile. ''Truly, I believe you are more angry with yourself than with Mr. Richfield. You must sorely regret that *you* were not there yourself to save William. Where were you? Safe here in England? You must feel awful that you live while your brother died. But I'm certain he'd not have wished you to blame his good friend...or yourself. You loved him very much, didn't you, sir?

Oldham's dark eyes began to tear just as hers were doing, and he turned away rapidly so that she lost her hold on him. She heard a strangled "Yes" as he stalked hurriedly from the room and disappeared outside the inn.

Hugh cleared his throat and Clarissa slowly turned to face him. "You're angry with me for that," she guessed.

"Not exactly," he said. "But I would like to know why you did it."

"What? Interfered?"

"Defended me in such a way. How could you possibly know what took place on the Continent? How did you know Oldham remained in England instead of fighting on another front?"

Clarissa shrugged. "He looked grieved and distraught, but he also looked guilty. I did not intend you to remain the object of a wrath he refused to turn on himself."

"I see," Hugh said. "Not that I deserved any absolution, but you probably did save him from a charge of murder."

She smiled. "It was Oldham's immediate survival I worried about. He would never have gotten that pistol out of his belt. I remember well how quickly you can move when the mood strikes. I figured you had seen bloodshed enough to last you awhile."

"Just so," he said quietly, looking away. "I should be furious, even somewhat ashamed, letting a woman fight my battles."

"But I guess you are not," she said with a saucy tilt of her head.

He looked directly at her then, his gaze burning into hers. "You have exceptional courage, Clarissa Fortesque."

"For a woman, you mean?"

Hugh shook his head. "For anyone at all."

"Be that as it may, if you would please order up some ale. My knees are pudding and my heart's still in my throat." She glanced toward the door, worried. "You don't think Mr. Oldham will come back, do you?"

"No," Hugh replied with a sad look and a sigh. "He won't be back."

THAT NIGHT and the next, Clarissa slept surprisingly well considering there was a man in her room. It should not have been so different from sleeping in the chaise beside him. But it was. Even though they were both fully dressed, there was something about lying prone in bed as one normally did when retiring for the night that somehow made it seem more intimate.

She supposed it would not have mattered if they

had been intimate. In the eyes of the world, she was compromised beyond redemption. If anyone bothered to ask, there were witnesses aplenty to their cohabitation. Oddly enough, Clarissa felt safer because of that.

Fully committed, she could not turn back, and no one could stop events from unfolding as she had planned. She must marry Hugh now whether she wished to or not.

All that considered, she had to confess she was a bit put out that he had not even tried to kiss her.

BY THE END of the next day's travel, she had completely lost her fear of their being followed. Tomorrow they would reach Scotland.

Hugh had worked hard to distract her with entertaining stories of his youthful scrapes—some Banbury tales of the highest order, she was certain—and pulled from her a recounting of her own school days. They shared their memories of times spent with the Dicksons, the antics of Phyllis, Harry and the others who had visited there. The conversations remained light and amusing, never touching on his days as a soldier or her worries about her future.

But Clarissa realized he was putting up a cheerful front for her benefit. Something weighed heavily on his mind. Something tragic, and it took no great intelligence to decipher what that must be. The awareness did nothing to help her resolve it. Perhaps deal-

ing with the aftermath of the war was a thing Hugh
must deal with himself.

After their fourth stop of the day, they dozed, his
head resting against the wall of the coach, hers lying
against his shoulder. She realized he was holding
her hand and smiled at the warmth of their position,
the sweet suggestiveness of it.

Suddenly the chaise lurched sharply to one side.
The wheels bumped wildly as they left the road. She
grabbed onto Hugh as they halted, tilted perilously,
rocked side to side and then settled with a bone-
jarring thump.

Someone shouted but with the jerking of the
chaise and frantic neighing of the mounts, she understood nothing.

"Stand and deliver!" a deep voice boomed, much
closer by and readily comprehensible. Clarissa
cringed.

"We only needed this to make a perfect day,"
Hugh muttered, disentangling himself from her
clutches and reaching beneath the seat for his pistol.

Before he could retrieve it, a wicked silver barrel
appeared in the window. "Out!" the voice commanded.

Hugh complied, muttering darkly, "There goes
my watch." He seemed less than upset, more angry
about the inconvenience and probable loss of his
timepiece. "You, stay right here," he ordered her.

Clarissa remained where she was, hoping the
highwayman had not seen her, huddled as she had

been, practically beneath Hugh. She risked a peek and saw Hugh standing well away from the door of the chaise, most likely to draw the mounted man's attention away from her. Indeed he had. The black-garbed, masked man did have his back to her, his pistol pointed directly at Hugh as if he planned to shoot him dead. Where was their driver? Where were the post boys?

Since the robber was speaking to Hugh and not looking her way, she stood and leaned out the door. Their driver and his sons lay prone on the grass beside the road, but she could see they weren't dead and most likely not even wounded.

The best she could discern, they must have fallen when the coach lurched and had been ordered to stay where they were.

"Lie down on the road!" the highwayman was demanding of Hugh. The dark horse danced closer to the chaise as the fellow aimed and repeated his order.

Oh, no! Clarissa could see Hugh's intent. He'd bent his knees and was about to leap. Close as he was, he might manage to unmount the brigand, but there was the pistol! If only she could—

The horse danced closer. Clarissa thought of jumping. No, she'd probably land in the dust and be trampled. The dark mount's tail twitched high, brushing her hand. She grabbed it and yanked hard.

Simultaneously, the pistol discharged and the horse kicked, catching the bottom of the doorway where Clarissa stood. The chaise rocked and she pitched forward, landing on the man's back with a screech of terror. Her legs dangled to one side of the horse's rump. She clung to the man's throat with one arm and batted at his gun arm with the other, determined to foul his second shot.

Its report echoed through her. She prayed he'd missed Hugh. The highwayman shouted and struggled wildly to dislodge her. Clarissa clawed at his neck, losing purchase as the horse reared.

She screamed as she fell. Thundering hooves beat the ground nearby as strong arms caught her. She landed atop Hugh and they rolled from the roadway into the grass.

He shoved her aside like flotsam and dashed to the chaise. In seconds she saw him level his own weapon and fire. The fleeing horseman jerked, yelped and leaned forward, tearing around a curve in the road and disappearing.

"Damn! He's escaped," Hugh cursed. Dusting angrily at his trousers, he turned to her. "Have you lost your mind?"

She ground her teeth, then retorted, "Have you lost your watch?"

The driver's laughter boomed as he scrambled to his feet and helped up the lads. "Godamighty, I never seen nothin' like it!" He threw back his head and howled. The boys joined him, gleefully slapping their knees.

Hugh strode over and offered his hand to her. She

could see he was biting his lips together. Whether to suppress laughter or to keep from blistering her with foul language, she couldn't say. He helped her to stand and examined her visually. "Are you hurt?" he asked.

"Oh, such sudden concern, sir? What prompts it, I wonder." She yanked her hand from his and stomped back to the chaise.

"Look," Hugh said as he lifted her inside from behind, "you scared the hell out of me. I could have had him off that horse in another two seconds if you'd stayed where you were."

She glared at him over her shoulder. "And had a bullet in your chest for your trouble. You're quite welcome, by the way."

He pocketed the pistol, climbed in behind her and all but collapsed, rocking the chaise. When she opened her mouth to chastise him, he grasped her face with both strong hands and kissed her.

All the fight drained right out of her and she melted against him like a puddle of wax. His mouth stole every thought in her head, every single, solitary thought except how dreadfully glad she was to have saved him for this. Oh, my, their one other kiss paled in comparison to this. How desperate it was, how invading, how totally inappropriate. How gloriously wonderful.

His mouth ground against hers, demanding and forceful. The kiss went on forever and she prayed he'd never stop. She slid her palms along his chest and felt his heart beating strong and true beneath her fingers.

At last he drew away, leaving her wanting, waiting for more. Finally she opened her eyes and saw him regarding her with consternation. "Wh-what is it?" she gasped.

"You," he whispered. "You are magnificent. Foolish...but magnificent."

He looked quite serious. She felt a swelling of pride that very nearly outstripped the disappointment that he'd stopped the kiss. "Me?"

"You," he said softly. He frowned then. "But you could have been killed!" He brushed her forehead with his lips.

"So could you," she argued, but without heat. "I couldn't let him shoot you." She traced a finger along his cheek, following the line of his jaw.

His arms slid around her and held her close, his face buried in the curve of her neck. For some time he simply held her as if he would never let her go.

Clarissa memorized the feeling, held it like a precious jewel to be swathed in silk and hidden away, to be taken out and treasured for the rest of her life. No one had ever, ever held her like this and might never again.

Surely today's occurrence was rare as an eclipse of the sun and what else could ever move a hero like Hugh Richfield to hold a woman this way?

WHEN THEY ARRIVED at Peven's Close where they were to pass the night, Clarissa decided she was completely comfortable with the idea of spending another night with Hugh. After all, she had watched him sleep, had allowed him to fasten the buttons at the back of her neck, which she had loosened in order to sleep, and had even seen him shed his waistcoat and shave his face. She fancied they were almost like a married couple already.

Mostly, he teased, amused and even casually flirted. But now and again she would catch him wearing an expression that betrayed his inner thoughts. Sometimes those were very dark, no doubt to do with tragedies he had witnessed, such as the death of Will Oldham. But at other times they seemed more speculative and centered on her. Oh, he tried to conceal them, but Clarissa knew he was regarding her, not as a partner in a mutually beneficial arrangement, but as a woman. A woman he had kissed and held.

Though she had never been the object of any man's desire before, she instinctively knew that he wanted her. But then again, she was the only female handy and probably the only one ever who had not begged him to take her to his bed.

"I spoke with the local constable," he informed her as he returned to the dining room where he had left her. "He says they have not been troubled by highwaymen before in this area. Anyone asking for a surgeon hereabout will be suspect. I'm sure I hit the fellow."

"You did," she agreed. "Have they vacant rooms here?"

He dragged out a chair and sat down. "Yes. There are two chambers available so that you may sleep alone tonight."

"Alone?"

He nodded. "I think that might be advisable."

"Well...all right," she said. Then without thinking, added, "Why?"

Disappointment must have clouded her features because he smiled knowingly, leaned closer and tugged playfully on the ribbon of her bonnet. "If not, we might anticipate our vows."

Though he grinned and wiggled his brows when he said it, Clarissa had the distinct feeling that he was not joking.

"You think so, do you?" she asked. "Then you overestimate your charm, Richfield. You always have."

He laughed. "Ah, Clarissa, you are a delight. How can I possibly resist you much longer?"

"Little danger that I can see."

"Sounds like a dare to me," he said, still grinning. He lightly tapped her nose with his finger. But deep in those golden eyes of his, she clearly saw something other than the humor he pretended or the admiration he had declared. Need. The sheer starkness of it frightened her. Want was expected, but he was not supposed to *need* her, for heaven's sake. Perhaps the need was only physical.

Both hands planted firmly on his chest, she pushed him aside. "Order up our meal, Richfield. Hunger makes me cross."

He shook his head and shrugged. "Small bother, indeed, compared to what it does to me, I can tell you."

Clarissa was at least sophisticated enough to know they spoke of a different sort of hunger. She could not hide her smile. Another kiss might be in order, after all, but not in the public room of the inn. Perhaps later when she bade him good-night, she would allow it.

"Aha. I knew it was a dare," he whispered.

Had he read her thoughts that clearly? Clarissa tossed her head and groaned. "You can be such a dolt!"

He merely grinned, not in the least put off by her insult.

Though the ale proved excellent, the joint of mutton was underdone and the peas quite crunchy. Despite that, they made short work of their supper and it was time to retire. Hugh escorted her up the two flights of narrow stairs and saw her to her room. He came in with her, looking around as if to make certain everything was in order.

Then he closed the door and leaned back against it. "Do you mind teasing so very much? You didn't used to," he said, placing one hand on her arm, caressing it as if to soothe her. "You scarcely spoke all through the meal and now you look terrified I'll pounce on you."

Clarissa shrugged, very aware of both his hands now cradling her upper arms, squeezing gently. "You mistake my mood if you see terror. I am only beleaguered by doubt."

"Doubt about what?" he asked, a small frown creasing his brow. "The marriage?"

"No, of course not that. About whether I should invite you to kiss me good-night is all." She ducked her head, embarrassed, then looked up at him again. "I have no experience with men whatsoever, much less a fiancé. If you would really like to, I suppose I shouldn't deny you. But if you are content to wait until—"

His mouth fastened over hers so quickly, she had no time to draw a breath. His warm, wonderfully mobile lips pressed against hers. Tenderly at first foray, then open at the next, his tongue coaxing her to invite him in. Caution deserted her completely as she threw herself into it with all the fervor she possessed.

His hands slid to her back, clutching her pelisse, grasping her to him in an embrace that melded their bodies from chest to knee. One palm smoothed down to the base of her spine, pressing her tightly against him.

Fully aware of how his body changed, hardened against her, Clarissa arched closer and closer still, greedy for the brand new feelings encompassing her.

She wanted more, wanted a keener spear of pleasure, something deeper to assuage the sweet insistent ache building inside.

He broke the kiss, angled his head the other way, renewed and deepened his assault. They had been moving from the doorway, she realized, as she felt the backs of her knees touch the softness of the bed.

"Let me stay, Clarissa. Let me stay with you," he whispered.

Unable to speak, she quickly kissed him again. Madly, deeply and without any reservation whatsoever. She wanted this man and she wanted him now. Devil take it, she cared nothing about society's rules or possible scandals or unspoken vows. She'd had no idea such ecstasy as this existed. "I am lost," she gasped. "Lost."

"Oh, no, sweetheart," came the sibilant growl against her ear. "You are found."

Her heart thundered in her breast, his words echoing like a blessing all around her, around them. He had found her.

When he lifted her onto the bed, she quickly made room for him beside her, hardly waiting until he cleared the floor before she reclaimed his mouth. His hands were everywhere, behaving as impatiently as she felt, tugging at her buttons, untying her ribbons. Adding her efforts to his, they soon discarded her pelisse and gown, his jacket, waistcoat and shirt.

Her fingers threaded through the crisp curls on his massive chest, reveled in the feel of his hot skin. He kissed her deeply, grasped her wrists and moved them to either side, and brought his chest to hers. His heart thundered against her, the thin batiste of her chemise the only impediment.

A furtive tug and it no longer was. Clarissa writhed with eagerness, wishing he would hurry and…

He pulled away, almost gasping for air, and issued a mirthless little laugh. "Wait."

"No," she argued, and ran her hands down his bare, flat stomach to the buttons on his flap.

He had already reached them and had two undone. In as inelegant a move as she had witnessed by him thus far, he kicked off his boots and shed his breeches. This time she laughed, but he buried the sound with another scorching kiss that made her forget everything. Every single thing except his mouth and hands and that strong, fine body now covering hers.

Oh, yes, she had seen him. Briefly, but in detail. He was better formed than any nude statues she had seen in books, putting those creations to shame. And his touch…. Nothing on earth equaled the sheer pleasure of his seeking hands on her breasts, her waist, her thighs and in between. She shuddered when he invaded her, providing in small measure what she sought in depth. "Please," she cried.

Suddenly his hand was gone and she felt him settle in the cradle of her, probing, seeking, finding. She rose to meet his thrust and took him into her.

All of him. The pain she had expected was nothing, the joy she had not expected was everything.

In tandem they moved, as if made one for the other. His mouth left hers and he looked down on her, his heavy-lidded gaze meeting hers, divining her every thought, but she couldn't care. She wanted him to know how she felt, wanted him to feel this way, too. Somehow she knew that no other man would ever bring her such a feeling. Not ever. No matter how many lovers she might have or how skilled they might be.

"You are mine," he whispered, his voice shaking with passion. He stopped the pleasuring and lay heavily against her, holding her still. "Say it."

"Yours," she agreed, willing him to continue before she died of need. "Always."

He kissed her thoroughly, but it was not enough. Beneath him, she moved, urging him to love her.

He growled and increased the pace, driving her to some unknown height she had not imagined and could not credit. Her entire world centered on the place they were joined and the sudden explosion of ecstasy took her wholly by surprise. She cried out, grasping his shoulders until her nails bit into his flesh.

His own sound of completion blended with hers. His body tensed, hard as marble, as his fire poured into her, a heat she welcomed like another breath when dying.

For a long while they lay motionless, his body

covering hers, his arms cradling her while his rapid breathing slowed and tickled her neck.

There should be love words now, she thought, worried because neither of them had any to offer. Not yet, anyway, and perhaps never. They had only just gotten to be friends. Devilishly awkward, this aftermath of the storm that was their passion. Did all married people suffer this silence at first? She felt compelled to say something, no matter how inane.

Should she give way to the overwhelming emotion their lovemaking had evoked from her? Or should she resort to something more lighthearted to cover her feelings entirely? No question which a man like Hugh would prefer.

She drew in as deep a breath as she could with his weight pinning her down, and said, "This cannot be good for you."

Laboriously it seemed, he pushed himself up, braced on his elbows and frowned down at her. He looked confused, deeply troubled and quite at a loss.

"This," she said, by way of explanation, glancing down between her breasts to where his lower body lay pressed against hers. "Anything so sinfully delicious cannot do one any good. Like mounds of sweets gorged by greedy children. I feel like…a greedy child."

He rolled away, disengaging himself, and sat up, raking a hand through his hair. But he said nothing. Clarissa reached for the edge of the counterpane and dragged it up and over her nakedness. "I'll wager something dire will result from this. Nothing should feel this good without consequence."

He tugged her close, counterpane and all, and kissed her fiercely, hungrily, as if his very life depended on it. Then he released her. His eyes were still clouded. "Consequence?" he muttered.

Clarissa nodded. "I could grow to love you because of it. We cannot have that," she told him. "It is not what I had planned."

"Do not love me." His voice sounded tight, too controlled. Was he upset? What had she done to anger him? she wondered.

"Why not?" she asked, feeling foolish to have mentioned it.

"I cannot…love you back." The words were bitten off one by one as if it pained him to have to say them, as if she should already know.

"Oh." She swallowed with some difficulty, trying to digest his confession. "I see."

"No." He shook his head violently, then rose from the bed and strode to the door that separated their two rooms.

"Where are you going?" she asked. "Won't you stay now that… There's no reason for you to leave."

Again he shook his head, refusing to face her. He did not speak again. He lifted one hand as if to silence her, lowered it, and then he was gone.

She knew she wouldn't sleep a wink. The entire night she would be reliving every second he had spent with her and trying to figure out why he already knew so definitely that he could never love her.

But she knew it would be best if he did not. It made no sense for her to want him to. Hadn't she chosen him because he seemed such a freedom-loving sort and would be likely to leave her to her own devices and go his own way? It would certainly be best if she did not love him in the event he did just that. If he chose to care deeply about her, he would be underfoot all the time, telling her what she could and could not do.

So where was her problem? They did very well together in bed. *Very* well, she thought, shivering with pleasure at the memory of it. He could make her dizzy with passion, wild, fulfilling her in a way she had never dreamed possible.

And except for his strange behavior just now, he was proving to be a highly entertaining companion and a good friend. That should be enough for anyone. But she could not deny she yearned for more.

Could it be that he did, too? She suddenly recalled the look of need in his eyes, the one that was clear and yet so fleeting. The one he tried to hide.

This was not going at all as she had first envisioned.

CHAPTER FIVE

Now Hugh knew he had made a huge mistake in wanting to feel things again. He'd been desperate to do so, hating the emptiness so much, doing anything to fill it. But how could he have known he wasn't hollow at all?

Somehow during that nightmarish time on the battlefield—death and dying all around him—he had shut down. His emotions had retreated to a secret place inside him and locked a stout door. It had only taken the right woman with the right key to unlock and throw it open. He was having the devil of a time getting it shut again before everything spilled out at once and left him a candidate for Bedlam.

He almost hated Clarissa for doing this. For trusting him so, for putting herself in his hands, for making him love her and in so doing, unleashing all these other things. Things he could no longer contain. He felt suddenly buried beneath the weight of them as surely as he had been on the field of mire and blood, trapped and writhing in vain beneath the tonnage of that dead horse.

Since that day when they had found him half buried beneath the corpse of his mount, since he had regained his senses and looked around him on that battlefield, Hugh had felt nothing. Not grief, not guilt, not horror, not happiness at being alive. Nothing.

After returning, it seemed his life's quest had become a dedicated search for pain, excitement, pleasure, fear, damn near anything that might make him feel alive again. To escape the dreadful emptiness. He laughed, caroused, drank, raced and behaved exactly as did his friends, taking his cue from them as to what might be normal for a survivor of hell. He had wanted to die, but could not stomach the cowardliness of that course.

Grief racked him, stretching him to the breaking point. So did guilt. He should have saved his men. Somehow, he should, though logically he knew he had not possessed the power to do that. The decision to attack had not been his. But he had been the one to order them to advance, to shout and encourage and lead them straight to their slaughter.

And then he had not died, had awakened with only a knock to his head, a couple of cracked ribs and a dead mount pinning him to the rain-soaked ground. Even the looters had missed killing him or taking anything from him but his shako, since nothing more of him than his head was visible beneath his mount. By rights, he should be dead along with his men.

Pain, harsher than any a sword's thrust could inflict, encompassed him completely. Oh, God, he *felt* now. He felt too much and too keenly to be borne, too deep even for tears. His muscles contracted, his lungs squeezed out all breath and he clenched his eyes against the horrible visions that swept through his mind. No use.

He wished he could weep for his brave men who had given their all and the families who would miss them, for the French soldiers he had killed, men like himself only doing as their generals had ordered them. Weeping seemed the least he could do, but there it was, an inability to perform even that mean feat. He lived. He loved. And they could not.

Soul sick, he sat on the bed, facing the window, staring out at the darkness while he drank heavily from the flask of brandy he'd pulled from his pack.

Hugh jumped as a soft hand touched his shoulder. "What's wrong, Hugh?" Clarissa asked. "Are you ill?"

Unable to help himself, he turned and grasped her around her lawn-clad hips, burying his face in the softness of her abdomen. He hated her and yet he loved her more. Probably always had, even when she was a sad-eyed child watching him from afar.

He couldn't speak. What could he say? She would no more welcome his love than she would his hate. He knew why she had selected him to marry. She thought him a fool, an irresponsible rakehell who would take her bribe and not interfere with her life. He had deceived himself when he thought he was saving her. Now he had taken her innocence and there was no one to save her from him.

Her fingers combed through his hair, caressed his neck and came to rest on his shoulders. "Hugh?"

Slowly he raised his head. Moonlight bathed her in soft blue so that she appeared an ethereal vision, an angel come to comfort.

"May I stay with you?"

Without a word, he drew her down to the bed beside him and wrapped her in his desperate embrace. If he could not save her, then perhaps she could save him, pull him out of this pit of despair she had shoved him into with her ready acceptance and confounded trust.

At the moment he was just too overwhelmed to mind the unfairness of it. What was one more regret in the scheme of things?

CLARISSA SCARCELY recognized Hugh that next morning. The day before and into the evening—precisely, until they had become intimate—he had gone out of his way to be charming, funny and set her at ease with him. Today, this last day of their journey to Gretna Green, he was nothing if not morose and uncommunicative, obviously overcome by dark thoughts.

When his mood had not lifted by midafternoon, she felt obliged to make an issue of it. "You are a different person today, Hugh."

He quirked one eyebrow, but still refused to look

at her. "Two men for the price of one. What a bargain."

She sniffed. "Hardly that. Credit me five thousand back and keep the present fellow away from me then. You're in a foul temper and you must realize to which event I attribute that change in your spirits."

Hugh stared at her as if he had never seen her before. He reached for her hand and held it with both of his. "It's nothing to do with you."

He was lying. Now was no time to play the blushing virgin and go all mishish, she decided. As with her students, she knew that confronting a problem at the outset went a long way toward preventing its escalation. This called for plain speaking.

"I was in that bed with you, Hugh. Even given my status as a novice in the ways of intimacy, I know what happened between us affected you adversely somehow."

He withdrew one of his hands from hers, brushed it over his face as if to wipe away the miasma that had him in its grip, and managed a small laugh. "Trust you to cut straight to the heart of things. And to think I once believed you shy."

At least she had him talking to her again. "So, what is the problem then? Had you had rather I had been more reticent? Did I disappoint you?"

"God, no!" He turned slightly and leaned his forehead against hers, kissed her cheek, a perfunctory peck. "I neglected to tell you how wonderful you were. How sweet and giving. While we loved, I thought of nothing but how precious you are, how generous. I was humbled, happy..." His voice drifted off as he drew away from her, squeezing the hand he still held and caressing it with his thumb. He carried it to his heart and held it there.

"And then?" she prompted softly.

"All of a sudden, I knew that I loved you," he replied. "And that I have no right."

"Ah. Well, *that* makes a great deal of sense. Who would want to love their wife, for heaven's sake? Not the thing at all. Chances are that would create a scandal worse than this elopement of ours when we return to town. Society would crumble all around us!" She forced a laugh. "Why, all the husbands in London might suddenly follow your lead and then what would happen? No adultery, no beatings, no overindulgence in drink! How horrid!"

He smiled.

She returned it. "There's no need for you to dissemble, Hugh. I am perfectly capable of enjoying you just as you are, fair moods and foul, without any lies to justify our sharing a bed. I will be your wife regardless of whether you love me, praise me, ignore me or shoot me daggers." She held her smile to show him she was sincere.

He looked at her and shook his head, her hand still clasped to his chest. "You have no earthly idea what you have done to me and I'm not even certain I can explain it myself."

"Well, I suppose we had best address it before we proceed any further. I need to prepare another course for myself if you plan to bow out at this juncture." But she knew he would not. His crisis, whatever it had consisted of, seemed to be over or at least eased for the present. "You won't renege, will you?"

"And have you sue me for breach of promise as I threatened to do to you?" he asked, his good humor partially returned or at least well pretended. "We'll see this through, Clarissa. I apologize for my megrims. Will you forgive me?"

She straightened her skirts with her free hand and tossed her head. He was pretending. She might as well risk all and demand the truth. Otherwise they could be dancing this particular tightrope for years. "I'll forgive only if you make a clean breast of it. Does this falling into despair have to do with your experiences these past few years? Don't bother to lie. I know it does."

He released her hand, sat back against the squabs and stared out the window at the passing scenery. "Yes."

"Will you tell me?"

"I cannot. It has nothing to do with you."

"So you said before, but I think it must. Why else would that dark time intrude during the…consummation of our, uh, betrothal?" She paused, then added, "For lack of any finer way to phrase it."

"Not during. After. The instant I realized how deeply I felt for you, it loosened some restraint inside me. The admission of it seemed to demand I recognize all sorts of other, not-so-fine feelings I had apparently…shut away."

She pondered that for a moment, then met his gaze. "That was difficult for you."

"But certainly not your fault," he hurried to add. "And again, I am so sorry I did not stay to praise and comfort you." His eyes softened even more. "Instead, it was you who came to comfort me throughout the night. I shall never, if I live to be two hundred, forget that, Clarissa. But I will make it up to you, I promise."

She grinned and pinched the hand that held hers. "Selfish man, I daresay I shall hold you to it."

He slipped his arms around her and kissed her soundly, waking her need for him so that she did not notice the slowing of the chaise until he drew away and looked out the window. "It appears we are near our destination."

"So soon?" she asked, and he laughed, sounding comfortingly like her merry Hugh.

The chaise came to a stop and he opened the door and got out. "Here we are at last," he said, holding out his hands to lift her down.

They were in a courtyard surrounded by several buildings, including the requisite blacksmith's shop where she understood all those clandestine weddings she had read about had taken place.

"Where are we to go?" she asked, studying at length the small, quaint structures that surrounded them. The whole of it looked rather bleak, she decided. Not at all the sort of place one would think to begin a happy life together.

A lad still in short pants had appeared out of nowhere, ostensibly to greet them. "Welcoom, sar, leddy! Lookin' fer a priest, are ye?" he asked with a gap-toothed grin.

"Aye, we are," Hugh said, reaching into his pocket for a coin that he flipped in the air. The urchin caught it and tested it with his remaining teeth.

"This way," the little fellow said, darting past the chaise. Clarissa realized that there would probably be no overnight stay, no lingering at all. Couples came here to say vows and hie off elsewhere to spend the wedding night, she supposed. She felt faintly disappointed at the thought of resuming their travels immediately afterward. The post boys had alighted and were fetching water for the team.

At the door of the cottage where the boy led her and Hugh, a portly man of about seventy years greeted them. "Come to marry?" he asked with a gentle smile.

"That we have," Hugh said.

The man nodded as he invited them in, propping the door open to take advantage of the warm breeze. "I'd be Laing, who'll see to yer ceremony." Without delay, he took a sheet of paper from a simple unadorned box on the table, unstoppered the inkwell and picked up a pen. "And you'd be?"

"Hugh Richfield and my bride, Clarissa Fortesque," Hugh replied.

Scratching words that would serve as the written record, he slid the paper toward them. "Go on and make yer marks."

After they signed, he entered their names in a clothbound ledger, stoppered up the ink and replaced the pen in its holder. "I'll summon th' witnesses. Have a tot while ye wait. Water of life. Settles th' dust." He gestured idly at the bottle and glass sitting beside the ledger.

He seemed in no rush at all as he limped over and retrieved his hat from a hook on the wall, then took forever settling it just so on his wild shock of white hair. He smiled at them, then crossed the room yet again at a snail's pace and exited through the back door.

On the table, to one side, a Bible lay open. "I wonder if we'll be married in here. Better than over the anvil, I suppose," Hugh said with a smile. "Perhaps they've discontinued that practice in favor of something a bit more in keeping with the occasion. In any event, he doesn't strike me as a smithy."

"No," Clarissa mumbled. "None of this is what I expected."

"Truth to tell, I'd pictured worse," Hugh commented as he perused the label on the bottle of spirits. He set it down again without pouring any out.

He paced, glancing around at the contents of the comfortable, if humble, cottage.

Clarissa remained still. She felt if she moved at all, she might turn and run as far and fast as her legs would take her. Could she really do this now that she was here? Could she *not* do it, now that she had shared a bed with this man, promised him a small fortune to accompany her here, and foolishly grown to love him in a few short days?

But it had been more than the time they had spent together as adults that made her care so much, she knew, else she would not have dreamed of him so often during the intervening years since her childhood. She would not have built this plan around him, never seriously considering another for it.

Hugh was examining a small plaque attached to the wall when a shadow fell across the main threshold. He turned to face the new arrival, as did Clarissa.

Trenton stood in the doorway, holding a pistol aimed at Hugh's heart. "Not to put too fine a point on it, Richfield, but I believe you have abducted my cousin. Not a soul in Christendom would deny I have the right to blow a hole in you the size of my fist."

Hugh held out his hands to the side as if inviting his fate. "Or you could hang for it. I do believe we met on the road."

"Did we?" Trenton asked with an evil smile.

Clarissa saw the scratches she had inflicted on his

neck during the incident. The blackguard would not admit he was the one. That was why he had not faced her when she was in the coach. He had meant to kill Hugh then, ride away and claim her later, thereby hiding his identity as the highwayman. She knew it was so!

Trenton sneered. "I expected you here sooner. I've been waiting."

"How...how did you know we were coming here?" Clarissa asked.

Hugh remained motionless. "He was in the corridor at Dickson House, outside the library, and heard us making plans."

"How clever of you. How else would I have known? Even after she nearly unmanned me, I still wanted her. I'll have her, too."

"Like to wager on that?" Hugh asked calmly.

Trenton snorted. "Your infamous bets. This is one you'd lose, Richfield. By the way, what delayed you? Stop along the way to have a taste before your grand meal, did you?"

"How coarse of you, *cousin*," Hugh taunted. "Where are your manners? If you put away that nasty cannon you have there, we'll invite you to the wedding breakfast."

Clarissa could not find her tongue. Why on earth did Hugh keep provoking Trenton? Did he *want* to die? Oh, God. Perhaps he *did!* She had to do something. But what? If she rushed at Trenton, the surprise might cause him to fire. She could never reach him this time to deflect his aim.

"Here now!" thundered a deep voice from the back portal. "We'll have no shootin'!" exclaimed Mr. Laing. "Lads?" He said, moving inside so that the two burly fellows behind him could enter.

"I'm afraid you're too late, anyway," Hugh announced to Trenton. "I, Hugh Richfield, am here to take Clarissa Fortesque as my lawfully wedded wife and she intends me to be her husband. Is that not true, Clarissa?"

When she merely gaped at him, he prodded her. "Well go on, say it's true. Loudly, if you please."

"I…yes, that's true," she stuttered, nodding, looking from one to the other, dreading what might come next. Trenton looked fit to kill, his breath rushing in and out between his teeth as he scowled. The pistol shifted dangerously, as if his hand trembled trying to hold it steady.

"Done and witnessed," Laing said gruffly, apparently recognizing the need for speed and lack of formality. He shuffled around them and shoved the paper they had signed into Hugh's hand. The priest, as he called himself, now stood directly between Hugh and her cousin.

With a growl, Trenton rushed farther into the room, attempting to get Hugh directly in his sites again. He snarled at Clarissa. "You stupid little fool! I'm trying to save you! Now I'll have to kill—"

Hugh leaped and struck. His hand came down so fast on Trenton's wrist, she hardly saw the move before it was over. The cocked pistol hit the floor beside her foot, discharged and blew a hole in the wall.

Trenton cried out in agony as Hugh grasped his arm, twisted it behind his back and dropped him to his knees. Hugh's other hand grasped Trenton's hair, forcing the head back at an unnatural angle.

"Stop!" Trenton cried. He groaned and began to sob.

Hugh huffed in disgust. "Control yourself, man. You'd think I broke your arm the way you carry on!"

"It's the bullet wound! My shoulder," Trenton gasped. His breath hissed inward. "You can have the chit! For all she's worth, take her and be damned!"

"I *do* have her," Hugh growled. "And you'd be wise to not forget that. Mr. Laing, summon your constable."

"No need. No need," Trenton pleaded. "You have my word—"

"Worth spit, I'm sure," Hugh muttered, giving Trenton's pomaded hair a hearty yank.

"I'm quit of this. Of *her!*" Trenton promised, his voice an octave higher than usual. "Let me go. Just let me go."

Hugh released him with a shove that dashed Trenton prone on the floor. "You're a lucky man, Fortesque. It's my wedding day and I feel benevolent.'' He raised one eyebrow and hefted Trenton's empty weapon, holding it out, butt first. "I might still change my mind if I ever see you again. Get out of here."

Her cousin raised a hand, palm outward, and took the pistol. He scrambled to his feet and cradled his arm protectively. "I should have known it was pointless, trying to save her."

"Save me?" she asked with a scornful laugh. "Was that what you were trying to do? As it happens I'm here doing this because I needed someone to save me from *you!*"

He glared at her with what could only be described as malice. "Don't come crawling to me in tears when he abandons you for someone who actually *has* money. Just remember, I would have taken you without it."

"What do you mean?" she demanded, the fear she should have felt before now hitting her full-force. "What are you saying?"

He straightened his coat and brushed at his sleeve, trying unsuccessfully to keep his eyes off the threat that was Hugh. "That our dear, mad uncle has poured every pound you had and all that is left of his in some stupid venture that cannot possibly succeed."

"In what did he invest?" Hugh asked.

Trenton spat to one side, then answered, "Steam travel. Yachts! Can you fathom that? Foolish old addlepated fart. Now the money's tied up in the building of the damned things. The novelty will have worn off completely by the time they're done. *If* they ever are.'' He sneered at her. "So you have nothing, little cousin! Nothing for you or for *him*.'' He bared his teeth at Hugh.

"That…that can't be true!'' she exclaimed, looking from him to Hugh and back again. "How could he?''

Trenton laughed bitterly. "Easily enough. Uncle lies there in that pillowed nest of his reading scientific journals, dreaming his dreams of quickly made wealth, and corresponding with all manner of charlatans he believes will provide it. His man of business must be in league with them. It's gone, Clarissa. He has put it where neither you nor I have a prayer of getting it back.''

"He…everything?'' she asked in a small whisper.

"I had a bit put by, so I could have afforded you.'' He shot a dark look at Hugh, then fastened his angry gaze on her again. "But you're ruined now. Even I won't help you. You've made your bed. Go and lie in it.'' With that, he strode out the front door.

"Wait!'' Clarissa called, running after him, fully aware that Hugh was right behind her. "Trenton, wait!''

He halted abruptly and whirled around to face her. "It's too late, Clarissa. You can't come with me. I've given *him* my word.''

Hugh threatened him with a pointed glare, promising more of what Trenton had so recently escaped. "You will hear her questions and you will answer, Fortesque. Are we understood?"

Trenton inclined his head. "So ask away for all the good it will do you."

"Why did you pursue me at all if you knew I had nothing to inherit?" Clarissa demanded.

He grimaced, paused and finally said, "I fancied you, as badly as I hate to admit that now. Since we were children, I thought of you as mine."

She placed her hands on her hips and stared at him with disbelief. "A fine way you had of showing that with your pawing and threats! All you succeeded in doing was making me despise you!"

"All women wish to be mastered!" he argued hotly.

"Not this woman! I thought my knee should have made that perfectly clear!" She ignored the gasp of the men behind her as well as Trenton's chest heaving anger.

"Why did you not simply tell me what Uncle had done?" she asked, spreading her arms wide. "I could have declined your offer. All of this…this subterfuge would not have been necessary if you had simply talked to me in a civilized way!"

He tugged impatiently at his too high collar. "Explain finances to a woman? Ha. You would not have understood. Hell, you don't understand even now what a pickle you're in! And this *subterfuge,* as you call it, is all your doing. I told you outright that we must marry, that you had no other course! But you found one, didn't you? Flying off to Gretna with a penniless, cutthroat *soldier!*''

Hugh pushed her aside and planted his fist in Trenton's jaw. "That was for the insult to my wife."

He waited for her cousin to struggle to his feet before addressing him again. "One more word to Clarissa—save for your apology, which I now demand—and I'll be requiring the ultimate satisfaction." He narrowed his eyes, grasped Trenton's foulard in his fist and gave him a shake. "Evenly armed, you'd not like to face down a cutthroat soldier trained to kill, now would you? I promise your choice of weapons would hardly matter."

"No," Trenton croaked, backing away quickly as Hugh released him. He spat on the ground, then touched his bleeding lip with one finger. "I won't chance death for any woman, especially *her.*"

"No chance involved," Hugh promised. "Now leave before I change my mind."

Trenton risked shooting him a nasty look, then sketched a small bow in her direction. "My apologies, Clarissa," he snapped. "May I be the first to wish you happy." His words were bitter, his expression even more so. She did not even bother to acknowledge either.

They watched him stalk off, slapping his hat against his leg. He mounted a saddled gelding hitched to a post near the smithy's shop and rode away south.

"There's an end to that unpleasantness," Hugh said brightly, dusting his hands together before taking her arm. "Shall we repair to the inn here and commence with our celebration?"

"Oh, Hugh," Clarissa said, very nearly wailing. "I am destitute." Her knees felt like they would collapse beneath her as the reality of it sank in.

"Well," Hugh said with a sunny smile, "even poor people need sustenance. Come along now."

"Are you mad?" she cried, tugging out of his hold. "I don't want *food!* How can you imagine any sort of celebration? I'm so mortified, I want to die right here! What a mess I've made of things! I—I can't keep my promise to you, Hugh," she cried. "You have kept your end of the bargain, but I cannot."

"Of course you can." He smacked his palm lightly against his forehead. "Small wonder you're upset after what I forgot."

"What?" she asked, sniffling, wiping her eyes with the edge of her sleeve.

"Something that will make everything all right and solve all our problems," he explained. And then he kissed her.

How she regretted that the pure ecstasy of his mouth on hers, his body pressed against her, his long fingers sliding through her hair and dislodging her bonnet, could not resolve their dilemma. They were poor, she had nothing to offer him and he was bound to her as surely as if they had wed in St. Paul's before hundreds of witnesses. His honor would never allow him to deny their marriage happened, however informal it had been. There were papers. It was recorded.

When he finally released her, leaving her shaking while he appeared more than a bit disconcerted himself, she informed him breathlessly, "I fear we've only created more problems, Hugh."

"So we did," he answered with a grin, "but we have a ready solution to these." He took her hand and looked down at her, then over at the inn, his amber eyes sparkling. "Do we not, Mrs. Richfield?"

CHAPTER SIX

HUGH WAS STILL pouting at the end of the day when they arrived at Hartcastle, forty miles southeast of the Scottish border.

There had been no available private rooms at the small inn at Gretna. It seemed the marriage trade was busy, and not all the couples were outrunning irate relatives. Unfortunately, Hartcastle's direction was by way of a byroad where there were no posting inns and Clarissa had insisted they travel on to his brother's estate to pass the night.

Aside from the delay in consummating their marriage, Hugh was in no mood to confront the unpredictable Nigel. If offered the same welcome as the last time he was here, Hugh feared they might very well have to sleep in the chaise.

Had Nigel forgiven him for returning alive without the two Archer boys? Though he had never said as much, Hugh knew his brother held him responsible for them. They had been tenants of the estate. Neighbors and friends.

The guilt Hugh suffered over the deaths he had witnessed at Waterloo still troubled him, but he knew he could have done no more than he had and must live with that fact. He had decided that, in their honor, he must make his life count for something instead of grieving uselessly.

Clarissa had, in her direct and sensible way, urged him to that conclusion. With her trust in him and her insistence on his openness, she had helped him to put it in better perspective. How was he ever to thank her for that? Certainly not when they were tearing through the north of England looking for a place to light.

Devlin and the lads followed directions to the letter and the chaise was now approaching the ruin Hugh had once called home.

"Do not expect much," he warned Clarissa as they wound their way up the long drive.

The moonlight revealed signs of further dilapidation in the main house as they approached. "Damn," he said on a sigh, noting several black rectangular holes across the front where there were once windows. The abundant ivy that had covered a multitude of cracks in the facade had been ripped away, leaving the time wounds bare. Abandoned scaffolding stood affixed to one side of the entry where someone had obviously attempted repairs.

Clarissa covered his hand with hers, offering comfort without words.

They alighted and Hugh pointed out the stables to Devlin so that he could water and rest the team. Then he escorted Clarissa to the door and raised his hand to knock.

Before he could, the stout oak door—which on closer inspection Hugh saw was new—opened. Nigel himself stood there, tall and pale, a much older, sicklier version of Hugh himself. His brother still bore the ravages of the scarlet fever that had invalided him when he was twenty. Given the difference of fifteen years in their ages, Hugh could not even recall when Nigel had been hale. Or happy.

"Hugh!" he cried, holding out one arm while the other held a lantern high. "My God, boy, how did you get here so quickly? I only sent word to London two days ago!"

Mystified at the effusive greeting and the unexpected welcome, Hugh allowed himself to be hugged, pounded on the back and drawn across the threshold. "Nigel," he said. "You sent for me? Why?"

But his brother was looking past him, smiling. How long had it been since he had seen Nigel smile? Belatedly, he recalled that Clarissa was still standing there. "Oh, this is Clarissa Fortesque…Richfield. My wife. Clarissa, my brother, Earl Hartcastle."

She curtsied beautifully. Bedraggled as she was in her wrinkled carriage gown and creased velvet spencer, she appeared regal as any queen. "My lord," she acknowledged brightly.

"Wife?" Nigel croaked. He stared openmouthed at her and then at Hugh. "Dash it all, you've married! How wonderful!" He reached for Clarissa's hand and stepped back, tugging her inside. "Well, come in, my dear, come in!'' He kissed her on the cheek. "Oh, this is too grand, isn't it just! Mind the tools there and don't trip. We've a bit of a jumble here what with all the renovations.''

"Renovations?'' Hugh parroted, only then noting the plethora of instruments scattered about and the stacks of rolled paper for doing the walls. "What…what is all this?''

Nigel laughed as he ushered them into a parlor bare of all but two settees and a small table set in between. "We've come into blunt, m'boy. The gamble's paid off at last. Sit, sit. Drinks are in order and then you shall eat. Or have you eaten?''

"No,'' Hugh admitted, "but I'd as soon have an explanation. What gamble do you mean?''

"A moment, please.'' Nigel seated Clarissa, then reached for the bellpull. Only after a stiff-kneed butler appeared and disappeared with an order for a late supper and rooms to be readied did Nigel sit down and explain. "First of all, I must apologize for all but ordering you away when you came home last, Hugh. I was in a sorry state then, horribly guilty for having risked everything. I wanted you well away so I did not have to face you with my foolishness.''

"But I thought it was because of the Archers. That you held me accountable.''

Nigel frowned, leaned forward and shook his head. "Oh, no, Hugh. That never entered my mind. They were grown men, as old as you were at the time, certainly capable of making the decision to become soldiers. No, it was my own folly that preyed on me. You see, George Notting had in mind to finance an expedition to the Orient, a private venture, as it were. He was quite persuasive and I fear I wagered everything. The ships were delayed beyond hope, but if they had been captured or gone down, well…"

"But I take it they recently arrived?" Hugh said with a grin. "You are flush again. Rebuilding. Replanting?"

Nigel nodded emphatically. "*We* are flush, Hugh. All's right with Hartcastle and I can't tell you how relieved I am."

He then turned his attention to Clarissa. "I thought *I* had come into luck, but it appears you have put my good fortune to shame. How is it this lovely creature has surrendered herself to a muck-about such as you?"

Clarissa replied, "He married me for my money."

Nigel threw back his head and laughed. That, Hugh had never seen him do. Probably foxed, celebrating his newfound wealth.

"However," Clarissa quickly added, "it has come to nothing, you see, which is why we are here imposing upon your hospitality. The uncle who had charge of my inheritance made much the same gamble as you did, my lord, but without like results."

"Oh? His ships sank, did they?" Nigel asked with all concern.

"No. As far as I know, they are not even built

yet.'' She dropped her voice to a woeful whisper and shook her head. ''Steamships. Pleasure yachts. Whatever was he thinking?''

Nigel worried his brow for a moment, then leaped up and strode out of the room without a word.

''Now I've done it,'' Clarissa said, exhaling sharply. ''He's probably ordering Devlin to hitch up the team and haul me away. No doubt he believes I've tricked you into marriage.'' She raised her hand to her forehead and pressed her fingertips to her brow. ''Would you mind terribly if I forego supper and excuse myself before he comes back? I have a bit of thinking to do.''

''Sweetheart, you mustn't worry. Not at all. I suppose I should have reassured you sooner about—''

''Later, perhaps,'' she said, interrupting him as she stood. ''But I would like to retire now.''

''Of course. I'll see you upstairs. We'll most likely be staying in my former room. That is, if the windows aren't knocked out.'' He grimaced.

''No, please. Stay and visit with your brother. The butler is just there,'' she said, gesturing toward the open doorway. ''He will direct me. Do stay, Hugh. And wish Lord Nigel good-night for me.''

''If you're certain,'' he said, wanting nothing more than to carry her up the stairs himself, but realizing she was right. He needed to discuss everything with Nigel.

No sooner had Clarissa disappeared up the stairs than Nigel strode back into the room and tossed a periodical into Hugh's lap. "Page twelve," he said, pointing and nodding, obviously excited. "The article by Isaac Weld, Esquire. Read it."

Hugh examined the cover of the *Journal des Mines,* dated September, 1815, turned to the correct page and read aloud.

"'A newly launched ship, *The Thames,* has successfully completed her maiden voyage. The steam vessel traversed, in spite of contending seas and opposing winds, 758 miles in 121 hours. This voyage has established the utility of vessels so propelled, and the reliance that may be placed in them when controlled by skillful persons. Several other vessels, on similar principles, are being constructed and will be employed in conveying persons to Richmond, Sheerness, Southend and Gravesend, as well as to Margate from London. Vessels with steam engines will doubtless become adopted in various other parts of England as a commodious and pleasant means of travel."

Hugh looked up at his beaming brother and smiled. "It seems her ship has come in as well as yours."

"Half of what I've gained belongs to you, Hugh. I wagered everything you sent from your army pay that was intended to support the estate. Foolish, I know, but fortunately it's turned out well in the end. The funds are in your account."

"I could have supported her in comfort, if not

luxury,'' Hugh said by way of defense. "I have a tidy sum put by.''

"I heard how you got it, too,'' Nigel said, frowning in disapproval. "That sort of thing must cease. You've gained a reputation for foolhardy risks, boy.''

"Foolhardy, profitable risks, old man. The tendency must run in the blood.''

Nigel shrugged. "Brandy?''

Hugh grinned and glanced meaningfully at the ceiling, above which Clarissa rested in his former room. "No, *bride.*''

Nigel embraced him again, then gave Hugh a playful shove in the direction of the door. "Then go on and make us an heir, you scapegrace. Supper can wait.''

WHEN HUGH SLIPPED INTO his familiar old bed and took Clarissa in his arms, she sighed with pleasure and snuggled back against him. "You know, I have been lying here thinking of what we might do,'' she whispered.

"Have you?'' he growled. "I've been giving it a bit of thought myself.'' He slid one palm down her midsection and cradled her intimately.

She groaned a low sultry laugh and covered his hand with hers pressing him to her. "We should return to town. I have a notion how we could replenish my lost fortune now that I am used to adventuring.''

Hugh kissed the curve where her exquisite shoulder met her swanlike neck. "Have you? And here I had expected to let a small, comfy cottage and live frugally with you into our cheese-paring dotage." He had quite looked forward to it if the truth be told.

"Racing," she declared. "I believe I should like to race." Her breath caught fetchingly as he cupped one pert breast and caressed it through the thin lawn of her chemisette. "Ah. You could...could teach me to drive a high-perched phaeton. Bet on me and I'd win. Not a soul would ever expect a female to know how to race one. And shoot. You could instruct me in...all your games of chance. Um," she hummed as he stroked her, the sound of her pleasure exciting him to a fever pitch.

"Whatever you wish to learn," he assured her as he raised the hem of the one garment she had not removed for the night. "Here's a lesson you'll love."

She reached back and smoothed one hand along his hip. "Why, Richfield, you're not wearing any clothes," she whispered with a lazy giggle.

"First rule in this race," he told her, slipping the soft filmy fabric over her head and tossing it away. "Now on to the next, if you don't mind."

"Such an eager teacher...and willing student," she crooned, turning in his arms and pressing full against him, her lips open and trailing across his chest while her hand wandered in dangerous territory. "I do believe I have some small notion how this goes."

"The trick is not to rush your...fences," Hugh warned, "or the race will be over all too...soon."

"Wrong sort of race, my darling," she advised him. "I believe I already know how to ride."

"You think so, eh?" he asked as he drew her on top of him and smoothed his palms down her lithe, firm body, encouraging her to fit hers to his in a way she had not yet experienced. "You want adventure, do you?" he dared. Was there anything she was unwilling to try? he wondered.

She sank onto him, encompassing him completely, turning his grand plan of instruction to ashes as she began to move, sinuously, slowly, with an eroticism he had not dared hope for in one so untrained. Her mouth found his, devouring him as he constantly dreamed of doing to her. As he had done too few times. Her breasts grazed his chest, leaving twin paths of sensation he arched to recapture. Her scent filled his senses, rosewater and something indefinable that was hers alone. Essence of Clarissa, intoxicating.

Leisure was not her intent, he soon found out. Though he'd intended to draw out her pleasure, make up for their first hurried encounter and his near abandonment of her afterward, she had other ideas. Hugh relinquished any semblance of control, gladly allowing her to set the pace, helpless to devise any measure that would grant any greater ecstasy than she provided. The best he could do was try to rein in the urge to finish until she demanded that, too.

Her sweet cry of completion forced his complete surrender and he filled her, groaning both in blessed defeat and keenest victory. Ribbons of sheer feeling stretched to the limit, burst in stages, their remnants curling through him like slithers of rich, smooth silk.

"Beginner's luck," he gasped, laughing breathlessly.

"Not so." She lay draped on top of him, one hand tangled in his hair, the other resting bonelessly on his shoulder. "I am a natural," she argued softly. "Anything you can do, I can do as well."

"Can you box?" he asked, teasing her.

One small fist bounced playfully off his head. "Anything."

WHEN HE COULD BREATHE normally again and held her securely in the curve of his arm, her silken, sated body nestled against his side, Hugh toyed idly with the long, dark curls that had come loose from her chignon. He twisted and untwisted one about his finger and gave it a gentle tug. "We should marry again, don't you think? Here, at Hartcastle. There's a beautiful little church in the village. A kindly old vicar. Neighbors we could ask to attend."

"If you like," she said with a heavy sigh. "And then we should return to London."

"Why? I had thought we might stay on. The old

dowager cottage down the way is empty. We could set up there.''

She shook her head, then snuggled closer. ''We cannot live upon Nigel's charity, Hugh. We must make our own living now. I see no other avenue but to join forces and win what we may. You were doing rather well at it, weren't you? With me at your side, who knows how successful we shall be?''

Hugh sighed. He knew her better than she knew herself. Winning her fortune back was secondary. After living the mundane, restricted existence she had for so many years, it was excitement and adventure Clarissa craved. Now that she'd had a taste of it, she obviously had acquired a taste *for* it. And whatever Clarissa wanted, she should bloody well have.

Not that he would always give in to her, but a bargain was a bargain. He had promised to marry her, take what she offered and ask no more. He had done that. But he had also promised to continue doing exactly as he pleased in order to amuse himself, not to give her orders and to leave her fortune alone.

He could do that, too. A gentleman always kept his word. No need to bring up the crass subject of money at this juncture. At present they still had nothing but what he had put by. His longing for the quiet life could wait awhile.

So he simply smiled, kissed the tip of her pert little nose and murmured, ''Yes, dear. You shall take London by storm. I do believe you were meant for it."

"And this," she said, stretching a bit to reach his lips with hers.

"And this." Perhaps he *would* always agree with her, after all. She certainly did agree with him.

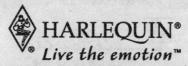

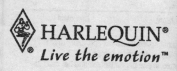

If you enjoyed what you just read,
then we've got an offer you can't resist!

Take 2
bestselling novels FREE!
Plus get a FREE surprise gift!

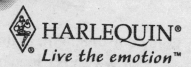

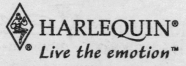

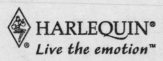